Dog

"The supernatural lives, and it lives in a San Francisco where the dog days don't just get you down; they eat you alive."
—Rob Thurman, author of *Madhouse*

"A compelling magical mystery, filled with twists and some uncomfortable turns as it follows a likable new character through a mostly familiar San Francisco . . . I thoroughly enjoyed *Dog Days*. It's proof that there's still a heck of a lot of potential for variation in the urban fantasy genre, and it's a highly satisfying read . . . an excellent start to a promising new series."
—*The Green Man Review*

"Appealing, fully rounded characters . . . Levitt promises to be a novelist worth watching . . . Readers will enjoy the roller-coaster ride through dangers both magical and mundane. Anyone who likes solid storytelling will enjoy *Dog Days*. Here's looking forward to the next adventure."
—*SFRevu*

"Levitt has envisioned a lively world . . . [a] delightful take on good versus evil. Mason's character, with his self-deprecating humor, beat-up van, and list of odd associates, is entertaining and engaging, and will certainly leave readers looking for more from this unlikely hero and his dog."
—*Monsters and Critics*

"Dog lovers don't get many fantasy books geared to them, so finding one is a pleasure . . . Fans of Harry Dresden will enjoy the tone this story sets."
—*Huntress Book Reviews*

"A great little cross-genre read; I highly enjoyed this . . . I highly recommend this book to anyone who likes urban fantasy . . . [It] came together exceptionally well and had more than enough surprises to keep it interesting."
—*FantasyBookSpot.com*

Ace Books by John Levitt

DOG DAYS
NEW TRICKS

NEW TRICKS

JOHN LEVITT

ACE BOOKS, NEW YORK

THE BERKLEY PUBLISHING GROUP
Published by the Penguin Group
Penguin Group (USA) Inc.
375 Hudson Street, New York, New York 10014, USA
Penguin Group (Canada), 90 Eglinton Avenue East, Suite 700, Toronto, Ontario M4P 2Y3, Canada
(a division of Pearson Penguin Canada Inc.)
Penguin Books Ltd., 80 Strand, London WC2R 0RL, England
Penguin Group Ireland, 25 St. Stephen's Green, Dublin 2, Ireland (a division of Penguin Books Ltd.)
Penguin Group (Australia), 250 Camberwell Road, Camberwell, Victoria 3124, Australia
(a division of Pearson Australia Group Pty. Ltd.)
Penguin Books India Pvt. Ltd., 11 Community Centre, Panchsheel Park, New Delhi—110 017, India
Penguin Group (NZ), 67 Apollo Drive, Rosedale, North Shore 0632, New Zealand
(a division of Pearson New Zealand Ltd.)
Penguin Books (South Africa) (Pty.) Ltd., 24 Sturdee Avenue, Rosebank, Johannesburg 2196,
South Africa

Penguin Books Ltd., Registered Offices: 80 Strand, London WC2R 0RL, England

NEW TRICKS

An Ace Book / published by arrangement with the author

PRINTING HISTORY
Ace mass-market edition / December 2008

Copyright © 2008 by John Levitt.
Cover art by Don Sipley.
Cover design by Annette Fiore DeFex.
Interior text design by Kristin del Rosario.

ISBN: 978-0-441-01656-3

ACE
Ace Books are published by The Berkley Publishing Group,
a division of Penguin Group (USA) Inc.,
375 Hudson Street, New York, New York 10014.
ACE and the "A" design are trademarks belonging to Penguin Group (USA) Inc.

PRINTED IN THE UNITED STATES OF AMERICA

10 9 8 7 6 5 4 3 2 1

ACKNOWLEDGMENTS

Once again, I'd like to thank my ever-patient editor, Jessica Wade, for all her help. And also my agent, Caitlin Blasdell, who routinely steers me in the right direction when I go off course.

ONE

ON THE CORNER OF MARKET AND CASTRO, HALF-hidden in the shadow of a doorway, stood a vampire. Not just any vampire, mind you; one with a dark cape and four-inch protruding fangs. And tons of hair gel. A few door-ways down, a werewolf chatted amiably with a sickly green-hued zombie. All around them, demons and divas swirled giddily together. It was, of course, Halloween in the Castro.

But Halloween in the Castro is not entirely what it seems. On the surface it's simply San Francisco's largest and gayest party, a hundred thousand costumed revelers crowded into a few square blocks. Mardi Gras, condensed in time and space, a time of celebration, freedom, and ex-cess.

In past years there had been violence though, sudden and unexpected. Nine partyers had been shot, although thankfully no one had died. So this might well be the last Halloween party the Castro would see for many years. But another current flows underneath, less ominous. We in the magical practitioner community tend to blend in and keep a low profile. We hold jobs and go to clubs and football games just like everyone else. A few ordinary citizens know we're around, but for the most part civilian society is oblivious.

So, for the practitioner community it's the perfect time to let our hair down and have some harmless fun. Halloween has always been my favorite day of the year, and the pretend darkness hovering over the sense of gaiety is half the fun. And I was ready for some fun. I'd been through some dark days.

Dark days indeed. No money. No girlfriend. No gigs. No desire to play gigs. For a jazz guitarist, that's unthinkable. I'd even had to go back to work for Victor to pay the bills.

Sherwood, my ex, was dead almost a year now. She'd been killed by a practitioner gone bad. Campbell, my most recent ex, was seeing another guy. Another practitioner. I couldn't decide if that made it better or worse.

Victor, of course, had little patience with my moods. Even Eli, who'd been so supportive, was tired of my deep sighs and hangdog looks. I didn't blame him. I was sick of it as well. So I finally pulled myself out of that funk and my self-imposed torpor. When Eli called to suggest we attend the Castro festivities, I jumped at the chance.

All the practitioners were in costume, only their costumes weren't cloth and tinsel, but clever deceptions. The unspoken rule is to come up with the most convincing and imaginative illusion using the minimum amount of talent.

Eli was dressed as an Arabian Djinn. Eli has been my mentor and best friend ever since I was a raw teenager with no idea of my own talent. He nurtured that talent and gently introduced me into the practitioner community, and most of what I know I owe to him.

The odd thing is that although he's a genius at theory, he doesn't have much innate talent himself, so the costume rules were easy for him—he was used to doing more with less. He has a solid template to work with, though—African-American, six feet four, almost 260 pounds, and a former Division I college lineman. A quick spell to take the gray out of his beard and transform his thinning hair into a gleaming bald pate, another to create the illusion of scanty robes that would have left him freezing if real, and a final conjuration to transform his middle-aged body into that defined rippling mass of muscle that can only come from hours at the gym. Or so it would appear. He looked a lot like Shaquille O'Neal in *Kazaam*, but if I told him that, he might have tossed me across the street. Not all of that considerable strength is illusory.

The crowd on Castro Street was packed wall-to-wall, making it difficult to move even a few feet, much less an entire city block. I'd walked over from my flat in the Mission, realizing the near impossibility of parking. I stayed away from the middle of the street, where the crush was most claustrophobic, and tried to navigate along the edges. Lou of course had no such problem—a one-foot-tall dog who weighs only twelve pounds can easily worm his way through shuffling feet.

Not that he's exactly a dog. He's an Ifrit. Usually Lou looks just like a miniature Doberman, black and tan with uncropped ears and undocked tail. Tonight, however, he, too, was in costume. I'd refused to go in costume myself—I just threw on a short leather jacket to keep off the chill. Otherwise, I was the same old me—dark, shaggy hair, brooding expression, angular face. Sort of like Jack Kerouac in the early days, before the hard living caught up with him. On my right forearm is a tattoo of two twining briars—the only outward sign there's anything different about me, but only to those who would know that anyway.

But at least I'd made an effort to dress up Lou. I had to spend a lot of time on him, illusion not being one of my stronger talents. However, since most of the practitioners in the city were present, pride, if nothing else, dictated I put forth a credible effort.

I could have easily made him into something wildly exotic, but the rules did call for subtlety. So, I softened up his sharp muzzle, enlarged his eyes, mottled his coat into a dappled beige, turned delicate paws into delicate hooves, and added two tiny, straight horns on the top of his head. When I was done he was a perfect replica of an African dikdik antelope. I was proudest of the horns, since they weren't completely imaginary. They were functional, which is far more difficult to do than a simple illusion. Lou was delighted with them and even jabbed me a couple of times in an excess of high spirits. He wouldn't stop until I threatened to change his appearance to that of a precious rainbow-colored lamb.

Victor was waiting for us opposite the Castro Theater. Most of the time he's all business; in fact, Victor at a party is much like broccoli on a birthday cake. Even his fun has to be carefully choreographed. Ever the perfectionist, he'd come up with a cool and understated outfit. It was a standard devil illusion, complete with red skin tone, switching tail, and small horns growing out of his forehead. Not as good as Lou's horns, but not bad. Victor's neat twist was a variation on a standard aversion spell. It produced an aura of real evil.

He was his usual dapper self, neat and compact and wiry. His dark beard, once all angles and fine lines, now covered most of his face. It was trimmed close, giving him a theatrical satanic air. The closer you got to him, the more reasonable it seemed that he might indeed be an actual devil. Of course, considering his personality, he also has a solid basis to work with. Even with the crush of revelers, a clear space remained around him. People felt uncomfortable and didn't want to get too close.

"Mason," he said, acknowledging me with a nod. "Eli." He ignored Lou, and Lou ignored him. We were just one big happy family. Victor is the unofficial head enforcer in San Francisco, someone who keeps an eye on the practitioner community, reining in those who occasionally step over the line. At one time I'd worked for Victor full-time, a minion on his magical enforcement squad, but I wasn't really cut out for the job. But someone had to do it. A rogue practitioner can cause a lot of trouble in a civilian society that barely understands people like us even exist, so people like Victor are an unfortunate necessity. It didn't make him lovable, though.

Two young men dressed entirely in tinfoil edged by, followed by a giant sunflower. Victor glanced past them, lifting his hand in a desultory wave. I looked over my shoulder and saw Janet, a minor practitioner I knew casually. She was dressed tonight as Dorothy, complete with ruby red slippers, and her own twist was that when she skipped, it took longer than usual for her feet to return to the ground. Again, it was subtle. People in the crowd kept watching her, unable to put their fingers on exactly what was so unusual about the way she moved. Very nice.

Lou put his paws up on my knee and gave an annoyed bark. From ground level he couldn't see a thing except legs and he was getting bored. He doesn't have the longest attention span. I bent down to pick him up, but Eli intervened.

"Allow me," he said, picking up Lou and placing him on one large shoulder. Eli's bulk and height dwarf mine, although I'm about six feet tall myself, and it was a great platform for Lou. He loves a party, and now he had the best seat in the house. He certainly garnered a lot of attention. Even with the abundance of outrageous costumes, he stood out, with people stopping and pointing while he reveled in the attention.

A striking figure dressed in only a loincloth with arrows sticking out of his chest and sides came up to us. I had to look twice before I recognized him as Jay, a practitioner I hadn't seen for a while. He'd done a bang-up job on his costume, a mock-up of St. Sebastian, the Christian martyr. A folded loincloth was all he wore, and he'd glamoured his body in the same fashion Eli had, only his was wiry, toned, and ripped. He was getting more than his share of admiring glances from both women and men.

The best part of the illusion was the numerous arrows that pierced his side and back, like a human pincushion. Whenever he stood in one place for too long, drops of blood dripped onto the pavement. Somewhat of a turnoff for some, an added attraction for others.

St. Sebastian is sort of a gay icon, so it was particularly appropriate for the Castro, though I wasn't sure if Jay knew that. He's a born-again Christian, which I always thought odd for a practitioner, considering our use of magical talent. It didn't seem to bother him, though. I asked him once in all sincerity if he believed Jesus was a practitioner, what with the water into wine and all. He laughed so hard he almost choked on a hotdog he was eating.

"You have a peculiar view of what being a Christian means," he'd said, shaking his head, and that was all he had to say.

"I thought St. Sebastian was just for Catholics," I said. Jay pulled on one of the arrows to get a little more blood flow.

"No group has a monopoly on suffering. But I'm surprised you even know who St. Sebastian is."

"I saw him on a postcard once."

"As I thought. A deep thinker." He turned to greet Eli, who was uncharacteristically brusque.

"Where's Pook?" Eli asked. Pook is Jay's Ifrit, a sweet and small soot gray cat.

"She's at home, sleeping probably. She hates crowds, you know." Eli relaxed, almost imperceptibly, but Jay picked up on it. "You still worried about Ifrits?"

"No, just wondering," Eli said.

He *was* worried, though. Not about specific Ifrits, but about Ifrits in general. He insisted there were fewer of them of late—not that Ifrits were disappearing, but that no new ones were appearing on the scene. He thought it might be a sign of something more serious, sort of a magical global warming problem. I hadn't noticed that myself, but since it's not that common for a new Ifrit to appear anyway, maybe I was missing it.

Jay wandered off through the crowd, and Eli watched him, distracted. Eli didn't seem to be having as much fun as you might expect. He kept glancing at his watch every few minutes and frowning slightly.

"You expecting someone?" I finally asked. He nodded abstractedly.

"Sarah. She was supposed to be here an hour ago."

Sarah. I hadn't seen her in a couple of years. Sarah and I went out for a while some years ago on a semiserious basis. She'd spent half of the time on her cell—one of those people who simply has to be in constant contact. Like if she weren't talking to someone, she didn't fully exist. She was a practitioner, a very smart woman, and very sweet, but unaccountably insecure. If the cell phone hadn't been invented, I don't know what she would have done. We didn't last long. It would be nice to see her again, though. I had been very fond of her.

"Sarah, late?" I said. "Isn't that one of the signs of the apocalypse, like the Cubs winning the World Series?"

"It's certainly not like her," Eli said.

That was an understatement. Sarah had an almost pathological sense of responsibility. If she said she'd call, she called. If she said she'd be somewhere at nine, she was.

"I've called her, several times," Eli said. "All I get is the recorded message."

Ordinarily this wouldn't mean much of anything. But it was so out of character for Sarah it was worrying. And after last year's events, we all were hypersensitive to anything out of character.

Victor added something that didn't make me feel any better.

"She called this afternoon. Said she'd come across something odd that she wanted to talk to us about, so she was going to meet us here."

Now I wasn't having any fun, either. We watched as the

crowd eddied around us, protected from the crush by Victor's unsettling persona. Every few minutes Eli checked his watch again, took out his cell, and hit the redial button.

"She was supposed to be here at nine," he said.

It was ten thirty at least. Eli's concern was contagious. I didn't like the feel of this.

"Maybe we should go looking for her," I said.

Eli reached up to touch Lou, who was still happily ensconced on his shoulder, and gave me a questioning look. I nodded.

"He remembers her well, I'm sure."

One of Lou's talents is his ability to track people. Not exactly like a dog—he's an Ifrit, after all. That's just what we call them, although nobody knows exactly what they are or where they come from. If you're a lucky practitioner, though not necessarily a deserving one, sometimes one will hook up with you. I have Lou. Victor has Maggie, who manifests as a relatively unpleasant Persian cat. Once they show up, they're with you for life.

Lou has two limitations in tracking someone, though. One is that he has to start somewhere reasonably close—he can't just waltz out the door and find someone wandering around in the Oakland hills.

The second is that he has to know the person. The better he knows them, the easier it is to find them and the farther away they can be. Lou could locate me halfway across the planet, but that's different. It's a shame I can't return the favor.

"Any idea where Sarah was when she called you?" I asked. "We could start there."

"Marina Green," Eli said. "She was watching a volleyball game with some friends."

"Let's stop at my house first," Victor said. "I need to pick up some things. Just in case."

AN HOUR LATER, ILLUSIONS GONE, WE WERE standing on the sidewalk outside Marina Green, looking out down the trail toward Crissy Field by the dark water of the bay. A dark mist had crept in from the water, chilling us and adding to my unease.

Victor wore a fanny pack, a bad sign. At home he kept all his magical tools in a black old-fashioned doctor's bag, but when he went out he transferred them to a fanny pack for convenience. It wasn't encouraging that he thought he might be needing them. Worse, he didn't need his tools for spell casting or protection. He mostly used them for magical forensics, and forensics usually means unpleasant things have already happened.

Lou sat patiently beside us. His usual jaunty demeanor was gone. He understood something serious was up. I was on edge, nervous and jumpy, until I made myself get hold of my emotions. We were all grimly assuming something dreadful had happened to Sarah without a shred of evidence to back up that feeling. But I had to admit it was getting to me.

Usually Lou is clowning around and I have to grab him by his muzzle to get his attention. This time, he sat quietly, looking back and forth at the three of us. I squatted down to his level.

"Lou," I said. "Remember Sarah? Long ago. Our friend Sarah?" He stared fixedly at me, usually a good indication that he's following what I'm saying. "We can't find her. Can you do it? Find?"

Of course, he can't understand exactly what I'm saying, but he has a pretty good understanding of the sense of it. God knows I've made him understand things a lot more complicated than this.

I always expect him to nod when I explain something to him. It's easy to forget he's really just a dog. Sort of. He stood up on his hind legs and did a little pirouette, like a circus dog, sniffing the wind. I don't think scent has anything to do with it—it's just his personal ritual to help him focus on whatever passes for talent in an Ifrit, the same way some practitioners will use a crystal to focus theirs.

After a minute he dropped back on all fours, glanced

over his shoulder to make sure we were following, and trotted off north along Marina Boulevard. The mist had become a light rain. I hadn't bothered with a hat, so I just
hunched my shoulders and turned up the collar of my
leather jacket. Victor, of course, had a small travel umbrella
that he unfurled. Eli walked alongside him, expression grim,
oblivious to the rain.

We hadn't gone far, just to the point where Marina
Boulevard curves past the Palace of Fine Arts, when Lou
broke off and headed toward it.

The Palace of Fine Arts was inspired by Greek and
Roman architecture, though it always looked more like a
Baha'i-influenced structure to me. In front of the main
building lies a small lagoon, and Lou carefully circled the
edge of the water, hesitating, but never quite stopping. Not
as if he'd lost the trail; he clearly didn't want to continue.
Another bad sign. The last time he'd done that, the eventual outcome had not been pretty.

He worked his way around to the temple building, paused
a moment, then resolutely headed down to the water's edge.
By this time the rain had let up, and patchy clouds revealed
an almost full moon. It's usually a pleasant area, a great favorite for tourists and weddings, and there should have been
at least a few people around, especially on Halloween. But
there weren't. Tonight it looked bleak. And dangerous.

Halfway to the water, Lou stopped and sat down, looking intently at the shoreline. As soon as I reached him, I
saw what he was staring at. A solitary figure, motionless on
a bench by the edge of the water. It was hard to see in the
gloom, but I could make out long blond hair under a cap.
Sarah had long blond hair. The posture of the woman
seemed stiff and unnatural, almost as if she were about to
topple off the bench at any moment.

Lou refused to go any closer. I didn't want to get any
closer myself, but I had to. Victor and Eli came up beside me
and together we warily approached the bench. The woman
must have been able to hear us coming, but she didn't turn. I

walked around the bench to get a look at her, but her head was down and she didn't look up. I had to crouch in front of her to get a look at her face. I let out the breath I'd been holding.

"Sarah?" I said.

There was no response. I reached out and touched her on the shoulder, and she flinched as if someone had touched her with a hot poker. I lifted up her head and this time there was no reaction, but when I looked at her face I saw eyes wide open, staring sightlessly into the darkness. Both hands were clenched tight. In the center of her forehead was a dark smudge, like a Catholic's cross on Ash Wednesday. Probably part of the working of a spell, although not one familiar to me.

Eli gently pulled me away. "Let Victor take a look at her, Mason," he said.

I was more than glad to relinquish the examination. I felt sick to my stomach. All the troubles of last year seemed to be resurfacing.

Victor squatted down beside Sarah, oblivious to the mud and grassy damp. He reached into his pack and pulled out the tools of his trade: several crystals, small pyramids of different metals—copper, iron, silver, etc.—a sort of stethoscope with an engraved disk, and a very mundane flashlight. I walked to the edge of the lake and stood with my back to them, staring out across the dark water. I hadn't seen Sarah for a long time, but I'd liked her a lot. After a while, Eli called.

"Mason. We're done."

I walked back over to the bench. "What's the verdict?" I asked, although I knew the answer.

"Not good, I'm afraid."

"Is there any chance? Some kind of healing? Something's happened to her mind, right? There must be something we can do for her."

"No. Usually there's a way to treat this—it's typical of what can happen when a practitioner tries to take over another's mind, but this is worse."

"How could it be worse?"

"There's nothing left to heal. She's empty."

"Empty? How can she be empty?" I raised my voice. "What about that mark on her forehead? Won't that tell you something about the type of spell that was used, something that could reverse it?"

Victor was busy putting his tools back in the fanny pack. "It's not a mark," he said curtly. "It's blood." He handed me the flashlight. "Take a look."

I walked over reluctantly, bent down close, and shined the light on her face. The pupils of her eyes didn't react at all. She just kept staring into the distant void. I told myself it was not so different from someone with a medical condition, someone in a coma, but her staring eyes and slight exhalation of breath gave me the chills. Her breath carried the faint odor of peppermint. She always did like peppermint.

Victor was right; it was blood. But what he hadn't told me was that the blood came from a neat little hole drilled in the center of her forehead. Someone had trepanned her, for God knows what reason.

Eli came up and stood beside me. "Whoever did this had no success with possession. So I think he decided to go one step further: drill right into the pineal gland—the third eye—and see if what couldn't be done by psychic means might be accomplished with brute physical force. That failed, too, but now there's nothing left at all. It's not only her mind that's been destroyed; it's her brain as well."

"What are we going to do?" I asked. Eli and Victor said nothing, just stood there, looking at me.

"We can't," I said. "That's *Sarah* for God's sake."

"Not anymore," Eli said gently.

Victor didn't speak. He didn't have to. The horrible thing was, they both expected me to do it. I'm the one she'd been closest to, so it was my responsibility. That's one of the unwritten rules of practitioner society—and many other societies as well. You take care of your own. You do what needs to be done, even if it twists you up in a knot and gives you nightmares ever after. I remember joking about it with Eli once—he'd called it the Old Yeller rule. It didn't seem so funny anymore.

Sarah was still sitting in that unnatural rigid position. I thought back to when Lou had faced a similar situation. He hadn't hesitated. If he could do it, so could I. I walked over to the bench and my legs started to tremble. I took several deep breaths, but couldn't seem to catch any air. I raised my hands, breathed deeply again, then lowered them. In the dark, she looked almost normal, the Sarah I had laughed with and argued with and slept with. I stood there paralyzed for an eternity.

A hand on my shoulder made me almost jump out of my skin. I turned to find Victor standing behind me. His expression was difficult to read, a mixture of sadness and compassion, but with almost a hint of contempt.

"Go back, Mason," he said. "I'll take care of it."

I shook my head. "I can't let you. You know that."

A trace of a smile flickered over his face. "Very noble. But you know you can't do it. You don't have it in you."

"But—"

"No buts. I didn't know her well; it's not as hard for me. Tradition be damned. Just go."

There wasn't any point in arguing. He was right. I just didn't have it in me. If she'd been suffering horribly, I could have done it, but she wasn't. She was sitting calmly and staring out across the vastness. Not that there was a "she" anymore.

I joined Eli and we walked silently back to the path near the main building. The clouds closed in and the rain started up again. Lou got up from his vantage point, stretched, and accompanied us. I listened fearfully for a scream, or a gasp, or something to let me know it had been done, but there was nothing.

Two minutes later, Victor joined us. He didn't say a word. But he did hold out something in his hand.

"She dropped this when—she dropped this."

It was a flat and angular green stone, similar to jade. Eli peered at it through rain-streaked glasses.

"It's like a rune stone," he said. "A power object. Usually for divination, as in the I Ching. But there are darker uses for them."

"Like power transfers," Victor said. "And control."

Lou sat at my feet, shivering as I stared out at the cold rain. I didn't say anything. There was nothing to say.

TWO

"SO WHAT ARE WE GOING TO DO?" I ASKED.

I was sitting in Victor's study, looking at a familiar scene: the dark-paneled Victorian room, the crackling fire in the wonderful fireplace cutting through the chill of a cold November day; Maggie curled up on the hearth, Victor seated behind his giant mahogany desk, and Eli impatiently pacing by the tall windows overlooking the Pacific.

Lou had plopped himself down by the fire. Maggie was already in the best spot on the hearth, and when he did, she half opened her eyes and then closed them again. The snarling and spitting that usually manifested between them whenever Lou showed up wasn't happening for once.

"There's not much we can do," Eli said. "Except to be extra careful. And spread the word, of course. Someone was trying to take over Sarah's mind, to possess her. That much is clear. But as to who or why—" He shrugged his massive shoulders.

"I thought that couldn't be done except in extraordinary cases."

"Usually, it can't. Even the very attempt can destroy the

victim's mind. You saw the result. This might be an iso-
lated incident, but I doubt it. The entire practitioner community will need to be on their guard."

I got up and moved a little closer to the fire. "Has there
been anything else like this?"

"Not here," Victor said. "But there have been similar incidents recently in Portland. I've already called for some
help."

I didn't like the sound of that. The last time Victor and
Eli had asked someone for help, we were almost helped
right into the grave.

"No, not like last time," Eli said, seeing my expression.
"An old friend. As soon as he gets here we'll start looking
into it. In the meantime, just be careful."

The sound of steps coming up the stairs interrupted
him. Timothy, Victor's latest, strolled in, jacket slung over
his shoulder. Lou pulled himself up from the warmth of the
hearth and ambled over, tail slowly wagging. He doesn't
usually bother much about nonpractitioners one way or the
other, but Tim was on his short list of good people. Maybe
it was Tim's habit of carrying liver treats and handing them
out to every dog he saw.

Tim threw his jacket toward a nearby chair, barely
reaching it and drawing an exasperated look from Victor. I
walked over to shake his hand. Lou wasn't the only one
who approved of Timothy. He was a quantum leap forward
in the ongoing Victor boyfriend parade. For one thing, he
was older, somewhere in his midthirties. He worked at a
South of Market Internet company, doing some sort of
software development. He wasn't bad looking—dark, un-
ruly hair, rows of small gold loops in both ears, a wide
mouth that was usually open in laughter—but he was miles
from the typical pretty boy Victor usually favors.

Mostly, Victor ends up with more shallow, short-term
relationships. His last, Danny, had been more serious, but
after seeing a disturbing confrontation with a truly horrific
creature, Danny had moved out the next day. Victor tends

to date nonpractitioners who have no idea of who he really is or what he does, and sooner or later something nasty and supernatural is bound to happen. And that's the end of that, as far as they're concerned. I suspect Victor likes it that way—if nothing else it avoids a lot of messy breakup scenes.

But for once, he'd told Timothy up front exactly what the deal with him was. I wish I could have been there to see it. I could imagine, from my own experience, how it had gone: first, the belief that it was a peculiar joke; then the gradual awareness that the person telling you about magical powers was dead serious and thus crazy as a loon. Then, figuring out a way to humor the madman, while easing quietly toward the door. Finally, a small demonstration of talent, and the dawning realization that the universe might be, after all, far stranger than you ever could have imagined.

Timothy took it well, a lot better than I would have if I'd been in his shoes. Of course, he was a lot more grown-up than I was. He wasn't in awe of Victor and his powers. In fact, he mostly treated him with a certain fond tolerance. He was smart, too; Victor occasionally asked him for advice and even listened once in a while.

"Mason," he said, grabbing my arm. "Perfect. I was just going to call you."

"Here I am."

"You know my friend Robyn? The one with the band?"

I nodded. "Dagger Dykes, right?"

"Right. Well they're supposed to play a gig at Goldie's Bar tonight; it's a big deal for them. Then, just yesterday, their guitar player gets drunk and falls off the stage. Broke her arm. They desperately need a fill-in, and you're the best guitar player I know."

I could see why they might be bummed out. Goldie's is one of those clubs where every up-and-coming band wants to play. It's a dive, but it's got a certain something and it's launched several careers.

"That's a nice compliment," I said, "but I'm a jazz player, remember."

"Yeah, but you can play anything. I've heard you. They need someone good enough to pick up the songs without any practice."

"Thanks for the vote of confidence. But aren't I the wrong gender for the band?"

"They don't care. Goldie's is a tranny bar on Thursdays anyway, so it hardly matters."

"Thanks, but I don't think so. I've got a lot on my plate right now."

"They're paying good money."

This put a different face on it, since I was broke. You'd think I wouldn't have money problems, considering my magical abilities. I could easily hand a store clerk a one and get change for an illusionary twenty. But I don't like cheating people, not to mention that my job with Victor was mostly about preventing practitioners from doing just those sorts of things.

Of course, I could always transmute iron into gold if I got desperate. I really can; so can any practitioner who possesses a respectable amount of talent, and everyone tries it at some point just to see if they can. The problem is, it's a lot harder to actually transform something than it is to play with illusions, and metals are notoriously difficult to work with.

At today's prices, one gram of gold is worth maybe twenty-five dollars. Transforming a gram of iron or lead into gold would take at least four hours of extended effort, plus another four hours to recover. Not very cost effective.

"How much are we talking?" I asked. Timothy named a figure that was double what I usually get from a jazz gig. "Do they have charts?"

He laughed. "Not likely."

It didn't really matter. Dagger Dykes are an indie rock band, all sweet melodies and basic chords. It shouldn't be a problem. It would help take my mind off Sarah; sitting around at home and brooding wasn't going to help anything. Seeing I was considering it, Timothy pushed.

"You'll do it, then?"

"Sure," I said. "Why not?"

"Great. I'll tell them. Ten o'clock tonight—two sets. I can swing by about nine and give you a lift to the club if you like. You should be able to fit your amp in the backseat."

That sealed the deal. No parking hassles to worry about. There wasn't much else to talk about, so I signaled to Lou and headed home.

Victor's house is in the Sunset, right across from Ocean Beach, a faux Victorian mansion constructed a few years ago using plans from a London original. It has a courtyard where you can park, with an ivy-covered wall along the back to make it seem less sterile. It was warded of course, and the warding around the house is powerful—all sharp angles and crisp lines of power, humming with energy. It makes my own protection look feeble by comparison.

But Victor needs the protection. When you spend your career telling powerful practitioners what they can and can't do, you have to expect occasional unpleasantries. The warding is good enough to make the house not only the safest place in San Francisco, but probably in all of California. And the wards were not only proof against magical energy; they were also as effective a physical barrier as a steel door. Of course, Lou and I were exempt; we could stroll right in with no problem.

I walked toward my van, which was parked by the corner of the back wall. Lou was pacing alongside, head down, lost in his own doggy thoughts, when he stopped short and stiffened, almost imperceptibly. I stopped as well, scanning the area around the house for threats. I didn't see anything, but Lou had now focused on a section of the back wall. I couldn't make out anything but low bushes and ivy, but if he thought something was there, you can be sure there was.

The smallest flicker of movement was enough to give it away. Now I could see it. Plastered against the wall, standing in plain view, was a man. But it wasn't easy to make him out; chameleonlike, he had altered his body parts to blend in with the background. Not just color, but texture as well. Where the ivy covered the wall, his head and shoulders were a dappled tangle of glossy green leaves. His right arm and torso were a rough and sandy brick; his feet were the mottled green and brown of the ground beneath him.

If this were a practitioner bent on harm, which seemed more than likely, shouting out, "Hey, you! What are you doing here?" wouldn't be the best plan. I bent down to retie my shoelace, stalling for time, a clever ploy if ever there was one. The smart thing to do was to go back inside and return with Eli and Victor by my side. On the other hand, he might slip away if I did. Besides, I had the advantage. He didn't know I had seen through his concealment ploy. I should be able to surprise him, and he was standing in the perfect spot for it.

If you want to trap a fellow practitioner, you'd best do it in a way that prevents him from speaking or gesturing. An all-purpose immobilization spell would be great, but I don't have that sort of thing handy. Victor, I'm sure, could whip one out at a moment's notice, but I have to work with what's around me.

That's where the ivy came in. Campbell had helped me a lot in strengthening my organic magic, so I could now work easily with all types of plants. I pulled in some natural energy from the sun and drew on the life force of the ivy itself. That was easy for me, but it was sure hard on the ivy. I could see it wilting, and it would take a day or two for it to recover.

I straightened up, whirled around, and shouted, "Bind." The tendrils of ivy shot out like stop-motion animation and whipped around the man's body, securely trapping his arms. At the same time, other shoots twined around his head, muffling him as surely as duct tape.

I strolled over to see exactly what I had caught. I hadn't gone more than a few steps when I heard Lou warning me, but instead of his usual high-pitched bark it was a low baying sound. At the same time, the air around me thickened and closed in. It was liked walking underwater, then like trudging through syrup, and finally, I was stuck solid like a fly in amber. I would have shook my head in disgust, only I couldn't move it. It was a time dislocation spell, where my personal time had been slowed down to the point where I was effectively immobilized. Sure, I could still move some, only it would now take me a couple of hours to scratch my nose.

I didn't understand how he had managed it, until part of a flower bed dislodged itself and moved toward the man trussed up on the wall. Ahh, mystery solved. There were two people. I had ignored the basic rule of confrontation: identify all of your opponents before charging blithely ahead.

A distinctly nonmagical knife made its appearance, and very shortly after the man was free. He took the knife from the other's hand, brushed off some remaining leaves, and approached me. Where the hell was Lou? Maybe for once he'd shown some restraint and scampered back to alert Victor and Eli.

It was hard to get a good look at the guy; the camouflage spell caused his outline to waver and flicker as he passed through the courtyard. It made me dizzy even to look at him. He stopped in front of me, made several gestures, and released the time spell that was holding me. I staggered forward, having been caught in midstep when it hit, and as I did, he took the camouflage spell off of himself, revealing a Hispanic man with long, frizzy hair scrunched up into a bushy ponytail. I stared in amazement.

"Rolando?"

He held out his hand and pulled me into a hug when I grasped it. "Mason. Good to see you, man. You've kept your sharp eye, but you still don't think things all the way through, do you?"

Lou ran up to greet him. I eyed Lou suspiciously, wondering if he'd known all along who it was but thought it would be funny to see me get my metaphorical ass kicked. I looked around to see who Rolando's partner might be just as she removed her own camouflage spell.

It wasn't anyone I knew, but I wished that I did. She was small, no more than five-two, with masses of dark curly hair. Delicate features, with a swath of freckles dusting the bridge of her nose, atypical for such a dark complexion. She was smiling, her face radiating good humor mixed with a slight air of satisfaction at having so neatly caught me. She seemed . . . well, merry is the only word I can think of.

It's often said that after you know someone for a while, you don't really see them anymore. They just are who they are. But sometimes the same thing happens the minute you meet them. She was more than attractive, downright stunning in fact, but after the first few seconds she just looked like herself, as if I had known her for years.

She was wearing jeans, a dark top, and a light jacket. At first I would have pegged her at twenty-five or so, but as she came closer I could see the fine lines around the corners of her eyes. So she wasn't so young after all. Even better. And talk about chemistry. I was, in the old-fashioned sense of the word, instantly smitten.

It could have been an enhancement spell, but if it was, it was the best I'd ever seen. And I couldn't think of any reason she'd bother with such a thing. She came up to Rolando and ruffled his hair with affection. He put his arm around her shoulder. Rolando always had a way with women, though he never got very serious about them. He was worse than I was; at least I'd had a couple of real relationships, even if they hadn't lasted all that long.

"That was big fun," she said to him. "I didn't believe he'd even see you."

"I told you," he said.

"I didn't at first," I admitted. "It was Lou who tipped me off."

"Oh," she said. "An Ifrit. Lucky man."

"Don't I know it. But don't tell him that; it'll just go to his head." We stood looking at each other until Rolando jumped in.

"Oh, sorry. Josephine, this is Mason. An old friend. Mason, my sister, Jo."

When you think of words that bring you pleasure, it's most often words like "love," or "chocolate," or "Is it okay if I pay you in cash?" I now added the word "sister" to that list.

"What are you doing here, anyway?" I asked. Then I got it. Victor. Problems in Portland. He'd said that he was getting some help. I'd worked with Rolando in the past, and not only was he a friend; he was one of the better practitioners around. He noticed the look of comprehension that flitted across my face.

"Exactly," he said. "Victor called me." He stopped and offered me a sympathetic half smile. "He told me about Sarah. I'm really sorry."

"Yeah, me, too," I said.

"Something similar was going on in Portland a while ago. More than similar, almost identical. I've been out of the enforcer game for a while, but it was nasty enough to pull me back in. We never did find out exactly what was going on, and after a while it just stopped. Now it looks like it might be starting up again here."

"Any ideas?"

"One very big idea, but no way to prove it. Anyway, I'll run it by you later. Right now I'm late. I promised Victor I'd be here as soon as I could. What are you doing tonight?"

"Playing a gig down at Goldie's Bar on Folsom. Not a real gig, just helping out an indie band. But you should come by and we can talk before the gig." I looked over toward Josephine to make sure she understood the invitation included her.

"What time?"

"We start about ten. Come a little early and we can catch up."

Rolando and Josephine made their way into the house, and Lou and I climbed into my van and headed home. It was good to see Rolando again. He and I had been tight back in the day, although apparently not as tight as I'd thought. I hadn't even known he had a sister. We had a lot in common; like me, he had fallen into the enforcer game almost by accident, and like me, his real passion had nothing to do with the world of magical talent. I consider myself a jazz musician at heart, just one who also happens to have a magical talent. Rolando had his own dreams and they had nothing to do with magic, either. He wanted to play professional soccer.

He was good, too, good enough to play with the old semipro San Francisco Seals, a team good enough to beat several MLS teams back a few years ago. He had several tryouts with MLS teams, but he never quite made the cut. He definitely had the skills and he had the body, but he lacked that indefinable extra that separates the amateur from the pro.

Of course, he could have used his other talent to become a star. It wouldn't have been difficult. He was right on the cusp anyway. A slight nudge, one that would tuck the curving shot into the corner of the net, or a momentary disruption that would enable him to sprint past a defender would have been enough to put him over the top. But he wouldn't do it. I never asked him why not. I knew why not. For the same reason I don't use talent to amplify and sweeten my tone. If you have any respect for yourself and your passion, that kind of thing is simply out of the question.

THREE

BY TEN I WAS ON THE BANDSTAND, READY TO PLAY. Timothy spotted some friends and drifted off to join them. Rolando and his sister hadn't shown up yet, but I guessed they'd be along sooner or later. I'd left my Gibson Birdland at home, opting instead for the Stratocaster that had been sitting in my closet for a year. I'd also dug out my effects board, a wooden plank with individual effects glued down and hooked together into a master. This wasn't jazz, after all.

I did have to leave Lou at home. Dogs are not welcome in clubs, even dogs who aren't really dogs. Not that he cared. There's a dog door in the back and he was more than happy to go off on his own doggy/Ifrit business. I don't know the half of what he does when I'm gone.

I chatted with the band members as we set up. Goldie's is basically a large, bare room with a scuffed wooden floor and a bunch of rickety tables. The small bar at the very back is always overwhelmed, and drinks are always a long time coming. In fact there's very little to recommend it, except that somehow it had become the favored bar for new hot bands trying to come up in the world. Certain bars gain that particular cachet, for reasons that are unfathomable. It's the same with bands. Nobody really knows why one band or bar becomes hugely popular and another, equally good, falls by the wayside. If anyone could figure out why it happens to some and not others, they'd be a millionaire.

If nothing else, the Dagger Dykes were an eclectic group of women. The lead singer was tall and slinky, with a sequined floor-length gown straight out of the forties. The bass player was African-American, slightly overweight, with frizzy hair, thick glasses, and beige coveralls. Keyboards were handled by a blond girl who looked like she was just out of high school. I was hoping she'd be able to at least run through the tunes with me, since keyboard players usually know at least some musical theory. But no, it turned out she played strictly by ear.

I was saved by the drummer, of all people. Drummers are much maligned, with some justification. (What do you call a person who hangs out with musicians? A drummer.) But surprisingly, she was the one person in the band who actually knew how to write a chord chart.

She was small and wiry with a lined face, shaved head, and short black Mohawk. A sleeveless top showed off arms and neck covered with tattoos, along with black crescents inked behind each ear. She looked at me skeptically from behind her kit.

"I'm Megan," she said. "How you doing? Do you think you can carry this off?"

"I can give it a try."

"Timothy says you're a guitar guru."

"Timothy tends to exaggerate."

She tightened up the ride cymbal. "Not usually."

She did a couple of quick rolls to loosen up, then ran through the set list with me.

"Listen," she said, "the first tune is the most important. It sets the tone, you know? If we can jump right in and grab the audience, the rest of the set will be cake. But if we fumble around . . ."

I nodded. "I know. I have played a time or two before."

She paused for a second to decide whether I was copping an attitude, then decided getting off on the wrong foot wouldn't be the best thing for the upcoming gig.

"Great," she said, running through the chord changes of the songs for me. "First tune is simple, but after the second verse we need a killer guitar solo. Jane was awesome. Mostly drunk, but still awesome."

I smiled. I was starting to like her. "Well, I'll certainly do my best."

We started off with an up-tempo rocker. The bass player was solid, the keys were tasty, and the singer was on her game. But what really made this band was Megan. She sat hunched behind her drum kit, not too busy, but with perfect time and the pop that makes a good drummer. Just like some sax players have a sweet tone or a singer has a compelling voice, some drummers hit the skins just right. A good drummer has an electric snap that can carry a whole band. In fact, a good band with a great drummer will often sound better than a great band with a merely competent one.

I was lying back, trying to get a feel for the melody. A good solo, especially in rock or pop, is built around melody. Otherwise, no matter how fast your runs and how flashy your effects, you're just playing a bunch of scales.

Megan looked over at me and nodded her head as the singer wrapped up the second verse. I started out my solo with a single sustained note, bending and letting it end with a fast vibrato. Then I built quickly—pop songs don't give you a lot of time to ease into it. Nothing complicated—just a variation of the hook, then the same line played down the neck, then a high-energy double-note run ending on a high note.

The rest of the band picked up on the energy and kicked

it up. I hadn't played anything but jazz for a while, and I was having fun. Not all jazz musicians are good rock players. Sure, rock is a lot simpler. Any jazz guy can play the notes and do some interesting stuff, but there's more to it than that. Just like jazz, rock takes a certain feel, and just because it's simple doesn't mean it's easy. But my first guitar heroes, before jazz caught me, were Jimi and Stevie Ray, and I still had those roots to rely on. I backed off as the singer came in with the final verse:

> Southern breeze
> Phosphorescence in the seas
> And the nights are oh so warm
> I can't sleep
> Sharks are circling in the deep
> And they wait so patiently.

Megan had wanted to grab the crowd on the first song, and we'd certainly succeeded. People sitting at the crowded tables were whistling and clapping enthusiastically. She looked over at me, smiled, and mouthed the words, "Want a job?"

I saw that Rolando and Josephine had slipped in and were sitting at a tiny table in the back of the room. Josephine caught my eye and clapped her hands high over her head, half mockingly, half seriously.

As Megan had predicted, the rest of the set was a breeze. The crowd was on our side. They wanted to like us, and although I did miss a few licks, the audience was forgiving, especially since I made up for it with some slick guitar work.

After the first set was over, I carried a beer over to Rolando's table and pulled up a chair, almost knocking over a drink on the table jammed in next to us. I don't usually drink when I'm playing, but if rock doesn't call for some alcohol, what does? Josephine greeted me with a wide smile.

"I'm impressed," she said. "Rolando told me you were good, but most of the time he doesn't know what he's talking about."

Rolando smiled good-naturedly. "Only most of the time? Your opinion of me must be mellowing."

"No, sometimes you do get it right. In fact, I think I do remember another time, back in the nineties."

Rolando took a swig of beer. "Ah, family. Nothing like it."

I noticed they were wearing matching bracelets, silver and antique looking. I guessed they were a lot closer than the average brother and sister.

"So what have you been up to?" I asked. "It's been a few years, no? How is Portland treating you?"

"Great. I love it there. It's like San Francisco fifteen years ago. We've been on vacation for the last month—just traveling around, nothing special. Then Victor got hold of us and here we are." He stopped and pointed a finger at me. "I hear you had quite a time this last year, though."

I made little circles on the wet table top. "You could say that."

They both saw it wasn't anything I wanted to talk about. Josephine had finished her own drink so she reached over to take a sip of Rolando's beer.

"Well, it looks like there might be a problem here again," she said.

"So it seems." I turned to Rolando. "You said something about having an idea?"

"Yeah," said Rolando. "Have you ever heard of a practitioner named Byron? A dark arts guy?"

"Don't think so," I said. "Is Byron his real name?"

"I doubt it. You know, a lot of practitioners still are hesitant about letting their true names be known."

I knew. It comes from the old days, when practitioners believed that knowledge of true names conferred special power over another. It doesn't; that belief is just so much nonsense. Even practitioners can be superstitious, though. It's still considered impolite in some circles to use someone's name directly unless you're a friend. Which can make introductions at parties somewhat difficult.

"Who is he?" I asked.

"He's a black practitioner out of Portland. When we had some similar incidents there, his name kept coming up."

"Like what?"

"I'll tell you later. It wasn't nice."

"Byron moved down to San Francisco," Josephine put in. "Coincidentally, the problems in Portland stopped about the same time he left."

"That is a coincidence, isn't it? How long ago?"

"Just last month."

"Probably why I haven't heard of him."

"He's young. Slicked-back hair and pointed sideburns, and even a soul patch for God's sake. A very image-conscious guy, always stylish."

An extraordinarily attractive waitress with a tongue piercing stopped by the table to see if I wanted anything else. I shook my head no. I didn't want to get hammered, even for a simple gig like this one. I looked over to where the rest of the band was sitting with friends and groupies. They apparently had no such qualms, since they were slamming down shots of Jack Daniels as fast as they could.

Rolando surprised me by refusing the refill offer as well, something not like him. The Rolando I was familiar with seldom, if ever, turned down a drink. He smiled at me, knowing exactly what I was thinking.

"I've backed off some in the last couple of years," he said. He pointed over at Jo. "I attribute it to her bad influence."

"We've got to go in a few minutes, anyway," Jo said. "Victor's asked us to check on a rumor that's been making the rounds. Something about a weird person. Or monster, or whatever, hanging out under one of the access ramps to the Bay Bridge."

"A troll, no doubt," I said.

Josephine laughed. "Well, Victor wants us to check him

out. I think he's grasping at straws, looking into anything that sounds peculiar. It shouldn't take long, though; it's right over by where we live. Actually, he almost ordered us to check it out. Rolando says you both worked for Victor for a couple of years, back when. How did you manage to last?"

"Oh, Victor's not so bad," I said, amazed that I was defending him. It was like when someone starts trashing the brother that you yourself can't really stand. Then it's time to pull in ranks against the outsider. Although I was hoping she wouldn't be an outsider for long. "He's just . . . well, he's just Victor."

"Is he ever," said Rolando. "Besides, Mason was never much of an enforcer, anyway."

"You're too kind."

"You know it's true. Telling people what to do and not do isn't your thing." He turned to Josephine. "But Mason is pretty smart. Sooner or later, he figures out what's really going on. Always, though it might take a while. More of an investigator than an enforcer. Me, I'm just the muscle."

Josephine looked at me thoughtfully. "Good to know," she said.

Rolando took another swig of beer. "Anyway, back to Byron. He didn't get down here much, mostly stayed up in Portland, but there was one person here he was friends with, another black arts guy. Want to take a guess?"

"Harry Keller," I said.

"Right in one."

Harry Keller had been the premier black arts guy in San Francisco until he bit off more than he could chew. I was there; what he bit off almost chewed me up as well. Also interesting, Harry had been connected to Christoph, and Christoph had been, among other things, an expert at possessing other practitioners.

"Have you talked with this Byron guy lately?" I asked.

"We just got here, remember? I'd like to, but I have no idea where he is or how to find him. I've been away from San Francisco too long to have any contacts here. Maybe you can help." He drained the last of his drink. "Or, what about Lou? I seem to remember he was quite good at finding people."

"Only those he knows," I said. "If he's never met someone, he can't locate them."

"Oh, of course. Now I remember. That figures; we wouldn't want it to be easy, would we now?"

"I'll see what I can dig up," I said. "Unless of course you can pin it on the troll tonight." Rolando laughed.

"Sounds good. Let's get together tomorrow then. You have got to see our new place. It's a condo over on Beale Street. Right downtown by the Bay Bridge with an incredible view. Tenth floor. We're finally living the high life."

That was unexpected. Condos there were hard to come by, and cost as much as a small house. There was no way he had that kind of money unless things with him had changed drastically. Or maybe if he were doing things he shouldn't be.

"You must be doing well these days," I said.

Rolando picked up on my expression and smiled a second time. He knew me well enough to understand exactly what was going through my mind.

"Oh, I'm doing pretty well. I found a way to use talent in a way that makes one horse run faster than another."

"Great."

"Yeah, it is. Only problem is, I still can't figure out which horse it is."

"Must be frustrating," I said. He laughed.

"Seriously, I've been working for the city of Portland for a while now, trying to get an MLS franchise for the city. It's a natural; soccer is big up there. The only thing standing in our way is Seattle. Jo's been doing some PR part-time, but she's going back to school."

"Never too late to learn," she said.

"The city owes me a lot of vacation time, so the call from Victor came at a good time. And no, we're not paying for the condo. It's a sublet, free, courtesy of Victor. I figure it's the least he can do since he wants our help. Call me to-morrow and we'll set up a time."

He scribbled down his phone number and address on the back of a napkin, drained the rest of his beer, and waved as he and Josephine headed out the door. The rest of the band was tuning up for the second set, so I wandered back to join them.

I was a lot more relaxed for the second set, and now that I had a feel for the band, I started using a lot more of my effects board. You have to be careful with effects; if you use them just because they sound cool without any regard for the shape of the tune, you can ruin the sound of the band. But a little here and there goes a long way and really adds to the music.

About halfway through the second set I noticed a short, dark-haired woman with a cast on her left arm sitting at a front table. She was looking daggers at me under heavy brows, slamming down shots and glowering. I couldn't fig-ure what her problem was until it dawned on me that she must be the injured guitar player, and I was playing far too well for her liking. I eased off a bit. I wasn't going to be playing with Dagger Dykes on any regular basis, and piss-ing off their regular player and shaking her confidence wasn't going to help anyone in the long run.

The crowd was still into it, though, and by the time we had finished the set, they were on their feet, calling for an encore. Meg, the drummer, shook her head.

"Always leave them wanting more," she said. "That way, they'll be sure to come to the next show."

I collected my very welcome check and located Timo-thy. I expected he'd want to hang out for a while, but he was ready to go.

"I'm not as young as I used to be," he said. "These days I'm pretty much done by midnight."

He left to retrieve his car and I packed up my guitar and hauled my amp and my board out to the sidewalk. As I waited there, I cast around for any psychic activity in the area. My troubles last year had started after just such an otherwise uneventful gig, and I had no desire to repeat that performance. Especially since more troubles seemed to be on the way. This time, as far as I could tell, there was nothing out of the ordinary.

Timothy pulled up in his Subaru and I loaded my gear in the back. Before I got in, I took one last look around, this time on a more mundane level. Still nothing. But just as I was about to climb into the passenger seat, I saw a movement in a doorway down the block, as if someone had just pulled back. I stood there with one hand on the door handle, considering. Probably nothing, maybe just a drunk or a homeless guy. Or both. Still . . .

"Hold on a sec," I said, and walked back over to stand in the door of the club. Inside, people were still drinking, talking, and in some cases, getting a bit raucous. I let the surging life wash over me, absorbing the vitality of the crowd, then walked back to the car. I searched along the sidewalk until I found a disgusting piece of gum mashed flat by passing feet. Luckily I didn't need to touch it. I took the sticky property of the gum and cast out the life force from the bar. The idea was that the force would stick to any living thing in the area. Sure enough, points of burning light started to appear wherever I looked. Timothy, being the nearest, burned brightly. Down at the corner, a couple stumbling arm in arm twinkled like Christmas lights. Several smaller lights, close to the ground, showed where cats were prowling in the dark.

I leaned against the car door and looked up the street in the opposite direction. I could partially see into an alley halfway up the block, and was baffled by a myriad of tiny lights scurrying back and forth. Oh, of course. Rats. They say that there are as many rats in the average big city as there are people. We just don't see them most of the time.

I turned around and stared at the doorway where I had seen movement. It was as dark as ever, not a glimmer of light. But that didn't mean there was no one there—quite the opposite. Sometimes what you don't see is as revealing as what you do. The whole dog not barking in the night thing.

I'd definitely seen someone there, so the lack of light meant that he was shielding. And shielding extremely well, which indicated a certain level of power and expertise. I didn't think I was being paranoid, not after last night.

It seemed quite possible that whoever was shielding in that doorway was there because of me. It's not like a doorway on Folsom Street is a major tourist attraction. And there was something familiar about the person. No matter how well you shield, once the shielding is discovered something will escape. Not enough to identify who it was, but enough to make me wonder if it might not be someone I knew.

But if it was a practitioner, my first instinct to rush over and confront him might not be the best idea. For one thing, he could be stronger than I was. Second, there was Timothy. If he were to get caught in a magical cross fire, it wouldn't be so good for him. If anything were to happen to him, Victor would never forgive me. I wouldn't forgive me, either.

But maybe I could at least get a look at whoever it was. That might well clear things up right now, or at least give us a good starting place. There was no way I could just stroll over to the doorway; he'd either slip away or it would spark the exact confrontation I wanted to avoid. There was another way, however. There usually is.

I focused on one of the small lights that indicated the presence of a cat. I needed to get close to do what I intended. In fact, I needed to be touching it, preferably holding it. That might be difficult. Feral cats are not known for their willingness to warmly cuddle up to strangers.

I walked over to a trash can that sat outside the club door and started rummaging through it like a starving homeless person. The door guy looked at me curiously, but decided it was none of his business. Toward the bottom I found the perfect concoction: the last remains of what was once a tuna melt. I reached out and absorbed the essence of the half-eaten delicacy, a very peculiar magical operation.

I was expending a lot of energy, though, especially after playing two sets of music. Playing takes some of the same energy as utilizing talent, although two jazz sets would have taken a lot more. Slowly, I walked over to where the lights showed me the cat, crouched between two parked cars. I squatted on my heels and made encouraging noises. The cat was wary, but the figure of a threatening human had been replaced in its mind by something nonthreatening, something that projected the very essence of tuna fish and melted cheese.

It hesitated, then streaked forward with very short, quick steps. Soon it was rubbing against me in an orgy of purring delight. I gently picked it up, walked back to the van, and slid into the passenger seat. Timothy looked at the two of us.

"Where did you find that cat?" he asked. He took a closer look. "And why?"

The cat was missing most of one ear and the other had several ragged notches in it. Its back was covered with scabs and it smelled strongly of garbage. It kept rubbing all over me, purring constantly, trying to find the source of the enticing essence of tuna and cheese.

"I'm going to borrow it for a while," I told him. "I need to follow someone, so I'm going to transfer my consciousness into the cat." Luckily Timothy had been with Victor long enough so he didn't even blink an eye at this statement.

"Couldn't that be dangerous?" he asked.

"Not really. Not unless I stay in there too long."

This wasn't exactly true. Eli had warned me about this sort of thing. It's not something you can do to another person. Even if you could, the results wouldn't be good.

A cat is easy, though, relatively speaking. Possession isn't difficult because their brains aren't much bigger than a walnut and it doesn't take much to overwhelm them. Unfortunately, that also means their brains are too small to hold a human ego together for long. If you stay for too long, your ego starts to dissolve. What happens next is un-clear, since to my knowledge no practitioner has ever tried such an experiment. Equally important, the other unknown factor: just how long is too long? If Eli knew I was even considering this, he'd throw a fit.

So it was dangerous, but it was worth it. If this really was someone I knew, it might well mean we had a spy in the middle of Victor's organization. There might not be a better chance to uncover him, and if I passed it up, more people could die before we discovered who it was.

I should be able to pull it off. This unknown person was shielding against practitioners, not animals. Why would he be? I could creep down under the parked cars to the occu-pied doorway, take a quick peek, find out who it was, and be back at the van inside of a minute.

"It will look like I've passed out," I told Timothy. "Don't worry; just keep me propped upright. I should come out of it in a minute or so."

"And if you don't, what then?" He'd definitely been hanging around Eli too much.

"Don't worry. I will. But if something does go wrong, just take off with my body and head back to Victor's. He'll know what to do."

Or maybe not. But I didn't anticipate any problems.

The first thing I did was to put some preventive wards around my body. With any kind of transference magic you don't want to leave yourself untenanted and unprotected. The most succinct advice on this subject came not from a practitioner, but from an old-time jazz player who claimed he had traversed the entire universe by means of astral pro-jection. He had never exhibited even the least smidgen of talent, but his advice was still sound.

"You got to be careful when you're traveling," he'd ad-vised, "mighty careful. Or when you get back, you're liable to find something else has set up housekeeping while you've been out."

I held the cat, which was still squirming and nuzzling,

and focused on its essence of catness, reaching out and letting my consciousness flow into it. A moment of intense nausea and pain, another of truly horrific dislocation, and suddenly I *was* the cat. I could feel the cat's awareness, curled up quietly somewhere in the back of its consciousness. A human would have been struggling and freaking out, but the cat ego just went to sleep. My human body relaxed and slumped back against the car seat.

I peered around, curious. I'd never attempted anything like this before. I do sometimes use a little trick where I can see through Lou's eyes, but when I do I'm just a passenger. I can see only what he sees, look where he wants to look, and dogs and practitioners often have very different ideas as to what's of interest.

The first thing I noticed was how bright everything seemed, more like a dark, cloudy day than nighttime. The second was how all the colors appeared washed out. The third was that there was a truly horrible taste in my mouth. God only knows what this cat had recently been snacking on.

I pawed at the door to be let out, unable to resist the temptation to try a meow at the same time. It came out as a strangled cry that sounded more like a cat about to throw up. Timothy leaned over and opened the passenger door, looking a lot less blasé about the situation than he had while I was explaining it.

I jumped down into the gutter and instinctively flattened out, ducking under the car for protection, checking across and down the street with my newly acquired night vision. Sure enough, I could see right into the doorway where my watcher waited in shadow. One thing I hadn't counted on, though—cats don't have much in the way of distance vision. Or maybe this particular cat was nearsighted. I could just make out a figure in a hooded sweatshirt, but it was fuzzy, without detail. And from my unaccustomed vantage point next to the ground, I couldn't even make a guess at his build or height.

I scuttled underneath the cars that were parked along the

street, trying to get close enough for a good look, stopping at each new car wheel to check for danger. A motorcycle whizzed by, scant feet from my protective cover underneath an SUV. Again, I froze, instinctively hunkering down. I might be in control of the cat's mind, but apparently its body had a mind of its own.

Finally I reached the car directly across from my target. I edged out from under the car, and now I could see into the doorway. The hooded sweatshirt still obscured his face, which unfortunately was now turned away from me as he stared down at the van which held Timothy and my unconscious body.

I started shifting position toward the back of the car, hoping to get an angle, but halfway there I stopped, confused. I knew I needed to reach the rear tire, but I'd forgotten why. I crouched there, lashing my tail, nervous but not understanding why.

Then I remembered. The figure in the doorway. I wanted to know who it was. As I reached the rear tire and peeked around, a quick movement on the curb to my right caught my attention. Another cat. I recognized him, a scarred tom that was constantly trying to move in on my territory. He had found something choice in a trash can, and was dragging it back to where he could eat it in peace. Fat chance. I exploded out from the cover of the car and came at him full speed. Usually he wouldn't back off, and we'd had some fierce battles, but this time, taken by surprise, he panicked and leapt up on a nearby ledge, leaving the spoils to me. Chicken bones. Not too old, lots of meat left. I tore into them, keeping an eye out for his return.

Another movement. Rat this time. Rats are dangerous. Another. They stalk me, careful not to get too close, but not afraid. Time to retreat. Not that hungry anyway.

Rain. Cold, wet, nasty. Shelter, back under car. Car was important, but why? Water, rushing down the gutter. Wet. Cold. Time to leave. Ready, ready. Wait . . . Wait . . . DOG! Freeze; be invisible.

Back around the car. Twist, turn, backtrack, down the alley. Around the corner, up onto the ledge. Off the wall, fast, fast, fast. There. Through the hole. There. There. Box. Safe. Sleep. Sleep.

FOUR

SUNLIGHT GLARED IN MY FACE. MY HEAD ACHED and I tried to turn away without opening my eyes. Victor's sarcastic drawl pushed its way into my consciousness.

"Come on, Mason. Time to wakey-wake."

I opened my eyes cautiously. I was lying on a futon in Victor's study, which was odd. Futons are not part of Victor's decor. Eli was towering over me, eyeing me with silent concern. On second look, it wasn't so much concern as it was anger.

Victor was standing behind him, clearly amused. Timothy was sprawled out in a chair across the room and Lou was sitting quietly next to me. He had several long scratches on his muzzle and a bright red one on his left ear. It was like everyone had gathered for an intervention. Eli finally spoke.

"What in God's name did you think you were doing?" he said, trying to keep his voice under control.

"Uhh, I'm not really sure," I said.

Truth was, I hadn't the slightest idea of what he was talking about. The last memory I had was of playing at the club, having a grand old time. I looked around the study, searching for some clue as to what had happened and how I'd ended up back here. Besides the group, the only thing I saw was Maggie, curled up in a patch of sunlight on the floor. It was hard to believe she was really an Ifrit. Lou is invaluable to me, clever and dedicated, whereas Maggie spends most of her time sleeping and eating, although I have to admit she did help bail me out on one occasion. But where Lou is an Ifrit who happens to also be a canine, Maggie acts more like a cat who just happens to be an Ifrit.

A cat. Oh. A cat. My memory rushed back: creeping under cars, slinking down alleys, totally forgetting what I was trying to do and eventually even who I was. Victor noticed the change in my expression.

"Starting to come back now, is it?" He was thoroughly enjoying the situation.

"Some of it," I said. "What exactly happened?"

Eli relaxed a bit. "Timothy waited in his car for you—or rather, the cat—to return." Timothy gave me a nod from his chair. "Then, when a half an hour had passed and there was still no cat and no you, he got scared." He broke off the recitation. "Mason, how could you? You, of all people? You know better, or at least I thought you did. Have you even half listened to anything I've ever tried to teach you?" His voice grew louder and my head started throbbing even more.

"It was just supposed to be for a couple of minutes," I said defensively. "Someone was waiting in a doorway, shielding. I thought if I could just get a glimpse at whoever it was, it might clear a lot of things up. Did Rolando tell you about Byron?"

"He did," Victor said. "You think it was him?"

"I never got a clear look. Things unraveled too quickly."

"Precisely," said Eli. "That's why you don't try stuff like that, especially when you're alone. You're a very lucky man, son."

"Did you get anything at all, even an impression?" asked Victor.

I shook my head and instantly regretted it as the throbbing started up again. "Not a thing. Someone in a hoodie is about it."

"Well, that's not much help, is it?" Eli said. "Not worth risking your very existence for, was it now?" His anger had faded and he was looking at me more in exasperation now. "Well, what's done is done."

"How did I get back here?" I asked. "I assume you came and got me?"

"Yes, sort of. After the worst half hour of his life, Timothy drove back here with your comatose body and woke up Victor."

Timothy spoke up. "Actually, I was screaming my head off. I was totally freaked out."

"As well you might have been," said Eli. "Victor called me, of course, and then drove back to the club with Timothy. I expected we'd need some assistance finding you, so I stopped by your place to pick up Lou. Only he wasn't there.

"So, I drove down to the club as well, and as we were standing in the street trying to figure out just how we were going to locate one particular cat in an urban jungle, Lou showed up."

It was lucky for me that San Francisco is such a small city, geographically speaking. Goldie's couldn't have been more than four miles from my house in a straight line. And it was even luckier that Lou can tell when I'm in trouble— clearly the Ifrit/practitioner connection we have saved my hide yet again. Eli reached down and gave him an affectionate pat.

"He was breathing hard from a long run, but it didn't take him more than five minutes to find the cat. It was in an alley three blocks from the club, hidden in a cardboard box under a pile of junk. We never would have found you without him. Still, we almost lost you again. The cat was out of that box and streaking down the alley before anyone but Lou could react. He took off after it, two feet behind, but it kept its lead and darted across Folsom Street, right through oncoming traffic. Two feet one way or the other and we would have lost both of you under the wheels of a minivan.

"He caught up with it on the sidewalk and pinned it down by the scruff of its neck, but by the time we came up, he'd paid a price." He pointed toward Lou's battle scars. "Victor immobilized the cat with one of his handy spells and we carried it back to the car. He managed to pull your consciousness out of the cat and put it back into your own body, but it was a close thing. There wasn't that much of 'you' left in that cat. Another hour and you would have lived out your days wishing you knew how to operate a can opener. You've been asleep since then."

"Thanks, Victor," I said, for once meaning it. He gave an offhanded shrug.

"Anytime. I like cats." I didn't quite catch his drift, but I was sure I'd been insulted in some fashion.

"What happened to the cat?" I asked.

"Oh, we released it. It ran off fifteen feet and then stopped and started cleaning itself."

AN HOUR LATER I WAS HOME. TIMOTHY HAD GIVEN me a ride back, and despite my headache I spent some time checking and updating my wards before I went inside. I didn't used to be so diligent about maintaining them, but after what happened last year I had become somewhat anal about the whole thing.

A few cups of coffee eased my head some and I started feeling better. It was already close to noon when I dug out the crumpled napkin Rolando had given me and punched in the number. Josephine answered.

"Josephine? Mason."

"Mason! How'd the rest of your gig go?" Her voice sounded like she was especially happy to hear from me, but maybe I was projecting.

"Great," I said. "The crowd loved us. Did you find your troll?"

I heard a muffled snort on the other end. "Yeah. He was curled up in a sleeping bag next to a support tower, doing a credible imitation of a homeless man with incipient psychosis."

"They can be clever, can't they? I hope Victor appreciates your brilliant investigative abilities."

She muttered something uncomplimentary and slightly obscene. I wasn't sure if she was directing it toward Victor or me.

"Speaking of odd people, I ran into someone interesting when I left the club after the gig. Someone waiting in a doorway, a practitioner, shielding."

"Really? Could you tell who it was?"

Apparently Eli hadn't told them of my misadventures, and since it didn't reflect much credit on me I decided to finesse it.

"I tried," I said, "but he got away before I could get a look at him."

"Byron, I'll bet."

"Maybe. But what makes you think that?"

"It just makes sense. Stuff happened in Portland. Then he moves to San Francisco. Now things are happening here. You're one of the people looking into it. And he is a dark arts guy, after all."

"Well, we should get together and talk about it. Is Rolando around?"

"He just ran out to the store. He'll be back in a few minutes. You want to come over?"

I didn't really feel like driving across town. Also, I suddenly realized I was starving.

"Why don't you guys come over to the Mission?" I said. "We can go for lunch, and talk things over there."

"Sure," she said. "Where exactly are you?"

I gave her my address and spent the next half hour straightening up the place. For once it wasn't too bad, but I did have to vacuum up the dog hair that Lou sheds daily. It turned out I didn't even have to do that, since when Rolando pulled up outside the house in a gold Civic, he just honked for me to come out.

"Where to?" he said, as I climbed into the back with Lou.

I directed him to Tashi's, a small family-run restaurant at the top of Noe Valley. It's one of my favorite haunts, with great sushi and home-style Japanese cooking, things you don't often see on a Japanese menu, like marinated fried catfish. Bonnie, the woman who owns and runs the place, is a shrewd businesswoman; she calls all her customers by name and makes each one feel that they, and they alone, are her special friend. You know it's all an act, but she's so good at it you can't help but feel flattered anyway. Her husband mans the kitchen by himself, and the busier it gets, the faster he moves, but he never looks hurried.

"Mason! Where have you been so long," she cried, rushing up to greet me. "I never see you anymore. And Lou." I hadn't been there for maybe two weeks. "These are your friends?"

I introduced Rolando and Josephine as we sat down and ordered miso soup and some hand rolls. One of the reasons I like to eat at Tashi's is that Lou is always welcome. The health department frowns on dogs in restaurants, but Bonnie doesn't care. And if any customers complained, which wasn't often, she told them he was a certified therapy dog, and could therefore stay. I had to keep an eye on him so he didn't go from table to table, sitting up in his cute-dog begging stance, but as long as I slipped him an occasional treat he behaved himself.

"So," I said, after giving them an edited version of last night's events, "what now? Track down Byron, you think?"

Rolando drummed his fingers rapidly on the tabletop, then waited for my response.

"Sorry," I told him. "Not getting it."

"It's a drumroll, idiot. Ta-dah! Already done."

"Already done, what?"

"Byron. I know where he lives."

Jo broke in. "Yeah, it was brilliant detective work on Rolando's part. A friend of ours in Portland called this morning and gave us the information. Apparently Byron left a forwarding address at the post office."

"That seems a bit odd for an archvillain," I said.

Rolando shrugged impatiently. "Who cares why he did it? We've got the address." He pulled a small notebook out of his shirt pocket. "One-oh-two Laidley Street. According to the Internet, that's close to here."

"Very close," I said. "Up around Harper Street, I think."

"Maybe time to pay a visit?"

I thought about it. "Couldn't hurt, I guess, though I'm not sure we'll learn anything."

One thing I've learned over the years is that bad guys never tell you anything unless you either have something they want or some means of threatening them. But at least I'd have a chance to meet him.

Rolando excused himself and headed off to the men's room. Jo looked at me appraisingly. She was wearing a simple black top and jeans again, and looked even better than I remembered. I figured I had maybe two minutes to dazzle her with my class and wit before Rolando returned.

"So, how are you liking San Francisco, anyway?" I suavely asked. Her mouth widened with amusement.

"Well, I haven't had a chance to see that much of it," she said. "I was hoping someone who knew the city could show me around."

Clearly I had impressed her. Well, at least she had decided to take pity on my feeble opening.

"Maybe we can find time to do the tourist thing," I said. "We can't chase bad guys twenty-four seven."

"I'd like that," she said. This was too easy. I had the sudden suspicion she was just setting me up for some future humiliation. Let it not be said I lack confidence in dealing with women. Rolando came back before I could think of anything else clever to say.

"Let's do it," he said.

We found a parking space a couple of blocks away from the address. The first thing I saw was a spectacular Victorian, all turrets and spires, painted a bright lavender. I thought for a moment that was Byron's house until I noticed the row of mailboxes along the front. It had obviously been chopped up long ago into flats and apartments. Byron's place was slightly farther down the street, a brightly painted, modernistic house with random angles jutting out and huge windows affording a great view of the city. It was small, but with that view and neighborhood, we were still talking a million and a half or so.

"Where does this guy get his money?" I muttered.

Most of the practitioners I know, much like musicians, have day jobs. Victor of course is an exception. He has so much money it's obscene—that's how he can afford his full-time enforcer gig. Where he comes by his money I haven't a clue. It's not the kind of question one asks, even of a good friend, and that's not how I would describe our relationship. Rolando overheard my muttered comment.

"Nothing mysterious there," he said. "His parents own half the real estate in Portland. Not a trace of talent evident in either one of them."

I altered my vision, using the small shift that enabled me to see the wards around the house. Although you don't exactly *see* it—it's more subtle than that. You can tell quite a bit about a practitioner by the warding they construct. Rigid or sloppy? Clever or forceful? Victor's house is sheer power, crackling lines of force like an electrical grid. Even he doesn't have enough power to maintain them, but he has a lot of help.

My wards are like my music—nothing showy, always shifting and adapting to whatever comes along. There were places where the warding might seem vulnerable to pressure, but if you concentrated your efforts there, you'd find the rest of the wards would shift over and lock into place.

Byron's wards were unusual, and unpleasant, like barbed wire dipped in poison. Most wards are designed for protection; they keep out unwanted guests. These wards looked like they were designed as much to wound as to guard. Rolando and Josephine stood quietly, examining them with me.

"Nice fellow, wouldn't you say?" Jo chuckled.

Rolando knocked on the front door, more loudly than was strictly necessary. No answer.

"Maybe he's out," I said.

"Maybe."

He pushed the doorbell a couple of times and knocked again, and this time we could hear footsteps from inside the house. A second later the door opened and there stood the elusive Byron. A strange thing, the door swung outward, toward the street, exactly the opposite from what is normal in most houses. Maybe Byron was just trying to be contrarian, appropriate for a black practitioner. Or maybe his contractor wasn't all that competent.

His appearance was precisely as Jo had described: black slicked-back hair; long, pointed, carefully trimmed sideburns; a mustache; and a goatee. Dark silk shirt, and expensive slacks. Very much the fashion plate. The effect was somewhat spoiled by what appeared to be a nasty cold. His eyes were watery and behind him I saw a wastebasket filled with used tissues.

His eyes passed over me quickly and focused on Rolando. I watched his face carefully, looking for signs of concern or worried caution, but all I saw on it was annoyance. He stood there without speaking, then his shoulders slumped.

"I might have known," he finally said. He heaved a theatrical sigh. "You may as well come in."

Inside, black leather couches and expensive-looking artwork dominated. It looked more like the home of an investment banker than a black practitioner. It reminded me of Victor's place, although I couldn't say why—the two houses were as different as could be. Then it clicked, what they had in common. Money, and lots of it.

Byron gestured us toward one of the leather couches.

He stayed on his feet, leaning against the mantel of a white marble fireplace that had never seen a fire.

"What do you want?" he asked, wearily. "Just happened to be in the neighborhood and decided to drop in for old time's sake?"

"Good to see you, too," said Rolando. They stared at each other. "As to what I want, a damaged practitioner, to start with." Byron's lip actually curled, reminding me of Lou when he's disgusted.

"Can't let it go, can you? I left Portland to get away from your crap."

"I'm not talking about Portland. I'm talking about San Francisco." Byron straightened up, pushing himself off the mantel.

"Christ on a crutch!" he said. "Not again. Do I have to move to Bora-Bora to be done with this?"

Josephine leaned forward on the couch. "You were in Portland during the last troubles. Now you're here, and it's started up again. And you are a black arts practitioner, after all—is it really such a surprise that we're interested in what you've been doing?"

Byron laughed. "You're one to talk," he said. "Oh, wait—that's right. I'm a dark arts guy. Any time there's a problem, find a dark arts guy."

"That's not the only thing," she said. "You were a friend of Harry Keller's, right? Used to come visit him from time to time?"

"So?"

I put in my two cents' worth. "So Harry was involved in some pretty bad stuff last year. People died. Practitioners died. Including Harry."

He looked over at me, taking note of Lou curled up by my feet. "I see. And you are . . . ?" He politely waited for me to name myself. If nothing else, he had manners.

"Mason," I said.

"Ah, yes. I heard something about that. What exactly happened to Harry, anyway?"

"He tripped and fell down some stairs."

Byron waited a moment for me to elaborate. I didn't, deliberately leaving the impression that I had been responsible, which was completely untrue. But it wouldn't hurt to put that thought in his mind. If he really was targeting me, it might make him think twice.

"I was sorry to hear about Harry," he said. "But he wasn't exactly a friend. He was a colleague—that's all. I didn't have that much to do with him because, to be honest, he wasn't all that bright." That much was true. "Besides," he continued, "you're acting like all we dark practitioners do is spend our days plotting evil and murdering children. I would expect that from the uninformed, but you're practitioners, for God's sake. You should know better than that. We're no different than you; we just use different methods to achieve the same results."

"I heard much the same line from Harry Keller," I said. "I didn't buy it then and I don't buy it now."

"So all of us are automatically suspect. Is that it? What about that other practitioner, then? Christoph, wasn't it? Yeah, I heard about that, too. He was one of you guys, right? And how did that work out for you?"

He had me there. I snuck a quick look at Lou to get his take on the guy. Not that it would be necessarily helpful. Ifrits are very good at sussing out danger, but unfortunately it needs to be imminent. If someone is at ease, smiling and joking, all the while planning to murder you later, an Ifrit won't necessarily pick up on that at all.

"And another thing," he said. "Do you really think black practitioners, or anyone for that matter, go around doing evil just for the sake of it? People do things for reasons. Find the motive and you'll find the person." He stopped and looked at each of us in turn, slow and deliberate. "You might want to look a bit closer to home."

Byron was not what I had expected. But a lot of dangerous individuals can be charming and personable and persuasive unless you are a particular problem to them.

They love their pets; they love their kids; they're loyal to their friends. That doesn't mean they won't kill you in a heartbeat if they have reason to. Or if they think they do. There isn't any way to tell, not just by talking. We were at an impasse until Rolando decided to up the ante.

"I know one way to find out if you're involved," he said.

"And what would that be?" Byron asked.

"Well, if something unfortunate were to happen to you, and you were to end up out of the picture and the attacks then stopped, why, then we'd know, wouldn't we?"

"So it's like that, now?"

"Just saying."

I didn't like the direction this was taking. I've never been a fan of preemptive action, no matter what the stakes, even after what I'd been through. Byron didn't look thrilled with the turn in the conversation, either. He got very still and his face lost all expression. I had the sudden conviction that whether he was our bad guy or not, he could be a very dangerous person to mess with.

"I see," he said. He walked over and opened the front door. "Get out."

There wasn't anything else we could do but leave. We weren't even sure if he was our guy, or at least I wasn't, and it wouldn't be wise to attack a practitioner on his own territory even if he was.

"What was that about?" I asked Rolando, kind of pissed. "I don't see that threatening him like that was a good move, even if he is our guy."

"Oh, he's our guy. Make no mistake," he said. "I was just rattling his cage a little."

"I'm not so sure things are that simple," I said. "He made some good points. I'd like to find out a little more about him before we start acting like judge and jury, not to mention executioner."

Rolando just shook his head in disgust and disagreement.

"Who else could it be?" said Jo. She repeated what she'd said, like a mantra. "He's a black practitioner. He leaves Portland, practitioner attacks stop. He arrives in San Francisco, they start up again. Do you really think that's coincidence?"

They both seemed set on the idea. It made me wonder if there wasn't another agenda involved, maybe something that had happened back in Portland. I'd have to look into that.

"I get your point," I said. "But it still looks too easy, too pat. Things aren't usually that simple."

"Maybe not," said Jo. "But don't forget, most of the time the simplest answer is the right one."

I still didn't like it, Occam's razor or no. And equally worrying was Rolando's attitude. This was not the Rolando I remembered, easygoing and sensible. He was acting more like one of those cops who spends too much time on the job and ends up escalating every situation he encounters into a violent confrontation.

As we walked back toward the car, Jo linked her arm in mine. Rolando didn't comment, but I got the distinct impression he wasn't pleased. Another side of him I'd never seen. In the past we'd actually dated some of the same women, though not at the same time. He'd never had any problem with it, or shown any jealousy. Maybe it was different because this was his sister.

They dropped me off at home, and right before they left, Jo handed me a card.

"My cell," she said. "Give me a call. I'd love to see more of the city."

As I went inside, I reflected that intimating to Byron that I'd offed Harry Keller just might backfire on me. I'd meant to make him hesitant about tangling with me, but along with Rolando's veiled threat, I might have simply given him the idea to do something about me instead. Self-preservation is a wonderful motivator; he might not have been out to get me before, but he surely would be considering it now. That's one of the reasons I'm a better musician than I am a magical investigator. At least as a musician I know when to lay out and keep my mouth shut.

I had a phone message waiting for me. Campbell. She was my most recent ex, and probably the sanest girlfriend I'd ever had. That might have something to do with why it hadn't worked out between us.

I hadn't spoken to her for a couple of months. The last time we'd talked she had just started seeing a new guy, someone she liked a lot. I was happy for her. She deserved a good man, but I had no desire to make his acquaintance—not that I had anything against him; I'd never even met him. But just the fact that "she" was now a "they" made a difference. You're not completely over it until you can genuinely enjoy meeting the new boyfriend or girlfriend. I wasn't there yet.

When I called back, her unfeigned tone of pleasure at hearing my voice was heartwarming. We talked for a while before I asked her what was up. Maybe she'd called just to chat, but I didn't think so.

"I had a visitor last week," she said. "It was odd."

"In what way?"

"Well, just odd. I didn't think much of it at the time, but I talked to Victor this morning and he told me about what happened to your friend. I'm truly sorry."

"I am, too," I said. A brief uncomfortable silence followed. "This visitor, do you think there's some connection?"

"No, not specifically. But I've learned that when two strange things happen around the same time, it's something worth looking at. You taught me that."

I was glad I had at least taught her something. Other than not to get involved with people like me.

"So what was the deal?"

"Well, he was a practitioner. He'd heard of me, that I've had some success at healing, and he wanted help."

"I'm glad to see you're finally getimg your due. Were you able to?"

"I didn't try. There was something I didn't like about him—not that it would have mattered if I thought I could have helped—but there was something very wrong about him. Not just physically, but . . . Well, I can't really explain it. Anyway, I referred him to someone else."

"Palmed him off, did you?"

"Basically, yes. I thought my . . . friend Montague would be better able to deal with it. He's had a lot more experience. And not much throws him."

Ah, yes, the "friend." And what kind of name was Montague? Already I didn't like him.

"And did he?" I asked.

"Not really. But later, when I told him what I'd heard about your friend, he got very quiet. Then he said he'd really like to talk to you about it if I could get you to come up here."

"He knows who I am?" I asked.

"Oh well, you know. We talk."

"Maybe he could call me."

"No telephone. Phones don't work where he lives."

"No cell coverage?"

"No, it's just—well, it's complicated. But if you want to talk to him, you'll need to come up here."

"I could come up tomorrow," I said. "It's kind of late now. I doubt if I could make it up there before dark."

"I know, but he's leaving tomorrow morning for a while. It's up to you, but I think it might be important."

Campbell lives up in Soda Springs, a three-and-a-half-hour drive from the city. I wasn't eager to make the drive, but if she thought it was important, it probably was.

"Okay," I said. "I can be up there by seven."

"Are you bringing Lou?"

"Do you have to ask?"

"Great. I'll make pancakes," she said. "See you then."

After she hung up, I turned to Lou. "We're going out to see Campbell," I told him. "Pancakes."

Lou managed to look excited while still yawning. He

liked Campbell a lot, although I sometimes think it was as much her pancakes as her personality. He is a mercenary creature at heart.

I thought about her choice of words. *Odd,* she'd said. Campbell wasn't exactly conventional herself, being a healer and a Wiccan, so it made me wonder. It promised to be interesting. But I had become wary of interesting.

FIVE

CAMPBELL LIVES IN A SMALL CABIN UP IN SODA Springs, a small town right below Donner Summit. The first time I'd been there, a year ago, I'd run into a vicious snowstorm that almost did me in. This year it was mild and dry, all bare earth and scraggly trees alongside the highway instead of snowdrifts and howling winds. Maybe it was global warming.

I got there just before seven. Her familiar Land Cruiser was parked at the bottom of the steep driveway that led up to her cabin. As I pulled up, the door to the cabin was flung open and Campbell ran down to meet me, blond hair flowing and health and vitality pouring out of her. She was a Telemark skier, among other things, and always in shape. Seeing her usually made me feel pale and wan by comparison.

Inside, the square woodstove was pumping out heat. The well-remembered futon sat on its frame in one corner, and shelves of colored jars lined the back wall, stuffed with plants and herbs.

When I'd first met Campbell, I'd had some doubts about

her abilities. Magical operations are about using talent to manipulate energy, plain and simple. Practitioners use all sorts of items to focus that energy, but it's exactly that—a focusing device. There's nothing intrinsically magical about any object. Whether or not you're successful has nothing to do with the words you speak or the objects you choose to employ. It's all about accessing the place talent resides. As long as you're confident, it makes no difference whether you use willow bark or lavender, or chocolate sprinkles for that matter.

That's what I'd always believed, what I'd always been taught, but these days I was no longer so cocksure. The magical world was apparently a lot more complicated than I'd smugly assumed. Campbell insisted that particular plants have specific properties, and since she could accomplish some things that were beyond me, who was I to doubt it?

And then there was the talisman—an ancient figurine of carved ivory and wood that she'd given to me for protection. The carved image looked vaguely wolflike—supposedly the wolf was my totem animal, my protector, and this charm would call up help when I most needed it. I'd taken it just to make her happy, but secretly scoffed. Right up to the moment when it suddenly glowed with power and three wolves appeared over a hill to save my butt. Being skeptical is all well and good, but you don't need to make a religion out of it.

A flannel shirt hung over the back of a chair, far too large to be hers. I looked at it curiously, keeping my eyes on it just a moment too long.

"What?" she said.

"Nothing."

"You're an idiot. No, no one's living here. Why would you care, anyway?"

"I don't. Not really. Just sort of, I guess."

Lou interrupted our conversation before it could get too serious by throwing himself against her hip and then running into the kitchen, where he started barking insistently.

"Pancakes," I reminded her. "He's expecting pancakes."

"Ah, yes. It's so nice to be loved simply for oneself. But we might want to get going. I told Montague we'd be there sometime after seven."

"And where is 'there'?"

"That's a good question. Just a short walk from here. Usually."

I thought for a minute she was being cryptic, but then I remembered that her new guy was a practitioner. So she was probably just being matter-of-fact. We went out the back door and started up the hill that leads away from the cabin. The moon cast enough light for us to avoid tripping over random objects, and Campbell seemed to know where she was going. The weather was mild for November, but we were still at a hefty altitude and it was getting cold. All I had was my leather jacket, so I hoped we wouldn't be going too far.

Lou had his nose out of joint from being denied the promised pancakes, but he got over it quickly and scampered around sniffing at rocks and bushes just like a real dog.

"Where did you meet this guy?" I asked as we walked along.

"Montague? I was looking for someone with some plant knowledge and his name kept coming up. He's taught me a lot."

"I thought he was a practitioner."

"He is, or at least he was. I don't really know what you'd call him now. But he can do things with plants I never even imagined."

Considering Campbell's talents in the same direction, that was high praise coming from her. She suddenly laughed.

"What?" I said.

"There's a surprise waiting for you when you meet him. I won't tell you, but you'll be amazed. That, I promise."

Our conversation turned to more personal things. Campbell was worried about her mom, who was having some health issues that the doctors couldn't get a handle on.

"I'm going to see her as soon as the new test results are in," she said. "Even if I can't help, I might be able to figure out what the problem is."

We talked of other, more pleasant topics, and I lost track of time as we walked through a forest growing denser with every passing minute.

"I wouldn't have expected so much wilderness so close to a town," I said, waving a vague hand at the dim trees surrounding us.

"Oh, fuck," she said. Not a response I'd anticipated. "I missed the tree."

I resisted the obvious question of "What tree?"

"Is that bad?" I asked.

"I hope not. Montague's house is hard to access. There's a certain small dead tree along the way, and when I reach it, I walk three times around it, widdershins. Then the way is easy to find. But I got so involved talking that I walked right by it."

"Widdershins," I said.

"You take that sarcastic tone and I swear I'll leave you here. We'll see how long it takes you to find your way back."

I wasn't worried. I knew she wouldn't, and anyway, I had Lou with me. I still apologized, though—I knew better. We made our way up a small rise and Campbell relaxed.

"I recognize where we are now," she said. "The house is just over the top of this hill."

But when we crested the rise, nothing but unbroken trees stretched out in front of us.

"Hmm," she said.

"Maybe the next hill?"

"No, this is the right place. But we got here by the wrong path, so his cabin isn't here." I'd heard stranger things.

"What now?" I asked.

She looked over her shoulder, nervously. "I should probably try to find our way back home—if I can. These woods aren't entirely safe if you stray off the path. That's what Montague told me."

"No problem," I said. "Lou can find his way back."

I whistled sharply to catch his attention. "Lou. Let's go back. To the cabin. Home."

He did his dog equivalent of a shrug. If we wanted to take a stroll in the woods at night for no reason, that was fine with him. He whirled around and trotted confidently back the way we'd come.

"I'm not sure I understand," I said. "Does Montague shield his cabin?"

Campbell shook her head, just visible in the moonlight. "Not exactly. I don't completely understand it myself. It's not exactly *here*, at least not all the time. It's kind of out of phase with our world, if you get my drift. If you went looking for it, you wouldn't find it. It gives him privacy, but it's kind of a drag that I can't just give him a ring anytime I want. Telephones won't reach there. He provided a path for me, but I missed it. So now I think we're somewhere in between his corner of the world and our own."

We walked in silence. Nothing looked familiar, but Lou still seemed to have his confidence, so I assumed he knew what he was doing. Just when I was starting to relax, Lou started moving more slowly and then stopped, turning his head from side to side, irresolute. When he started moving again it was without his usual sense of purpose. I didn't like the implications.

We reached an open grassy area that I didn't remember from the trip in. The trees now were scrubby and twisted, close together. They didn't look like any of the trees I had seen earlier. Not good.

There wasn't much choice but to follow, though. Finding our way back without Lou's help would be next to impossible. A narrow path made an appearance, winding through unfamiliar trees which were thicker now but not so thick as to cause problems. We crested another small rise, and on the other side was a fork in the path.

"I don't remember a fork," Campbell said.

Lou stood there, indecisive again. Then he veered toward the left-hand path, trotting confidently, tail high. He wasn't fooling me. The path continued to the left for a while and, before too long, split in two once again. Lou glanced up at me as if for guidance. Good luck there.

"Okay," I said. "This is not working. I think we'd better retrace our steps." We turned and traipsed back along the way we'd just come. A half hour later, we still hadn't reached that first fork in the path. To make things worse, around the next bend a small brook cut across the trail. It didn't pose much of a barrier, but we certainly hadn't crossed any stream on the way down. I'd already accepted the fact we were lost, but now we were *really* lost.

"Lou!" I called. He bounded up to me, happily oblivious. I didn't think he was taking things seriously enough. He didn't think of it as lost—more like an extended outing. He didn't seem to care whether we got home or not. I crouched beside him and got stern.

"Home," I said. "We need to get back. Now. Stop screwing around, okay?"

A sharp bark, and he spun around and started back the way we had just come. I called to him to make sure he had understood. "Home? Back home?" He barked again, this time impatiently, as if to say, "Yeah, I got it already."

By now it was getting serious. I unconsciously increased my pace, and that was where I got into trouble. Instead of climbing over a deadfall that blocked the path, I tried scooting up on the bank to go around and save a few seconds. The bank was slick and mossy and my feet went out from under me as I crashed down into the logs and branches. A sharp pain lanced through my ankle, and when I tried to stand upright, I couldn't put any weight on it. I hobbled over to the stump of a dead tree and leaned against it for support. Campbell bent down beside me.

"Let me take a look at it," she said. She's great at the

healing arts, truly gifted; in fact, she once saved Lou's life. She took off my boot and examined it briefly.

"Not broken," she said. "Just a slight sprain. If I had my plants, I could make it good as new. Still . . ."

She wrapped her hands around my ankle and looked up at the night sky. She spoke a quick invocation or prayer, too softly for me to hear, then blew across her hands. I felt the trademark surge of her particular energy roll over my foot. A moment of intense pain, and then it subsided to a dull ache. I tried putting some weight on it. It still hurt, but now at least I could walk on it.

"Sorry," she said. "That's the best I can do for right now."

"It's fine," I assured her, although it wasn't. "Thanks."

We started off again. The moonlight was stronger now and the surrounding landscape took on a subtly threatening aspect. I'm not overly suggestible, but there was something unpleasant about these woods.

When another half hour passed with no sign we were getting anywhere, I started considering alternatives. It was getting even colder and I'd been hearing faint noises for a while now, barely audible but subtly disturbing. Campbell was looking more nervous by the minute. Maybe it was time to hunker down for the night.

We passed an outcropping of rock fifty feet off the trail and I stopped to take a good look at it. It looked solid, granite or maybe limestone, with a depression cut into the back. Not quite a cave, but a rounded area that would at least offer some protection against the cold and perhaps worse things. I pointed up in that direction.

"We're not going to make it out of these woods tonight," I said. "We may as well stop here where we have some shelter. Tomorrow morning we'll be able to better see where we're going."

Campbell didn't look thrilled with the idea, but she didn't have anything better to offer. We clambered over to the rock face and spent the next twenty minutes gathering dead wood from the surrounding area. A simple ignition spell started a small fire burning, as much for morale as for warmth.

I spent the next hour setting up protection around the perimeter. I used my own uneasiness, the pain in my ankle, and a couple of intensely bitter berries Campbell located to fashion a serious aversion spell. If anything dangerous was lurking in the darkness, it would now take an extraordinarily strong motivation to entice it to cross over into our space.

All we needed now were some freeze-dried rations for a romantic firelight dinner, but we had nothing. Lou was beginning to rethink his earlier devil-may-care attitude now that he realized there was no dinner in the offing. You'd think with my abilities I could whip up a five-course gourmet dinner, but it doesn't work that way. Talent has many uses, but creating something out of nothing isn't one of them. Oh, I could make a tree branch look like a giant sausage, and with enough expenditure of energy, maybe even make it taste like one. But you'd still be eating leaves and bark.

The fire was reassuring, since I could hear faint rustling noises coming from beyond the circle of firelight. Fires are a mixed blessing, though. They provide warmth and comfort, and the light that drives back the darkness has been a solace to mankind ever since our earliest ancestors huddled in caves. Come to think of it, much like we were doing right now. But fire destroys your night vision and you can't see a thing beyond its glow. Just about anything could be crouched thirty feet away, invisible outside the ring of flickering light.

I had no idea what might be out there. Conventional wisdom has it that the waiting is the worst part, and that things you imagine are far worse than the reality. Personally, I've never found that to be the case. Maybe I'm just lacking in imagination.

But whether it was the long, cold walk or the comfort of the fire, I found myself growing sleepy. Campbell showed no such inclination, staring out at the darkness and feeding the fire whenever it began to grow small. But the continual rustling noises weren't enough to keep me from resting my eyes from time to time, and before I knew it I had dozed off. I was awakened by Lou pulling quietly but insistently on my shirtsleeve. Campbell had finally dozed off as well but came instantly awake when I sat up. She gazed out beyond the fire and stiffened.

"Mason," she hissed. "Look!"

Outside the ring of fire, glowing eyes blazed in a semicircle in front of us. They were tiny, like the eyes of a rat or a ferret, no more than a foot off the ground, and there were hundreds of them. Thousands, for all I knew, since I couldn't see much past the circle of the fire. I straightened up slowly.

"What are they?" she whispered.

I peered into the darkness. "I have no idea. The aversion spell seems to be keeping them away. Or maybe it's the fire."

Lou had walked over to the edge of the firelight and was standing still as a statue, staring intently into the night. He didn't look comfortable. I hauled myself to my feet and tried to get a better look but it didn't help. I pulled Campbell close and whispered in her ear.

"I'm going to provide some illumination," I said. "I want to see what these things are."

With the firelight still flickering it was an easy task, more a redirection than a true creation spell. I mumbled under my breath and gestured expansively. The immediate area lit up as if from a giant low-wattage night-light. Lou gave a strangled bark and Campbell screamed. I can't say I blamed her.

Lined up shoulder to shoulder, not just around the fire, but as far back as I could see, were rows upon rows upon rows of armored crustacean-like creatures. Not regular crabs, but things that looked like giant horseshoe crabs, each the size of a garbage can lid. From their ranks came a constant, impatient rustling and chittering sound.

Now, horseshoe crabs are harmless. They were here long before humankind. They were here before the dinosaurs. They were here even before the flowering plants, sporting in ancient seas with their trilobite cousins. But I didn't say these things were horseshoe crabs; I said they looked like them. Except that horseshoe crabs don't possess bright red eyes gleaming with intelligence, nor are they the size of garbage can lids, nor do they have gaping mouths with sharp teeth.

I shuddered. When I was a child I spent a summer with my grandparents, on the Delaware coast. The shores there teemed with the creatures, and my greatest fear when wading barefoot was that I would step on one, break through the horny carapace, and plunge my foot into the squirming body and claws beneath. It would then become stuck on my foot and strip my bones of flesh before I could manage to dislodge it. Logic, as well as my grandfather, told me it was an absurd fear. They don't even have claws. But since when has logic held any sway over primal terror?

Maybe that fear came from some foreknowledge of this very day. Maybe it was coincidence. But one thing was obvious: these creatures had the ability to strip flesh from more than just a foot. The aversion spell was holding strong, but as the creatures in the back pressed forward, the ones in the front would be propelled through the barrier whether they wished to be or not. Once through, there would be nothing between them and the tasty morsels of flesh gathered round the fire.

The light spell faded somewhat as it lost energy and we were left inside the circle of firelight. What to do? If we could climb a tree, we'd be perfectly safe; there was no way these things would be able to climb. But the area around the rocky outcrop I had so cleverly chosen was clear of anything larger than bushes and saplings.

I looked desperately around, hoping to come up with some brilliant idea before the things broke through the protective circle.

Off in the distance I saw something so peculiar that at first I thought I must be having a delusional episode brought on by stress. Something was moving quickly through the massed ranks, something small, bounding from back to back over the horseshoe things as if they were rubber tires strewn over a marshy field. It was hard to tell in the dim illumination, but as it got closer I could see it more clearly, and it looked an awful lot like Louie. Automatically I spun around, half expecting him to be gone, but he was still at the edge of the fire. He stood up on his hind legs to get a better look at whatever was coming toward us and then started barking in that high-pitched, piercing tone that always hurt my ears. Identical barking sounds echoed back from the dog which was now almost up to the circle. Except it wasn't any more of a dog than was Lou.

It bounded off the last of the creatures and broke through the aversion perimeter without even flinching. Clearly an Ifrit, as if the bizarre backfield run through the creature minefield hadn't already given me a hint. He was slightly smaller than Lou, with almost identical markings, but stockier and with a shorter muzzle. Louie ran up to him and they stood nose to nose in the firelight like magnetic twin Scottie dogs, calmly wagging their tails. Of all the insane things I have seen, in some ways this was the most bizarre. I stood there gawking stupidly. I sometimes find myself at a loss for words. Now I was at a loss for thoughts. In another few seconds I think my mind would have simply imploded, but I was saved by the sound of a voice calling from down the hill.

"Willy! Willy! Get back here!" A few moments' silence, then, "Oh, you found her, did you?" Then, "Good God, look at the buggers!"

I heard more cursing and scrambling sounds until finally a man strode out of the darkness and made his way up to the edge of the firelight where the aversion spell kicked in. He stopped and wedged himself between the horseshoe crabs that were bunched up there, pushing and kicking them aside to gain a little space for himself. From what I could see of him he looked like nothing so much as a Hell's Angel, complete with long hair and leather jacket, minus the bike.

"Hey!" he yelled, staring straight at me. "Get rid of that spell, will you? Man, that's nasty."

I waved weakly toward the crabs. "But what about . . ."

"These things? Don't worry; they're harmless. Scavengers, mostly."

"But those teeth?"

"They use them to chew up rotten logs and eat the worms and beetles inside. What, you want a natural history lesson while I'm standing in the middle of a whole school of them?" He kicked at one of them to get a little more room. "They can nip a bit, you know. Just move away from the goddamned fire and they won't even notice you. Fire is what attracts them; they're like moths. What do you think brought them here, anyway?"

I took down the barrier spell and wordlessly moved off to the side. The horseshoe crabs, freed from their disinclination, poured through like gigantic lemmings. I moved to one side as they ignored me and crowded as close around the fire as they could get without going up in flames. The Hell's Angel strolled over to Campbell and gave her a brief hug.

"Got a bit lost, I see."

He took a couple of steps back and put out a rough hand toward me. "I'm Montague."

Of course. Who else could it be? Along with the surprise Campbell had promised: an Ifrit very much like Lou.

"Mason," I said, taking his hand.

He looked down to where Lou and the other Ifrit were now trading information in some complicated fashion far beyond my understanding.

The man chuckled. "Found a friend, have you, Will?"

"What are those things?" I asked.

"That's a long story, but this is no place to stand around and swap tales. Pretty soon a few of those delightful creatures will get squeezed into the fire, and before they smother it, one or two will get toasted. They go up like blowtorches and they stink to high heaven. Come along. I don't live too far from here." As he led us back down to the trail below, he looked up for one last glimpse at the makeshift campsite.

"A fire," he said in amazement. "What were you thinking?"

SIX

MONTAGUE'S HOUSE WAS LIT UP LIKE A CHRISTMAS tree. It was a single-storied log cabin, longer than usual but plain and simple. Until I got up close. What I'd taken for logs was actually one organic structure, a giant tree that had curved and wrapped in on itself, piled up cleverly so that the layers of each "log" were tightly bonded. The roof was a mat of thickly entwined coarse fibers, but whether they were alive or dead, I couldn't tell. The house was ablaze with light.

"Electricity?" I said. "How?"

"No, I'm afraid not. The light's my doing."

Campbell glanced over at me, a smug expression on her face that pissed me off. "Montague's good with plants," she said.

She was vicariously showing off. Bad enough that my replacement was a larger-than-life mountain man; he was also far beyond me as a practitioner.

The inside of the cabin was one large room with a comfortable-looking loft built up high, leaving plenty of space underneath. A separate small kitchen occupied one end, with wood countertops and the ubiquitous wood-burning stove. Another door led out the back of it. Large, glowing potted plants rested in every corner of the house, like living chandeliers. Mystery solved.

"I found these a few years ago in a swamp," Montague said, pointing at the plants. "They're naturally phosphorescent, so I used some talent to encourage genetic shift and in a few generations they were pumping out ten times the light. Then a simple spell to change their original cold light into something warmer and brighter, and presto—instant lighting. The upside is that they never burn out. The downside is that there's no way to turn them off. I have to throw covers over the pots to get any sleep." He led us into the kitchen, still warm from the heat of the woodstove, and opened up a cooler that had wooden doors. He pulled out a slab of bacon. "You guys look hungry."

Campbell got three plain brown bowls from a cabinet, showing a familiarity with the place that gave me a pang, somewhere between jealously and regret. She took the bacon from him and put the slices in a cast-iron skillet. Montague scooped three cups of oatmeal from a large tin and put them in a pot of water, then placed the pot on the hot stove. Soon, oatmeal was bubbling away and the smell of sizzling bacon wafted through the kitchen. Lou was already licking his lips in anticipation.

Standing in his kitchen, Montague seemed larger-than-life, taking up space like someone twice his size, and he wasn't small to begin with. When he took off his leather jacket a plaid flannel shirt showed underneath. With the shirt and his full dark beard he made the perfect Hollywood version of a steely mountain man. All that was missing was a ragged collection of smelly furs draped around his shoulders. Montague. That name had been gnawing at me since I first heard it, and it finally clicked.

"Wait a minute," I said. "You're Montague."

"I thought we'd established that."

"No, I mean you're *Montague*. You used to be an enforcer. Victor mentioned you once."

"Ah, yes. Victor. And how is dear Victor?"

"The same, I'd imagine. But didn't you just up and disappear about ten years ago?"

He nodded. "That I did."

"And you ended up here?"

"Well, this is my base. I don't spend much time in any one place anymore. Too many things to see. Too many things to do."

Montague regarded me with benign amusement, which immediately got my back up. It reminded me too much of someone else: Geoffrey. Geoffrey had that same fond, bemused way of looking at me like I was a child constantly asking, "Why is the sky blue?" Eli thought highly of him, but I thought Geoffrey was basically a loon. He was brilliant in his own odd way. But for someone supposedly so spiritually evolved, he had no idea how annoying he could be.

Montague must have picked up on my reaction, because his bemused expression was quickly replaced by one of appropriate interest and concern.

"So, has Campbell told you much about our visitor?" he asked. Campbell shook her head.

"No, not much," she said. "Just that I thought there was something wrong with him, not just physically, so I brought him to you."

He stirred the oatmeal and put the lid back on the pot.

"He was a very sick puppy. He'd heard about Campbell and her healing arts, and as she said, she brought him to me."

So far, I saw nothing strange about this.

"What was it he wanted?" I asked.

"Well, he needed a healer, of course. The plant magic I've learned has opened up some fascinating avenues in that direction. Not all magical operations are simply about accessing talent, you know." I thought about Campbell and some of the things I'd seen her do.

"Could you tell what was wrong with him?"

"Oh, yes. Cancer, I'm afraid."

"You can cure cancer?"

Montague laughed, amused. "I wish. I'd be giving Mother Teresa a run for her money. No, healing has to do with putting the body back in balance, helping it heal itself. I'm best at outside problems, like if someone's been poisoned, or if there's an infection. Then it's just a matter of neutralizing the intrusion. That's where the plant knowledge comes in so handy—it combats the problem.

"But cancer is a very different animal. The body has gone haywire; it's fighting itself. I can't do much to help because the basic structure of the body is distorted and there's nothing healthy I can work with. Theoretically it's possible, but I don't have those kinds of skills. I don't think anyone does. I was able to give him some relief, maybe even slow down the progression, but that's about it."

"And then what?"

"He just thanked me and left. Haven't seen him since."

"What am I missing?" I asked. "This all seems pretty normal to me."

"Well, for one thing, he was a practitioner. And for another, he was shielding, projecting a complete illusion. He didn't want me to know who he was or even what he looked like."

"Couldn't you see through the shielding?" I asked.

"Didn't try. None of my business. At the time, it didn't seem important—there are a lot of reasons people, including practitioners, want to keep their medical conditions private."

"But what does that have to do with what happened to Sarah? And others, apparently?"

"That's what I'm wondering. Tell me exactly what happened. Every detail."

After I did, he nodded. "That, unfortunately, makes sense."

"In what way?" I asked.

"Well, I'm not positive, I but I think the cancer was centered in the brain, so that's what I focused on. And I found something peculiar, something I've never run across before. There were remnants of other personalities present."

"You mean multiple personalities? Like that movie *Sybil*?"

"No, they weren't formed at all. More like little wisps, like something left over, almost like a memory."

"I don't get it," I said.

"I didn't get it, either, not at first. But consider what happened to your friend. Clearly an attempt at some form of mind control, or possession. Or, and this is just a thought, maybe an attempt to switch bodies. That would certainly explain the other personality traces."

"Why on earth would anyone want to do that?" I asked.

"The cancer. What better way to escape it than to leave it behind?"

"Could that actually be done?"

"Probably not. But it could be attempted; that's for sure. And even if it didn't work, the intensity and commingling of personalities would leave a psychic imprint. This woman—she was blond, am I right?"

"She was," I said, feeling like I was a subject in a mentalist act.

"And sort of anal-retentive? Sorry, no offense."

"None taken. She was."

"That's all I could get. But there were a few others in there as well. You never quite shake your enforcer paranoia. Terminal illness, shielding of identity, and damaged practitioners. Something's very wrong here. To be honest, it was incredibly creepy. That's what Campbell picked up on. If I'd known about your friend at the time, I would have at least made sure I got a good look at him."

"What if you saw him again? Would you recognize him?"

"Saw him unshielded? No, there'd be no sign."

"So it's a dead end?"

"Maybe not. When I worked on him, some of my energy

became absorbed into his system. If I touched him again, I'd feel it."

"That's not much help. If I knew who it was, I wouldn't have to haul him up here for you to identify."

"No, but other things would work, too. If you wanted confirmation, then a bit of hair from a hairbrush, a toothbrush, anything like that would be enough. One drop of blood and I could tell you immediately if it was someone I'd ever worked on."

"Sounds like voodoo to me."

"More like DNA, actually. But it works. Voodoo priests wouldn't use that stuff if it didn't, would they?"

Montague broke off the conversation and ladled large dollops of oatmeal into the bowls Campbell had set out. He added some butter and deftly shoveled bacon from the hot pan onto a stoneware plate, tossing a couple of pieces each over to Willy and Lou. Willy finished off both of his before Lou was even through with his first, something I would never have believed possible.

"How did you know where we were?" asked Campbell. "And that we were in trouble? Or at least we thought we were."

"Well, actually, you might have been," he said. "There are a few things around here far worse than those scavengers you encountered. A particularly nasty predator the size of a wolf, for example, but a member of the weasel family. They hunt in pairs. Very useful for dealing with practitioners holding grudges from the old days who would dearly like to catch me unawares."

"Not to mention innocent bystanders who have lost their way," I said.

Montague looked a bit abashed. "That shouldn't have happened. You ended up between spaces, in a manner of speaking. You shouldn't have been able to do that."

I pointed at Lou, who had given up on the possibility of more bacon and was lying by the stove with his eyes closed, soaking up warmth.

"Blame him."

Willy was sitting next to Lou, like a protective older brother. I noticed for the first time he had quite a bit of gray in his muzzle, like an older and wiser Lou. Lou had his head turned slightly to one side, exhibiting an uncharacteristic deference. Montague watched them both fondly for a moment.

"He's got some talent, that one," he said. "Even Will had some trouble navigating when he was younger." I felt obscurely pleased by the compliment, as if it were a reflection on me.

"Anyway," he continued, "I got worried when Campbell didn't show up as promised. But I didn't find you; Will did. How he does it I have no idea. Will's been with me close to thirty years, and I still don't have the slightest idea how he operates." He smiled at me. "I'm sure you can relate to that."

"Can I ever," I said. "Well, you've given me a lead, at least. I appreciate it."

"Glad to help."

"Now if only we can find our way back."

Campbell didn't get up from the table. "I think I'll stay for a while," she said, looking somewhat uncomfortable. "As long as I'm here anyway."

"No problem," I said. "I'll just wander around in the dark until I run into some of those giant weasels Montague was talking about."

Montague laughed. "Will can show you the way back."

"Thanks again," I said. "And for breakfast." I got to my feet. "Come on, Lou. Time to go."

Lou twitched an ear and half opened one eye, but didn't stir. He was in no rush to leave the comfort of the kitchen stove. Montague laughed again.

"I see you and Lou have the normal Ifrit working relationship."

After Lou had sufficiently embarrassed me, he pulled himself up, yawning, and strolled toward the door. The moon was high in the sky, casting shimmering light over the surrounding terrain, but the woods no longer seemed threatening, just quiet and peaceful.

Willy trotted back into the woods with Lou close and me trailing behind. He picked out a broad path I hadn't noticed on the way to Montague's, keeping a steady pace. In what seemed like no time at all, I could see the lights of Campbell's cabin in the distance. Will touched noses briefly with Lou, then turned tail and took off at full speed back the way we had come.

As he ran, his form faded in and out, flickering and wavering like a heat mirage on a hot day. But before he disappeared into the darkness, a flash of red and gold replaced his form. And something else. I can't be sure what I saw, but it was something. I might just have got a glimpse of the true form of an Ifrit.

On the drive home, I almost fell asleep twice. It had been a long day, and a hard one. Seeing Campbell again, and meeting Montague, reminded me that I had no one in my life. Not that I really wanted anyone right now. I couldn't even imagine living with a woman, not for a while, maybe not ever. But there were times when it would have been nice to have someone waiting at home after a long day, and I had no one.

Turns out, that wasn't entirely true.

SEVEN

TO HAVE SOMEONE WHO AWAITS YOU AFTER A
hard day's work or a long night's journey can be a wonderful thing. Even more wonderful is when that person happens to be a beautiful woman. And the woman who waited
to greet me as I climbed out of the van was beautiful, tall,
and slender, dark hair shimmering in waves halfway down
her back and white teeth gleaming in the light of the setting
moon. But sadly, it was not wonderful at all.

"Mason?" she said, tentatively.

I've never claimed to be that quick on the uptake, but neither am I the stupidest practitioner on the planet. Lou can see
through illusions better than I can, but this time he didn't
even bother warning me. He just gazed up at me calmly as if
to say, "Well, if you can be fooled by this, you deserve whatever happens to you."

The woman glided toward me, hair flowing behind her,
moving gently in the breeze. Only there wasn't any breeze.
When she spoke, her voice was low and pleasantly husky.

"Eli told me to wait here for you," she said. "He thought
you might be in some trouble."

That part, she had right. I wasn't sure what she was, but I seriously doubted if she had my best interests at heart. I sidled away from her approach, trying not to be too obvious about it.

A year ago I was complacent, secure in my extensive knowledge of magical operations. Magic, I devoutly believed, was all about accessing energy sources and then manipulating them properly—no more, no less. The various spells that practitioners employ, all the talismans, gestures, and the like, are mere focusing devices, useful but having no intrinsic power. Monsters, werewolves, demons—all are manifestations of energy without an objective reality. But that was last year. Since then I'd seen far too many things I couldn't explain.

I tried to think of what this creature might be. The beautiful-woman ploy is a staple of folk legend, with the damsel usually revealing herself as a corpselike hag at the appropriate moment, gleefully sucking marrow from the bones of the besotted victim. I started preparing a spell to strip it of illusion, though I wasn't sure how much I wanted to see its true colors.

"Trouble?" I said. "Why, no, no trouble here."

I was still edging sideways. She followed, so we were now circling each other like boxers in a ring. Moonlight spilled over the empty streets, making it difficult to uncover her true aspect. Moonlight, after all, is the traditional stuff of dreams and illusion. I tried to focus on the ordinary and banal: streetlights, street signs, parked cars, the faint sounds of rumbling trucks and buses. Then, the trees lining the street, simple natural things. I drew it all in together and cast out a wave of energy strong enough to cut through any illusion. Her outline trembled and wavered uncertainly. But as I stepped back to admire my work, I stepped on a greasy half-eaten hamburger abandoned on the sidewalk. My foot went sideways, tweaking my still-sore ankle once again and sending me sprawling backward onto the sidewalk.

Before I could get up she was kneeling beside me and had taken one of my hands in hers. Up close, I could see her clearly, even in the weak light thrown by the moon. Her faced glowed with the soft aura of pale gold. I realized I had been mistaken. She was no monster at all; she was exactly what she appeared to be—a beautiful woman, full of life and lust and wholesome goodness. She pulled me gently up until we faced each other on our knees, tilted her head, and smiled quizzically, half in sorrow, half in invitation. She reminded me in an obscure way of Campbell, and even more of Sherwood, back when we were new and in love. Without thinking, I reached for her.

But this mood was quickly shattered as the ever-helpful Lou, growling and snarling, charged forward and flung himself at the woman. I automatically interposed my body to protect her, fending off his attack. I didn't blame him; he was just doing his job, trying his best to protect me. But he didn't understand. There was no danger here.

Except he wasn't attacking her at all. He ducked under my outstretched hand and dove toward my feet. A second later, he had hold of my ankle, the sore one, the one I'd already twisted twice. I was expecting to momentarily feel the sharp tearing of teeth, but he barely broke the skin. Instead, he took a firm hold on my boot just below the ankle and, using his surprisingly strong jaws, gave it a powerful wrench, then shook it back and forth like a terrier with a rat. Intense pain shot up my leg. It would have hurt in any case, but with the injuries I'd already suffered, the pain was excruciating.

I yelled, involuntarily straightening up. I hopped awkwardly on my good foot and let go of the woman's hand. As soon as I did, my anti-illusion spell cut in, full force. A moment ago the woman of my dreams had been kneeling before me. Now in her place a minor nightmare hunched down at my feet. Leathery skin, dark and mottled, covered it completely. The mouth was lipless, the head devoid of hair, the eyes large and liquid, and the pointed ears furrowed with deep grooves. Best of all, huge leathery wings were folded over its back like a medieval gargoyle.

Lou let go of my foot and stood beside me, immobile. Revulsion gripped me. My God, I had been just about to kiss this thing. After which, no doubt, I would have ceased to do anything at all.

I didn't have a killing spell handy. I'd never prepared a fatal spell of any kind, and preset spells are not my thing anyway. Even though I still work with Victor from time to time, I'd never had to use anything like that. The odds of needing such a thing are about the same as the odds of a cop having to use his gun. There's always the chance, but most cops never even fire their guns, not in their entire careers. But cops don't have to deal with creatures of the night, at least not this kind.

I gathered all the strength I could, using my fear and disgust as a template, molding those emotions into a packet of sheer energy. I added Lou's sharp teeth and the cutting shards of broken glass littering the ground. This was no time for subtleties. I raised my hand, then hesitated. Truth is, I'd only once deliberately killed another person, and he was actively trying to kill me at the time. This was different, and although this wasn't exactly a person, it wasn't just some abstraction of evil, either. Repulsive and dangerous it might be, but it was still a sentient being.

And at the moment, it wasn't attacking at all. It remained crouched before me, wings wrapped around it as if for protection, huddled miserably on the cold pavement. It looked up at me with its large, night-seeing eyes, and what I saw in them was not so much rage, or hate, or hunger, but simple fear. It was afraid. It didn't want to die on this dark night any more than I did.

Lou gave a short bark, urging me to get on with it. There aren't any shades of moral gray in his world. If it's a friend, you protect to the death. If it's an enemy, you kill it. Nice and simple. I raised my hand again, and the thing whimpered softly and closed its eyes. Shit. I couldn't do it. I knew I would regret it, but I couldn't do it.

"Get out of here," I said. Its eyes opened and it looked at me, but didn't move. "Go on," I said again. "Get out of here."

It stood up slowly, stepping away so I could see it was no longer a threat. The leathery wings slowly unfurled, huge beyond what I'd expected when they were wrapped around its body. Then, suddenly, shockingly, it launched itself into the air and flapped off clumsily into the night sky. I watched until I lost it in the darkness. Lou was looking up at me in disbelief mixed with resignation. I shrugged.

"You wouldn't understand," I said. "Let's get some sleep."

NEXT AFTERNOON, I WAS CONFIDENTLY RELATING my little adventure to Victor and Eli. They were concerned with Montague's story, but I wanted to know about the creature. To my surprise, neither one knew what kind of creature Batgirl might have been.

"I could research it," Eli said, "but I think what's more important than what it was is what it wanted."

"Well, to suck out my life's blood, I imagine."

"Maybe, maybe not. Maybe it wanted to take you somewhere, a willing slave."

"For what purpose?"

"Well, if Montague's ideas are correct, you might have been the next in line for a brain transplant."

"Montague's no fool," Victor added. High praise, coming from him.

"So what now?"

"Rolando's convinced that our black practitioner friend Byron is involved with this," Eli said. "You say Montague could identify him, given the right material. So I would think collecting something of his would be a good place to start."

"Maybe I could ask him for some fingernail clippings.

I'm sure a black practitioner would have no problem handing over something like that."

"No, it won't be easy. In the meantime, we've been examining that green stone that Sarah was holding. The rune stone. It's odd—made of some material I'd never seen—clearly mineral, but almost organic. And it's completely inert, magically speaking. I don't understand how it could be employed for anything involving talent. We've examined it six ways from Sunday and learned nothing. Victor even asked Timothy if he could help."

That made me raise my eyebrows. Asking anyone for help was unlike him, much less a nonpractitioner.

"What could Timothy do?"

"Well, Victor could use talent to download information from the stone onto a hard drive. Theoretically, it should work. DNA from a single cell contains all the information about the entity that produced it. Every piece of a hologram contains the entire picture, although not from all angles. He thought Timothy might be able to write a program that would pull it up."

"Clever," I said. "What did Timothy say?"

"Maybe, if he had a few months to organize the information in a meaningful way. Otherwise, no."

"Too bad," I said. "But I'm sure you guys will figure out something."

WHEN I GOT HOME, I PUTTERED AROUND FOR A while, thinking about what Montague had said. And about Campbell. Mostly about Campbell. After a while I picked up the phone and called Josephine. I know you're supposed to wait a couple of days before calling, or at least that's what they say these days, but I didn't see the point. She knew I was interested.

"What do you think about dinner?" I said, after a few pleasantries.

"Dinner is good. I like dinner."

"Dinner tonight?"

"Let me check my calendar," she said. She waited a half second and then said, "Good news. I'm free. Where are we going?"

"I thought maybe the Cliff House. A bit touristy, but a San Francisco landmark. Very iconic, and great views."

"Sounds lovely. Dressy or no?"

"Not really. It helps if your jeans aren't torn. How about seven? That way we'll still get the last of the light."

"Seven is fine."

"Great. I'll pick you up at six thirty." There was a slight pause on the other end.

"Why don't you call right before you leave?" she said. "I'll wait for you downstairs, in front. Parking's not really an option that time of day."

After I hung up, I wondered about that. It was almost as if she didn't want me coming up to her place. I was being paranoid again, probably.

I hadn't been to the Cliff House in quite a while. Most natives have never been there at all; they consider it too much a tourist attraction and take perverse pleasure in avoiding it, much like a New Yorker might be proud of never having visited the Empire State Building.

They're missing something, though. Sure, the food isn't up to the standard of restaurants like Masa's or Chez Panisse in Berkeley. Not that I've ever been to either; they're out of my price range. But the food's good, and more importantly, it sits up high at the far end of Ocean Beach, with window tables overlooking the Pacific Ocean and waves crashing dramatically over the sea lions frolicking on the rocks below.

A first date isn't about food anyway. It's about finding a place with ambience and color, a place where both of you can relax and find out over a seafood platter if there's any connection besides physical attraction.

About six, I called again and headed downtown. Lou sat beside me in the passenger seat. I couldn't bring him inside the restaurant, but that wasn't all bad. He tends to be a third wheel on a date anyway, demanding to be in the spotlight and distracting attention from what is truly important—me. But I'd decided that until things were sorted out, I wasn't going anywhere without him. He could either curl up and sleep in the van, or wander around as he saw fit.

I picked up Josephine outside her building. She was wearing a three-quarter-length red coat and long red gloves against the chill, looking positively elegant. Lou hopped in the back, agreeable for once.

Seeing how good she looked, I was glad I had dressed up somewhat, at least for me. I actually do have some nice clothes, courtesy of the wedding gigs I sometimes play. If you want to make a living as a musician, wedding gigs are the way to go. You can play with a trio and make three times as much as you would for a club date, with half the effort. At first it bothered me that, unlike club audiences, people at weddings don't actually listen to the music—to them it's just background noise. I quickly got over that when I saw the size of the checks they handed out.

I had decided not to ask about the whole meeting outside thing, but on the way over to Cliff House Josephine brought it up herself.

"Sorry about having you pick me up outside," she said. "Rolando is home and I didn't want a scene."

"He has a problem with me? We're good friends, or at least we used to be."

"No, it's not you specifically; it's anyone. He doesn't like it when I go out. I mean, with men."

This struck me as odd. Big brothers often feel protective toward their sisters, but Josephine was a strong practitioner in her own right, well able to take care of herself. For all I knew, she might be stronger than Rolando. And neither one of them was a kid anymore. I wondered if maybe there wasn't some deeper, less healthy reason for his concern.

"Has he always been that way?" I asked.

I saw her shake her head out of the corner of my eye. "No, that's the funny thing. It's only been in the last year or so. He's changed. Most of the time he's the same old Rolando I grew up with, but sometimes . . ." She let it trail off and we talked about family for a while. She couldn't envision growing up without a sibling, just as I couldn't imagine what it would be like to grow up with one.

When I pulled up to the Cliff House all the parking was taken, so I parked up the hill in the lot overlooking the Sutro Baths. We got out and I sniffed the chill salt air coming off the ocean. I let Lou out but left a window down so he could jump back in if he wanted. There wasn't anything worth stealing in the van and I seriously doubted that anyone would care to steal the van itself. I put a slight aversion spell on it, just to play it safe, nothing strong enough to sap my energy, just enough to make people disinclined to approach it.

We opted for the Bistro, less formal and more intimate than the main Sutro room, but with equally good views. It has a long bar and small tables along a row of windows, giving patrons a great view of the Pacific, dark and mysterious in the last of the early winter light. But by the time it grew totally dark we weren't looking at the view anymore.

Some people are good at first dates, at ease and full of charm. It's only after a few weeks that you realize it's all an act and the person you were so attracted to is not who you thought they were at all.

Others are uncomfortable and tongue-tied, their personalities stifled by insecurities, but if you give them a chance there's something great underneath that nervous babble.

I'm more the first type, and so was Jo, which meant we had a great time, regardless of anything that might follow. I ordered the cioppino, a Mediterranean fish stew made with the catch of the day. Jo opted for grilled salmon, along with a bottle of overpriced but still tasty Chardonnay. We avoided talking about anything heavy for the moment. I didn't feel I knew her well enough yet to tell her everything I'd been through. We might have been working together, but I'd learned long ago not to completely trust anyone, except Eli.

And sometimes Victor. And Lou, of course, but that doesn't count because he's a dog. Sort of. Ironically, I got the sense Jo might feel the same way.

So she told me amusing stories about growing up with Rolando, embarrassing stories that I'm sure he wouldn't want told. I told her stories about, Lou that he wouldn't want anyone to know about, either, like the time he'd got his head caught in a restaurant-sized plastic mayonnaise jar trying to get at the last few dollops on the bottom and couldn't get it off.

We laughed a lot, partly because the stories were funny, partly due to the wine. Romance is supposed to be hot and steamy, with deep soul gazes and earth-shattering emotions. But in truth, laughter works far better. It breaks down barriers and hints at possibilities. It connects people, and when you feel that connection, other things seem not only possible, but often desirable. Several times Jo put her hand over mine in such a natural manner that it was almost like we were an actual couple. So far, so good, but we did have some other things to talk about.

"So tell me," I finally said over coffee. "What exactly was going on up in Portland?"

She sighed at the sudden serious turn in the conversation, put a sugar cube in her coffee, and stirred it idly for a while with her spoon.

"The first indication was what happened to Yvonne. She was a sweet woman; everybody liked her. And she was stunning—African-American, five feet ten, and slender as a willow reed. She worked as a fashion model for a while. She didn't have much talent, but nobody cared about that." Jo picked up her spoon and started stirring again. "One day she was fine. The next she was found wandering the streets aimlessly, unable to even talk. It was upsetting to everyone, but no one realized she had been attacked. It was just a mystery—some thought she might have tried a spell too strong for her to handle—she really wasn't much of a practitioner.

"But then, three weeks later, the same thing happened, this time to a friend of Rolando's, Jimmy Tam. That's when Ro started looking into it seriously. Finally, a month after that, another practitioner, Sheila."

"I knew her," I said. "Slightly. She was a pretty strong practitioner as I remember."

"Yes, she was. That was one of the curious things. Each practitioner attacked was stronger than the last."

"Why would that be?"

"Rolando thinks it's because whoever was doing it was gradually testing his power."

"And that someone would be Byron? Why? And what was he trying to do?"

"Well, that's the question. As to why Byron is a good bet, we've been over the reasons."

"Did he know the victims?"

"He did. That doesn't mean anything, though. Portland has a small practitioner community, smaller than San Francisco even. But Sheila was hanging around with Byron right before she was turned into a rutabaga."

"Guilt by association?"

"Just another coincidence," she said dryly. Jo stopped and a look of intense annoyance passed across her face. "Look at that guy," she said, jerking her head toward a man sitting across from us at the bar.

He was wearing a dark suit, sitting next to another man wearing a similar one. The two were deep in conversation, and at the same time, the first man was trimming his nails with a nail clipper. There was an audible click, and a large piece of fingernail went flying over the bar. Another click, and this time the nail shot out toward a nearby table.

"Gross," said Jo. A third click sent a piece headed our way. I instinctively ducked, and it landed on the tablecloth between us, squatting there proudly. "Okay, that's it," she said.

She took her teaspoon from the coffee cup, emptied a sugar packet into it, added the offending fingernail and a few drops of coffee, and heated it all over the candle that burned in the middle of the table. Her deft movements reminded me of nothing so much as a junkie cooking up a fix.

"You know we're not supposed to mess with civilians, right?" I reminded her.

"Yeah, and I'd guess you're a big fan of rules, yourself." She gave me a mock glare and gestured toward the ocean rocks outside the window. "Rat me out and you'll spend the rest of your life as a lonely sea lion desperately looking for a mate."

She held the teaspoon over the candle flame until the mixture bubbled into a treacly paste. Then she blew on it until it cooled slightly, dipped one finger into the mixture, and rubbed it over her fingernail until the nail was coated. When she was done, she turned toward the man at the bar, who by now had started on his other hand.

Jo smiled wickedly at me and whispered, "Stick," at the same time flicking her finger out as if she were zapping a fat horsefly that had landed on her knee. She cleaned off her finger with a napkin and some water from her water glass before leaning back contentedly in her chair.

Meanwhile, the man at the bar clipped on, oblivious. After the last one, he examined his fingers briefly to see if they were ready for the nail file. A slight frown appeared on his face and he used the clippers on a nail again, sending another missile speeding through the air. He stopped talking and a look of serious consternation now crossed his face. He clipped the nail once again, looked at it, and quickly got to his feet, jamming his hand into the pocket of his suit jacket. Jo's little spell had obviously resulted in the fingernail growing back instantly the moment it was clipped.

"Sorry. Gotta go," I heard him say to his friend. "Not feeling well." He threw some money on the bar and bolted out of the restaurant.

"You probably shouldn't have done that," I said, laughing.

"It'll only last five minutes or so. He won't even be sure

it actually happened. Besides, it was a public service. The next time he decides to trim his nails, you can be sure it will be in his own bathroom, with the door locked."

So. Jo had talent, which I already knew. And skill, which is not the same thing. And best of all, a sense of humor. Things were looking good. I paid the check and we left, in great good humor. As we walked toward my van I whistled for Lou, who wormed his way from under a nearby parked car and looked at me expectantly.

"Sorry," I said, spreading my empty hands wide. "I had fish stew and there wasn't a doggie bag for it."

He looked at me in disbelief, thinking I must be joking, and when he realized I was serious, he turned around and stalked off ahead of us, stiff-backed and disapproving. We had just about come up to the van when Jo stopped.

"Listen," she said.

I listened. Faint sounds of wind and waves. "I don't hear anything," I said.

"Wait."

We stood there in silence. Lou was acting nonchalant, busily sniffing at a fascinating patch of scrub grass near the sidewalk. He appeared unconcerned with anything.

"If there was anything wrong, he'd tell us," I said.

Josephine hesitated, then relaxed and started walking again. "Just being paranoid, I guess."

She hadn't gone more than a few steps when she stopped again, turned, and pointed toward the trail leading out to Land's End.

"Look," she whispered.

At first I didn't see anything, but just as I was about to turn away, I saw a quick flicker of pale ghostlight halfway up the trail, just inside where the trees started. Ghostlight is the by-product of active magical operations, the leaking out of energy into the visible spectrum. You can't see it in daylight, and normal people can't see it at all.

Ifrits of course are particularly attuned to it. Lou had

abandoned his scrub investigation and was up on his hind
legs like a meerkat, trying to get a better look. Josephine
took me by the arm.

"What do you think?" she said. "Should we check it out?"

I wasn't so sure that was a good idea. My first instinct
was to make sure she wasn't rushing off into danger. She
was my date, after all. Then again, she was a practitioner,
and for all I knew as competent as I was, if not more so. It
was no time to play the chivalrous protector.

"I'm not sure," I said. "It strikes me as odd that we pick
up on this just as we're coming back from dinner. Did you
tell anyone where you were going?"

"Just Rolando," she said. "It strikes me as odd, too. I'm
not an idiot. But even if it's a trap of some sort, so what?
We'll find out who set it. If the two of us together can't
handle it, what good are we?"

She gave me a challenging look. There are drawbacks
to dating strong, competent women.

"Okay," I said, "but let Lou take the lead. Remember,
his senses are a lot sharper than ours."

She nodded agreement, and I gestured to Lou, giving
him a wave toward the trees. He trotted confidently forward, but kept glancing back over his shoulder to make
sure we were following. Sometimes I suspect he doesn't
completely trust me.

It was full dark as we crossed the parking lot that led to
the trailhead. Underneath the trees, it was even darker. At
dusk the trail is fairly busy, with tourists and residents
strolling along to catch the great views of the Golden Gate
Bridge as the sun sinks into the sea. It's also a favored gay
cruising spot, but never after dark. After dark it's scary,
even without any supernatural influence.

The trail winds along the top of steep cliffs, sometimes
approaching right up to the drop-off. Occasionally, Park
Service signs appear, warning of the dangers of getting too
close to the edge, using the same stick-figure icon you see
on Don't Walk signs. In this graphic, however, the figure is

plunging head over heels to its death as the cliff crumbles away beneath it.

We walked cautiously along the path, Lou slightly in the lead. He didn't show any real wariness, only alert interest. The path split, one side continuing along straight and the other veering off downward toward the cliffs. I could barely make it out in the gloom. Josephine stumbled over some unseen obstacle and stopped.

"We could use some night vision," she said.

Indeed we could, but it isn't that easy. I can use Lou's vision and look through his eyes, but I don't do it unless I have to. His night vision is good, but looking through his eyes makes me nauseous and always leaves me with a splitting headache. I can look only where he's looking anyway, and that can be frustrating.

And as far as coming up with a spell for vision enhancement, first, I'm not good at specific spells. And second, it's really difficult to do anything that directly affects one's own makeup. Healing someone else isn't that hard, at least for those who are good at it, but it's a different matter to heal yourself. It takes so much energy that you end up worse off than you were when you started. Eli has tried to explain the why of it more than once—something about closed systems and feedback loops—but I've never understood it.

And the same thing holds true for things like vision enhancement or superhearing. They can be done, but the energy expenditure is horrendous and they don't always work that well anyway. Josephine had demonstrated she was no novice; she had to know that.

Turned out she did. She fished in her coat pocket and pulled out an amethyst-like crystal. It glowed with a soft inner light quite unlike a normal gem. I looked at her questioningly.

"You prepare the proper spell and leave it out in the sunlight for seven consecutive days," she explained. "Not an easy thing to do in Portland, or here in San Francisco, either, for that matter. It absorbs and retains all the light until you need it."

"You carry that around all the time?" I asked.

"I carry a lot of things around. You never know when you're going to need something to give you an edge."

She held it up and pressed it against the center of my forehead, spoke a few words in Spanish, and let energy flow into me. My vision blurred, then came back stronger than ever. It was like the cat vision, shades of gray and black, but this time I could see perfectly, like dusk on a late summer's day. An obvious and elegant solution to the self-enhancement issue. The gem provided the vision enhancement; Jo provided the energy. As long as she was close enough to keep feeding me a trickle of energy, I'd be able to see clearly.

"Now me," she said, handing me the gem, which was now half as bright as before.

I was flattered at her assumption that I could match her spell, but it presented a problem. As a rule I don't use objects or presets; I draw on the environment around me and adapt to my surroundings. Most of the time that's an advantage. You can't foresee every eventuality, no matter how many things you have in your pocket, and it's no help having a handy spell to solidify water when you're lost in a burning desert. But improvisation has its own drawbacks. Like right now, where I was about to be exposed as a total incompetent by someone I would have liked to impress. I had the gem in my hand but no idea how to make it work.

I cast around, hoping something would spark an idea. Nothing came, but I did notice that the trail we'd just walked down now seemed narrower. I took my hands from her face and peered back along the trail. Definitely narrower. As I stared with my now-enhanced vision, I saw a bush move. Actually, it didn't so much move as it *grew*. Impossibly fast, like the stop-motion photography in nature films. Behind it, the rest of the path was rapidly disappearing under a mass of greenery.

"What is it?" asked Josephine. I'd forgotten she couldn't see it, courtesy of my lack of reciprocal talent.

"The path seems to be closing off behind us," I told her. "Nothing to worry about."

In truth, I wasn't worried. Campbell had taught me a lot about plant magic and I was confident that I could counter whatever was going on. I'd seen another practitioner handle a similar situation once, turning an encroaching tangle of jungle plants black and withered with one malevolent word. That wasn't my style. I'd simply convince the bushes that they wanted to grow in a different direction.

Before I could act, a long and flexible plant tendril snaked out of a bush and wrapped itself around Josephine's throat. She made a gagging sound as her hands automatically reached up to claw it away. "Mason," she managed to gasp out as she was dragged away.

Almost immediately, another tendril whipped out, this one coiling around my ankles. It jerked viciously and I went down, sprawling face-first on the dirt path. The gem I held went flying off into the underbrush. A thick vine, tough and woody, spiraled over my left wrist. It was like my earlier trick with Rolando and the ivy, but a hundred times deadlier.

Lou was instantly on the vine holding my ankles, tearing at it with sharp teeth. For a moment I was free. I scrambled to my feet just in time to see Josephine, bound by thick, ropy braids, being pulled into the bushes. Then everything went dark. I thought for a moment I'd gone blind until I realized Josephine must have lost consciousness, cutting off the energy flow that powered my night vision.

I managed to tear off the vine encircling my wrist and stood there irresolute. I wanted to go after Josephine, but with my vision gone I had no way to find her. It rapidly became academic, since more bushes were springing up between where I stood and where I had last seen her. And these bushes were thick with thorns, tough enough to draw blood, as I found out when I brushed up against one of them.

I turned and sprinted down the path as quickly as I could without losing my footing in the dark, headed down toward the cliffs. The soil there would be hard and rocky, leaving little purchase for plants, or so I hoped. Maybe if I had a moment's respite, I could figure out what to do.

Lou, as always, was one step ahead of me, leading the way, but when we got there it wasn't any better. Huge, mutant cacti were bursting out of the rocky soil, crowding in on us, sporting foot-long spikes that were capable of skewering either one of us clear through. I scrambled farther down, to the very edge of the cliff. The only hope was to reach the safety of solid rock, where not even these plants could follow.

Finally, almost at the very edge of the cliff, I found a small rocky outcropping that offered temporary refuge. I huddled there as close to the edge as I dared. I couldn't see the bottom of the cliff, but I remembered from previous trips that the cliff plunged down about a hundred and fifty feet to a base filled with large and pointed rocks. Lou, with his better night vision, sidled up to the very edge and scanned the drop, looking for an escape route.

I looked around for some way to calm the insane vegetation. If I could figure it out quickly enough, I might still be in time to save Josephine. Lou's precarious position was distracting me, so I called him back from the edge. As he turned to come back, the rock shelf he was standing on suddenly crumbled and dropped off into the night. He scrabbled frantically, paws working in a blur, but he was losing traction. I took a few quick steps and threw myself on my stomach like a rescuer on a frozen ice pond and grabbed a front paw. I was inching back, not daring to get to my feet until I was well away from the crumbling lip, when I felt the berserk plant energy once again, this time underneath me. The bare rock was instantly transformed by a thick cover of moss or lichen, oily and damp and slick. It was building up faster in the rear than it was in front, creating in effect a tilted ramp. Before I could react I was sliding helplessly down toward the cliff edge, unwilling to let go of Lou and unable to find any purchase with my free hand.

Lou gave a strangled yelp as we tumbled over the edge, falling through the dark air toward the jagged rocks below. Great, I thought. Now I remember why I don't go out on dates more.

EIGHT

IT TAKES SLIGHTLY MORE THAN THREE SECONDS to fall a hundred and fifty feet. Not enough time to even think of a protective spell, let alone cast one. Even if I had crafted a bunch of prepared spells, I doubt I would have had anything ready for this. There wasn't even time to pray, not that I do much of that anyway. I never thought my last conscious utterance in life would be the words "Oh, fuck," but I'll bet I'm not alone in believing that.

I instinctively twisted as we fell and pulled Lou close so he would be above me when we hit the rocks. That way he might survive, and it certainly wouldn't help me any if I landed on top of him. But it wasn't my day to die after all.

I heard a whooshing sound as something large and black swooped down and grabbed me with hands that felt more like talons. For just a beat our speed increased, and then huge bat wings spread out with a muffled boom. Then we were circling down, losing altitude like an overloaded hang glider.

We hit the rocks hard enough to gash my arm and tweak my bad ankle again, but I wasn't complaining. I lay there stunned for a moment, then lurched to my feet and looked around wildly for our rescuer. Ten feet away, hunched on a large rock, I saw a dark figure. I couldn't make out much in the darkness, but I could see enough. I limped over slowly until I was close enough to see its lipless mouth, pointed ears, and large and opaque eyes. I didn't speak, and neither did it. We stood there without moving for maybe ten seconds. Then it unfurled its batlike wings and launched itself out over the ocean waves, flapping clumsily and climbing up into the night sky.

"They say no good deed goes unpunished," I said, glancing over at Lou. "Maybe they're wrong."

I didn't have time to ponder the vagaries of karma, though. I had to get back up the cliff. I didn't have much hope for Josephine, but there was always the chance. There was no way to climb the cliff, but if I followed the rocky shoreline back toward Cliff House, there'd be a place where the slope evens out and I could clamber back up. What I was going to do once I got there was another question. Just as I turned to go, I heard a raspy shout from the cliff above.

"Mason! Mason! Are you all right? Where are you?"

It was Jo. To say that relief washed over me would be an understatement.

"Down here," I yelled back. "What about the plants?"

"Taken care of. Can you get back up?"

"I can, farther down where the slope isn't as steep. I'll meet you at the trailhead in the parking lot."

Ten minutes later we had both staggered back to the van. I was bruised and sore, but Jo was worse. She had welts across her face and bruises on both arms, and could barely speak from the combination of having a vine around her throat and then trying to yell. Only Lou looked no worse for wear.

When I opened the van door, the dome light cast enough illumination to show a matted patch of hair on the side of Jo's head. I reached up gently and found it damp and a little tacky to the touch.

"Somewhere along the way my head met a rock," she said.

I looked at her eyes, and although it was hard to tell in the weak light, one pupil appeared larger than the other. Never a good sign—almost surely a concussion.

"We need to get you to Victor's," I said. "You're hurt worse than you think you are."

She started to shake her head, then stopped as if she regretted the motion. "Just take me home. Rolando's good at healing, better than you would think."

I had my doubts, but I could hardly order her around so I drove back to her place without arguing.

"How did you get out of there?" I asked. "I thought you were a goner."

She smiled grimly. "Not quite yet. I'm tougher than I look. The real question is, what happened to you?"

I told her about sliding over the cliff, and how I'd survived. And the creature that had saved me. She didn't show any surprise, which astonished me.

"A dhougra," she said. "But that makes no sense."

Even Eli hadn't known what the thing was.

"What's a dhougra, and how do you know about them?" I asked.

"Dhougras? They're like Ifrits, but not quite as pleasant. I know they help practitioners, at least the practitioners who know how to compel obedience. I don't know where they come from."

"How come I've never heard of them?"

"They're rare. And they're masters of illusion." I could attest to that. "The only reason I know anything about them," she continued, "is that Rolando and I ran into one a couple of years ago when we were checking out a black practitioner." She looked at me significantly. "A black practitioner. Does that give you a clue about who might be responsible?"

"But it saved me," I pointed out.

"Yes, it did. That's why I said it makes no sense."

I could have enlightened her as to the exact reason, but I

was beginning to think that the less I said about anything, the better. Until I got a handle on what exactly was going on, I wasn't going to volunteer anything to anyone. Except Eli, of course, and maybe Victor. Jo was bound to relay anything I said to Rolando, and I wasn't sure just how stable he was these days.

When I pulled up across from her apartment building, I insisted on at least seeing her up to her door, but she was having none of it.

"I'll be fine," she said. "Rolando is going to have a fit about this, and your presence there will just make it worse." She smiled unexpectedly. "You do know how to show a girl a good time, don't you? At least I got a dinner out of it."

"Sorry," I said. "Not a great first date, was it?"

I didn't bring up the fact that she was the one who had wanted to traipse off into the dark in the first place.

"That's okay," she said, still smiling. "I've had worse."

I compromised by watching her until she got across the street and into her building before I drove away. Lou sat up in the front seat and peered out the window, totally at ease, watching with interest as the city rolled by. I envy his ability to live in the moment.

When I got home, the message light on my answering machine was blinking. Eli's voice boomed out when I pushed the play button.

"Mason. I guess you're out—I hope you're being cautious, since things are looking dangerous these days." Wait until I told him the latest. An almost smug tone entered his voice. "Anyway, come by Victor's tomorrow about noon if you can. An old friend will be dropping by, and I know you won't want to miss him."

Eli didn't usually play these kinds of games, but it worked. If he was going to do something so out of character, I absolutely wanted to show up and find out who he was talking about. I thought about it for a few minutes, but couldn't come up with who it might be.

I was bone tired, not to mention bruised and cut up. I

gave Lou some kibble, but he refused even to look at it, trying to guilt me for not bringing back anything from the restaurant. He scooted out the dog door in search of better rations. I tumbled into bed and was out in less than a minute.

The ringing phone woke me up next morning before I was quite ready to get up, which seems to be a universal law of nature. At least I'd had enough sleep to answer without being surly, which was just as well since it was Josephine on the line.

"How are you feeling?" she asked.

"Okay. A little stiff and sore; that's all. What about you? You're the one who got hit in the head."

"Oh, I'm fine. After Rolando got through ranting and raving, he fixed me up. He wanted to storm over and confront Byron on the spot, but I talked him out of it. I've still got a slight headache, but that's about it."

"Listen," I said. "I'm going over to Victor's at noon. Eli will be there and you should stop by, too—he'll be more than interested in what happened last night, and I'm sure he'll have some ideas about it."

"Okay," she said. "Noon, then."

Jo was already there when I arrived, talking to Eli. Eli looked up as I came in to the study, and broke into a wide smile of amusement. The reason for his amusement was standing by one of the tall windows that looks out over Ocean Beach.

Lou ran up to the figure standing there and rubbed up against him like a cat. I wasn't quite as thrilled to see him. Eli knew how I felt about Geoffrey; that's why he'd promised me a "surprise." Eli's a wonderful man and a brilliant scholar, but his sense of humor can be absolutely juvenile at times.

"Geoffrey," I said. "Good to see you."

Not entirely true, but not a lie, either. Geoffrey had been some real help last year in figuring out what was going on, but getting information out of him was like pulling teeth.

Not that he meant to be secretive; he just couldn't help himself. He was a "Transcendent," one of those practitioners who supposedly have progressed so far along magical lines that they voluntarily withdraw from the magical world altogether, like a Zen monk. They no longer do magic. Ever. Whether that's a matter of choice or something else entirely, I couldn't say.

And lately, according to Eli, Geoffrey had become a Breatharian—a discipline that claims one can live indefinitely without food or water on nothing but sunshine and air. Ordinary followers of this premise end up in the hospital suffering from malnutrition. The lucky ones, that is; the unlucky end up dead. Geoffrey, however, remained annoyingly heathy. Loon he might be, but he wasn't without real powers.

As a Transcendent, he supposedly possesses a deep understanding and knowledge of all things, magical and otherwise, but it seems that most of whatever information he has to impart is cloaked in ambiguity, like a Zen riddle. Eli held him in high regard. Victor couldn't stand him. I was somewhere in the middle. One of the things that kept me from believing he was a complete fraud was Lou's total approval of him. Geoffrey bent down to scratch Lou's ears.

"Well," he said, "how's your music coming along?"

"About the same. Yourself?"

Geoffrey played piano, although not that well from what I understood. But I should have known better than to give him an opening. He immediately started chattering happily away about the trials of learning chord inversions and how to properly use them. He would have gone on all afternoon if Eli hadn't interrupted with a gentle reminder, picking up what must have been the previous conversation.

"Geoffrey," he said, "getting back to the Ifrit problem, I still have some questions."

"There's an Ifrit problem?" Jo asked.

"No, not really," Geoffrey said. "Just the natural ebb and flow, I think."

"I'm not convinced," said Eli. "Statistics tell me the trend is definitely downward."

"I don't understand why you think this is so important," I said. "It's not like Ifrits are disappearing off the face of the earth."

"No," said Eli, "they're not. But there's another factor involved, and when two things happen simultaneously, it's not a bad idea to ask if they're related."

"And the other?"

"Talent is getting harder to access. Spells are weaker and less reliable."

"I haven't noticed that," I said. Geoffrey perked up and nodded his head.

"Eli's right," he said.

"Is it serious?" I asked. Eli rocked back and forth on his heels before answering.

"That's hard to say. The difference is so slight that you wouldn't even notice it. As you obviously haven't. I only noticed it myself when I was assisting Victor with some very delicate experiments requiring exact measurements. The energies didn't quite balance."

"What does that have to do with Ifrits?"

"I'm not sure. Maybe nothing. But maybe the same energy drain, whatever it is, affects why we're not seeing any new Ifrits. Or maybe it's the other way around. We lost a lot of Ifrits last year. The two things may be connected or they may not, but it's worth looking into. So, Geoffrey, why are there fewer Ifrits, do you think?"

Geoffrey was listening with polite interest. If anyone could explain it, he would be the man. But getting a straight answer out of him is a different matter. He smiled in his usual infuriating fashion.

"Because there haven't been very many around, I would suppose."

"Any helpful ideas?" I put in, unable to keep quiet. Geoffrey pushed my buttons in many ways. "The question was why, remember?"

"I would think that's obvious."

"Humor me."

"Well, have you ever wondered where it is Ifrits come from?"

"Of course. Who hasn't?"

"And have you ever seen a young one, a puppy or kitten, or whatever?"

"No."

"So they arrive fully formed, complete little entities?"

"It seems that way," I said.

"Well, there you have it."

I took a deep breath. I was not going to let him aggravate me. "No, there *you* have it," I said. "I'm afraid I don't get it at all."

Josephine had been listening intently to the exchange. She walked over to the window and stood close to Geoffrey, putting on a seductive air I hadn't known was in her repertoire. She didn't realize it would be totally lost on him.

"But why do certain practitioners acquire Ifrits while others never do?" she asked, all but batting her eyes at him. Geoffrey smiled.

"Exactly," he said, beaming at her as if she were a precocious child. "Excellent question. The very crux of the matter. And the answer of course is that they don't."

"Don't what?"

"Don't acquire them."

"You mean the Ifrits choose practitioners, instead?"

"No, no, not at all. Nothing is acquired. No one is chosen. Practitioners do magic; Ifrits are magic. What could be clearer?"

"A lot of things," I said. "Like, where do they come from? Can you at least give us some idea?"

"Well, that depends on what you mean by 'come from,'" Geoffrey said.

This conversation was beginning to sound a lot like the one I'd had with him the last time I'd asked Geoffrey to explain something.

"Well, they have to come from somewhere," I said. "They can't just appear out of thin air."

Geoffrey shrugged. "Whatever you say."

The conversation was interrupted by Victor's return. He overheard part of the last exchange and waved it aside dismissively.

"Figure out where Ifrits come from another time," he said. "Right now I'm more interested in practitioners and what's been happening to them. Josephine's story about what happened to you two last night is another escalation, and we need to find out who was behind it before something like that happens again."

"Agreed," Eli said. "First, was it targeted at Mason, at Josephine, or at both? Second, whoever it was, they were lying in wait. But how did they know where you were going? Mason, did you tell anyone about your dinner plans?" I shook my head. "Josephine?"

"No. Just Rolando."

"Could you have been followed?" Victor asked. "Or tagged in some way with a follow spell?"

"I suppose," I said. "I wasn't paying that close attention."

"No, I imagine you weren't."

"How about Rolando?" I asked Jo. "Does he have any ideas about this? Apart from assuming it's Byron's doing, of course."

"Well, after he finished reading me the riot act, he got all distant and thoughtful. When I woke up this morning, right before I called you, he was already gone. There's something stirring around in his mind, for sure."

Geoffrey sighed, clearly bored by the conversation. "Can we go now?" he asked Eli, showing a very childlike petulance. "I really want to see the exhibit."

"Japanese Bamboo Art at the Asian," Eli explained. "But Geoffrey, before we go, I'd like you to take a look at something." Geoffrey got a pained look on his face.

"Is this something to do with magic again?" he asked. "You know I don't—"

"Yes," said Eli, interrupting. "I know you don't do magic anymore. I just want to know if you can tell us anything about this green stone we came across recently."

"Like the Ifrit stones?" said Geoffrey. He might have been a flake, but he could be surprisingly astute sometimes.

"I don't know what it is," said Eli.

He took his hand from behind his pocket where he'd been hiding the stone, waiting for the right time. Geoffrey really didn't like anything to do with magical objects, or anything else involving talent for that matter. He took it from Eli, rather reluctantly, and rubbed it between his fingers.

"Well, it's been used," he said.

"We know that. But for what?" asked Eli. Geoffrey shrugged, but Eli was being patient. "Can you tell us where it came from, at least?"

Geoffrey looked over at me, with a glint of amusement in his eye.

"No," he said. "But I'll bet Mason could find out."

"And how could I do that?" I asked warily.

"Why, by using your talent, of course."

I was never quite sure whether Geoffrey was completely clueless or whether he knew exactly what he was doing, but either way he always managed to get to me. Eli saw my temper starting to rise and jumped in.

"Yes, Geoffrey," he said. "But do you think you might clarify that just a bit?" A look of resignation replaced the pained one on Geoffrey's face.

"Music," he said. "Mason has an extraordinary talent for music." This was no help, but I'd regained my composure and said nothing. "Music creates worlds, don't you see? Channel your talent through the stone and you'll find where it came from."

"Oh, now I understand," I said. "What could be easier?" Eli did seem to understand, though.

"Wait a moment," he said. "Mason. You remember when we created that construct world for you where you could meet Christoph?"

"Vaguely." It had only been the most intense experience of my life.

"Yes. Well, I think you might have come away with the impression that Victor and I did all the work while you were simply the instrument."

I glanced over at Victor, who was blandly examining a slight discoloration on the surface of his desk.

"Something like that," I said.

"Well, it wasn't quite that simple. The way you personally access power is through a process of pulling together various parts of the world around you, using them as extended metaphor. Now if you just had more dedication . . ."

"Yes, I know. I'd be able to just wave my hand and the pyramids would levitate."

I figured I'd reach that level about the same time I surpassed Mozart as a composer. Eli continued, sidestepping our long-standing argument over what I should be doing with my talent and my life.

"But your talent for improvisational magic also works on an unconscious level. We supplied the power and the template, but you're the one who created that construct. I don't know many practitioners who could have pulled that off. I think you can do the same type of thing here."

"I'm not sure what good that will do."

"I'm not sure, either, but I believe you can create a space analogous to the one this stone came from. It wouldn't be a real place, of course—again, more like an extended metaphor. But it may at least give us an idea of where it came from." Eli glanced over at Geoffrey, who was nodding in approval.

"Any ideas how I'm supposed to pull this one off?" I asked.

Geoffrey simply smiled his infuriating smile and no one else said anything, so I guessed it was up to me. The first thing that came to mind, naturally, was jazz. Maybe I could play my way into the space they were talking about. A jazz improvisation is not that different, after all. You start with a template and create a metaphorical world out of the basic form. But focusing my talent while focusing on creating music wouldn't be easy. It would be like playing two separate solos simultaneously, something well outside my abilities.

It had to be listening, then, someone else's composition. Use a piece of music as the pattern and build from there. My first instinct is always jazz, but this might work better with a classical piece. Classical music is more structured, which would give me a leg up, and more complex, although I could give you a list of jazz musicians who would argue that point.

All right. Classical, then. Solo instrument? Chamber music? Orchestral? I wandered over to check out Victor's CD collection, neatly stacked in storage racks alongside the stereo. No jazz. No show tunes. Surprisingly, quite a bit of world music, and lots and lots of classical.

I pulled out a few disks at random, careful to put them back in their proper slots so Victor wouldn't freak out. I figured I'd know the right piece when I found it.

Bach cello suites? Too cerebral. Well, actually not, since it's some of the most intensely emotional music ever written, but too pure for my purposes. I needed something more down to earth, something more direct and visually evocative, like Vivaldi's *Four Seasons*. Not quite right, though. *Afternoon of a Faun*? Too diffuse. I could find myself wandering lost in a fog of sensation. Mendelssohn's *Italian Symphony*? Closer, but still not quite it.

Then, almost as if it had jumped into my hand, I had it. *Pictures at an Exhibition*. Mussorgsky. Not the Ravel orchestration that is most familiar to people, but the original written for piano. And not just any piano. Victor had the reissue of the Sviatoslav Richter version, recorded in concert back in 1958. Someone in the audience managed to smuggle a tape recorder into the concert hall in Sofia, Bulgaria, capturing one of the great performances of all time. The sound was tinny, swinging between distorted and inaudible,

and you could hear the flu-stricken audience hoarsely coughing through the quiet passages, but all that mattered not a
whit. I hadn't heard it since back when there were still LPs,
but it's one of those performances that you never forget.

Victor walked over to see what I had chosen, taking the
CD out of my hand.

"I'm surprised," he commented. "I didn't realize you
knew anything but jazz."

"Yeah, I'm a cultural idiot," I said, taking it back and
walking over to his state-of-the-art stereo. It was going to
be a waste of technology since the recording was so technically poor, but it was the music that mattered. I popped it in
the changer and picked up the remote.

"Last button on the lower left," Victor directed.

I looked over at Eli for clarification. "How is this going
to work?" I asked. "Will I just have visions, or do you think
I'll actually be transported away? And if I am, what if I
meet something there I don't like?"

Eli looked over at Geoffrey, who again smiled and
shrugged. He didn't seem to be interested in the question.
Even Eli was getting annoyed with him, but it doesn't do
any good to get annoyed at Geoffrey.

"Those are very good questions," he said, giving up on
Geoffrey. "The short answer is I don't really know. The
long answer, unfortunately, is the same."

"Best guess?"

"I'll have to straddle the fence on that. I think you both
stay here and don't, as in a psychic projection. But I would
still be careful. If something were to happen there, I don't
think your body here would necessarily escape unscathed."

"Reassuring, as always," I said.

Lou sidled over and stuck his nose in the hollow behind
my knee. He'd find a way to follow if I slipped into some
other dimension. He always did.

"Well, no time like the present," I said.

NINE

I HIT THE PLAY BUTTON ON THE REMOTE, AND AF-
ter a slight pause, the familiar promenade theme filled the
room, ambling gracefully along like a comfortable friend,
shifting between 5/4 and 6/4 time, inviting me to follow. I
concentrated on the stone I was holding and let the music
take me. This was different from anything I'd attempted
before; I wasn't drawing from any outside influences, just
gathering the music and channeling it through the green
stone. The room grew dim, but apart from that, there was no
indication anything was happening. Then the promenade
ended and the first musical picture arrived with that sudden
arpeggio ending on an F-sharp, setting the hair on the back
of my neck bristling.

I felt a tremendous lurch as the universe rearranged itself
and deposited me in a dark forest. Huge trees surrounded
me, all but blocking out a faint and distant sun. Centuries-
old detritus underfoot muffled the faint dripping sound of
nearby water. I remembered vaguely that the first piece was
supposed to represent a gnome or something, but that wasn't
what I was seeing. I wasn't hearing anything, either, at least

not in the way that we understand the concept. The music was still echoing in my head, but I didn't hear it as sound anymore. The forest surrounding me had become the embodiment of the music, each shift in melody and tempo being expressed not by sound, but rather through some remolding of reality. If that doesn't make sense, let's just say that it was indescribable and leave it at that.

Lou was right at my feet. I've never understood how Ifrits travel; it seems that if Lou is near me, he can then follow me anywhere, even into a dream. He scanned the area and stretched carefully, head turning back and forth, keeping a watchful eye out.

To the left of us, a line of bushes grew thickly along a gentle rise. They sported pale, spiky leaves that looked sharp and brittle, more like crystal spears than soft plant matter. I could see leaves trembling on one of the closer bushes, as if something were hiding under it. A scurry and a jump, a flash of something small and brown, and a sense of something flittering from one bush to the next. Lou was after it like a shot. I started to call him back and then figured, what the hell, he probably had a better grasp on this place than I did.

He was back out in a second, though. Whatever was in the bushes was either too quick for him or was something he didn't want to mess with. He looked up at me, sharp-eyed, waiting to see what I was going to do. That's one of the great things about Lou. Despite all evidence to the contrary, he insists on preserving the illusion that I know what I'm doing.

Farther up the slope, the bushes were thicker and taller, growing to a height of fifteen feet or more in places. Several of them were swaying, even though there wasn't any wind. A rhythmic thudding shook the ground beneath my feet, as if some unseen elephant-sized creature were stalking ponderously along just out of sight. The little brown things were multiplying, flickering in and out of view.

All very interesting, to be sure, but I couldn't see it was

getting me anywhere. I felt the promenade theme return-
ing, and the forest faded away to be replaced by a different scene. The next picture in the series was supposed to be
something about an old castle, but again, what I was seeing
had nothing to do with architecture.

I was standing on a broad plain—what I imagine the
Siberian tundra must look like. Brown and sere, it stretched
away until it ran up against low-lying hills covered with
patchy snow. In the distance, a herd of reindeerlike animals
ambled slowly along. The wind whispered around my
head, cold, dry, and chilling. Lou was already shivering,
picking up one paw after another, not thrilled with our new
destination. Once again, this wasn't getting me anywhere.
It had been a great idea, but it wasn't working. I tried to remember how many different musical sketches there were
in the Mussorgsky piece. Ten? Twelve? Too many to wait
around for, anyway. Maybe I could speed up the process.

I tried simultaneously concentrating and relaxing, a very
Zen concept. Usually that sort of thing is beyond me, but it
worked. Scenes flickered by in a cosmic CD shuffle as each
sketch passed: thousands of ratlike rodents scurrying aimlessly; huge machines like giant water wheels grinding away;
millions of fireflies blinking over endless dusky meadows.

Then I found it. There. I stopped the shuffle, emerging
on a hillside overlooking a shallow valley. Cold, cold and
silence. That special ancient silence of a dead world. Bodies lay collapsed on the ground, thousands, maybe tens of
thousands, ancient as the silence, stacked in rows like some
enormous mortuary. But not human, not at all. Crystalline,
glittering, many faceted. And the bones, if bones they were,
consisted of a smooth green material that looked like jade.
I'd found what I was looking for.

A distant clinking sound echoed from somewhere to my
left, startling me. The sound was jarring, almost sacrilegious
in this quiet place of the dead. I could just make out a solitary figure, walking slowly among the brittle corpses, stopping every so often to pick out a random bone. The figure

was too far away to make out anything, other than whoever it was wore a long, bulky coat against the cold. A large canvas bag with a black-and-white pattern, like a messenger pouch, was slung over one hip, and the collected bones were being tossed casually into it.

I wanted to get closer for a better look, but I didn't want to expose myself. By the time I finally decided to cautiously ease down the slope, the figure had disappeared over a ridge. Lou jerked his head back toward me, asking if I wanted him to follow. Before I could say anything, the sound of carillon bells filled the sky, tinkling and twittering like a flock of ethereal birds.

Larger bells chimed in, increasing in volume. Then, the tolling of an impossibly huge bell which shattered my ears and shook the ground. The bell grew even louder, overwhelming me. I stopped, unable to move, and dimly realized that the Mussorgsky piece was coming to its climax. The tolling of the giant bell paralyzed me, driving out all rational thought. Finally, the bells all came together in a giant chord that echoed and hummed throughout my body. It went on seemingly forever, expanding until the whole world was nothing but sound and vibration. Every nerve in my body sizzled like an electric storm. I gasped for air as I felt myself growing larger without changing size and, at the same time, melting into myself. Then, just before my body turned inside out and my psyche dissolved, the world around me shattered and I was back at Victor's, flopping around on the floor like some epileptic fish.

I tried to stagger to my feet, but Eli knelt down and held me there until I regained some composure.

"Sorry," he said. "I didn't realize it would be so rough on you."

Geoffrey walked over, concerned for once, but I was in no mood to deal with him and in no mood for apologies. My nerves were still buzzing and my body felt infinitely fragile, as if my bones would snap if I moved too quickly. I checked my body for signs of bruising, but my skin was smooth and unbroken. It still hurt like hell, though. I pushed Eli away and climbed shakily to my feet. Timothy gave me a sympathetic look. Lou was sitting next to me composedly, not a hair out of place. Naturally.

"Next time, how about you doing the experiment and me taking the notes?" I said. "Better still, how about we don't do this anymore?"

Eli walked away to give me time to cool off. Victor must have realized I was seriously pissed because he didn't say anything, but he did start drumming his fingers impatiently on the desktop.

I walked gingerly over to the warmth of the fire and stood there glowering at both of them. Jo came over and stood next to me in sympathetic silence. My body was still sore, but the pain was fading, so whatever damage I'd incurred wasn't permanent. Finally, Victor could keep quiet no longer.

"Well?" he demanded.

"I found something, but I don't know what it means," I said. I described the scene in detail, and Eli nodded his head several times in satisfaction as if it all made sense to him.

"So it is organic in a sense, and yet not."

"But what were they? And where exactly was I?"

"Impossible to say. As I said, it's all metaphor. You weren't really anywhere, not in the traditional sense. But now I understand that rune. It had a residual life force; it could be used to enhance a transfer of personality, and probably a lot of other things as well. But once it's been employed, the life force is used up. What we have left is just dead bone, empty and inert. I'd love to get my hands on a fresh specimen."

"Sure thing," I said. "I'll see if I can't bring something back next time."

I WAS HUNGRY AFTER MY UNEXPECTED ADVEN-ture. Jo and I had lunch at a nearby café that serves expensive sandwiches of indifferent quality. Lou had to wait outside, but since everyone who left slipped him some sort of treat, he was perfectly happy. I'd have to get him out of there before he turned into one of those sausage dogs from all the extra food he was scarfing down.

I wanted to talk about what had happened to us last night. Considering we had both almost been killed, I thought it might be of some interest. But Jo wasn't interested in a postmortem discussion, nor was she that interested in the rune stone or my vision. Instead, she was more focused on Ifrits. Geoffrey seemed to have made quite an impression on her.

"How long have you had Lou?" she asked.

"Seven, maybe eight years."

"And you've never tried to find out where he came from?"

"Not really. I mean, we all wonder about it sometimes, but it's just part of magical life. There's no point, practically speaking. I might as well wonder where talent comes from. I leave that sort of speculation to Eli."

"And he seems to think the supply is drying up."

"If it is, I haven't noticed. But I admit I haven't heard of anyone acquiring a new Ifrit in quite a while."

Jo chewed on her overpriced sandwich and looked through the glass door at Lou. He was busy running through his gamut of tricks for a delighted child who just might have a spare french fry. Pretty soon he'd start in on the backflips.

"What do you suppose Geoffrey was getting at when he said Ifrits are magic?" she said, choking down a crust.

"Well, they are. It's obvious."

"Yes, but he phrased it quite specifically. 'Practitioners *do* magic. Ifrits *are* magic.'"

"So?"

She leaned in across the table and grabbed my hand. "What if what he meant was, practitioners *create* Ifrits?"

"But they don't," I said. "They can't. If they could, everyone would have one."

"No, I don't mean on purpose. I'm talking about something from the subconscious. If you need one and the circumstances are right, it just springs up from the unconscious mind and strolls through the door."

It sounded ridiculous. But when I thought about it for a moment, the idea had a certain appeal. It still left a lot of questions unanswered, but it also would explain a lot. Like why Ifrits are so similar in personality to their practitioners. I had always assumed it was just a more refined version of pets taking on the attributions of their owners, but maybe it was more than that.

"Interesting," I said. "But why then would it only work for some practitioners?"

"I don't know. What do the ones with Ifrits have in common?"

"That's always been the question. Nothing, as far as anyone can tell."

"Well, it's got to be something," she said, and lapsed into silence. After a while she shook off her mood. "Hey," she said, "let's go somewhere, take a walk, maybe."

"Sure," I said. "Anywhere in particular?"

"It's your city. Take me somewhere. Somewhere with water."

So we ended up walking along Baker Beach in the damp drizzle of a November day. The Golden Gate Bridge loomed romantically through the fog, visible one moment, hidden the next. Lou halfheartedly charged a group of sandpipers, indicating just how bored he was.

"I like sunsets and long walks on the beach in the rain," she said, looking up at me and batting her eyes.

"I like quiet nights by the fire with a glass of wine."

"And kittens?"

"Only for lunch."

She watched Lou trotting up and down by the water's edge, nose twitching at every gust of wind.

"It's hard to believe he's not just a dog, sometimes."

"You're not the first to say that."

We walked a bit farther, automatically linking our hands.

Strolling down a foggy beach, walking hand in hand, like two kids in love. Forever the blessed ones. But we weren't, not really, any more than Lou is just a dog.

"Do you think Geoffrey could be right about the Ifrits?" she said again. She seemed to have fixated on the idea. "That practitioners bring them into existence in some way? Maybe they're even an extension of a practitioner's psyche."

"I don't see how. Again, if that were the case, there'd be a lot more of them, for one thing."

"Not necessarily. What if it took a special talent to do that? Apart from magical talent, I mean."

"Such as?"

"That's what I can't figure. But you must have thought about it. You're the one with the Ifrit, after all. I'm just on the outside looking in."

A lot of practitioners feel that way. Most of them never voice those feelings because there's nothing to be done about it, but I know they think it's unfair. And it is. But it wasn't anything I spent much time thinking about.

"And Lou," Jo continued. "Eli says he's special, even for an Ifrit. So why would he find you? What's so special about you? What is it that you have that none of the other practitioners possess?"

"A 1955 Gibson Birdland guitar, for one," I said, turning it into a joke.

That's when it hit me. No ponderous chain of logic. No carefully researched theories. No late-night discussions. Out of nowhere I had the answer to an age-old question.

Like all great discoveries, it arrived fully formed—like an Ifrit. It would have to be tested. The details would have to be worked out, the implications thought through. But in my heart I knew I had it.

"Music," I muttered.

"What?"

"Music," I said, getting excited. "Oh, not just music—creativity, in all its aspects. Practitioners tend to be creative souls anyway, but there are degrees. I'm a musician—that's really my life; that's who I am. I'm certainly not the strongest of practitioners, but I do have creative talent. Quite a bit, in fact."

"And so modest about it."

I ignored the gibe. I was on a roll. I had dropped Jo's hand and started waving my hands, walking faster and faster, almost forcing her to jog to keep up. "And—" I stopped so quickly that Jo almost ran into me.

"What?" she prompted.

"Sandra. And Moxie. Moxie was the smartest Ifrit I ever knew. Smarter than Lou in some ways. And Sandra is an artist. She's hardly even a practitioner anymore. She just paints all the time. And she's good. Really good. It fits perfectly. And that explains Lou, why he's so amazing."

"Because you're such an amazing player?"

Her tone carried more than a hint of sarcasm, but it didn't bother me. Usually I'm the faux-modest sort, but the truth is, I really can play.

"Yes," I said. "I am. Just like Sandra is an amazing artist, and Moxie was an Ifrit genius."

"You said, 'was.' Moxie was. Did something happen?"

"Yeah, it did. Moxie's no longer with us."

I didn't say any more, making it clear I had no intention of talking about it. It was not a happy memory. I eventually had to tell Sandra what had happened to Moxie, but I never told her the complete story. It wouldn't have done her any good.

"And Montague," I said. "He's another. He built a living house, just by using talent and the good green earth, and lit it with plants he invented. If that's not creativity, I don't know what is. And guess what—he has an Ifrit, Willy, smart as a whip."

Jo looked at me, puzzled. "Who's Montague?"

I realized I hadn't yet told her about him and his theory about the sick practitioner. And the fact that Montague might be able to identify him if he had something to work with.

"That's great," she said when I explained. "But will it really be proof? Montague may think so, but can he be sure?"

"I think so. He doesn't strike me as someone who makes mistakes."

Jo looked unconvinced. "Maybe, but Byron is a slippery character. Even if Montague clears him, it wouldn't necessarily mean anything. And how are you going to get hold of something of Byron's anyway? Practitioners don't usually leave personal stuff lying around, especially black practitioners."

"I know," I said. "I'm working on it." That's what people say when they have no idea how to go about solving a problem—"I'm working on it." I had a feeling Jo knew that as well as I did. "Again, why are you so sure Byron is our guy? You seem to be awfully certain considering there's no real evidence."

"Because I know him. He might have you fooled with his oh-so-reasonable front, but I know him. He's slimy and he's cruel. You may need proof, but I don't. And if you knew him better, you wouldn't, either."

She let go of my arm and put some space between us. For the first time since I'd met her, I saw real anger.

We walked in silence for a while. Lou continued his pathetic attempts to amuse himself, sinking so low as to actually dig holes in the sand.

"Victor," she suddenly said. I had no idea what she was referring to.

"What about him?"

"He has an Ifrit, Maggie. Victor's a lot of things, but I've never thought of him as a creative type. So how does that fit in?"

For a moment I saw the whole house of cards crashing down. Victor is the least creative person I know. But I wasn't going to abandon my idea. Not quite yet. It was too good; it explained too much.

"How long have you known Victor?" I asked.

"I don't know. Awhile."

"And how well do you know him?"

She laughed. "Not very. Who does?"

"Exactly. No one, except maybe Eli. For all we know he might be writing romance novels in his spare time."

"Under what name?"

I thought a moment. "Victoria Savant?"

"Not bad. But really, how do you explain Maggie?"

I was watching Lou as we talked. He had turned his back on the shore and was focused on a fascinating piece of driftwood. An unusually large wave broke behind him, rushing up the beach.

"Lou, watch out," I called. "Rogue wave."

He turned just in time to catch it full in the chest. It swept him off his feet, and by the time he recovered he was soaked to the skin and covered with wet sand. He started pawing at his muzzle, trying to get the sand off, gagging from the salt water he'd swallowed and sneezing from the water up his nose. Jo looked at him, then at me, then at him again.

"Hmm," she said. "Perhaps this idea has some merit. I do see a definite resemblance here."

She was just giving me a friendly dig, but it triggered an idea.

"Yeah?" I said. "And who does Maggie remind you of? Supercilious, fastidious, never a hair out of place?"

"Well, sure, but that doesn't mean anything. Even ordinary pets tend to take after their owners."

"But nobody really knows Victor, not even Eli. Maybe Timothy, a little, though I doubt it. And you don't have to play music or write novels or paint to be a creative soul. 'Art in the blood is liable to take the strangest forms,' you know."

She nodded. "Sherlock Holmes," she said, catching the reference and rising a notch in my estimation.

"Exactly. Holmes was creative; detective work was the way he expressed that. Victor is a detective of sorts."

"Sherlock Holmes is a fictional character," she reminded me.

"The analogy is still valid. And Victor is an extraordinary

practitioner, even creative you might say, though I'd never tell him that to his face. It's not just that he has power; along with Eli, he's come up with some amazing discoveries. Eli is unequaled as a researcher, as a scholar, but Victor is the one with the flair."

"But still, you can't really call that *creative*, not in the way you are, or . . . What was her name?"

"Sandra. Sure, you can. And anyway, Maggie's not the Ifrit that Lou is, either. For a cat she'd be extraordinary, but as an Ifrit? Sleeping by the fire is pretty much her prime focus in life."

I'd slowed down enough by now so that Jo no longer had to hurry to keep up. We walked along until we reached the far end, the area where it becomes an unofficial nude beach, mostly for gay men. A few hardy souls braved the chill, sitting on the sand, but no one had their clothes off. Sweats or Levi's and sweaters seemed to be the preferred uniform this gray November day. Jo kept her head down, staring at the uneven beach, scuffing her shoes along the wet sand. She was thinking hard.

"Let's say you're right," she finally said. "Let's say that creative practitioners somehow produce Ifrits out of their unconscious. Why couldn't some practitioner without an Ifrit consciously choose to do that?"

So. There it was. The reason Jo was so interested in the whole subject. Like plenty of others, she wanted an Ifrit of her very own.

"Well, I'm sure it's been tried before, although I've never heard of it. But no one's ever succeeded—that's for sure. That, I would have heard about."

"But if you're right, there's no actual reason it *couldn't* be done, right?"

Jo was waving her hands excitedly. I grabbed one of them to calm her down.

"That's quite a leap, Jo. I mean, right now it's hardly a theory. More of a notion, and I wouldn't have the slightest idea how one would go about it."

"What about that woman?" she said. "Sandra?"

"What about her?"

"Well, you said she's an artist, a good one. And apparently she lost her Ifrit somehow, right?"

"Yes," I said, cautiously. I wasn't sure I liked where this was heading.

"Who better than to try out this theory, then? She's highly creative, according to you. She creates things; that's what a painting is, a creation. She once had an Ifrit, so we know she has the ability. Presumably she would like one again. Why not give it a try?"

"What, bring back Moxie from the great beyond? Apparently you don't read much horror fiction. Ideas like that never have a happy ending."

"No, not bring anything back. Create an entirely new Ifrit. You said yourself no one's ever tried anything like that. No one's even imagined such a thing."

I thought about the last time I had seen Sandra, when I broke the news to her about Moxie. She was already devastated, right on the edge, and for a while I feared the shock would push her the rest of the way over. But she got through it, and the last time I'd talked to her she was painting again. I felt guilty I hadn't been there for her back then, but at the time I was having troubles of my own.

But to barge in on her now, stir up old sorrows, and offer what was almost surely a false hope? No way in hell. Let sleeping dogs lie is good advice in more ways than one.

"Sorry," I said. "That's just not going to happen."

Jo started to argue, but she heard something in my tone that told her it was not open to discussion. She bit her lip and fell silent. We turned around and walked back the way we had come, this time in silence, and not a comfortable one.

TEN

I DROPPED JO OFF BACK AT THE RESTAURANT where she had left her car. I started back home, but as I drove along on Diamond Heights Boulevard, a sudden whim made me turn off toward Byron's house. I wanted to talk to him again. Something wasn't quite adding up, and without Rolando around to hijack the conversation, I might get a better feel for things.

No one was home when I got there. I rang the bell and knocked on the door, but no response. Probably out looking for virgins to sacrifice. I stepped back and examined the wards again. They were as grim as I remembered, more so if anything, and he'd added some extra frills. Our visit must have disturbed him enough so that he had spent some additional time working on protection.

But right by a side window I could see something off-kilter. A slight incongruity, like where two separate coats of paint meet on a wall, almost but not quite identical. I walked over to take a closer look.

Byron hadn't had the time to rework his wards. Instead, he'd simply layered over the new stuff on top of the old.

Sloppy work. And stupid, as well. Even I knew better than to cut corners that way. It was like wrapping a pipe with duct tape to fix a leak. It may work for a while as a temporary fix, but you're just inviting eventual disaster.

The window itself was no problem; it had an old retro brass latch securing it, classic but not very secure. It would be simple to slip the latch with a pocketknife.

A thin line shimmered where the old and the new wards met. There was no way I could dismantle those wards, but I could take advantage of this interface. Something similar had once happened to me; I had learned my lesson, but apparently it was a lesson Byron had not.

I stood outside, almost hoping he would drive up. I didn't really want to break into his house. The morality didn't bother me; it was just too dangerous to be undertaken lightly. Entering another practitioner's house uninvited is one of the most egregious offenses in the practitioner community. There's kind of a Wild West attitude about it—if you break into someone's house and you get caught inside, anything goes. And wandering around a black practitioner's digs wouldn't be the safest of occupations. If something fatal were to happen to me, Eli in particular would mourn my passing but he wouldn't be able to do a thing about it.

But like the decision involving the cat, this was too good a chance to pass up. Well, maybe that wasn't the best example, considering how the cat thing had turned out. At least I would be looking around with an open mind. Maybe I'd find something inside that would clear him. If Rolando broke in, I could even see him planting evidence; that's how sure he was of Byron's guilt. Rolando was always an ends-justify-the-means type of guy.

But maybe I'd find something damning, like a pile of green rune stones lying around. Or, if I could swipe some hair or soap, or something else personal, I could find out if he was indeed the practitioner who had visited Montague seeking help. Or not. If he wasn't, I'd actually be doing him a favor.

It took me a full two minutes to make up my mind. I didn't need a clever use of talent this time; enough of a discontinuity was present to simply reach into it and wedge it apart, using raw energy. I slipped the latch and slid the window open. There wasn't enough of an opening in the wards to let me slip through, however. Even this glaring flaw wouldn't allow that. But there was more than enough room for, say, a small dog.

Ifrits are notorious for their ability to squeeze through the smallest discontinuity, to ooze through dimensional cracks. I waved Lou forward and he bounded up through the window without hesitation. Now there was a path through the rent in the ward, and our connection made it easy to slip through after him. I envisioned myself as a rail-thin spectre, turned sideways, let out all the air in my lungs, and followed Lou through the open window. I felt a brief tearing sensation inside me, and then I was standing inside the living room.

The first thing I saw when I got inside was a collection of figurines laid out on a low table by the leather couch. They came in varying shades of green, jade probably, much like the rune stone, but when I picked them up they were disappointingly normal. If you consider a collection of jade animals with distorted human heads normal.

I didn't take time to examine them thoroughly. Like any good burglar, I immediately checked on potential escape routes in case of Byron's unexpected return. That's the first rule for burglars—check out the exit options. I looked back at the rent in the ward where I'd come through. It was still glowing, faintly but reassuringly.

I looked around trying to locate the bathroom, the best site for hair and such. But something better presented itself—the wastebasket filled with tissues at the end of the couch. Perfect. Actually, not so much perfect as gross. Snot and phlegm and saliva. But it would work, as surely as blood.

And the second rule of burglary is to get in and get out as quickly as possible. Wasting time searching aimlessly because you're squeamish about bodily fluids is a sure way to get yourself caught. I reached in the wastebasket and stuffed a wad of the tissues into my pocket. One good thing, he certainly wasn't going to miss them.

"Let's get out of here," I said to Lou.

I hadn't taken more than a step when the rent in the ward flashed and then smoothly melded together like a Ziplock baggie. The outline of the rip faded back into the featureless wall.

So Byron wasn't so sloppy after all. He was clever, and had set a clever trap. The only remaining question was whether the trap was designed simply to contain an intruder, or if it were more along the lines of a trip wire attached to a shotgun. And if so, where was the shotgun? And equally to the point, what would it be?

A noise from the next room, a heavy scraping sound as if something rough was painfully dragging itself across asphalt, answered the where. The what was going to be all too apparent in a moment.

The room wasn't offering much that I could draw on. My talent thrives on chaos; the more disorderly the area, the more things randomly scattered around, the better. Neatly manicured lawns and carefully arranged furniture and razor-straight pictures on the wall cramp my style. Still, you work with whatever is available.

Lou had retreated back to the wall where we'd entered and was pawing hopefully at where the rent in the ward had been. His ears twitched at every grinding bump that came from the next room. I tried to blank my mind and steady my nerves. Not the easiest thing, since whatever was coming through the doorway was bound to have its share of fangs, drool, and insatiable lust for blood. Breaking into the house of a black practitioner does have drawbacks.

When the thing came through the doorway, it was a huge anticlimax. Literally huge. It could barely squeeze through the doorway, but there were no fangs, no drool, no glowing satanic eyes. It resembled a giant walrus more than anything else, but with no tusks and an almost human-looking face. It regarded us placidly with what I would call a sweet expression, although that might have been overly optimistic. It lumbered painfully through the door, pulling itself along on rudimentary flippers, rough skin scraping against the floor with a raspy sound. This wasn't a guardian; this was a pet.

Even if it meant us harm, which seemed unlikely, it was too slow to accomplish much. Giant, slow-moving creatures are never much of a problem. It's the quick ones with sharp little teeth that you have to worry about.

It was big, though, bigger even than I'd first thought. It had managed to finally squeeze through the door and now was standing in the room, panting heavily and staring at us somewhat mournfully. Lou gave up on his futile scratching at the wall and sidled back over toward me. He didn't show much concern, but he wasn't going to get near the thing, either.

It settled down with a soft whooshing sound and spread out over the floor as if it were a giant bread pudding. Squatting there, it looked larger than ever. Certainly larger than when it first came through the door. I looked at it closely, trying to get a sense of just how enormous it was. A nagging thought skirted around the edges of my mind. Maybe it wasn't just perspective; maybe it really was growing. After another minute, I no longer had any doubts. It was definitely growing, slowly but relentlessly. It had already taken over another foot or so of floor, and was inching toward the ceiling as well. Before long it would fill the entire room and there wouldn't be any space left for a foolish practitioner and his faithful familiar.

I drew out some energy from the electrical current running through the walls and sent out a small pulse of electricity at the nearest fold of flabby flesh. There was a sizzling sound, and a burnt, fishy odor filled the room as the flesh jerked and quivered, but instantly another fold of plump meat flowed around the burn and smoothed it over.

Worse, the probe energized the thing and it began to expand even faster, flowing toward me like a giant wave of pastry dough.

Well this was just dandy. I'd fought slugs and hordes of rats and unstoppable demons, but I had no idea how to handle this. I backed into the farthest corner and went about setting up a protective shield. I didn't think any type of aversion spell would work—the creature's flesh posed the problem, not the creature itself. So it would have to be a physical energy shield.

The room had little I could work with, but at least I could use its order and rigidity for something. I used that order as my basis and constructed a shield as hard and rigid as the room itself. I poured all the power I had into it—I hated to deplete myself that way, but it's foolish to die with a reserve of power that you've saved for future battles.

Of course, if the thing kept growing exponentially, the shield would eventually fail under the pressure and collapse. But I had a safety valve. There's an old joke about two guys running from a bear. The first guy says, "You're crazy; you can't outrun a bear." The second guy says, "I don't have to. I just have to outrun you." My shield didn't have to be stronger than the ever-growing flesh pressing in on it. It just had to be stronger than the wall it was jammed up against.

Before long, Lou and I were huddled in the corner, surrounded by a mound of tissue and muscle. The power I was pouring in made the shield glow, so at least we weren't in total darkness. We spent the next couple of hours crouched on the floor. The pressure wasn't getting any worse, but my reserves were starting to run out. I could keep up the shield for quite a while longer, but I couldn't stay in the corner forever. I needed to come up with a plan, and quickly, before Byron returned.

The sound of a key in the front-door lock made the whole problem moot. Byron was home. With the creature filling the entire front room, I couldn't see how he was going to open the door, though. Then I remembered my last visit—the front door opened outward. I should pay more attention to details. At the time I'd just thought it peculiar, but there's almost always a reason for those odd little quirks that don't quite add up.

The door opened and the sound of a low chuckle was just audible. Then, a sharp command.

"Tobbo! Enough. Let 'em out."

Seconds later the surrounding flesh began to shrink back. In less than a minute, my little corner was free and a rapidly diminishing Tobbo made himself relatively small against the opposite wall. But I wasn't out of trouble, not by any means. A very pissed-off Byron was standing in the open front doorway. He looked at the two of us with what could be described only as disappointment.

"Mason," he said slowly, drawing out the name. "Not exactly who I was expecting."

I curbed the impulse to toss off a flip reply. For one thing, I'd just broken into his house, something even more unacceptable among practitioners than it is among ordinary citizens. Not that ordinaries are too keen on the idea themselves.

Second, a practitioner is strongest on his own turf, and I was weaker than usual after holding up that shield for the last two hours or so. I realized just how clever a trap it was. Not only had I been effectively immobilized until Byron's return, but the energy I'd been forced to expend made me as vulnerable as a kitten. He could pretty much do anything he wanted with me.

"This is not what it looks like," I said.

Byron smiled, with the smug expression of someone who knows he's got the upper hand.

"Oh? And what is it, then?"

I thought frantically and then gave it up. "Okay, it's exactly what it looks like. What now?"

He walked across the room and sat down stiffly on the couch, waving me over to a nearby chair. Lou plopped himself down at my feet and immediately went to sleep. So much for the faithful-dog-protecting-his-owner routine.

"I assume you were looking for something," he said. "Did you find it?" I could feel the bulge of tissue in my pocket.

"Well, I didn't really have time. That's quite a pet you've got there."

"Tobbo? Yes, very useful. Not too bright, though. But you didn't answer my question."

"I wasn't looking for anything specific," I told him, fudging a bit. "I just thought I might find something that would tell me if you're involved in this shit. Or maybe even something that would clear you."

I added that last part to indicate I was more than willing to consider him innocent. I gave him my best I'm-a-nice-guy smile, rueful and a bit sheepish. He wasn't buying.

"I don't need to be 'cleared,' not by you, not by Rolando, not by anyone," he said.

I was beginning to feel more at ease, despite the embarrassing situation. Byron seemed more annoyed at me than outraged. Despite some notable lapses, I'm pretty good at assessing people. Byron didn't seem dangerous, at least at the moment. And Lou would hardly have curled up for a nap if he sensed any imminent danger. True, Byron had set a clever trap, but it hadn't been a lethal one.

It was interesting that he'd brought up Rolando. Maybe the trap wasn't a random setup. Maybe he had been expecting someone in particular. That would explain the disappointed look I'd received.

"You seem to have quite a history with Rolando," I said innocently. "What's the deal with that, if you don't mind my asking?"

He didn't answer, just continued staring at me. I didn't say anything more. I just kept looking at him with what I hoped was a neutral and politely interested demeanor. After a while he shrugged.

"How well do you know him?" he asked.

"Not that well anymore. We were friends at one time, but I haven't seen him in a while."

"How long?"

"Four, five years."

"Well. About a year ago I crossed paths with him up in Portland. We had some issues; what they were isn't important, but ever since we've had trouble. Now he shows up here threatening me. So, yeah, I thought I'd take a few precautions."

"And his sister?"

"That's a very different story. But, no, she doesn't care much for me, either."

That was putting it mildly, considering what Jo had said about him.

"Why is that?" I asked.

"You'd have to ask her. But why isn't important. Rolando started a campaign to get me lynched, basically. It got so unpleasant for me that I finally decided to move down to San Francisco, just to get away from him. And then, he shows up on my doorstep."

I looked at him skeptically. "You didn't try to resolve it with the Portland community, or fight it out, or something like that? You just uprooted yourself and moved?"

Byron laughed bitterly. "Resolve it? How? I'm a black practitioner, remember? Who's going to take my side? And as for more direct action, well, Rolando had a lot of allies up there. Thanks to him, half of Portland believes I'm a monster of some sort. Look at you—whose word are you going to take, mine or your good friend Rolando the enforcer?"

He had a point. But there was one telling fact that wasn't being addressed.

"What about the practitioner attack we just had here? Exactly like the ones that stopped about the time you moved down from Portland?" I felt anger rising up. "That was a friend of mine, by the way." The wry smile on his lips faded.

"I'm sorry to hear that," he said. His gaze was level. "But I'm not the only one who's recently left Portland."

That threw me. The vague doubts I'd been having about Rolando jumped into focus. But then, a second later, I remembered who it was suggesting this. Byron might be acting sane and rational at the moment, but he was a black practitioner after all. Not all of them are as bad as you might think, but I hadn't had very good experiences with the ones I'd known.

Still, I was an uninvited guest in his house and my power had been mostly drained. He might be acting calm and composed and rational, but it still wasn't a good time to be challenging him about anything. I had one more question, though.

"That trap. Rolando?"

He shrugged. "I had hopes."

"What were you going to do with him?"

He shrugged again. "I hadn't decided."

"Well, you've certainly given me something to chew on," I said, getting to my feet. "I'm going to have to think on this." Lou was awake instantly and headed for the door. I wondered if he'd really been asleep at all.

Byron's eyes tightened and for a moment I thought there was going to be trouble. Instead, he put out his hand to Lou, who surprisingly walked over to him and sniffed it.

"You ever wonder where these guys come from?" he said, indicating Lou.

A lot of people were asking that question lately.

"I've given it some thought," I said.

"So have I."

For a moment it seemed as if he was going to continue, but instead he got to his feet, walked over to the door, and ushered us out.

"Come again anytime," he said. "Preferably when I'm actually at home." He followed me out the door. "By the way, you didn't happen to take anything away with you, did you?" I could feel the bulge of tissue in my pocket.

"No," I said. "Why would I?" I gave him my best frank and open look. When that didn't seem to be working, I held my arms out from my body. "You want to search me? Be my guest."

That seemed to satisfy him. He obviously didn't know any cops, who could have told him that the "Go ahead, search me" line is an almost sure indication there's something to be found.

"Never mind," he said. "Just one thing. This may sound strange coming from a black practitioner, but trust me. Rolando? There's something very wrong with that guy."

He went back inside and left us standing in the street. On the way home, I mulled it all over. He'd had me in his clutches, so to speak, yet hadn't taken advantage of that. So was he a bad guy or a good guy? Or as usual, something in between? I needed to have a serious talk with Rolando; that much was clear. I could only hope I could get some answers from him.

ELEVEN

I DIDN'T HAVE TO TRY VERY HARD TO FIND RO-
lando. He was waiting for me outside my flat, and he wasn't
happy.

"Get a goddamn cell phone, why don't you?" were the
first words out of his mouth.

I climbed out of the van and spread my arms wordlessly,
trying to placate him. I didn't think my lack of a cell phone
was his major concern.

"And what the hell were you trying to do?" he continued.

"You'll need to be a bit more specific," I said, although
I had a pretty good idea what he was talking about.

"You almost got her killed—is that specific enough? You
think this is some kind of game? Taking her out on a *date*,
for Christ's sake. Byron is picking off practitioners, and
you're out on a goddamn date?"

It didn't seem the best time to tell him I'd just come from
Byron's, much less that Byron was trying to finger him as a
bad guy. Luckily, he wasn't much interested in anything I
might have to say. Lou was edging away, not scared, just
more like the way people in the street edge away when they

see a homeless person waving his arms and talking angrily to invisible adversaries. Rolando paused and gathered his control. When he spoke again, it was quieter, but no less intense.

"I don't want you seeing her anymore, Mason. I mean it. We need to all work together, fine. But I don't want you seeing her."

Usually I don't take well to being told what I can or can't do. I've got a whole store of snappy comments for just such occasions. But Rolando was right on the edge, and things were liable to turn even uglier if I pushed it.

"We can talk about it later," I said. "When you've calmed down some."

"There's nothing to talk about. Stay away from her. If you don't, you'll regret it. I promise you."

I gave it one more try. "Hey, man, I thought we were friends. What happened?"

"I don't need friends," he said shortly. "I had a friend once. It didn't work out."

His statement was so off the wall that I couldn't control myself. I tried to keep a straight face; this was nothing to be taken lightly, but he could see me struggling. He continued to glare, then the absurdity of what he'd said struck him as well.

He tried to keep up the glare, but he couldn't do it. A little snort escaped him, and then we were both laughing out loud. Part of the laughter was no doubt a way of dealing with the tension, but it was still genuine. I was glad to see him back to rationality, but the sudden mood swings disturbed me.

"So what's the deal here?" I said, after we finally stopped. "Things didn't go well, I admit, but still . . ."

"Sorry," he said. "It's just, she's my kid sister, you know? And the minute you two get together, something bad happens."

"Not really anyone's fault."

"No, I guess not. But I don't think it's a good idea right now. There are more things going on than you understand."

"So tell me."

"It's complicated. Anyway, that's not what I came here about. I just got pissed off while I was waiting here. Byron's up to something—bet on it."

"What?" I asked. "Something specific, or just something in general?"

"He's set up a meeting tonight with a bunch of other black practitioners."

"What for?"

"That I don't know. I've got an in. I know someone who knows him and owes me a favor from long ago, but she couldn't tell me where or when. Just that it's a big thing, sometime tonight."

"And you want to do what?"

Rolando smiled at me. "Follow him, find out what's going on. I could use some help if you're up for it. I need someone who knows the city."

A challenge of sorts. He and Jo were definitely related. I still didn't mention I'd just come from Byron's. There were some trust issues involved.

"What about Jo?" I asked.

Rolando looked suspiciously at me for a second. "No, she's got her own things to do. Besides, the fewer, the better. It needs to be low profile, just a scoping-out operation. I'd go alone, but I might need some backup if things go wrong."

"Always a possibility."

"What do you say? Are you in? It'll be just like old times."

I wasn't sure anything was ever going to be just like old times again.

"Sure," I said. "I'm game."

"I'll swing by about six then and pick you up. I don't think he'll be moving until later, but we don't want to take any chance of losing him."

"How are you going to track him without him catching on?"

"Leave that to me," he said.

After he left, I called Campbell. I wanted to get back to Montague as soon as possible and bring him my precious snot-covered treasure.

"Sorry," Campbell said. "He's gone for a few days, remember?" I'd forgotten that.

"Any idea how long he'll be?"

"That's always hard to say. Why, did you find something?"

"That's what I want him to tell me," I said. "Give me a call when he gets back."

About five I whipped up an omelette and gave Lou some kibble, but again he was having none of it. He stared fixedly at me until I relented and shared. One of these days I'm going to put my foot down and remind him who's in charge.

After I ate, I dug out an old address book from the bedside table and thumbed through it. I know a few people up in Portland, mostly musicians, but a few practitioners as well. Like Jo said, the practitioner community there is small. Chances were good that Byron would be well-known.

My first thought was to call Wilson, an old acquaintance and general busybody, but I'd spilled coffee on that page and his number was illegible. But on the same page was the number for Whitney. It had been at least a couple of years, so I hoped the number was still good.

When she answered I almost didn't recognize her voice. She's one of those world-weary cynical types with a voice to match. When she says, "Good morning," it makes you wonder if that's necessarily so. This time, her voice was upbeat and bubbly, and she had news.

"Mason! How are you? Hey, guess what. I'm getting married."

"Well, congratulations," I said. "Anyone I know?"

"No. He's a journalist—we just met last year."

"A practitioner?"

"No, not at all."

That wasn't unheard of. Practitioners do tend to hook up

with each other because that's often their only social group, sort of like how people meet at work. And relationships with nonpractitioners often have problems. But sometimes it can work.

"What did he say when you told him?" I asked.

"Well, I haven't actually mentioned it as yet." I understood. It could be difficult.

"You're going to have to tell him sooner or later, you know."

"Yes, I know. The time just never seems right."

"I'm sure it will be fine," I said, though I wasn't sure at all. It was just too weird for some people. Sometimes it meant the end of the relationship.

"Hey," I said. "I'm actually calling for a reason. Have you ever heard of a practitioner up there named Byron? A dark arts guy?"

"Byron? Sure. He's kind of famous in Portland."

"Really. Why is that?"

"Well, first of all, he's a notorious ladies' man. A love-'em-and-leave-'em type. And then he was supposedly involved in something nasty where a couple of practitioners died." I could almost hear her shudder over the phone. "It was awful."

"Any proof of that?"

"Not that I heard. But he was basically forced out of town anyway. You were friends with Rolando, right?"

"Yeah," I said.

"Rolando was the driving force behind it all. He wouldn't let up. Of course, a lot of us thought it was more that other situation than anything about dead practitioners."

"What other situation?"

"Rolando's sister, Josephine. She and Byron had a fling, and Rolando went completely berserk about it. Then Byron dumped her, and Josephine went a little berserk herself. I don't blame him for getting out—they really had it in for him."

That explained a lot.

"Thanks," I said. "That's really helpful. And best of luck with your journalist."

How very interesting. Now their vendetta against Byron made a little more sense. It didn't mean they weren't right about him, though. I washed up the dishes and pondered. Right at six a car horn outside let me know Rolando had arrived. When I went out he was standing by the car, on the passenger side.

"You drive," he said, tossing me the keys.

That wasn't like him. I took the keys without comment, and Lou jumped in as I slid behind the wheel. Rolando plopped down in the passenger seat. He chuckled as he hefted a black leather attaché case.

"I was out by Byron's house earlier," he said. "I found his car and slapped a tracker on it. Now he can't drive around the block without my knowing where he's going."

"You put a tracker on him?" I asked. "Aren't you afraid he'll pick up on it? He's got to be feeling paranoid by now."

"I'm sure he is, and I'm sure he scans every inch of his car looking for the slightest trickle of magical energy. That's why I went high-tech."

He opened the case and pulled out a laptop. A couple of quick keystrokes and a map of San Francisco appeared on the screen.

"GPS system," he said. "Guys like Byron never think about technical innovations. They're too concerned with finding the proper toadstool for one of their dark invocations."

"Mushroom," I said.

"What?"

"Mushroom. There's no such thing as a toadstool." I realized I sounded just like Eli.

"Whatever. The point is, he wouldn't drive ten feet without checking for a follow spell. But he'll never think of simply looking under the rear bumper for a GPS device." He looked at the computer screen and hit a couple more keys.

"He's still home, so we'll park nearby and wait."

We sat and talked for the next two hours. The Rolando

of old was back. He slumped in his seat and told a series of entertaining tales about his doings of the last few years. But every time I tried to steer the conversation toward anything of substance, he deflected. I brought up the subject of Jo only once, and a stony silence convinced me to drop it. About nine, he straightened up suddenly and looked at the laptop screen.

"Okay, he's moving. North toward Portola. Let's hit it."

I navigated the side streets until I was maybe a quarter mile behind Byron's car.

"Turn west on Portola," Rolando said.

Byron's car passed Nineteenth Avenue and turned onto Sloat, so I assumed he was headed toward the beach, but a moment later Rolando made a little sound of puzzlement.

"He's just turned off the main road," he said.

"That's Stern Grove," I told him.

Stern Grove is a favored spot for dog owners. At one end there's a long, long, grassy mall with a lake. At the other is a broad ravine with woods and an outdoor stage, newly refurbished. Long stone benches bleed up into the hillside, and throughout the summer all manner of free concerts and performances take place there.

"Stern Grove is supposed to be closed at night," I said, "but we can park up top on the other side of the grove. Then we can make our way down through the woods and see what's up."

I drove around and parked, and from there we made our way cautiously on foot. We had a quick conversation about whether to shield and decided not. If you're shielding, you can get pretty close, but the least lapse in concentration and you're toast. The energy you use to shield can leak out, and a suspicious practitioner will pick up on the slightest spillage. Better to rely on the darkness and the cover of the trees.

By the time we were halfway down the grove, we could see cars pulling into the parking lot below. Quite a few people were already gathered on the stage and more were arriving every moment. Several carried heavy black robes complete with hoods, and a few had already put them on. Torches, flickering dramatically, illuminated the area. It looked like nothing so much as a bad Hollywood B-movie set.

"I don't fuckin' believe this," said Rolando. I reminded him what Eli has to say about black practitioner practices.

"They're big on tradition and ritual. It may seem silly to us, but it helps them to focus their energy. And it works. I knew one of them who used an absurd ritual to pull off something that almost killed us all."

Rolando grunted, not convinced. We got close enough to see the stage clearly and settled down behind two large trees that crossed, leaving a V we could see through while still providing cover. After a half hour, about fifteen practitioners had shown up, clearly all the dark sort. I hadn't realized there were that many of them in the Bay Area.

They gathered in a circle on the stage. Two Ifrits, both cats, sat on the stage. That was a relief. We were safe enough from discovery by practitioners with dull senses, but if there had been a couple of Ifrits who were also dogs, that might have been a different matter. Cats have their own talents, but long-range detection is not one of them. Lou was not so sure of our invisibility. He stood up on his hind legs to get a better look at them, then ducked back behind the tree.

A woman dressed in ordinary clothes picked up the two Ifrits and placed them in the center of the circle. Neither of the Ifrits seemed thrilled with the situation, but it might just have been because they were cats. Cats seldom are thrilled by anything.

One of the robed and hooded figures carefully placed stones all around them. Then he stepped back and began a chant, with the followers answering in a call-and-response fashion. I assumed the chanter was Byron, but it was impossible to tell under the hoods. The chant sounded like Latin, a big favorite in black practitioner circles.

"What are they trying to do?" I whispered.

"Not a clue. But nothing good, I'll bet."

We watched. The Ifrits seemed bored by it all. Then, fur started bristling and they bolted out of the circle to the edge of the stage. The area within the circle started to change. It swirled, gaining substance, growing plastic and thick like a huge bowl of multicolored syrup.

Lou was up on his hind legs again, staring fixedly at the scene below. Suddenly, without warning, he broke out into a quick volley of barks. Then, just as suddenly, he flinched, stopped barking, and looked over at me in mortification. His entire body language said, "Oops. Sorry."

"Jesus Christ," I said. "What is wrong with you?"

The second his barks rang out, the entire group on the stage lost concentration, and whatever was manifesting in the circle collapsed and vanished with a swirl of color. They all turned as one, looking toward the direction of the barking sounds. Oops indeed.

"Time to go," I said, and sprinted up the hill.

Rolando was right behind me, but Lou was lagging behind, not wanting to get too close to me until I calmed down. We made it back to the car, jumped in, and sped away as quickly as possible without actually squealing the tires. I thought Rolando would be enraged at Lou's faux pas, but he seemed more amused than anything else.

"Ifrits," he said, shaking his head. "What can you do?"

"Any idea what they were doing?" I asked. "Before the unexpected interruption, that is." Lou was staring out the window, pretending to be fascinated by the passing traffic.

"Trying to call up something, clearly. But I've never heard of using Ifrits to enable spells."

"That would seem counterproductive," I agreed. "Unless those Ifrits were helping to open a path, maybe."

"Maybe we would have found out if your stupid dog had been able to keep his mouth shut."

I thought he was joking at first, but when I glanced over at him his jaw was tight and his hands were clenched into fists. Another mood swing.

"He's not a dog," I said.

"He might as well be. Jesus."

Rolando fell silent until I reached my house and handed over the car keys. This had turned out to be an unproductive evening, thanks to Lou.

"Sorry," I said.

"No problem," he said, curtly. "Just remember, stay away from Jo." Before I could even think of a response, he drove off into the night.

I watched the taillights of the Honda as it drove away down the street. There wasn't anything I liked about this night. Not Rolando's mood swings, not the aborted ritual, which had told me nothing, not Lou's unaccountable idiocy. He was still a bit abashed.

"Come on," I told him. "We're going to get something at least out of this."

I fired up the van and headed back to Stern Grove. I wasn't sure what I could find, or what use it would be, but I was determined to get some return from the night's work.

By the time I got back there the nighttime fog had closed in. It comes off the ocean, and it can be cold and dank over in the Sunset while it's clear and pleasant in the Mission. Burglar weather. Fog can be very helpful if you're trying to keep hidden, but it's a double-edged sword. It also conceals the hunter.

This time, I parked across Nineteenth Avenue and crossed the street before heading down from the top of the grove from a different angle. It was quiet. Everyone involved had already left, but I stayed well back anyway, waiting to make sure.

Finally I walked down to the staging area and climbed up onto the wooden stage. I was looking for some sign of whatever it was they'd been doing there. A slight discoloration on the floor of the stage was all that was left. Any other evidence of their ritual had been cleaned up. A few scattered rocks were piled up on the ground in front of the stage, but they weren't the magical kind.

There had to be something, though. I went around to the

back of the stage, where the path leads up to the top of the grove. Nothing there, either, except for a couple of grungy tennis balls covered with ancient dog drool and an old plastic ball flinger abandoned by some forgetful dog walker.

It was just as well I had left the stage when I did, since the sound of twigs snapping and small rocks being dislodged warned of someone approaching from the opposite side. I peered through the latticework grill at the back of the stage.

A figure appeared and vaulted up onto the stage. Byron. Interesting. He took a few steps toward the stage corner, then stopped and stood motionless for a moment. Very slowly, he turned in a half circle, as if questing for something. When his eyes reached a direct line to where Lou and I crouched breathlessly, he stopped.

There wasn't much point in huddling there and pretending we didn't exist. If Byron thought he had located a source of lurking danger, his probable response would be to send something nasty our way. I coughed loudly to announce my presence and strolled casually around to the front.

"Hey," I said, giving him a little wave. As soon as he saw who it was, he relaxed. That was a good sign. He nodded slowly in comprehension.

"That was you, earlier, wasn't it?" he said.

"I'm afraid so. I didn't mean to interrupt, but Lou here got excited." There was a moment of uncomfortable silence, not surprisingly. "So what exactly was it you were trying to accomplish?" I asked.

"I could ask you the same."

"Me? I was just curious."

"You know what they say about curiosity and its effect on cats."

"That's why I've got Lou."

The fog had thickened even in the short time we'd been talking. It swirled across the stage in patches. It was the typical San Francisco early winter fog, smooth and gray. When it really closes in, you can't even read a street sign without getting out of your car and walking right up to it, and it settles thickest in low-lying areas. Stern Grove is down in a hollow, well below street level. I could barely even make out the shape of the trees on the opposite slope. It was going to be a bitch driving home.

Byron seemed perturbed by the thickening fog. You'd have thought night and fog would be right up his alley, being a black practitioner and all, but no. He peered out at the gray swirl settling in.

"This is not good," he muttered.

"Something wrong?" I asked.

He silently pointed at Lou, who was sitting quietly, tail curled around his backside. Only, he has two tail-curling positions. One is when he's relaxed and at ease. The other is when he's uneasy or scared. This was not the relaxed one.

"You might say so," he said. "Me, I'm leaving. Take my advice and get out yourself."

He hopped down off the stage and took three steps into the fog, almost disappearing before my eyes. Then he stopped, retraced his steps, and climbed back onto the stage.

"Too late," he said.

"Too late for what?" I asked. I had no idea what he was talking about.

Byron looked at me with what might have been condescension, but the effect was ruined by his constantly glancing back over his shoulder.

"Too late to avoid what's out there," he said. "There are a lot of odd things in the magical world, things you have no idea of."

"Oh, I don't doubt that for a moment. Care to enlighten me?"

He sat down on the edge of the stage and pulled out a cigarette. I assumed he was calming his nerves. When he lit up, the sweet tobacco aroma drifted over to me, setting off an instant wave of desire. I'd given up on cigarettes years ago, but cigarettes haven't totally given up on me. He took a deep drag.

"That ritual? The one you so rudely interrupted?"

"Yeah?"

"Well, it involved the use of a lot of magical energy, energy that was supposed to be focused on what we were doing."

"Which was?"

"Which is none of your business. However, when you lose focus in the middle of one of these evocations, the energy doesn't simply dissipate. It hangs in the immediate area for quite a while. It's still here. Can't you feel it?" I couldn't, but I was willing to take his word for it.

"I see," I said. "Then what?"

"It attracts . . . Well, I don't know what to call them, but they're not quite human and they're definitely not animals. Free-floating magical energy attracts them. Practitioners attract them, too, once they're in the area. And they can be dangerous."

As if to emphasize what he was saying, a flicker of movement out in the fog caught my eye just at the limit of my vision. Lou gave a slight growl.

"Okay," I said. "I'll buy that. Any ideas?"

"Why don't you two distract them, and I'll make a break for it?" he said. "Oh, wait—you probably meant ideas that don't involve using you as bait."

This was a new one. A black practitioner with a sense of humor. The fog moved in even closer, thicker than normal even for Stern Grove. I walked out a few steps to get a better look at what might be out there in the fog, and it was nearly the last few steps I would ever take.

"I wouldn't do that," Byron cautioned, and before I could reply, two shapes launched themselves out of the fog, snarling gutturally. Rough hands grabbed me and pulled me forward into the mist. I got a quick impression of damp fur and sharp teeth and crackling magical energy. I saw Byron make a gesture, and a sheet of fire erupted between me and the figures pulling at me. They let go and vanished back into the fog, snarling. I staggered back to the relative safety of the stage, face burning from the sudden heat.

"Very impressive," I said, shaken. "Thanks."

"They'll be back," he said. "And that stunt took most of what energy I had left."

He jumped off the stage again and started looking for something on the ground, picking up rocks and discarding them.

"What are you looking for?" I asked.

"Something I can throw, a good rock or even a piece of wood."

"Hold on a minute," I said. I made my way to the back of the stage and grabbed the tennis ball and thrower I'd seen earlier.

"Perfect," said Byron when he saw it. He took it from me and hefted it. "All right, this is what you need to do. Pour all the energy you can muster into the tennis ball. Don't try to draw energy from an outside source; the whole idea is to drain yourself of energy as much as possible and put it into the ball. I'll do the same, although I don't have that much energy left. I'll throw the ball and they'll be after it like a dog chasing a Frisbee—they'll follow the energy source. If there's no energy left in us, they won't be distracted by our presence. Then we can get the hell out of here."

"Won't that leave me without any protection?" I asked. I wasn't comfortable totally disarming myself, especially with Byron standing right next to me.

"You're already without effective protection," he said. "You just don't realize it. So do you want to follow directions, or would you prefer being torn into bite-sized bits?"

As usual, I didn't like being told what to do, but Byron seemed to know what he was doing. The other option he offered wasn't attractive. I considered briefly whether it might be a ploy on his part to render me powerless, but considering the wall of fire he'd sent out to help me, that didn't seem likely.

Byron held the ball tightly and concentrated, sending all his remaining energy into it, then handed it to me. I did the same, only I didn't have much more energy to put into it than he did. Mostly, I draw power and manipulate my surroundings; I actually don't possess that much intrinsic power of my own. The ball was now glowing faintly, but not very impressively. Now if Victor had been here, he could probably have made the tennis ball explode. Byron looked at me, disappointed.

"That's it? You're not holding anything back?"

"Just throw the goddamn ball," I said.

He set the ball in the claw of the thrower and with one quick motion raised it over his head and snapped it forward, finishing with a solid follow-through. The ball hurtled out into the fog, disappearing in an instant.

There was a moment of complete silence, then something uttered a cry, somewhere between a bay and a hiss. Lou crowded in closer to my feet. The call echoed through the grove and several others took up the chorus. The muffled sound of retreating footsteps, or paws, or something in between followed the flight of the ball.

"That's it," Byron said. "Let's book." He took off in the opposite direction toward the top of the grove without looking to see if I was following.

Running through the fog was disorienting, since I couldn't see more than ten feet in front of me. At any moment I expected to hear footsteps and hoarse panting behind us, and I wasn't disappointed. We'd only made it halfway up when the muffled sounds of clawed pursuit started coming up on us. There was no way we were going to make it to the top before they caught up with us.

Or at least, caught up with me. Byron's head start had served him well; he was already out of sight somewhere up ahead of me. I stopped and crouched low, wishing there was a wall or something I could back against. But there wasn't anything. I was out in the open, surrounded by the fog, vulnerable from all sides.

To make it worse, the fog had turned the world into a featureless, sound-muffled landscape, making it nearly impossible for me to use what talent I had left. When you rely on your ability to manipulate your surroundings to accomplish spells, an environment consisting of a featureless void is a serious handicap.

The sounds of pursuit had stopped, but that didn't mean they'd given up. They were within stalking range now. Lou was whipping around from side to side, focusing first in front, then behind, then back in front again. That meant they were circling us.

Byron was nowhere in sight. I couldn't blame him; he'd already saved my ass once, and if our positions had been reversed, I wondered if I'd be rushing back to his side.

Lou suddenly whirled around, growling. Three figures materialized out of the fog no more than ten feet ahead of me, between me and the safety of the street above. Before I could react, one of them held up a hand in a warning gesture. I could barely make him out, but from what I could see he looked more like a homeless street person than a ravening beast.

"Go," he said, his voice low and guttural, and stood off to one side. I hesitated until the sound of animal snarls from close behind helped me make up my mind. I sprinted past him, and as I did he and the two others closed ranks behind me.

When I reached the top of the grove, the fog suddenly thinned out into something more natural, still thick, but no longer impenetrable. Nothing was following, and Byron was waiting for me at the top.

"I wasn't sure you were going to make it," he said. "Well, that was certainly fun." He started to walk away. "See you around."

"Not so fast," I said. "I've got a few questions for you." He kept walking, turning his head back over his shoulder.

"Sorry," he said. "Not interested."

"There was someone else there," I said. "Who was that?" Byron shrugged, but didn't stop.

"And why were you still there, anyway, or did you come back? What were you doing there?"

This question didn't even earn a shrug. He just continued on his way, putting distance between us.

"All right, whatever," I called after him. "But tell me one thing. We're not exactly friends. I broke into your house, remember? In fact, we're on totally opposite sides. So why did you help me?"

Byron finally stopped and turned to me with a smile composed of equal parts bitterness and contempt.

"You really don't get it, do you, Mason? Let me ask you a question. If something with teeth had been dragging me, a fellow practitioner, off into the fog, what would you have done? Stood there and cheered?"

"No, of course not."

"Oh? You would have helped me, then? Why?"

"I don't know. It's automatic. It's just something you do."

"Exactly. But notice you can't grant me the same human reaction. I'm a black practitioner. I must be different. I must have had a hidden agenda, some ulterior motive for saving you. You're an asshole, you know?"

He turned and walked off before I could say anything else. He had a point, but I wasn't buying it totally. Maybe he was just being a normal guy, but the fact remained that now I owed him. And if nothing else, I now wasn't going to be very enthusiastic about helping Rolando take him down. Not without some solid proof, anyway. Which, luckily enough, I just might have. It was sitting on my bedside table in the form of a disgusting collection of tissues.

I drove home slowly though the murky streets. I still didn't know what Byron and his friends had been trying to do on that stage. And those shapes in the fog? What were they? What was the deal with Byron, anyway? I'd gone back out there to try to find some answers, but all I had now were more questions.

TWELVE

I CHECKED MY MACHINE THE MINUTE I WALKED through the door, hoping for some word from Campbell, but the message light glowed a steady red. Usually I'm happy at home, happy to be alone, but tonight depression was slowly sinking in. I'd pushed all thoughts of Sarah and what had happened to her aside. That's how I deal with things, but I'd noticed lately that wasn't working as well as it once did. It was weighing me down.

So I dealt with it the other way I do, by taking out my guitar—the old Gibson Birdland I'd had forever—and going over some charts. I had a well-paying gig coming up with Bernie Makoff, the Philadelphia trumpet player. Bernie has the name, but no band. What he does is book gigs in various cities and then pick up a rhythm section wherever he's booked. He keeps half the gig money and the locals split the other half. That was fair enough—it's his name that gets the gig, after all.

Since he plays mostly his own tunes, originals, he'd e-mailed me the charts to look over. I'm a good sight reader, but it never hurts to be familiar with a tune. In fact, you really can't play at top form unless you are. That's why I like standards—I know them so well I don't even have to think about the changes. I can just let my playing flow.

It was well past midnight when the phone rang. Midnight is too late for a random call, so odds were it wasn't anything I wanted to deal with. I was beginning to seriously entertain the idea that my phone was self-aware and actively malevolent—another sort of magic, and not the good kind.

A late-night call is seldom good news. I'd guess two calls out of three are ones I wished I hadn't answered anyway. I let it ring six times, sighed deeply, and then picked up before the answering machine could cut in.

"Mason here," I said.

"Mason? It's Jo. Did I wake you?" Her voice was tight.

"No, I'm up. Trouble?"

"Well, yes and no. I got home late and found a note from Rolando on the fridge, and it's weird."

"Weird how?" I asked.

"Not like him at all. Rambling and almost incoherent. Something about how I'd better be careful. And it was almost . . . threatening, in a way."

He must have left the note before he came to see me.

"Do you think he really might do something?"

"Rolando? No, of course not. But it's just so weird."

"Did he say where he was, or when he'd be back?"

"No, and he's usually very good about that." She paused a moment, as if forcing herself to say the next words. "Do you think you might come over? I'm kind of freaked out, to tell you the truth."

At last. A damsel in distress. All of my chauvinistic instincts cried out to jump at the chance. But Jo was no damsel, and if she were in distress, I'd probably end up in worse straights myself. Still . . .

"Sure," I heard myself saying. "I don't know what help I could be, but I'll be glad to drop by."

"Thanks," she said, and I could hear genuine relief in

her voice. Maybe she wasn't quite as self-sufficient as she made herself out to be after all.

Half an hour later I was standing in her building lobby. The security guard/doorman sat behind a raised counter, too large to be called a desk. A command post, maybe. He called upstairs, got the okay, and waved me through with a knowing grin. I didn't care for the place. Pink pastel walls decorated with modern prints attempted to soften the almost institutional aspect of the building, but without success.

I took the elevator to the tenth floor, turned right, and knocked at the proper door. Jo didn't answer right away, and I had a moment's apprehension, imagining, instead of Jo, an enraged Rolando flinging open the door and hauling me inside by my jacket collar.

The other fantasy was one of Jo opening the door wearing a sheer negligee, but it wasn't what you might think. That would have been more disturbing than erotic.

When the door finally opened it was Jo all right, and she wasn't wearing street clothes. But she wasn't wearing any negligee, either—she was wearing plaid flannel pajamas, loose and shapeless. She looked down at Lou, who was pressed close to my leg.

"Oh, you brought Lou," she said, with faint surprise.

I couldn't tell if her tone was approving or disappointed. Not that it mattered. I wasn't going anywhere without him until things improved significantly. Lou gave her one of his brief, noncommittal tail wags.

"Sorry about the pajamas," she said. "I was planning on going to bed and didn't have the motivation to get dressed again."

"Not a problem," I assured her.

Except, it kind of was. I'm not a big fan of sheer lingerie. To me, clothes or no clothes are the two best options. But flannel pajamas or a flannel nightgown is something else again. Flannel speaks of warmth, comfort, intimacy, home and hearth, and most of all, trust. It makes one consider options. It makes one see things in a new light. Or maybe it's just a fetish I don't want to own up to. One thing for sure—I hadn't had anything in mind when I arrived, but I was beginning to.

I brushed against her as I entered and felt that familiar tingling, that heightened awareness of another body. It seemed to me she purposely hadn't left much space to squeeze by.

"You okay?" I asked.

"Yeah, of course. I just had a momentary freak-out, and that's not like me. I shouldn't have bothered you." She gave me a strained smile. "It is good to see you, though."

That could mean a lot of things.

"Where's this infamous note?" I asked, looking around the apartment. It was another spare, minimalist space, eerily like Byron's house. Chocolate brown leather couch, soft as butter. Low tables of polished wood, long and narrow. A kitchen area full of high-tech appliances and a picture window overlooking the bay. The apartment didn't tell me anything about her or Rolando, though. It wasn't their place; they were just house-sitting, courtesy of Victor.

Jo went into the kitchen and returned, handing me the note. It was almost illegible, scrawled angrily in pencil with several cross outs. I couldn't make much sense of it, except she was right—it seemed to be a warning, and it also conveyed a sense of menace. At the very end, in larger and darker script, was another illegible sentence, ending with the words "I'm warning you."

"Warning you about what?" I asked, pointing to the last line.

"I have no idea," she said.

Her face looked careworn and suddenly older. That dusting of freckles across her nose that I'd thought was so cute now looked more like a disfiguring rash. Her shoulders slumped, and she shuffled more than walked. It worried me, and I felt an outpouring of affection for her that worried me even more. She took the note back, crumpled it up, and threw it into a wastebasket.

"I can't think about this anymore tonight," she said. "Let's just sit for a while and talk."

"Okay," I said.

"Anything at all. Anything but talk about Rolando, or damaged practitioners, or Byron, or any of that stuff."

That was exactly the stuff I wanted to talk to her about. Like why she hadn't told me about her relationship with Byron. But it could wait. We turned the chocolate leather couch around so that it looked out on the window. The Bay Bridge loomed large, and I could just make out a ship wisping out of the fog that hovered over the surface of the water. Jo rummaged around in the kitchen, opening cabinets, and eventually emerged carrying a bottle of Cabernet and two glasses.

She opened it with a few deft twists of a corkscrew, poured us a couple of glasses, handed one over, kicked off her shoes, and sat down next to me. She left enough space between us to tuck one foot under her other leg, and regarded me thoughtfully. I took a sip of wine and gazed back at her with what I hoped was a hip and ironic expression.

"You, know, you're really not my type," she said, as if discovering this surprising fact for the first time.

"How encouraging," I said. "Tell me more."

She laughed. "No, I don't mean it that way. I mean, I usually go for small, dark, and wiry. And with an edge. You know, the type who's just barely in control of his emotions?"

She had just perfectly described her brother, but I let it pass. "Bad-boy syndrome? That's a bit of a stereotype, isn't it?"

"It is, but I can't help it." She raised her glass and drank about a third of it, then eyed me speculatively over the rim. "That doesn't mean I couldn't change, though. Maybe I just haven't met the right type of person."

"And that type would be . . . ?"

"Don't know. Haven't met one yet."

We sat in meditative silence for a while, staring at the view out the window.

Lou stood quietly off to one side, staring out the window as well. Josephine uncurled her tucked foot and wedged it under my thigh. My hand automatically reached out and began to stroke her calf. After a while, I reached over and gently pulled on her shoulder. She swung around on the couch until her back was toward me and then leaned in against me, deftly keeping hold of her wine. She tilted her head back until her face was only inches from mine. I leaned forward to kiss her, stopping for just a moment before our lips met, giving her a last chance to change her mind.

I hadn't felt this way about a first kiss since high school, but this time there was no awkwardness getting in the way. Considering what I knew about her, I half expected an intense, almost devouring response, but it was nothing like that. It started out gently, almost innocently, and then gradually deepened. And yet, as the kiss grew more passionate, it still echoed with an ineffably sweet and almost nostalgic feeling. After a very long time, we drew back. Jo was staring at me, wide-eyed, as if she were startled to find me sitting there.

She placed her wineglass on the floor, never taking her eyes off mine. Lou glanced over his shoulder at us, then trotted off to a far corner of the room, curled up, and pretended to go to sleep.

"I think he wants to give us some privacy," Jo said.

"Not really. This sort of thing just embarrasses him."

She nodded thoughtfully, then said, "Rolando will be out all night, I'd guess." That was all she said, but the meaning couldn't have been clearer.

"Well, maybe so. But I haven't told you about his last visit to me. I don't think he approves of me. Or at least, of the idea of us together."

"He doesn't approve of anyone, when it comes to me."

"And if he comes back early?"

She gave me a quirky smile. "Come on, live danger-ously. You're not afraid of him, are you?"

Actually, I was. But testosterone was clouding up my instinct for self-preservation. She got up, reached out her hand, and let it hang suspended until I grasped it. One quick pull and I was on my feet. I'd say she was surprisingly strong, but it really was no surprise at all.

Inside the master bedroom, a king-sized bed on a plat-form frame dominated. On the wall behind the bed hung a large mirror. At least it wasn't on the ceiling. A small, at-tached bathroom was off to one side, and a single chair sat next to it. A small TV rested on a chest of drawers directly across from the bed.

Jo sat down on the edge and unself-consciously unbut-toned her pajama top and slipped out of the bottoms. I though it only polite to keep her company, so I did the same with my clothes. When she was done, she stretched out on the bed and I joined her. The freckles across her nose were mirrored by a dusting across the tops of her breasts. Up to now, I had thought of her as petite, strong but slight, but I had been mistaken. I felt a surge of lust that had nothing to do with Jo the person and everything to do with an incredi-ble and willing body lying next to me.

The next half hour or so was something that will stay with me until I'm old and gray. Technically, it was nothing but what is called foreplay—I did a lot of things to her and she did a lot of things to me. But each touch, every kiss, every . . . whatever was infused with a silent, intense pas-sion.

When I finally entered her, slowly, she kept her eyes locked on mine. Her mouth was slightly open and she was panting shallowly. Her expression was one of ecstatic awe, almost religious, a bewilderment at the intensity of the moment. Even though I was still moving slowly, my heart was pounding and I could barely catch my breath.

It's that emotional intensity that is the hallmark of great sex; technique is fine and dandy, but the purely physical ultimately just comes down to different methods of friction.

Then it turned subtly wrong. She moved slowly with me at first, then faster. I noticed a faint shift in her aspect; less emotional intensity, more animal need. Her head arched back and her soft moans became high-pitched screams, then shrieks. Her legs gripped me as she bucked frantically, and her sharp nails dug into my back. And she was strong. In seconds, she was tearing at me in a frenzy, gouging deep furrows, completely unaware of the damage she was doing. I could feel blood starting to trickle, merging with the sweat on my back.

For some, this would have been an overwhelming sexual experience. For many, the merging of sexuality and pain is the ultimate turn-on, the mingling of blood and sex the ultimate proof of overwhelming passion. Unfortunately, I'm not one of them.

Even my state of arousal couldn't completely block out the rapidly increasing pain, and the flow of blood from my torn flesh was a signal to my body of danger, not pleasure. And the body instinctively reacts to danger by pulling in on itself, like a turtle, with unfortunate and sometimes embarrassing results.

I was spared the inevitable humiliation when she suddenly gasped and spasmed, pulling me along with her. My release was sudden, and violent, and not entirely pleasurable. Spent, we turned on our sides and lay there without moving, both gasping for air. She was still shuddering, silently shaking from the aftermath.

It wasn't until I looked into her face that I realized she wasn't trembling with the aftermath of passion. Tears streaked her face, and I didn't think they were a result of joyous emotion. Her occasional quiverings came not from any orgasmic overload, but from a valiant attempt to suppress painful sobs. Abruptly, she disengaged herself, quickly jumped out of bed, and rushed into the bathroom. Through the closed door I could hear sounds of retching, then the unmistakable sound of vomit hitting the toilet. The toilet flushed, then more retching and more flushing. Finally, a long period of silence except for the faint sound of running water.

THIRTEEN

THE SOUND OF A KEY TURNING IN A LOCK AND Lou's muffled bark from the living room reached my ears at the same instant. I sat bolt upright with the panicky feeling of a man caught in bed with another man's wife. It could only be Rolando, and sitting naked in his sister's bed was not the way I wanted to meet him again. The streaks of blood left on the sheets weren't going to help, either.

I looked around frantically for my clothes, but the bedroom door flew open almost instantly. Rolando stood framed in the doorway like a man on a mission, anger pouring out of him so strongly it almost took visible form. Through the open doorway I saw Lou quietly moving up into place behind him, stalking him like a cat.

I put my hand up to signal Lou to cool it. He stopped midstalk, one paw off the ground, but ready to fling himself forward at any moment. Rolando, naturally, thought I was gesturing at him in supplication.

"You idiot. You fucking idiot." His voice trembled with rage. "I told you to stay away. You don't know who you're dealing with."

I had a damn good idea. A psychotic madman with sister issues. Lou edged closer as Rolando spoke, hearing the menace in his voice. This time I didn't signal for him to stay back.

Rolando clenched his hands together and started twisting them into contorted shapes. Either he was so mad he had to do something physical or he was preparing a spell. The room temperature dropped ten degrees, which answered that. I instinctively pulled the bedsheet close around me. Perhaps not the most effective defense shield. Now it was me who felt like the damsel in distress, and there wasn't anyone around to save me.

Wrong again. The bathroom door opened and Jo came out, still naked. It didn't seem to bother her. She stood between us and pointed an accusing finger.

"Get out!" she said, in a low, barely audible voice. The tone worked, though. Rolando flinched, but stood his ground.

"Not until we've settled this," he said.

"It's settled. Get out. Now."

For a moment I thought he was going to light into us both, but apparently he wasn't that far gone yet. Looking at the two of them facing off, I didn't think he could match up to Jo. She projected a crackling energy, a suppressed charge, restrained but powerful. I certainly would think twice before messing with her, and Rolando clearly had similar thoughts. Not to mention that I'd be weighing in against him as well. That didn't seem to be much of a factor, though. How humiliating.

He turned without another word and stalked out, almost tripping over Lou, who had worked himself up into teeth-sinking range. The front door slammed loudly, and Jo and I were left alone in the room. She sat down on the bed, trembling.

"He seemed a little tense," I said.

"I think he's finally lost it completely." She stared at the wall and avoided looking at me.

"You want to tell me what's going on?"

She turned her head and looked directly at me. "I have no idea. I was hoping you could tell me."

"I wish I could," I said.

When I straightened up the furrows in my back separated and began to bleed again. Jo looked at them and put a hand up to her mouth.

"Ouch," she said. "That must hurt. I'm really sorry, I don't usually get carried away like that."

I guessed she meant it as a compliment as well as an apology, but that wasn't our only problem. I briefly considered not mentioning anything, just scooping up my clothes and beating a hasty retreat, but it wasn't like I'd never be seeing her again. She saved me some awkwardness by bringing it up herself.

"About that other thing," she said. "After. That wasn't about you. It's just something that happens to me."

"Always?" I asked, before I thought.

"Always." She made a sound that could have been either a laugh or a muffled sigh.

I didn't know what to say. "How interesting" didn't seem appropriate. "That's a shame" certainly didn't strike the right note. I fell back on what we all say when there isn't anything to say, not really.

"I'm sorry."

"Don't be. I'm used to it. It does sort of limit my long-term prospects, though."

I could see that. I consider myself broad-minded and tolerant, and it wasn't as if she was a terrible person. But it definitely dampened my interest. That and the grooves along my back that were still slightly oozing. I hoped they wouldn't scar. Jo must have read my mind, or maybe my expression was showing my pain.

"I can help with your back," she said. "I'm not very good at healing, but I can do that much at least."

That's when I knew it was going to be a problem. You might think the other stuff would have given me a hint, but this was the real test. I'm very big on finding damaged women, thinking I can fix them. It's not a healthy way to be, but there it is. Perhaps, in time, I could help Jo—the bar was pretty low, after all. All I had to do was get her to the point where she didn't throw up after having sex with me. But unfortunately I didn't want her to even touch me, at least not right now.

"That's okay," I lied. "It's not that bad, and I'll get it fixed up later if it starts to bother me."

"Sure," she said, so sadly that I knew she understood. I felt like someone who had just kicked a puppy. I started gathering my up my clothes.

"Maybe I'd better go," I said.

She nodded. "That might be best."

On the way back home I sat up straight, trying not to rub my back against the seat. Lou gazed out the window. Just another ordinary night as far as he was concerned. Now what? I thought. You'd think by now I would know better. Well, live and learn, only I wasn't so good at that last part.

FOURTEEN

"WHY DIDN'T YOU TELL ME YOU'D BEEN TO SEE BY-
ron again?" asked Eli, rather grumpily.

We were sitting around the huge blond maple desk in
Victor's study; or rather, Victor and I were seated there while
Eli paced up and down by the front windows. My back was
worse, bad enough so I even considered asking Victor for
help, but the smug expression that would appear on his face
when he saw the marks would be worse than the pain. So far.

"Sorry," I said. "I had other things on my mind."

"And your trip to Stern Grove? What was Byron trying
to accomplish there?"

"I have no idea," I said, although in fact I did have some
thoughts about it. "What I want to know is what those
things in the fog were."

"Not enough information," said Victor. "If you'd managed to get a look at them, it would have helped."

"Helped you, maybe," I said, remembering the animal
sounds in the fog. "I don't think it would have been so
much help to me."

Rain had started in earnest. A fire was blazing in the big

fireplace and Lou was curled up on the hearth like a cat. Maggie, the actual cat, was stretched out on the other side of the hearth.

"Another thing to investigate," said Eli, eyes gleaming behind his glasses. Nothing made him happier than unexplained magical occurrences. He started to follow up, then got hold of himself with obvious effort. "But let's stick with more practical matters for now. Did you get anything useful from Byron's house?"

"I did."

"Then why haven't you tested it yet? This could be our proof, after all."

"Yes, I know. But I've got to wait for Montague to come back before I can find out anything. He's the only one who can make an ID. And I'm still not comfortable with this whole scenario of Byron as the only possible answer."

"Why not? He certainly qualifies." Eli repeated the mantra of coincidences, including the timeline.

"Byron's not the only one the timeline fits."

"Who else?"

"Rolando," Victor said.

Damn. I'd forgotten how sharp he could be. With his position he had to be. Eli momentarily went quiet, then shook his head.

"You must be joking," he said.

"He and Jo left Portland about the same time Byron did," I said. "And it isn't just that. I've known Rolando a long time. We were pretty tight for a while. And he's not the same person I used to know."

"A possession?"

"No, nothing like that. He's just . . . different. Yesterday he was practically frothing at the mouth. Told me in no uncertain terms to stay away from his sister."

Victor couldn't resist. "And you find that peculiar because . . ."

"Because he was totally irrational, completely out there.

And it's not the only time. Mood swings, paranoia, whatever."

I didn't tell them about Jo's affair in Portland, or Rolando's reaction to it. I'm not sure why, except that seemed almost like a betrayal to mention it.

"You honestly think Rolando could be involved in this?" Eli said. "That's absurd, Mason. I'd as soon suspect you."

"Sooner," Victor muttered.

"When Rolando was nineteen, he risked his life to infiltrate a group of rogue black practitioners who were planning human sacrifices. He never told you about that, did he?"

"No," I said.

"And remember when you thought you'd discovered a cave of ghouls? Who went in after you?"

"There were no ghouls. It turned out to be a pack of coyotes."

"Yes, but you didn't know that, and neither did he."

"I know, I know. I don't know what to think. But there's *something* wrong with the picture. He's not the same Rolando I used to hang with. Maybe he's just lost his mind." There was another silence, longer this time. "And another thing," I said. "Montague said the practitioner who visited him was shielding, so he had no way of knowing who it was. And that the visitor had an illness—cancer, remember? Probably brain cancer, which means a tumor."

"Not bad," Victor said. "A brain tumor would explain a lot of things. Irrationality. Impulse-control issues. And what better way to escape death than to switch bodies with another, healthier practitioner?"

"Theoretically possible," said Eli, "but in practice, I doubt it. You'd have to do a lot of experimenting first to be able to pull it off, and I doubt you'd find many volunteers."

"Exactly," I said. "Not willing ones. And maybe it would even take some magical help, like that rune stone Sarah was holding."

"Come on," Eli said. "This is sheer nonsense. I've known

Rolando a long time. Even if he were dying, he wouldn't do anything like this, any more than any one of us would."

"Charles Whitman," Victor said.

The name was familiar but I couldn't place it. Victor saw the puzzled look on my face.

"Read your history, Mason. Charles Whitman. Texas, back in the sixties. Back before every mass murderer was required to have his middle name included every time his name was mentioned on the news. Climbed up a water tower, killed fourteen people, and wounded a whole bunch more. The autopsy revealed a brain tumor."

"As I remember, he wasn't that stable to begin with," Eli said. "The tumor might have had nothing to do with it."

"Still, a tumor could explain personality changes."

"And so could simple stress." Eli shook his head in dismissal. "It's nice when all the pieces of a puzzle fit cleverly together, but simple is usually best. Speculation is fine, but let's just wait and see what Montague has to say."

BY THE TIME I GOT HOME, THE RAIN HAD STOPPED. The message light was blinking and the message was from Campbell telling me Montague was back. I called her immediately.

"When did he get back?" I asked.

"Last night. I was going to call you but it was late."

"That's fine. I can be up there by five."

"Well, you'll have to hurry. I got a call from my mom last night. She's taken a turn for the worse and I'm getting worried. I'm flying out from Sacramento tonight to see her."

"How serious is it?"

"I don't know, but I'm not taking any chances. So I'm not going to be able to take you up to Montague's after all."

"How long are you going to be gone?"

"It all depends. Awhile, at least."

That could be a problem. Lou had already been to Montague's once; ordinarily he could find his way there again.

But he hadn't done so well the last time. Not surprising, since the cabin was effectively between worlds.

"I'm not sure we can find his cabin on our own," I said.

"I thought of that. He's smoothed out a way through for tonight. You shouldn't have any problem getting there." How many times had I heard that particular phrase?

"Great," I said. "Maybe I can get up there in time to see you before you leave. I could use some of your healing arts."

"You okay?" she said, instantly concerned.

"I'm fine. Just a little marked up. That's all."

"What happened?"

"I'll tell you when I see you."

I MADE IT UP TO SODA SPRINGS BY FOUR THIRTY. I'd put on some heavy boots and a winter coat, since the rain in San Francisco meant there had probably been snow in the Sierras. A few inches did cover the ground, but the sky was clear and cold. I sat upright most of the way, again avoiding contact with the seat back. I wished I could have seen Campbell sooner. Half-healed gouges are harder to treat than fresh ones.

I put the now-dry tissues from Byron's house in one pocket and a well-worn folding Buck knife in the other, along with a small flashlight and some ancient beef jerky sticks. The very last thing I slipped in my pocket was the wolf talisman from Campbell, my totem. If I was going to be wandering around in the woods, I intended to be prepared for once.

Campbell was packing a small carry-on bag when I got there, so I didn't waste any time with small talk. I took off my jacket and shirt and turned around to show her the damage. She sucked in her breath in a half whistle.

"Well, you've been busy. How did you manage that?" I hadn't thought to come up with a good cover story.

"Umm," I said.

She looked at me with an expression that was hard to read. Another problem in our past relationship. I could never read her, but she had no problem reading me.

"Well, I hope it was worth it." She pulled up a chair from the kitchen table. "Sit down."

I followed instructions as she carefully gathered various plants from her collection, muttering to herself. A pan of water went on the stove and a mortar and pestle came out of a drawer. Lou sat watching with great interest. You wouldn't think a dog could smirk. You'd be wrong.

"Are you going to tell me about it?" Campbell asked as she chopped plants on a wooden board.

"Well, there's this woman I've been sort of seeing."

"That much I get."

"She's a practitioner, and possibly a bit troubled."

"You think?"

"It's not only this; it's the rest of what's been going on. She's right in the middle of things, and I think her brother might even be involved in some way."

"Oh. That's not good."

"No, it isn't. At least last year I had an idea of who I was fighting. This time it's a complete mess. I'm not sure about anything and I'm floundering around like a headless chicken."

Campbell put some plant matter in the mortar bowl, added a dollop of boiling water, and began grinding. Then she gathered a bunch of the glop she'd been mixing up and spread it over my back.

"This might hurt a little," she said. Immediately, a cool and soothing sensation flowed down the inflamed red lines, contradicting her words. "Not quite done yet," she warned.

She leaned over and blew a cool breath of air over the salve, and as she did I felt her distinctive surge of energy flow into my back. The coolness became a pleasant warmth. The warmth gradually increased until it was no longer pleasant, but definitely hot. Then scalding. I started to get up, but Campbell put her hand on my shoulder.

"It will pass."

"Easy for you to say," I said from between clenched teeth. "How long?"

"Just a minute or so."

Only pride kept me from whimpering. After what seemed more like five minutes, the pain eased and eventually vanished. Campbell offered me a hand mirror and I got enough of a look to see only faint traces like narrow tan lines remained.

"Thanks," I said. "But did you really need to use that particularly painful method?"

"No," she said. "But this way you'll think twice next time."

I started to get mad before I realized she was putting me on again.

"I will get even," I said.

"Oh, no. Remember, I'm delicate."

I slipped my shirt back on and turned to face her. Delicate was not the word for her. Attractive, yes. Athletic, with muscles toned from Telemark skiing, strong features, and immense vitality. She'd let her hair grow out, so it was as long now as when I'd first met her.

"Time for me to get a move on," she said. "I'm late already. You've got my cell number, right?"

I did. Campbell and I had been the last two people I knew without a cell, and she'd finally caved in, leaving me the last one standing.

The room was warm and comfortable. As she finished up packing I watched her move around the cabin and couldn't help but compare what I'd lost with her to what I now had. What the hell was wrong with me?

She glanced over, knowing as usual exactly what was in my mind.

"It was just bad timing," she said. "That's all. Some very bad stuff happened, remember?"

"I remember."

"Sorrows can make a relationship stronger. It can bond

two people together in a special way. But it can just as easily ruin things. It wasn't all your fault, or mine. Just bad timing."

I thought it was more than bad timing. I'm certainly not the easiest person to be in a relationship with, and Campbell has her own issues. It was interesting that she'd ended up with Montague, a man who was around only part of the time and whose residence wasn't even entirely in our world.

"I guess," I said.

"Things might have been very different if we'd met today, instead of last year."

"Except today you have a boyfriend."

"Well, yes, there is that. Again, bad timing."

"What if he were to meet with an unfortunate accident?"

"Not funny," she said.

"Sorry. I kind of like him, actually."

"He's a decent guy." She hesitated, then said, "One more thing, although it's not my place, really. This woman? She's trouble, you know. It's obvious you like her—I can understand that—but I don't know how good for you she is."

"Well, it doesn't take a genius to figure that out."

"But maybe that's exactly why you like her."

"Maybe it is," I said.

I WAVED GOOD-BYE AS HER LAND CRUISER PULLED away, leaving me alone by the cabin door. It would take about half an hour to reach Montague's cabin if everything went smoothly. I intercepted Lou, who was heading back to the warmth of the cabin.

"We've got work to do," I said. "Montague. His cabin. Let's go."

He looked toward the cold, dark woods leading up the hill, then back at the warm cabin next to us with a bland "I don't understand what you're saying" expression.

"Montague," I said. "And Willy, remember? Your friend?"

Ahh. That was different. He spun around and started trotting up the hill. The moon was just coming up, but I still needed my flashlight to keep from stumbling over tree roots. Lou found a trail of sorts and settled into a quiet trot, at a speed where I could just keep up with a brisk walk. He was confident this time, more sure of his direction. I guessed he had learned a thing or two from Willy.

I kept a sharp eye out, as best I could in the flicker of the flashlight. Montague had warned me that some not-so-friendly things roamed these woods. I heard subtle rustlings on each side of the trail, just out of view, but there is always rustling in the woods at night.

About twenty minutes later we passed a small knoll that I recognized—the site of the horseshoe crab debacle. So far, so good. Montague's place would be coming up shortly. Sure enough, I could see a gleam of light farther down, and as Lou quickened his pace, so did I.

We crested a small rise, and there, just at the bottom of the shallow hill where the trail curved, was the cabin. Lou bounded off down the trail, but he hadn't gone more than fifty feet when he came to an abrupt halt. I could barely make him out in the pale moonlight, but he was rigid and motionless, a tiny statue of a dog. He didn't move as I came up behind him. This was not a good sign.

I walked slowly past him and he fell into step behind me, head down. Another bad sign. If danger was imminent, he would have been alert, every sense quivering. But when he dragged behind, head down, it usually meant that something very bad had already taken place.

Nothing seemed out of place as we drew closer. I banged on the front door, loudly but without much hope.

"Montague! Are you in there?"

Nothing. Lou sat mournfully on his haunches, staring at the ground.

I tried again. "Montague!"

I stepped back and examined the house for wards. There

weren't any, or if there were, it was beyond my ability to perceive them. That wasn't much of a surprise—he'd basically retired from being a practitioner and could clearly take care of himself on any mundane level. There wasn't even a lock on the kitchen door.

I pushed open the door, slowly. The light from the glowing plants he'd installed was weak and spectral, not the cheery glow I remembered, more like phosphorescent fungus rotting in an ancient swamp. I cautiously walked inside and looked around. Two coffee cups sat on the counter, each half-full. A bag of onions hung from a ceiling hook, and half of them had spilled out and fallen to the floor. My eyes followed a trail of four or five of them into a corner, where a small, dark figure was wedged.

Lou pushed past me, walking hesitantly toward the corner. He sniffed briefly at the figure, then threw back his head and uttered a full-throated howl. I looked down and saw Willy. He was curled up in a familiar position, one that Lou has been in a thousand times. The sight of him lying there, so like Lou, made it hard to catch my breath. But his mouth was slightly open, his tongue partly out, and his head was cocked at that unnatural angle that always means the worst.

I bent down and ran my hand over his body. Cool, but not cold. It couldn't have been that long. Long enough so that whoever had done it was long gone, though. I straightened up and reluctantly moved to the living room. The faintest whiff of corruption was hanging in the air, an almost sweet smell, like rotted fruit. It had to be my imagination; it takes at least a day for even a trace of odor to surface.

The light from the plants was stronger here and I was expecting to see evidence of a fight: lamps knocked over, chairs upended, broken glass, but nothing was out of place. Except a booted foot and part of a leg peeking out from behind a worn and tattered couch.

I leaned over the couch and saw a plaid shirt and long, matted hair. It was Montague, all right. The back of his head was dark with blood, almost black in the greenish light from the plants. I didn't want to touch him, but I did. The blood was dried, but still tacky. He hadn't been dead more than a few hours. What in God's name was I going to tell Campbell? That little joke I'd made echoed in my head. An unfortunate accident, indeed. Unforgivable.

Next to Montague lay a large and heavy rock, what looked like granite veined with crystal, jagged on one side and also caked with blood. The murder weapon. *CSI* has nothing on me.

I looked around the rest of the house, hoping to find something, anything, that would help identify the attacker. Maybe he'd dropped his wallet. Lou traipsed along with me but didn't show much interest. But other than the living room and kitchen, there wasn't a thing out of place.

I had to get outside, away from the grisly scene, in order to think. It was times like this that made me regret having given up cigarettes. Not that there were many times even remotely like this.

The moon was now high, but the woods surrounding the cabin were still shadowed in darkness. It wasn't a threatening scene, though, as you might have supposed. It was calm, peaceful, an idyllic setting for a warm and comforting cabin in the far-off woods. Violence doesn't always announce itself with thunder and lightning.

I really wished Victor was with me, along with his bag of tricks. He was good at magical forensics. He would be able to run a bunch of tests and tell me a lot more about what had happened than I would ever figure out for myself.

The notion of forensics gave me an idea. A hundred years ago, the magical variety was without peer, even though it was sometimes fuzzy with lots of room for interpretation and mistake. What passed for science then was useless, but modern science has come a long way since. DNA analysis can put someone at a scene with far more accuracy than any use of talent, no matter how skilled the practitioner.

All I needed was some sweat or blood—not of the victims, but of the murderer. There was no sign of blood other than Montague's in the house, but I thought I knew where I might find some. I don't know much about crime scenes, but I do know about Ifrits.

Back inside, I knelt down by Willy. He wasn't much larger than a cat, and looked forlorn and pitiful lying there. Lou sat quietly across the kitchen, as far away as he could get. I carefully pried Willy's half-open mouth farther apart and looked inside. There. On his teeth. A gummy black substance that could only be blood. He hadn't gone down without a fight, and I could only hope he'd got at least one good slash and tear in.

I gently laid his head back down on the floor, crossed to the sink area, and rummaged around until I found a sort of muslin cheesecloth. Unfolding my Buck knife, I scraped off as much of the residue as I could from his teeth. With each stroke, the knife made a horrible scraping noise, and Lou whined uneasily at the sound. What I'd managed to collect went onto the muslin cloth, and I tied it up neatly so that it formed a small pouch. I put it carefully in my jacket pocket, looked around one last time, and called to Lou.

"Let's go," I said. He couldn't get out of the door fast enough.

I suppose I should have buried them both, but the ground was rock hard and I didn't have the time. Or a shovel. I'm not big on the whole respect-for-the-dead thing anyway. At least, not for the physical remains. I don't know what happens to us after we die—no one does for sure, and anyone who tells you they do is a fool in my book. But the physical bodies we leave behind are just that—dead flesh. Montague and Willy were gone, and whether they were buried or cremated or left where they were mattered not a whit to them.

I assumed we'd retrace our steps back, but Lou had other ideas. Instead of heading up the hill, he plunged off down a continuation of the trail that wound past Montague's cabin. It wasn't the same way we had left the first time we'd been there, either, but I had to assume he knew what he was doing. Maybe you couldn't ever use the exact same path twice. Maybe Montague's death had changed the way we had to go.

Montague's death might have changed other things as well. Any protections he would have set up for invited visitors should be rapidly degrading by now. Both he and Campbell had mentioned that it wasn't entirely safe to be wandering around this area uninvited. I urged Lou to pick up the pace. The sooner we were out of here, the better.

The moon was lower now. Snow crunched under my boots. The trail grew steeper, and the soil felt hard and rocky under the light cover of snow. We were now traversing a steep hill, and I stumbled a few times when loose rocks turned under my feet. The bushes and trees had thinned out and large areas of open terrain were now common. At least the rustling sounds I'd heard on the way in had ceased; there wasn't any cover to rustle in.

The moonlit landscape took on a spectral feel, becoming alien in a way it hadn't been before. The silence was complete, with only my breathing and the scrape of my boots on rock and the faint patter of Lou's paws to break the quiet. I was starting to feel spooked, but Lou was unaffected until a high-pitched whistle sounded from high up above.

He instantly flattened on the ground, making himself as small as possible. I did the same, dropping prone on the rocky soil. I had no idea what the whistle meant, or what it was, but standing upright in silhouette makes an easy target.

I lay motionless, listening for another sound. Again the whistle, but higher and in the opposite direction. So. Two of them, whoever or whatever they were. I lifted my head slightly, hoping to get a glimpse of them. Unfortunately, I did.

Barely visible in the moonlight, a large and sinuous form was loping toward us from up above. Behind it, another vague shape was drifting down. A quick memory surfaced of Montague, standing in his kitchen, stirring oatmeal, telling me of the dangers of the wood. "A particularly nasty predator the size of a wolf, but a member of the weasel family. They hunt in pairs."

Two more whistles sounded from behind us. So Montague hadn't been entirely correct. They didn't just hunt in pairs. They hunted in packs. A perfect end to a perfect day.

An open hillside on a moonlit night is not the most defensible position, and I didn't have much time before the first one reached me. Lou was still hunkered down, pretending to be nothing more than an odd rock formation. I didn't begrudge him that—there wasn't much he could do against carnivores ten times his size.

An aversion spell wasn't going to work. A fast-moving, hungry predator would be right on top of me before it realized it didn't want to be there. A shield is always an option, but they're harder to set up in open spaces, and sooner or later you run out of energy. Then you have to face the problem without any resources left. And of course, a shield works both ways. The weasels might not be able to get to me, but I wouldn't be able to do anything to them, either.

Bolts of sheer energy? I wish. Not in my skill set. Illusions were out—most predators rely on scent as much as sight. There were plenty of other things I could try, but I needed time. And you never do have the time. That's the rub. Most anyone can do simple multiplication and solve a problem. But quick, what's seventeen times thirty-seven? You have two seconds to come up with the correct answer. Sorry, too late. You're dead.

In a few seconds the first one would be at my throat. I gathered up as much of the essence of the rocky hillside as I could, all small stones and irregularities, and mixed it with the dappled pattern of moon and shadow and snow. But I was too late.

I got a glimpse of the thing as it launched itself at me. Short, dark fur, lighter around the throat. Tiny, round ears high up on the skull, a long face more pointed than an otter's, but not quite as sharp as a fox's. Like a giant wolverine, but slimmer and faster.

It hadn't noticed Lou lying flat on the ground, and as it leapt at me past him, Lou sprang up and went for its hindquarters. The unexpected attack threw it off enough so that it missed me and tumbled down the slope as I dove to one side, slipping on the snow-covered rocks. I worked both hands with a rolling motion, and put all the energy I could muster into the spell. The rocky ground below me turned loose and slippery, hundreds of tiny rocks surfacing like ball bearings and mixing with the snow.

The weasel tried to scramble to its feet, but couldn't find any purchase. It slipped farther down the slope, legs churning frantically. It would have been comical if it hadn't been a hundred-fifty-pound carnivore intent on making me its evening meal.

As I got to my feet I felt sudden warmth in my pocket. My forgotten wolf talisman was heating up, and just in time. I pulled it out and it was glowing brightly, which meant the lupine cavalry was on the way. Or so I hoped. And a good thing, too. Two more shapes were approaching from up above, and the slippery-slide trick wasn't going to work with an attack from above.

Then, just like once before, three wolves appeared on the ridge top. They stood motionless for an instant, silhouetted in the moonlight. They came scrambling down the slope at top speed, breath pluming out like little engines, heading for the two weasels above me. Lou uttered one quick bark of triumph, then ducked behind me to watch.

The two weasels turned to face the wolves, and two more weasels closed in from the sides to help out. The one below me gave up trying to climb the slope and angled off in an attempt to reach its pack mates.

The first wolf, running at top speed, got within ten feet of the weasels and launched itself in the air. It flew right over them and landed five feet behind. The weasels turned to face the threat and the other two wolves hit them from behind. In two seconds it was all a blur of fur and snapping teeth. The wolves were using a tried-and-true tactic: one of them would attack from behind, trying for a hamstring, and the minute a weasel turned to face the threat, another wolf would dart in at its now-exposed rear.

But it wasn't working so well. The weasels weren't as fast as the wolves, but they were stronger, and just as quick. And they possessed that weasel family trait of extreme flexibility. Their muscular bodies could bend almost double, so they could defend their rear without having to move their back legs at all. And they had the advantage of numbers.

One of the wolves managed to slash a tendon and cripple a weasel, but he paid for it. The weasel got him by the shoulder and hung on, then two more went for his throat as he tried to shake the first one off. The fifth weasel had made its way around the slippery area and was about to enter the fray. The wolves never made a sound apart from some hoarse panting, but the weasels kept up a constant chatter, interspersed with high-pitched whistles of rage.

This was starting to look bad. My talisman had once again called up the wolves to save me from danger. They had arrived fully ready for battle, but I just might have signed their death warrants as well as my own.

I stopped watching the fight and closed my eyes. A lot of my time and effort has gone into learning centering disciplines, crucial for maximizing potential. Proper breathing, calming of the inner dialogue, cleansing of negative energy—all ancient techniques that every yoga student knows. But try meditating with a fight to the death swirling around you.

I did the best I could. I let strength flow into me and absorbed the hardscrabble feel of the rocky ground and the solidity of the boulders up above. The chill of snow. Then, moonlight again, that classic transformer of all things mundane. Finally, the trapped feeling in my heart.

When I opened my eyes, one of the wolves was lying

motionless on the ground. The two remaining wolves were no longer attacking, but instead stood back-to-back in defensive mode, protecting their fallen brother. One of the weasels was down also, but the other four were circling patiently, waiting for an opening.

I could feel power dripping off my fingertips, but I was helpless. They were all too close together. I had to separate them somehow. I glanced down at Lou, and the second he saw me looking at him, he flattened himself on the ground again. He knew that look. That was the look that meant I was about to ask him to do something he really didn't want to do.

"You've got to," I said. "Separate them. Get the wolves away. It's our only chance."

He stared defiantly back at me, and for a moment I thought he was going to refuse to move. Slowly he stood up, giving me a look of his own, one that said, "You'll be sorry when I'm dead or crippled for life."

He loped off up the slope, but not toward the fight. He sheared off to one side and edged over until he was a good fifty feet above them. I could see him nerving up for the charge. He came down the slope straight at them like a bat out of hell, volleying off a series of high-pitched barks as he ran. The remaining four weasels and the two wolves stopped dead. It was such a bizarre sight that they couldn't quite comprehend. One of the weasels recovered more quickly than the others and lunged at him as he ran past, but Lou adroitly dodged him and made it through to where the wolves stood waiting. Instead of slowing up, he bounced off the nearest wolf at top speed as if he were using a wall to change direction. Then he circled the wolves twice and took off down the hill, still barking hysterically.

It wouldn't have worked if these were ordinary wolves, but they weren't. Any more than Lou is an ordinary dog. They caught on instantly, whirled, and broke through the circle. The first one got through unscathed, but the second received a slash down his back. But not enough to slow him up as they followed Lou down the hill.

The weasels took off in pursuit, but they were caught off guard and were slow to react. By the time they did, the wolves had a good twenty foot lead on them. And that was all I needed.

I clenched my fists as tight as possible and screamed, "Petrify!" at the top of my voice, with all the fear and rage I could summon behind the shout. I felt the energy roll off me in a wave, catching the weasels before they had moved ten feet.

If I were a stronger practitioner, the weasels would have instantly turned to stone. Even so, the spell did its job. One of them stumbled and fell; the others started moving in slow motion. The effect wouldn't last much longer than a couple of minutes, but that was more than enough time. The wolves saw what I'd done, turned back, and tore into the now-helpless creatures.

The weasels gamely tried to fight, but they were so slow as to be effectively defenseless. It was primal, savage, and bloody. I slumped weakly to my knees, partly from the energy drain and partly from the horrific slaughter being played out in front of me.

It was over in less than a minute. The wolves left the fallen weasels without a backward glance and came loping over toward me. For a moment I thought the bloodlust had got the better of them and I was going to be the next victim. Talk about an ironic demise.

But they pulled up short right in front of me. They were covered in blood, gashed up and down their bodies, and were panting heavily. The one on the left had a torn ear, but he hadn't got it in the fight. I recognized him immediately—the alpha male I'd first seen a year ago.

He turned and trotted off a few steps toward the wolf still lying on the ground, looking over his shoulder to make sure I was coming. I staggered to my feet and followed. I bent down over the fallen wolf and almost passed out, so I quickly plopped down cross-legged and braced myself with my hands on the ground. Lou approached and sidled up, curious, until a low growl from the big alpha warned him off.

The wolf was still alive, breath coming in labored gasps. His throat was torn and there was wolf blood on the ground, lots of it. The big alpha stared at me impatiently. Either I was getting really good at interpreting canine emotions or I was constantly projecting. He seemed to be saying, "You got us into this. Now you'd better do something about the consequences."

My talent was almost played out, I was exhausted, and healing is not one of my strengths anyway. But none of that mattered. The alpha was right: I'd got them into this, and if I couldn't save this guy, I'd forever feel guilty.

The first thing was to stop the bleeding. Any basic first-aid book will tell you that. I searched my pockets for something that might help, although I knew there wasn't anything in there I could use. Some freeze-dried jerky. My Buck knife. And of course, the muslin bag with the blood scrapings from Willy's teeth. But I did have a wad of the now-useless tissues.

I spread them over the wound. They didn't do much good, though they did staunch the blood flow slightly. Then I took out the muslin bag and held it gingerly, considering. Blood is a very powerful tool, and practitioner blood doubly so. But I needed the blood to nail the murderer. And blood-work in spells is almost exclusively the province of black practitioners. Not that it's necessarily evil, depending on the intended use, but it's always creepy and disturbing. But not as disturbing as watching my wolf friend bleed to death in front of me.

I unwrapped the bag, took out my knife again, and scraped the gummy flakes directly onto the wound in his throat. I pinched the last few flakes between my thumb and forefinger and rolled them around, absorbing the tacky consistency. Putting my hand on the wolf's throat, I smoothed the muslin bag over the wound and let a small portion of my remaining energy flow through my fingers. The dark flakes glittered and swirled, spreading through the fur until a protective mat formed over the open wound. I gathered up the very last dregs of energy I had left and breathed, "Absorb."

The sticky mat flowed *into* the wound, replenishing blood and pulling the edges of the gash together as it did so. The whole process didn't take more than five minutes, and at the end of it the wolf scrambled to his feet. He immediately fell over as his legs gave way. He might have been healed, but it would be quite a while before he was back to normal. He got shakily to his feet again, this time more carefully, and stood on quivering legs.

I didn't try to get up. I didn't think my legs would hold me, but I felt satisfied. You might have thought the alpha male would have acknowledged my help, but he was all business. He stood to one side of the injured wolf and shouldered him abruptly, not too hard but not gentle, either. The wolf took a few halting steps and then stopped. The alpha repeated his move, more insistently, then pushed his way in front and moved slowly up the hill. The injured one tottered gamely after him, with the third wolf bringing up the rear. I watched them until they crested the slope and vanished into the night. None looked back.

I hadn't expected social niceties, but it was becoming clear I had no idea how totem animals relate to their chosen. As if Ifrits weren't hard enough to understand. Still, I had no complaints. I was alive.

I wasn't happy sitting on the exposed slope, but there wasn't any help for it. I wasn't strong enough to even stand up, much less walk. If anything else were to come along, that would be that. I gave Lou half the jerky and gnawed at the rest, trying to replenish my energy. After an hour or so, I felt strong enough to at least get to my feet. When I did, I found I could indeed walk, like a very old man.

By the time we made it across the slope and into some woods, the sky was just beginning to lighten. I was feeling stronger, but I hoped we weren't going to do a whole lot of twisting and turning to find our way home. Luckily, Lou had a good handle on the route by now. We moved in a reasonably straight line until finally he veered off at a ninety-degree angle, up a small hill. When I reached the top I saw Campbell's cabin below.

It was a long drive back. By the time I reached my flat I was as tired as I'd ever been, emotionally and physically. The desire for bed and sleep was overwhelming. I half expected something dreadful to be waiting outside my front door, but for once I was lucky.

I thought about calling Campbell, but I didn't think about it very hard. I had to tell her, of course, but she'd want to know everything. A quick heads-up wasn't going to cut it. And I just couldn't face it right now. I could barely keep my eyes open.

Same went for Victor and Eli. It wasn't going to hurt Montague any to put off spreading the news. I turned off the phone, fell into bed, and slept for ten hours. I didn't dream at all.

FIFTEEN

BY THE TIME I WOKE UP IT WAS ALREADY CLOSE ON dark again. The message light on the phone was blinking merrily. Ten to one it wasn't anything I wanted to hear. I made coffee, head still muzzy, and gave Lou something to eat. I knew I should eat something as well, but I couldn't. Either my internal clock had been thrown off or I was still recovering from the shock of yesterday's events. Or both.

I finally nerved myself up to listen to the messages, which turned out to be not so bad after all. Two from Eli asking me to call, the second just starting to sound worried. One from Winnie Randolph asking if I was available to back her on a gig. Winnie's a fine singer, but she's not nineteen and blond so she has to scuffle just like the rest of us. Nothing from Jo. I didn't know if that was good or bad.

I called Campbell first, since that was going to be the hardest one. She wanted every detail, even the ones I didn't want to tell her. Her voice was tight, right on the edge of breaking.

"You think it was the guy I brought to see Montague, don't you?" she asked.

"I can't think of who else it could be." There was a long silence, broken only by the static of the cell.

"So if I hadn't introduced them . . ."

"Don't. You can't play the what-if game. *If* you hadn't introduced them. *If* I hadn't started looking into it. *If* we'd never met at all—that gets you nowhere."

But whenever someone close to you dies, especially by violence, it's impossible not to play that particular game. I know.

We spent an hour on the phone and it would have been longer, except she had to get to the hospital to see her mom. I promised her I would track down whoever had done it, but that didn't give her much comfort.

Eli was next, and that call was a lot shorter. He grunted, cursed, and told me to meet him at Victor's right away. An hour later I was relating my story. The eternal fire was blazing again, with Maggie curled up nearby. Timothy was sitting cross-legged by the hearth, pulling her tail gently whenever it twitched. He was a braver man than I, but Maggie seemed to like him.

Timothy was almost one of us, but even so I wasn't sure just how much I could reveal in front of him. Victor didn't make any sign, so I started talking. When I described finding Montague, Eli let out a huge sigh. Victor uttered a short obscenity, left his chair behind the desk, and walked over to the window. For him, that was the equivalent of throwing a major fit.

By the time I got to the part about the wolves and the giant weasels, Timothy was riveted like a five-year-old hearing about pirates and ghosts. Eli didn't say a word. He knew about my wolves as protectors from last year, and ordinarily, he would have had a million questions: Where do they come from? How do they get there? What are they, exactly? But he just sat there in stony silence.

When I was done, Victor walked over to a cabinet by the front windows and took out a crystal decanter half-full of what looked like Cognac or brandy. He set out three large snifters, then, after a moment's hesitation, a fourth.

"*L'Esprit de Courvoisier*," he said, pouring out a small amount in each glass.

I don't know anything about Cognac, but Eli and Timothy were clearly impressed. Victor handed the glasses around, raised his, and said, "To Montague."

I felt a little awkward—toasts to the departed have always struck me as a bit superfluous, but Victor is all about tradition and it clearly was important to him. We all drank, and I have to admit, I'd never tasted anything quite like it. Apple, spice, oak—all the flavors of a fine wine, but very, very different. I watched Victor surreptitiously to see if we were expected to throw the glasses into the fireplace or something, but apparently not. He simply collected the empty glasses and placed them on the top of the cabinet.

"One thing I don't understand," said Timothy. "This Montague was a powerful practitioner, right? How could someone manage to get the best of him like that?"

"A black practitioner has all kinds of tricks," said Victor.

"Possibly," I said, "but I think Timothy's on to something. Montague was an enforcer for years. He'd keep a careful eye on any black practitioner, no matter what the situation. But he was expecting someone. Me. Or someone who looked like me. A shielding, a quick illusion—it wouldn't have to fool him for long—just long enough for him to turn his back."

"Maybe," Victor said. "But who knew you were going up there?"

I had no answer.

Eli gave another sigh. "It's too bad you had to use up those scrapings of blood. That would have settled things." He patted me on the shoulder. "Not that I blame you. You had no choice. It's just too bad."

Victor was still standing by the window, staring out at the night. He turned suddenly and pointed at me.

"The knife," he said. "You scraped the blood off with a knife, yes? Where is it?"

"The knife?" I felt in my pocket. I hadn't bothered to take it out when I'd returned home. "Here," I said, taking it out of my pocket and showing it to him. "Why?"

"The blade. There's still going to be some traces of blood on it."

I shook my head. "I wiped it clean."

"That's not good enough," Timothy said. "Unless you scrubbed it with soap and water and bleach, there's still going to be some traces on it."

Eli lumbered over to look at the blade. "He's right. And magical traces need even less material than DNA. We can use this."

"Wouldn't you need a blood sample to compare it to?" I asked. "Like DNA?"

"No, that's the beauty of it. It's not only the material; it's the action. You see, the blood comes from the scene of a ghastly crime, a murder. It has an affinity for the person who committed it. If you'd read Haskins on this subject, you'd realize that any material—"

"Okay," I said. "I'll take your word for it."

I handed the knife over to Victor, who regarded it thoughtfully. He spread out some sheets of newspaper on his desk, unfolded the knife, and snicked the blade into place. Then he placed the knife carefully on the paper. It looked perfectly clean to me.

As expected, his old black medical bag came out from under the desk, but he also opened the safe and brought out a few more items. A small, shallow dish of Japanese or Chinese origin with dragons curling around the sides made an appearance. Setting it next to the knife, he filled it carefully with a green liquid poured from a flask he'd also taken from the safe.

Eli was now hovering over him, offering advice.

"Crystal, do you think?" he said.

Victor shook his head. "I don't think so. Not with the liquid."

"But the focus will be stronger."

They went back and forth on it, citing books I'd never heard of, and a few I had, but never read. An old tarot deck was next out, cards worn and frayed, with designs that were familiar but different.

"That deck looks old," I observed brilliantly.

Victor favored me with a quick disgusted glance, but Eli nodded. "Fifteenth century," he said. "Hand painted."

Victor shuffled through and selected a card. "The Moon," Eli said. "Good choice. Paranoia. The subconscious. Things unseen."

Victor placed it above the knife. By this time I was puzzled. Talent is all about accessing magical energy. The only practitioners who relied on props and symbols were black ones, as part of a whole belief system that was screwy to begin with. Victor didn't need this stuff; he was as strong a practitioner as I'd ever known. Eli explained.

"Magical forensics is a different kettle of fish," he said. "Don't ask me why; it just is. Victor actually knows a lot more about it than I do."

That was quite a statement, since Eli is an unqualified expert in all things magical, at least as far as theory goes.

Victor was still busy, laying out various other objects. A bit of what looked like black tar. A silver chain. And some salt. Salt seems to makes its appearance in all kinds of magical rituals. A universal substance.

When he seemed about done, Victor straightened up and called out sharply.

"Maggie! I need your help." It wasn't a request.

Maggie had meanwhile ensconced herself in Timothy's lap, where she was getting her ears scratched. She didn't seem pleased by the peremptory summons. If I'd used that tone with Lou, he would have made me pay. She jumped down off Timothy's lap and stalked over, just slowly enough to show she couldn't be ordered around. Victor waited patiently.

She gracefully leapt up onto the desk and immediately sat down. Victor took the knife and sawed off a bit of her long fur. If I'd tried that, she would have had my fingers off. Victor rubbed the fur between his palms, circled his hand three times around the dish of liquid, and let the fur dribble out into it.

Even Eli was nonplused by this. Victor glanced over at him as Maggie jumped down and resumed her spot in Timothy's lap.

"Cats are hunters," he said.

I wasn't sure I got it, but apparently Eli did, since he gave a grunt of approval.

"Where the hell did you learn all this?" I asked, unable to keep quiet any longer. Victor usually ignores my questions, especially if they're of a personal nature, but he was so focused on what he was doing he forgot to dis me.

"London," he said abstractedly, "when I lived there. A practitioner named Sean, a round little Irish guy. Best man ever for forensics. But they don't refer to themselves as practitioners there; they call themselves sorcerers." He shook his head in disbelief at the strange ways of those across the pond.

Finally he was ready. He swirled the silver chain through the green liquid before discarding it. The knife was dipped in the liquid, then carefully pressed into the salt, as if breading a veal cutlet. A small bit of tar went onto the knife blade, then he held up the knife between his two index fingers, one finger on the end of the handle, the other on the knife tip.

"Be careful," I said. "It's sharp."

I didn't understand precisely what he was doing, but I knew enough to realize that additional practitioner blood would screw things up royally. He didn't bother to reply. He held the knife and spoke three words. "Seek. Find. Tell." Energy crackled around him. After a moment, he said, "It's not enough. Mason, you'll have to help."

Those words had to cost him. He would rather have

asked Eli for assistance, but what he needed was an infusion of talent, and I was the only one in the room with enough to help.

"What do you need?" I asked, resisting the natural temptation to mock.

"Energy. Into the knife. And it's got to be an attraction-based type."

That I could do. With Lou in the room, it was easy. We're almost two separate parts of a whole anyway. I called him over—politely—and ran a loop of energy through my fingers, through him, and back through my fingers again. He sneezed as the energy coursed through his body. I did the loop a second time to build strength and finally let it go into the knife.

It flashed once, brightly, and the salt and tar melted away, leaving it as clean as ever. Victor closed it with a snap and handed it back to me.

"It's ready," he said.

"Ready for what? Will it now fly like an avenging arrow into the chest of the murderer?"

"It's primed, set on whoever's blood was on it," Eli said. "If you get near that person, it will glow like a firefly."

"I'm afraid not," Victor said. "If there had been enough blood on the blade, yes. But with such minuscule traces to work with, the best we'll get is a faint, phosphorescent glow. You might not even notice it under full light."

"Does that matter?" I asked. "Just so long as there's something."

Eli rubbed his chin with a discouraged motion. "No, that wouldn't matter. But because the spell is so weak, it's not totally reliable. Even if it does glow, it won't be conclusive. To extend the DNA analogy, this is more like the older method of blood typing. Like AB negative, a relatively unusual blood type. Maybe one in two hundred people is AB negative. A glow will be a strong indication, but it won't be a sure thing, just as blood types don't have the accuracy of a DNA match."

"One in two hundred?" I said. "I can live with that."

"More like one in fifty. And living with it is not what I'm worried about."

"Well, I just might drop by and pay Byron a visit, anyway."

"Don't bother," Victor said, handing me the knife. "He's not there anymore."

"What do you mean?"

"I was at his house earlier. The place is empty. Blinds open, no furniture, no wards even. He could be across town or across the ocean—the latter, if he's smart."

"So Byron's gone," I said. "And no way to check on him. How convenient."

AT HOME, I TOOK CARE OF A FEW CHORES, CALLED Winnie Randolph to confirm the gig, and wondered what to do with the rest of the night. Checking on Byron was no longer an option. I was in no mood to go out; the current problem was weighing on me too heavily. I had trouble getting the sight of Montague and Willy out of my mind, the two bodies lying dead in their own home. When I did, Sarah, blank-eyed and mindless, would take their place. It was one of those things that's so disturbing that you can't process it right away. You think you're all right, you think you're handling it just fine. You push it away. But there's no getting away from it; it sinks down in the mind and festers, surfacing every so often when you least expect it.

I paced around, unable to sit still. I didn't even try picking up my guitar. Lou curled up on the bed and pretended to be asleep. He's seen me like this before and doesn't care much for it. I had just started to calm down some when the phone rang. When I picked it up, I didn't even bother with "Hello," uttering a curt, "What?" instead. I had no desire to talk to anyone right now.

"Trouble, that's what," said the voice on the other end.

It was so unexpected it took me a second to recognize who it was.

"Rolando?"

"Yeah. Bad news. There's another practitioner down."

"Dead?"

"No, but as good as."

"Who is it?" I asked.

"No one you know, I don't think. But it looks very similar to what you said happened to your friend Sarah." More bad news.

"Have you called Victor?"

"No answer," he said. "I left a message. I thought you might want to come down and take a look, though. See if you think it's the same thing."

"Where are you?"

"At my apartment."

"Is Jo there?" He hesitated half a second.

"Yeah."

"Ten minutes," I said.

He hadn't said a word about the other night. It was like nothing had ever happened. Maybe it was just that it took something real to knock some sense back into his head. I grabbed my jacket, but before I left I slipped the knife into my jacket pocket. Whatever else was going on, at least one thing would be cleared up.

There was plenty of parking across from their building that time of night. All the residents have assigned spaces in the underground garage. I took the elevator up to twelve, got off, and took the fire stairs back down two floors. Probably overkill, but it never hurts to be cautious. Lou thought it was some sort of game and started prancing up and down the stairs until I had a quick talk with him.

I wanted a quiet moment beforehand to check on the apartment wards. They weren't as strong as wards usually are. They couldn't be; an apartment isn't an entirely self-contained unit. A house is easiest to ward because you can wrap energy completely around it. That's what I'd done with my place. Even though my space is a small in-law, I'd covered the entire house; it was more secure that way. My landlord was totally unaware that he, too, was protected against all manner of magical attack. Not that he needed the protection—he was blissfully ignorant of the magical world around him.

But an apartment building is a trickier proposition. You can hardly ward twelve floors containing a hundred apartments. And none of the apartments is entirely separate— they connect to others, those others connect to more, and so on. So there was a weakness there, one I might need to exploit one day.

The door was warded strongly, of course. The wards looked secure—but there was other security that wasn't. The last time I had been to visit, the deadbolt hadn't been latched. Maybe it was only because Jo had been expecting me, but practitioners often rely too heavily on magic for security. They tend to be cavalier about physical things like locks. One of the many things Eli has pointed out to me over the years.

These wards were strong. They were also thin. The energy loop they formed was impervious, but it was two-dimensional. It could be squeezed, and it could be bypassed. I formed a very basic ward of my own, beginner stuff really. Once it was set, I folded it into a small package.

"Lou," I said. "Whoever opens the door, distract. Got it? Distract them." I waited until I was sure he understood before finally knocking on the door.

It was Jo who opened the door, which deactivated the wards around it. Lou instantly jumped up on her and started barking playfully. She took a step back, and as she did so I placed my hand against the doorframe and let slip my own ward, so weak as to be undetectable. When the other ward was reactivated, mine would blend in unnoticed. I now had a backdoor into the system, and could manipulate it at will if ever I needed to.

"Lou!" I said sharply. "Stop it!"

I stepped through the doorway and gave her a short hug, to show I had no hard feelings or lingering uneasiness. Which was not entirely true.

"Sorry," I said, pulling Lou away from her. "He's been a little out of control lately."

Lou turned and took a little nip at my calf. He was getting tired of my instructing him to do things, then blaming him. Rolando was seated on the couch, and as soon as I came in he jumped to his feet.

"Let's go," he said. "We can walk. It's not far, just over on the Embarcadero. I'll fill you in on the way."

Downstairs, he started off down the street at a good clip before I had a chance to say anything, so I just took off after him. Jo looked at me and rolled her eyes in an exaggerated fashion, then fell in behind us. Lou brought up the rear, though I wasn't sure if he was keeping an eye out for danger from behind or if he wanted to be last in line in case of trouble up ahead.

"Do you remember I told you I had an in with Byron's San Francisco group?" Rolando said as I caught up with him.

"Someone who owed you a favor, right?"

"A little more than that, actually. A woman named Martine. Not that much talent, but someone who really wanted to be special. That's how she got hooked up with the black arts crowd in the first place."

That was an all-too-common story. Practitioners who weren't satisfied with their level of ability often turned to the dark arts in the hopes of learning new methods to enhance their prowess. It didn't often work, though; talent tends to find its own level no matter which path you choose.

"And she's the one in trouble?" I asked.

"Exactly. She called me earlier and said we had to meet, that she'd found out something incredible. Something I wasn't going to believe. There's an area on the Embarcadero we used as a meeting place. She was way too paranoid to come up to the apartment. She even freaked out if Jo answered the phone."

"Why didn't she just tell you over the phone?" I asked.

"Good question. I think she just loved the whole cloak-and-dagger thing as much as anything else. That had a lot to do with why she helped me, I'm sure. It made her feel important, like a spy or a secret agent, and she insisted on all the trappings. We even had to use code names whenever we talked on the phone."

A homeless guy sitting in a storefront entryway saw us coming and held out his hand to Lou, making kissing noises. Lou surprised me by stopping and letting the guy give him a brief pat on the head. It made the guy's day; Lou can be sweet at the oddest times for no apparent reason. He scampered to catch up with us.

"So what happened?" I asked.

"I don't know. She was already waiting when I got here. But she wasn't much help. Something has happened to her—she's still alive, but totally unresponsive, basically catatonic." That sounded all too familiar.

"And you just left her there?" said Jo, sounding a bit outraged.

"What was I going to do? Sling her over my shoulder and carry her back to the apartment? I put an aversion spell around her, enough to discourage anyone from approaching, and called Victor. And then Mason."

By now we were crossing the Embarcadero, headed for a small rest area beside one of the piers. A solitary bench was in the middle, and with an awful sense of déjà vu I saw a woman sitting on it, back turned to us. She had short dark hair and a tan beret perched on her head that must have looked jaunty at one time. Now it was just ineffably sad. Lou huddled up next to me, no more than six inches from my knee.

"Is that her?" I whispered.

Rolando didn't answer, just kept walking toward the bench. As we got closer I felt less and less inclined to go any nearer. Rolando's aversion spell, to be sure, but in my case it was hardly needed. He took it off as we approached, which made me feel only slightly better.

I walked around to the front to get a good look at her. She was dressed elegantly, very San Francisco chic with a long suede coat, high boots, and that tan beret. Her head was bent forward, and when I tried to lift it up to see if that same dreadful hole was drilled into her forehead, it took all my strength. Sarah had been limp and boneless, but this woman had every muscle tensed, rock hard and rigid. She was breathing hard, rasping a little. When I finally got her head up, I saw that the skin on her forehead was smooth and unbroken.

There was another difference. Sarah's eyes had been vacant, staring off into the distance at unseen worlds. This woman's eyes were rapidly flickering, madly darting from side to side, as if she were trapped somewhere inside her brain. Disturbing, but one good thing about that—it meant that something was still there, and maybe that something could be salvaged.

"Is it the same thing?" Rolando asked.

"Not quite. I'm not sure what it is," I said.

Her hands rested in her lap, and both of them were curled into tight fists. I thought I could see something in the right hand, but when I tried to uncurl her fingers, it was like trying to pry open an oyster.

"Help me with this, will you?" I said to Rolando. "I think she's got something in her hand." I looked over my shoulder to where Jo was hovering. "Grab hold of her shoulders so we don't just pull her right off the bench."

I was being a little brusque about the situation, trying to distance myself like a cop at a crime scene or a doctor in the ER. It's a lot easier to act matter-of-factly when you don't know the victim personally.

Jo took her shoulders and Rolando grabbed onto her wrist while I tried to pry her fingers open. For a moment her breathing stopped completely, and then, without warning, she let out a high-pitched keening wail, like the demons of hell were after her. We all automatically let go and jumped back. And as soon as we did, she was on her feet and sprinting toward the water. Lou reacted the quickest, catching up with her before she'd gone more than a few steps, trying to slow her down by nipping at her feet, but it was like he didn't exist. In five seconds she was at the water's edge. Without pausing, she hurled herself headfirst into the dark, chilly water.

We were only seconds behind her, but when we looked down at the water there was nothing, no sign at all. We stood there listening to the waves lapping against the concrete and smelling the mix of salt, fish, and diesel fuel. After a minute, Rolando leaned out over the water.

"She's got to come up sometime," he said.

She did, bobbing to the surface and slowing rolling over like a giant sturgeon before sinking again. That was the last we saw of her.

We waited another ten minutes, then another five just to be sure, but she was gone, another victim of the cold bay waters. Eventually we made our way back through the streets to the apartment on Beale. Rolando and Jo were discussing what had happened in low voices, but I was silent, thinking hard. I didn't understand what had happened, but it had the feel of a setup. And this woman, Martine, had been silent until Rolando had touched her. Two seconds later she'd been galvanized into action, throwing herself into the bay. It didn't feel like coincidence.

"We should talk about this," said Jo.

For once, I totally agreed. And I had more than talk in mind. We nodded to the security guard and took the elevator up to the apartment. As soon as we were inside, Rolando threw himself down on the sofa.

"This is just so totally fucked up," he said. Jo sat down next to him, one foot tucked under a knee in a familiar position.

"What are we going to do?" she said.

I walked over to the window and looked out. The fog was starting to roll in again off the bay. The other night it had seemed romantic; now it had taken on a vaguely ominous aspect. I put my hand in my pocket and fingered the knife I carried. Maybe Byron was out of reach, but Rolando wasn't, and he was looking better all the time.

"I told Ro about Montague," Jo said. "About the visitor he had, and the sickness, and how we might finally get some proof about Byron."

"Is that true?" Rolando asked. "For real?"

"Well, it was. But there's been another complication."

"What's that?" he asked.

"Montague's dead."

I kept my eye on Rolando's face, hoping for some reaction. I heard Jo's gasp of indrawn breath, but Rolando just looked thoughtful and concerned.

"What happened?" he asked.

"Very mundane. Someone hit him on the head with a rock."

"Byron. He knew he could be identified. Damn. Now we'll never prove it was him."

"You'd think, but we still might," I said. "He left behind something of himself."

I walked over in front of the couch a bare two feet away, and pulled out the knife. Jo looked puzzled, but I thought I saw a shadow of concern flicker over Rolando's face.

"What's that for?" Jo asked.

I didn't answer. Slowly, I opened the blade until it locked into place. I kept my eyes on Rolando, not even looking at the blade yet, but there was still no reaction from him. Finally, I glanced down at the open knife. At first, nothing. But then I saw it. A thin green line of phosphorescence limned the edge of the blade, glowing faintly but distinctly.

Until that moment, I hadn't actually believed it. My head had told me it was possible, logic had told me it made sense, but in my heart I never really believed it. Not Rolando.

He saw the glow the same time as I did, and his face

changed. I glanced over at Jo, but she either hadn't noticed the faint shine or had no idea what it signified. Rolando met my eyes, and I finally got the reaction I'd been waiting for. He knew what it meant. He stood up slowly, and I tensed. But instead of exploding into rage, he spoke slowly and quietly.

"I think it's time for you to go, Mason." Jo looked at him in confusion.

"Go? What are you talking about, go? We've got stuff to talk about. Lots of stuff. Why should he be going?"

I backed up against the wall. Lou started his warning growl, a little late if you ask me. This was the man who had killed Montague. And Willy. And left Sarah a mindless husk. I could take him. I knew it. Usually emotion is a hindrance in any fight. But I burned with a cold rage that would only focus my power. I could put an end to it, right now.

But what had Eli said? That it wasn't a sure thing. The knife blade wasn't absolute proof. I had to consider the possibility, however slight, that I had the wrong man. There was still Byron to be considered. I didn't believe that, but as I wavered the moment passed.

"Stop it, right now," said Jo. "What's going on?"

I couldn't strike at Rolando now. Jo would instantly leap to his defense, and I couldn't fight both of them any more than Rolando could have when he caught us in bed. And this was certainly not the time to try to convince her of the truth.

"I think maybe I will go," I said for the second time in two days.

I eased back toward the door, never taking my gaze off Rolando. I almost tripped over Lou, who was protecting me by taking up his usual position behind my knees. Rolando stood frozen, moving only his eyes. Jo looked at us both in turn, in total bafflement.

Once through the door, I took the stairs down all the way this time and didn't relax until I was well clear of the building. What a gigantic mess this was turning into.

As I walked toward my van, Lou stopped and stared across the street at a bare hillside that ran up the south side of the building. I couldn't see anything except some plastic sheeting that had been laid over the slope to prevent erosion. Behind it, just under the high access ramp to the bridge, construction work was in progress. I was in no mood to linger, but Lou refused to budge.

That made me think twice. He isn't usually recalcitrant without reason, like if there's a bacon cheeseburger in the offing. He stood there, nose twitching, and then I saw it. A figure came around the corner of the building and quickly walked away down the street. He was wearing a worn navy pea jacket and moved quickly, almost loping rather than walking. He turned the corner at Harrison, and Lou glanced up at me.

"Definitely," I said, and we took off after him. It wasn't that I had sensed anything magical about the man, but I knew he wasn't normal. Everyone has that sense—cops develop it quickly, or at least the good ones do. Something about the guy just seemed out of place, and these days anything out of the ordinary cried out for investigation.

When we reached the corner of Harrison he was already out of sight, but Lou headed west with no hesitation. We had almost reached Fremont Street when he stopped outside a construction site that extended from the street to right up under the roadway for the bridge access.

The site was surrounded by a wire mesh fence and a locked gate, but Lou found a small hole where the fence corner didn't quite meet the ground and squeezed himself under. He ran back over to the gate and stared expectantly at me from inside the site.

"Yeah," I muttered. "Easy for you."

No one was nearby and traffic was light, with only a few cars randomly whizzing up Harrison Street. The gate was seven feet high, easy enough to climb over, but it had the obligatory strands of barbed wire on the top. A clump of coarse hair had been snagged by one of the strands. Or maybe it was fur. Something had already climbed over that gate.

I bent down and pulled hardness from the concrete, letting it flow into my hands. In seconds, they were hard as rocks, and almost as stiff. Usually that would take too much energy to accomplish, but this was a fluid spell, not a static one. As long as I concentrated, my hands would keep their protection, but as soon as concentration wavered they would revert back to soft flesh.

I reached up and pulled the wire flat, then swung up and scrambled over, keeping my focus on my hands. The pant leg of my Levi's caught on the way over and ripped, breaking my concentration. I lost the protection on my hands and got a nasty gash before I could let go. A short and heartfelt curse relieved some tension. Lou sat watching with interest, trying to look concerned, but the slight involuntary wag of his tail told me he was highly amused.

I waved him on with a snarl, following as he picked his way through piles of debris, pallets of lumber, stacks of steel pipe, and silent backhoes. I stumbled over several unseen objects before I realized I wasn't going to do any good this way. I needed some night vision.

I called Lou back and thought about it for a couple of minutes, trying to remember the feel of what Jo had done over by the Cliff House. I wasn't going to be able to come up with anything that good, but I needed to at least be able to see well enough to keep from breaking my neck.

I grabbed hold of Lou and looked into his eyes, collecting as much of his night vision as I could manage. Then I let it flow into a circular loop, through his eyes and into my own. There was a moment of wrenching dislocation, not as bad as when I actually use his eyes to see through, but bad enough to give me the usual splitting headache.

It worked, though. Not as well as I would have liked—I could see about as well as a nearsighted man at dusk. And, of course, that little trick had used up a large portion of my available energy. Self-spelling always does. If we ran into anything unpleasant, I was going to be at a huge disadvantage.

Still, I could now see. I looked up at the concrete footings that anchor the bridge access. Even before the bridge crosses the water it's larger than it looks, huge in fact. Standing next to a bridge support pylon is like standing at the base of an enormous skyscraper. I could see why many of the homeless made it their home base; it was easy to stay invisible and overlooked under its shadow.

I looked around curiously. Random mounds of dirt were piled up and scattered around, awaiting some sort of construction project. Piles of broken rebar and scrap metal nested between neat rows of new material.

Lou quartered back and forth among the heaps of rubble like a sheepdog searching for a missing lamb, and after two minutes or so he stopped and got up on his hind legs, peering toward where the bridge sailed out over the bay. Then he was off, moving with more purpose.

He stopped by a makeshift fence by the east end of the site. A small patch of undisturbed ground led away from the site, clean and inviting, with pine trees providing cover and pine needles carpeting the ground underneath. At the top of an incline, a small, flat area made a platform on the hill, and as I got closer, a dark figure rose up from the ground and bounded away down the hill. Lou automatically started after it, but a quick word brought him up short. I don't think he was that anxious to close with it anyway.

I didn't want to go after it, either, but for a different reason. Right where the figure had risen up, another figure lay in a sleeping bag. Over it, a tattered tarp had been stretched low to the ground between a small tree and a rusted iron pole. The figure took notice of us and sat up quickly, keeping a wary eye on me.

I climbed over a wide ditch that separated the flat area from the construction site and approached cautiously. A pleasant expression on my face projected what I hoped was a nonthreatening and harmless demeanor.

"Hey," I said. "How's it going?"

The man considered the question for a moment. "Not bad," he answered. "Yourself?"

"Can't complain."

I walked a little closer and he quickly squirmed out of the sleeping bag. Living on the street teaches you very quickly not to be caught in a vulnerable position. He squatted on his heels, seemingly relaxed but ready to spring up at a moment's notice. He didn't seem to be having any trouble seeing me.

His long, graying hair was dirty and matted, hanging loose, but he'd braided his equally long beard into dreadlocks of a sort. A hooded sweatshirt covered the upper half of his body and loose pants completed the ensemble. He wore several pairs of socks on his feet and a pair of worn and sturdy work boots had been carefully placed next to the sleeping bag. He looked familiar, but I couldn't place him. Which was odd, because it's not like he would exactly blend into a crowd.

"Got a cigarette?" he asked.

"Sorry. I quit."

"Smart man." He looked over at Lou, who was regarding him with interest. "Nice dog," he said.

"Yeah, I like him. He's not that smart, though."

Lou threw me another disgusted look. I wasn't sure what I'd come across. This man seemed as unremarkable and normal as could be. Until he spoke again.

"He's an Ifrit, ain't he?"

"Yes, he is," I said. There didn't seem any point in pretending I didn't know what he was talking about.

"Thought so. Those other two, they didn't have one."

"Which other two?" I said, although I knew who he meant.

"You know. That guy and his girlfriend." I didn't bother to correct him.

"What did they want?" I asked.

"Same thing as you, I guess. Wanted to know who I was,

what I was up to." He laughed, genuinely amused. "I didn't care for them, so I just played dumb."

"I see," I said, although I didn't. This must be the guy Victor had asked Jo and Rolando to check out. Something about a monster hanging out under the Bay Bridge. He didn't seem like much of a monster, but he wasn't just some homeless guy, either.

"Nice spot you've got here," I said inanely, as if trying to make small talk. He looked at me as if I were slightly retarded. A smile flitted across his face. "Who was your friend?" I added casually.

"Friend? Oh, him. Just a ploy, just a ploy."

"For what?"

"I used to be just like you, you know." A definite non sequitur.

"Oh?" I said.

He held up his arm to show a faded tattoo just below the elbow.

"You don't know what this means, do you?" he said. "Even though you've got one like it."

"No," I admitted. "I do know what mine means, though."

"Do you? I wonder. Just remember, it's more than just a mark, more than a symbol. It has power of its own, and you may well find that out someday." He gave me another smile, just short of condescending. "You don't have much discipline, though, do you? I'm surprised you're not dead yet—you tend to get in over your head, I'd say. Although you did do a good job last year. Of course, you did have some help."

He waved a large hand in Lou's direction. Whoever this was, he knew a great deal too much about me. I was completely out of my depth here.

"You're a practitioner then?" I said, surprised. "What happened?" Not the most tactful of questions, but he'd caught me off guard.

"Used to be. Hard to say what happened, though. I always was a bit different, and now I'm . . . well, more different." He smiled again, but this time it had an edge. "Anyway, the main difference is that unlike you, I never had an Ifrit. Some folks say that's the reason we end up like this."

I hadn't the slightest idea what he was talking about. I sent out a small probe, trying to find some talent in him, some trace of a practitioner, but I got nothing. It just seemed to slip off of him, like it would an Ifrit.

I glanced over to see how Lou was taking this, and as I did I caught something with my peripheral vision. The man shimmered briefly and in his place stood a gnarled and leathery being. When I focused back on him, I saw nothing but an eccentric homeless man. I couldn't be sure what I'd seen, but my earlier joke about a troll under the bridge didn't seem so far off the mark now.

Geoffrey's words concerning Ifrits jumped into my mind. "Practitioners do magic; Ifrits *are* magic." Maybe this guy was something similar—no longer a practitioner of magic, but something of a magical being himself. I'd never heard of such a thing, but there's a lot I don't know about the world of magic and magical beings.

"Just what are you, anyway?" I asked, deciding on the direct approach. He laughed, again with real amusement.

"Me? I'm just a homeless guy who lives under a bridge." He smiled, showing surprisingly strong teeth, and a lot of them. "*My* bridge."

The way he said that made me uncomfortable, so I resorted to my default position, flippant sarcasm.

"And you charge a toll to cross, I suppose."

"No," he said. "There are toll booths up there for that." Score one for him.

"You're not technically under the bridge anyway," I pointed out.

"Close enough," he said. "Trust me."

"So what is it do you do here, then?"

"This and that. Sometimes I provide information to those seeking answers."

"An information service? How useful. And you do that out of the goodness of your heart?"

"No, of course not. Usually I do ask for something in return."

"Such as?"

"Depends on what you have to offer. In your case . . . Well, first you'd have to tell me what you want to know."

Fair enough. "Well," I said, "here's one. If I wanted to switch bodies with another practitioner, how would I go about it?"

I wasn't serious, of course. I didn't expect an answer. But I wasn't entirely joking, either. He was so odd, in a deeply peculiar way, that I was ready to believe almost anything.

"What would you want to do that for?" he said. "You're not sick."

An unexpected response, and did I hear just the slightest emphasis on the word "you're"?

"Hypothetically," I said.

"How badly do you want to know?"

"Just curious."

"I'll bet." He stood up and twisted from side to side, loosening up. "Tell you what. I'll ask you a question, and if you can answer it, I'll answer yours."

"And if I can't?"

"You leave your little . . . dog here with me for a while."

This was straight out of folk mythology. Solve the riddle, get your answer. Fail, and suffer the consequences. I laughed.

"Well, that's just not going to happen. Besides, he doesn't actually belong to me, you know. He wouldn't stay even if I told him to."

"Oh, he might. You never know. Anyway, that would be my problem, wouldn't it? So what do you say? Deal?"

I actually considered it. It was a cheap enough way to get information. If I figured out his riddle, I'd get an answer. If I didn't, I wouldn't be out anything. Lou wouldn't stand for it, and there was no way this guy could enforce the deal in any case. But something about the situation made me uneasy.

"What do you want Lou for?" I asked. "You can't just pick out an Ifrit and make him your own. If you were a practitioner, you must know that."

"Again, my problem," he said. "Well?"

Lou was looking over at me with disapproval. Whichever way this went, he was going to remember my hesitation. Still, it wouldn't cost either of us anything. If this guy wanted to play riddle games, why not? Maybe I really would learn something.

I was just about to nod my acceptance when I saw something in the man's eyes that gave me pause. A quiet confidence, and underneath it what could only be described as outright glee. His form wavered again for a moment, and this time I was sure of what I saw. Or rather, I was very sure I had seen *something*, even though I still had no idea what it was.

I broke out in a cold sweat, as if I'd been merrily walking along about to step right off a cliff and had seen it just in time. I didn't understand what was going on, but I knew I'd almost made a big mistake.

What had Eli said about folktales? That every archetype, no matter how disguised, contains a certain core of truth. And a universal caution is that whenever you try to cheat uncanny creatures, whether fey, trolls under a bridge, or even the devil himself, things do not turn out well.

"No, I don't think so," I finally said. "I don't think that would be a good idea."

He shrugged, disappointed. "Well, perhaps that's just as well," he said.

"What was your riddle going to be, anyway? I'm pretty good at riddles."

"Yeah? Well, here it is. Who won the 1955 World Series?"

"That's not a riddle."

"Who said anything about a riddle? I said a question."

"So you did. I just somehow thought, considering . . ."

"Yeah, well."

He sat back down again, reached over into the sleeping bag, and pulled out a limp cigarette. He lit it with a snap of his fingers and sucked down a deep drag.

"Tell you what," he said. "I'll help you anyway—if you'll help me."

"Sure," I said. "Always glad to help. But not if it has anything to do with Lou, here."

He stared fixedly at Lou, who was beginning to get nervous. I was about to remind him again there was no way, but he forestalled me.

"We need his presence. Not him, just his presence. We're going to try something, and it will be a lot easier if there's an Ifrit present. You, too, of course, if you like. I wouldn't expect you to trust me."

He was right. I didn't.

"Who is we?" I asked, avoiding the trust issue.

"A group of us." Well, that was enlightening.

"I hate to be difficult," I said, "but it doesn't sound like a smart idea for us to be in the middle of a group of, well, whatever it is you are."

"That's not a problem. You'd be perfectly safe, under my protection." He raised both hands, spread his fingers wide, then interlocked them. "By my blood and my soul, I give my word."

I'm not usually impressed by these types of pronouncements. Promises can, after all, be abandoned at will. This was different. I could feel the elemental force of the words, hooked as they were into the magic of the world, and I had no doubt that this was a promise as binding as death itself.

"Okay, then," I said, somewhat shaken.

"And to show good faith, I'll answer your question. To switch bodies, you would need a power object. Even then it would be difficult, though. Something, ideally, from a magical being—a bone, or a body part. Have you ever heard of a Hand of Glory?"

A Hand of Glory is the preserved left hand of a hanged

man, very popular among would-be sorcerers with no magical talent.

"A Hand of Glory is a phony magical prop," I said.

"Of course. But where do you think the idea came from? All legends contain some truth." He flickered again as he said that, as if making a point. "Your Ifrit for example—a witch's familiar. And you can do a lot of things besides body switching with the proper object." He pointed at Lou. "His dried ears would make fine charms, believe me."

Or his eyes, I thought grimly. Or maybe the bones of some long-dead being, transformed into green rune stones.

"I'll keep that in mind," I said. "Although I'd guess only black practitioners would use that sort of thing."

"You would think. The one who was here earlier certainly was curious about it."

This was becoming more interesting by the minute. "A black practitioner?" I asked.

"Seemed like. Kind of a fussy-looking guy. At least he didn't have any trouble recognizing what I am. Those dark arts guys never do."

"How did he find you?"

"No one finds me. I found him."

"*I* found you," I said.

He smiled, amused. "Oh, is that what happened? Anyway, he wanted to know some stuff."

"About what?"

"Ifrits."

"Did you help him?"

"I told him some stuff. I don't think it helped him much."

"He didn't have an Ifrit, did he?"

"Nope."

"But I do."

"Yes. And that's why I need your help." He gestured at Lou. "Actually, his help."

"Well," I said. "I appreciate the information. But what exactly do you have in mind? I'm not putting Lou at risk, not for you, not for anyone."

"Lou," he said thoughtfully. "A good name."

He hunkered down on his heels and held out a hand, palm down and fingers curled, the way you would greet a strange dog. Lou didn't move away, but he didn't go any closer, either. After a while the man straightened up again.

"There's a homeless encampment over on Cesar Chavez," he said, "where it goes under the One-oh-one Freeway. Do you know it?"

"Sure, but I thought the cops had chased everyone out of there."

"They come back. They always do. Tomorrow, at dusk."

It always had to be dusk. Or dawn. At least it wasn't midnight.

"That's all well and good," I said, "but you haven't answered my question."

At first I thought he hadn't heard me. He stared off into the distance, clenching and unclenching his hands. My vision enhancement was starting to wear off, but the hands now looked larger than they should have, with a vague suggestion of claws at the end of strong, thick fingers. I became acutely aware of my depleted reserves.

Then, disturbingly, he began to flicker, almost too rapidly to follow. His troll-like persona and the human one alternated so quickly it was like watching a strobe light.

"You'd better go," he said, voice thick. He was having trouble articulating the words.

"You okay?"

"Just go. I'll explain when I see you tomorrow. But go now."

The voice uttering "Go" triggered my memory. I'd heard that voice before, thick and guttural. Now I knew why he had seemed familiar.

"You were at Stern Grove," I said. "You helped me get out of there."

"Of course. I had to see if it worked."

"If what worked?" I asked. I was getting frustrated again. He didn't answer.

"Go!" he said again. This time his guttural voice deepened, and now it sounded dangerous.

I hadn't promised I would show up tomorrow, but leaving now did seem like a good idea. It was as if I had been innocently swimming in the ocean, only to suddenly realize a giant shark was silently gliding ten feet beneath me. One thing for sure, Eli was going to have a field day with this one. I jerked my head at Lou and started walking away, moving a little faster than absolutely necessary.

"Hey," I yelled, stopping for a moment after I'd gone far enough to feel safe. "Dodgers over Yankees. Seven games. *Brooklyn* Dodgers."

SIXTEEN

I'D CALLED VICTOR AND ELI WITH THE NEWS ABOUT Rolando as soon as I got home. Victor immediately called Jo and found that Rolando had left the apartment right after I had, and hadn't returned. Eli wasn't that concerned anyway—he still didn't believe Rolando could be involved. Eli has tremendous loyalty, which is great, but it can produce blind spots.

The next morning, Rolando still hadn't shown up. Victor, Eli, Timothy, and I met for lunch to talk it over.

"So as far as I'm concerned, that's all we need," I said. "The knife blade glowed as soon as I took it out. Rolando was no farther from it than you are to me right now."

We were having lunch at Ti Couz, the Mission crepe house. Timothy sat next to me, having temporarily escaped from his SOMA dot-com responsibilities. Eli and Victor sat across from us on the bench, backs to the wall. Victor never sat with his back to the entrance; he pretended he was just being careful, but I think he'd really picked up the idea from a James Bond movie or something like that. Lou was annoyed because he had to wait outside, but he calmed down when I promised to bring him something.

"That is troubling, I grant you," Eli said. "But as I said before, a false positive is always a possibility, especially since we had so little material to work with. It doesn't look good, but it's still not proof."

"But what about his reaction to it?" I asked. "That's almost enough for me right there."

"Well, it's not enough for me," Eli said. "At least I'll need to talk with him first, to see what he has to say for himself."

"Good luck with that. Ten to one we won't be seeing him again anytime soon."

Victor took out his cell and hit a speed-dial number. I could hear faint rings buzzing from the phone. After ten rings, he gave up.

"No answer," he said, unnecessarily.

"We'll get hold of him," Eli said. "If it is him, which I doubt, he'll be long gone by now. If it isn't, things will get straightened out eventually. Until then, Mason, I don't want you doing anything on your own. I mean it."

"Fine by me," I said. "I have no idea where he is, anyway."

Eli scowled. This was not the kind of thing Eli enjoys dealing with. Then again, who does?

Our waiter came by and I ordered my usual mushroom crepe. Not very adventurous, but always tasty, especially when washed down with a bottle of microbrew.

"Now for something else entirely," I said, as soon as the waiter walked away. "After I left their apartment last night, Lou noticed someone odd. We followed, and ended up talking to a homeless guy living under the bridge—the same guy you asked Rolando to check out, Victor. But he wasn't just some homeless guy."

"What, then?" Victor asked.

"Well, I don't know exactly, but I don't think he's completely human. I don't know what he is. But he told me some things, and he had a proposition."

"And that was?"

I told them. Timothy was transfixed. This was the real perk of hanging with Victor, the thing he'd never be able to replace—the entree he'd gained into the world of the supernatural. It was very like an addiction. He had been introduced into the inner circle and seen and heard things that his normal friends could never even conceive of, much less believe in. For him it was like being in the middle of the best book you had ever read, but one where you could actually talk to the characters, Holmes and Watson and Van Helsing. Without Victor, all that would be gone, and I wasn't sure he'd ever be satisfied with a normal life again.

I had a passing moment of sorrow for him; if Victor's past history held true, this relationship wasn't going to last forever. It had already gone on longer than any of his others.

Not that Timothy would exactly pine away. Victor was lucky to have him—Timothy would find plenty of others eager to console him were he to become suddenly unattached. He was a good-looking, interesting guy, and his head was a lot more together than any of ours. It would have to be to put up with Victor.

Eli leaned back, took off his glasses, and carefully cleaned them with a handkerchief. He acted matter-of-factly, but I knew him better than that. The stuff we'd been dealing with lately was hugely important. People had died. And despite Eli's reservations, my money was now firmly on Rolando.

But to Eli, important didn't equal interesting. To him, it was all a huge pain in the ass, something that had to be dealt with so he could get back to his beloved research. But this was different. *This* was interesting.

"Any ideas?" I said. "Theories? Ancient books of magical lore that will unlock the key?"

Surprisingly, Victor was the one who spoke up first.

"I've heard of these people," he said. "Ex-practitioners. I should have considered it when I sent Rolando and Josephine down there to check him out. But I always assumed it was an urban legend, at best."

"So did I," Eli said. "Although I always meant to investigate someday. But I never seemed to be able to find the time. There are just so many things that need looking into."

I stifled my natural desire to demand information. It wouldn't speed things up. Instead, I managed to look politely interested, usually the best way to get them talking. Timothy unwittingly helped me out.

"But what was he?" he asked. "That whole thing Mason saw, the shifting back and forth. Is he human, or something else?"

I knew what Eli was going to say before he said it: the same thing he always says when I ask him an either/or question. I'm not sure if that says more about how the world is or about how Eli sees it.

"Well, both, I think," he said, confirming my expectations.

"How can that be?" asked Timothy. Bless him for that naïveté. I settled in for what I hoped would be an illuminating lecture.

"Back in the Middle Ages," Eli began, "legends abounded about all types of half-human creatures, things that were as normal as you or I in the daytime, but that underwent horrible transformations at night. The most common of these legends, the one that has persisted to this day, is the werewolf, of course."

"But there aren't any werewolves," said Timothy. His voice grew hushed. "Are there?"

The waiter returned with our food, which left Timothy hanging. Eli sectioned off a large slice of crepe, popped it into his mouth, and chewed it thoroughly before finally answering.

"No, there aren't," he said with a definitive tone. "The werewolf is nothing more than an archetype, a concept."

"You positive about that?" I said.

That annoyed him. He doesn't like it when I interrupt

his lectures. He didn't mind Timothy playing the role of the inquisitive student, but he knew I was just trying to be difficult.

"Yes, I'm quite sure," he said, curtly. I knew he wasn't, not really, not after the things we'd both seen this past year, but I let it pass.

"But there are plenty of other things that have entered our collective consciousness. Nymphs and satyrs for the Greeks. Banshees, little people, and especially the fey for the Irish. Trolls and such for the Germanic peoples. Each culture has its own counterparts.

"And they all have two things in common. One, that they either can pass for human, or they are a distorted or idealized version of a human. And they have the same motivations and desires as do humans—lust and greed being the two most prominent.

"Second, they are creatures of the fringes. In the old days it was the forest and the hidden cave. Now it's more the fringes of society, but still the fringes."

"As in the homeless, today," Victor said.

"Yes. And don't forget, there once were a lot more practitioners than there are today. And far fewer Ifrits, which is another thing worthy of some investigative research. Back then it wasn't as clearly understood what it meant to be a practitioner. The practitioners of those days were unfocused, more elemental, closer to their talent but less able to control it."

"They didn't *do* magic so much as they *were* magic," I said, paraphrasing. Eli didn't realize I was quoting.

"Yes, yes. Very good, Mason, very good indeed. And I think that after a while, living with their uncontrolled talent changed some of them. They became something less than human, or maybe more. And over the years, they were enshrined in folklore as beings not quite human—goblins, fairies, apparitions—all the aspects of the uncanny."

"And you think they're still around today?"

"It's certainly possible. And not all practitioners are so

lucky as to be in control of their talent. If they're not, it usually leads to trouble. That's why it's so important to mentor those youngsters we discover, right after puberty when talent usually makes its first appearance.

"Remember, practitioners are no more immune to mental problems, social difficulties, and general dysfunction than is anyone else. That's one of the reasons Victor keeps so busy. Most of the practitioners we deal with are not criminal, after all. They're just damaged, messed-up people."

"What are you saying?" I asked. "That if no one's around to guide them, these youngsters don't only become confused, they change in some way?"

"No, not all of them. Not even most of them—it must be rather uncommon, actually. But if conditions are just right, yes, I could see it happening. Talent can manifest in a myriad of ways. There's no reason, theoretically, an individual couldn't morph over time into something not quite human."

Victor finished his crepe, some sort of Gruyère and hazelnut concoction, and pushed his plate to the side. "I'm not sure I go along with Eli on this one," he said. "But I'll be interested to meet them."

"You want to come with me?" I asked, surprised.

"You can hardly show up there alone. It could be dangerous for you. Not to disparage your talent, but . . ."

Disparage, my ass. According to Victor's way of thinking, the only thing that has kept me alive so far is running to him for help every other week. Even worse, that isn't so far from the truth.

"I'm not so sure about that," said Eli. "Only Mason was invited; that was the deal. If you'll keep the folklore in mind, it might be just as well not to break that agreement."

"I didn't actually agree to anything," I said. "But I've got to go, don't you think?"

"Absolutely. This is an incredible opportunity." For Eli, maybe. Not necessarily for me, though. Eli continued, oblivious. "I think it'll be perfectly safe. Again, think about all the folktales. Legends. One of the prime motifs that runs through all of them is that once a supernatural being's word is given, it can be counted on absolutely."

"Well, as I said, I never actually agreed to anything. But you might be right. If he thinks there's a deal, breaking it probably isn't a good idea."

Victor did not look convinced. I didn't care. He wouldn't be the only one to suffer consequences if things turned ugly.

"One thing for sure," I said, getting up to leave and picking up the doggie bag I'd snagged. "It's bound to be enlightening."

WHICH IS HOW I FOUND MYSELF STANDING ALONE in the middle of a homeless encampment at dusk. Anyplace where freeway ramps converge is a potential homeless camp. There's always space, there aren't any businesses or residents to piss off, and it's never a very attractive spot for others anyway. No well-groomed woman walking little Fluffy is going to accidentally pass by and be horrified.

Another important and often overlooked perk is the availability of concrete abutments and walls. If all you have is a tattered tent or an old tarpaulin, it's reassuring to have a solid bulwark covering your back. When you can face a potential threat head on, it provides a certain measure of security, and every little bit helps.

The ubiquitous shopping carts were everywhere, filled with personal possessions and recyclables. Most of the homeless stayed in their own private spaces, although a few groups of two or three gathered together, talking. Most were men; I thought I saw a couple of women, but I couldn't be sure. Several small dogs scarcely bigger than Lou lay in the front of tents or next to shopping carts. None had leashes; none were barking; none were running around out of control. Those dogs probably had a pretty good life. They seemed well fed; they got to be outside all day every day, having one grand adventure after another. Their owners were with them twenty-four seven.

Contrast that to the pampered house dog who gets a half hour walk twice a day if he's lucky. An owner who leaves at seven in the morning and doesn't get back till dinnertime, then spends the evening watching television. It's ironic, but the harsh life of a homeless man isn't half-bad for his canine companion.

The dog nearest to me, a black-and-white Jack Russell mix, looked curiously at Lou. He couldn't quite decide whether to growl or not. Dogs can't usually tell that Lou isn't really a dog, but this one looked like he wasn't so sure.

I'd dressed down to avoid standing out, wearing scuffed boots and my oldest and most disreputable army jacket. But as far as the residents were concerned, I might as well have been wearing an Armani suit and tie. They knew I didn't belong, and even if I'd used some talent to give myself the proper look, they would have known there was something not quite right about me.

I got a few wary looks, but nothing actively hostile. So long as I kept my distance and minded my own business, no one was interested in me. It took me a minute to locate my friend from the bridge, in the back of the camp, away from the freeway. He raised a hand to motion me over.

He was standing with two others, which hardly qualified as a group. He seemed embarrassed by the lack of support.

"Yeah, I know," he said as I came up to them. "But I couldn't get all seven of us together so quickly, and the only other number that's of any use is three."

He appeared totally normal, as if the weirdness of the day before had never happened. It would have been smart to follow his lead and go along, but my curiosity got the better of me.

"What was that little show yesterday?" I asked, casually. "When you told me to 'get out.' And when you started looking . . . different."

His eyes narrowed and I thought for a moment I'd made a mistake. Then he laughed and punched me on the shoulder.

"You should have seen the look on your face," he said.

"But it was just as well you listened. I'm usually under control, but sometimes it slips for a moment. I never know just when it's going to happen." He gestured at his two friends. "We're all like that. That's why we live like we do—we're not safe to be around other people all the time. So we live on the edges."

"And what were you doing at Stern Grove?" I asked. Again, I thought for a moment I'd pushed him too far. He didn't seem the type who enjoyed someone prying. But he needed me, or at least he needed Lou, so after staring at me long enough to make me uncomfortable, he answered.

"Same thing as you, I expect. I wanted to see if that black arts guy had come up with anything. But he got interrupted. I don't think it would have worked anyway." He smiled. "It's a good thing for you I did, no? And a good thing I had my friends with me."

I had a lot more questions, but he walked away from me and joined his two friends. I looked closely at them. I was tempted to try viewing on the psychic plane, but I had a feeling if I did, I would regret it. They both appeared distressingly normal. The one closest to me was rough and unshaven with dirty, thinning hair and bad teeth. When he moved, he reminded me of someone. It took me a second, then I got it. He was the same guy I'd followed to reach the bridge guy. Or rather, had obviously been lured by.

The other guy was very different, strikingly handsome, even under a layer of grime. He turned away, and as he moved it seemed almost as if he glittered when he walked. He was busy collecting stones and pieces of scrap wood, considering each one carefully, choosing some and discarding others.

"Richard Cory," the bridge guy said, walking back up to me with a smile that made it obvious the name was a private joke. I didn't get it. Not his real name of course; it would have been gauche to identify a friend by name to a stranger. He still hadn't told me his own name, for that matter, nor had he asked for mine.

"Time to get started," he said. It was getting dark.

"About that," I said. "I know I said I'd help, but not unless I get some idea about what it is you're doing. Specifically, how does Lou fit into it?"

"Well, I can't tell you exactly. It's unclear. But I do have a theory."

Except for the dreadlocked beard, mismatched clothes, and general air of danger and insanity, at that moment he reminded me exactly of Eli.

"You didn't have a mentor growing up, did you?" I asked, remembering Eli's comments. "Someone to explain things, to show you the ropes?"

He snorted like a horse. "Hardly. I grew up in a small town in Oklahoma. I started showing talent by age thirteen, and it scared the crap out of me. At first I thought I was going crazy, and after I decided I wasn't, I pushed that talent away and buried it as deep as I could. I was sure that if anyone discovered my dreadful secret, I'd be burned at the stake or something."

"Not an unreasonable fear," I said.

"Still, talent will out, though it may take years. By the time it did I was having other problems. I found myself . . . changing."

"Changing how?"

"You saw. It isn't all bad, once you get used to it. I can do things, more things than you know."

"But you'd still rather be—" I almost said "normal," but thought it might not go over well. "Rather be more in control," I finished.

"That's it exactly. I'm tired of living on the edges, unable to live like everyone else, afraid of what I might do. What I have done, for that matter."

"I see," I said. I didn't want to know details.

"And it's not just a matter of self-control. At a certain point the change becomes complete. I'm still human, mostly. Richard there, well he's mostly not, although he can fake it pretty well. But there are others I've known who have gone all the way. You wouldn't want to meet them. They're not entirely safe to be around, even for me."

"Are there many of them?" I asked. "I've lived here most of my life and seen some strange things in my time, but nothing like what you're describing."

"Are you sure about that?"

"No," I said, thinking of Stern Grove and those shapes in the fog. More pieces of the puzzle.

"They're hard to find, hard to see, even for practitioners. They've lost the ability for rational thought, but they're crafty. Like wild animals. There are a lot more of them than you'd think. They have their places. People just don't know they're around."

He drifted off momentarily and the outline of his body started to go fuzzy.

"Well," I said, loudly and heartily, "you seem to have yourself under control right now."

He looked at me as if he had no idea who I was, then snapped back into focus.

"Anyway," he said, "eventually I moved to San Francisco, a big change, but at least here I met people like myself."

"Those guys?" I asked, indicating his friends.

"Among others. And as I learned more about what I am, I realized two things that we all have in common. One is that we all have a strong talent that we never learned to handle. Most of us didn't even realize what it was."

"And the other?"

"None of us had an Ifrit."

"That's not so surprising. Most practitioners don't."

"I know, but you'd think at least one of us would. But no, not a single one."

"And you think there's a connection?"

"I do. I think the talent we bottled up inside overloaded us, and I think that Ifrits can act as a type of safety valve, with talent flowing into them instead of building up. Maybe if I'd had an Ifrit, I wouldn't have ended up the way I have."

This was an odd spin along the lines of what I'd been

thinking about myself, so I was one step ahead of him for once.

"You think you can create one," I said.

He looked at me in surprise. "So you figured that out."

"And you need Lou as a template."

"Something like that. I think more as an anchor to keep the energy from going off in random directions."

"I'm not sure I like the sound of that," I said. "I've seen spells go wrong more than once, and it's never good for whoever's in the middle of things."

"I understand that. But he won't be involved in the actual ritual. He'll just be used as a focusing device beforehand."

That didn't sound so bad. And in truth, I was dying to know if it was possible.

"Well, it's really up to him," I said.

Lou had been following the conversation with what appeared to be intense interest. There's no way he could have understood everything that was said; he's smart, but not that smart. But in some way I don't quite understand, he seems to get the gist of what he needs to. The bridge guy looked down at him.

"What do you say?" he asked him. "Want to give it a try?"

Lou twisted his head around and looked up at me. I shrugged.

"Up to you."

He stretched, walked over to Bridge Guy, and sat down in front of him.

"I guess it's a go," I said.

The other two came up and they squatted around him in a circle. Lou doesn't like having anyone behind him, but he stayed put. Bridge Guy put his face down right next to Lou's muzzle and looked into his eyes. Lou looked back without flinching. Then the one named Richard Cory did the same thing, which made Lou extremely nervous.

Fey, I thought. He's where the idea of the fey comes from. Not to be trusted. Finally, the third guy crouched, after which they all withdrew to the very back of the encampment. None of the other homeless was paying the slightest attention to any of this. I wondered if the three had unconsciously cast a deflecting spell around themselves.

They formed a triangle around the small pile of stones they had gathered. The bridge guy started mumbling, trying a chant of sorts, I imagine, but the rhythms were all wrong. Then Richard Cory joined in, then the rough guy. Again, this seemed familiar. Of course. Now I understood. It reminded me of Byron and his group in Stern Grove. They had been trying to do the same thing, in their own fashion. Maybe Byron was concerned about a connection between Ifrits and magic as well, and was trying to create his own.

At first there was no indication they were getting anywhere. Then a faint glow, barely visible in the darkening light. All three were flickering in the same way the bridge guy had done the night before, only this time there was no sense of menace about it. I saw the troll again, and a being of unnatural grace and light, and something else that seemed to have pointed ears and too much hair.

The glow flared red, then gold, then started coalescing into a swirling mass of color that reminded me of that last glimpse I'd had of Willy scampering down the trail, before his sad ending. But then, just when it seemed something must surely manifest, the mass of color wavered and collapsed in on itself. For a moment, the riot of color concentrated itself into a tiny sphere, and then it winked out like a candle flame in a strong wind. Nothing was left but the cold gray of worn stones and broken pieces of wood. The three of them slumped dejectedly.

"So close, this time," one of them whispered. I wasn't sure which one. "We need the runes."

I wanted to ask, "What runes?" but I had a good idea what they were referring to. I stood there awkwardly, not knowing what to say. Better luck next time? It didn't matter, though; the three of them walked away, ignoring me. I was no longer relevant. Richard Cory bent down to give Lou a pat as he passed. Lou flinched involuntarily; the guy still made him nervous. I would have thought the rough guy would cause more concern, but Lou actually went over to him for a friendly sniff as they passed by.

A minute later Lou and I were standing alone in the middle of the homeless encampment. One of the regular homeless suddenly took notice, as if we'd appeared out of nowhere.

"Hey," he said, walking over toward us with an artificial smile of friendliness. "You got a cigarette?"

SEVENTEEN

"WHAT DO YOU THINK?" I ASKED ELI OVER A CUP of coffee the next day. We were at the Café France in West Portal, one of our standard meeting places since it was halfway between our two houses.

Byron was still underground and Rolando was nowhere to be found, either. Since we couldn't find either of them, Eli was more than happy to focus on this new and interesting development instead.

After what I'd seen at the homeless encampment, I couldn't get my original idea about Ifrits out of my mind. Could they really be called up out of nowhere? Was Lou simply some projection of my own psyche, made corporeal? I found myself constantly looking at him, trying to see a connection between us. It started making him nervous; every time he looked up I was staring at him and then quickly looking away. After a while he decided he wanted no more of it and refused to come near me.

"So they were trying to create an Ifrit," he mused. "Fascinating."

"Or evoke one. Or something. I think Byron was trying to do the same thing in Stern Grove."

"But of course they couldn't."

"Why not?"

"You don't think it was the first time it's ever been tried, do you?"

"I never thought about it. Well, it didn't work, but it wasn't far off, either. And I'm not so sure it can't be done." I took a deep breath. "And here's why."

I launched into my previous epiphany concerning Ifrits, about how they come into being, about how creativity is the key. As I repeated it all, it didn't seem quite so compelling as it did earlier. Still, I forged on.

"One more thing. Remember last year, when I was checking out Sandra's aura on the psychic plane?" He nodded. "Well, I could see an energy flow between Lou and myself, between our auras. At the time I thought it was just because of how close we are, but now I'm thinking it's more that we share an aura, or at least parts of it. And that would make perfect sense with this theory."

Eli grunted, got up from the table, and left me sitting there as he went for another latte. Lou was sitting quietly by my chair, trying to look inconspicuous so he wouldn't get thrown out. When he wants, he can be almost unnoticeable, even without magic. Of course, he *is* magic, in a sense. That was what this was all about. The thought that he might be part of me was not reassuring. In fact, it was downright creepy.

When Eli returned, he sat across from me and started slurping, rolling the coffee around in his mouth. This was his most annoying habit, the one that usually drove me up the wall, but this time it didn't bother me. It meant he was thinking, and thinking hard. Finally he broke into a broad smile.

"I'm glad to see you're finally learning to think critically," he said. "But I think you may have taken this idea a little too far."

"So I'm totally off base here?" I said, disappointed.

"No. Not entirely. Others have come up with similar ideas, although your twist on it is pretty clever. But it's not that simple." Of course. It never is. He slurped more coffee and continued. "You see, the problem is that we're all stuck in the paradigm of either/or. Let's head back to the seventeenth century for a moment."

"Oh, let's do," I said.

Typical Eli. If he'd been a music professor and you were to ask what key a particular piece was in, a half an hour later he'd be explaining the medieval art of encoding secret messages in the text of motets. Interesting, but really beside the point. This time, however, I was intrigued.

"For a time, intense controversy raged over the exact nature of light. What was it, scientists wondered? Isaac Newton thought it was made up of tiny particles. Huygens, on the other hand, believed it was a wave phenomenon. Both theories had their adherents and their detractors."

"So who turned out to be right?"

"Well, that's the point. Quantum theory came along to posit a state of matter that has characteristics of both, but is neither. It wasn't either/or. And quantum theory defied our conventional either/or thinking. You'd think, for example, that an electron would have to be either here or there—it couldn't be in two places at the same time. Turns out it can."

Eli was just getting warmed up. I could see this heading into places I wouldn't follow.

"So how does this apply to Ifrits?" I said, hoping to keep him somewhat on track.

"Ah. Now if you'll remember, last year we had a similar discussion. Are the things that black practitioners sometimes call up 'real,' or are they just constructs of will?"

"I do. And I remember you said it's not an either/or proposition. Which is what you always say."

Eli laughed. "Exactly. I've long thought that Ifrits are, in a sense, created by practitioners. But just as importantly, I also think that they aren't. They clearly are totally independent beings. After all, if you have a child, you've created it, but it's not part of you. It's too bad Lou can't speak. He might have some answers for us."

"Oh, he's learned to speak," I said. "So far, though, the only words he knows are 'bacon' and 'cheeseburger.' But as soon as he learns a few more, I'm sure he'll have some choice words concerning you."

"I'll bet." He reached down and scratched Lou's ears. "You know, I never even considered the idea of creative energy in the artistic sense. An interesting proposition. Though again, I doubt it's quite as straightforward as you've made it out to be."

"Perish the thought," I said. "What fun would that be?"

He looked at me suspiciously over the top of his tiny glasses. Another affectation; he can't see much without them. But I was pleased to note that even after all these years, he's not entirely sure when I'm being sarcastic.

"It's quite possible that the same factors that go into determining whether someone has an artistic bent also create the unconscious mental state necessary for an Ifrit to appear. It isn't necessarily a direct causal relationship."

"Well, the bridge guy sure thought he could create one. Just because it hasn't been done before, are you really so positive it can't be?"

A range of emotions played over Eli's face—interest, curiosity, hope, and even some fear. Eli was no more immune to Ifrit envy than was anyone else.

"Well, I'm fairly confident. Mostly because if it were possible, someone surely would have figured out how to do it by now."

"What if you needed something special?" I said. "Like a power object. One of those rune stones, for example?"

That brought him up short. He stared off into space for a moment, then nodded approvingly.

"You *have* been thinking," he said.

"Well?"

"I'd have to give it a lot more thought. But my gut reaction is still no. And even if it were possible, it wouldn't be advisable to try it."

"Why not?" I asked. It was interesting that his reaction about attempting it was the same as mine, but I wanted reasons.

"Well," he said, "the unconscious is the place of dreams, of artistry, of unlikely connections that our conscious self never puts together. I think the conditions have to be just right to call up an Ifrit. That's why it takes years, and sometimes never happens. A deliberate attempt might well bring forth something very different from what one intended."

"But when I play music, it's a conscious act. The best music always comes from somewhere else—almost as if it's channeled. But it's still a conscious effort to create something meaningful."

"And do you ever make mistakes?"

"Of course. Everyone makes mistakes."

He pointed his finger at me. "But when you do, those mistakes don't move in with you."

He obviously hadn't met all of my former girlfriends, but I took his point.

I spent the rest of the day at home, mostly thinking. The last time I'd had a puzzle to work on, my main problem had been lack of information. It's hard to make clever deductions when you have nothing to go on.

But this time it was worse. I had so much information that I didn't know where to start. It's always easy afterward to tell the wheat from the chaff, to see which bits were crucial and which were mere distractions. If you're still around to see it, that is.

Rolando was behind the practitioner attacks—that much I was sure of. Well, almost sure. If nothing else, that eerie glow of the knife blade provided a strong indication. But a few things still didn't add up. Why would he try to kill me up by the Cliff House? Jo could have easily been killed as well. Why was he so obsessed with Byron? It went way beyond merely deflecting suspicion.

Still, these were side issues. It came down to the telltale knife, after all. Even if it wasn't 100 percent accurate, it was still compelling evidence.

I was so deep in thought that at first I didn't hear the soft knock on the door. Lou nudged me with his nose to alert me, which meant that whoever it was, there wasn't any danger.

When I opened the door, Jo stood there, looking small.

"Can I come in?" she asked.

"Of course."

I stepped back and she tentatively stepped inside, looking around curiously.

"This is nice," she said.

"You sound surprised."

"Well, the way you described it, I'd envisioned you living in an abandoned garage with oil stains on a concrete floor."

"Not quite that bad," I said.

I cleared off some sheet music from the bed and she sat down on the very edge, back straight.

"Okay," she said. "What's going on with you and Rolando? He's taken off somewhere and I haven't seen him since. Victor's looking for him. Eli's looking for him. And I have no ideas, except that it has something to do with the other night."

This was a problem. If I told her what I thought, she'd either laugh at me or fly into a rage. Blood is thicker than logic.

"Yes, that," I said. "I'm beginning to think he doesn't care much for me."

"And why would that be?"

"Well, it's complicated."

"Oh, no," she said. "You're not getting off that easily."

"You know, I think—"

"I don't care what you think. You're going to tell me what's going on, and you're going to tell me now. I'm not leaving until you do. If you leave, I'll follow. I'll stick to you like white on rice."

"I mostly eat brown rice," I said. Like most of my attempts to defuse tense situations with humor, it didn't work.

"Well?" she said, ignoring my feeble attempt. "Are you going to tell me?"

"Okay," I said, "but you're not going to like it." I took a deep breath. "I'm not so sure Byron is really our problem. I think it just might be Rolando."

"You can't be serious," she said. "Have you lost your mind?"

I went over everything, every link in the chain, every indication that Rolando could be involved. She listened politely with amused disbelief until the very end when I explained about the significance of the glow on the knife blade.

"Okay, I admit that's weird," she said, chewing her lip. "But there's bound to be an explanation."

"I wish I could think of one."

"It's insane. If it were true, don't you think I would have noticed something about it before now?"

"You're not exactly an unbiased observer," I pointed out. "Haven't you said that Rolando's been acting strangely for the last couple of weeks?"

"Yeah, he has, but how long have these troubles been going on? Months, if not longer. I tell you, Rolando has nothing to do with this. That's ridiculous. It's got to be Byron."

"You seem awfully positive about that," I said. "Are you sure there isn't something you're not telling me?" I thought for a moment she was going to say no, but then her shoulders slumped.

"You found out about it, didn't you?"

"A while ago," I said.

She reached over to give Lou a pat on the head, which he adroitly avoided without seeming to do so.

"I was bored in Portland," she said. "Byron was interesting—charming, good-looking, and definitely out-of-bounds for the likes of me. He was fun. He was interested in what I had to say. And he taught me a lot, things I wouldn't ordinarily have learned. But when Ro found out, it turned ugly. He told Byron to keep away from me—very big brother about the whole thing."

"And did Byron listen?"

"Well, that wasn't the issue. *I* didn't listen, and that's what mattered. It's not like I had nothing to say about it, although Ro liked to think that was the case."

"So what happened?"

"Ro was visiting me, over at Byron's house, trying again to tell me what I should be doing. The next day, Byron said something was missing and accused Ro of taking it. When I told him Ro would never steal anything, he turned on me, intimating that maybe I'd been involved as well. Things went downhill from there. He started acting nasty, cruel even, and we stopped seeing each other. After, I realized Rolando was right; there's something wrong with the guy."

Just what Byron had said about Rolando.

"And that's it?" I said.

"Not quite. A while later is when the practitioner attacks started. Ro was convinced that Byron was behind them—he didn't have any proof, but by that time he didn't seem to need any. I didn't believe it at first, but I do now. Byron's capable of such things.

"I see."

Jo had kept her eyes down the entire time, but now she raised her head and looked me in the face.

"I know I should have told you about it, but to tell the truth I was embarrassed. I mean, Byron *is* a black practitioner after all. I thought if you knew about us you wouldn't want anything to do with me." She smiled wanly. "I was starting to like you."

"I was starting to like you, too," I said. I switched gears. "What exactly was it that Rolando was supposed to have stolen?"

"Byron never would tell me right out. But I'm pretty

sure they were charms of some sort. Power objects. He had a wall safe, and I saw inside it once. The only thing in it was a pile of odd stones."

"Green stones?" She looked at me in surprise.

"How did you know that?"

"A lucky guess."

She got up from her seat on the bed and wandered around the tiny bedroom, examining things at random, not really seeing them.

"There's one more thing," she said. "I came here for another reason." I waited patiently for her to continue. "Byron called me this morning."

I hadn't expected that. "What did he want?"

"He still thinks Rolando has those stones. He wants them back."

"Understandable."

"I told him he was right, that I'd found them, and he could have them back if he'd just leave me alone."

"And did you?"

"No, of course not. Rolando doesn't have any stones."

"Kind of a dangerous game, don't you think?" I said.

"That's why I came here. I need help; I can't face him alone. Usually I count on Rolando, but that's not an option now. But I thought between the two of us . . ."

"That we could take him down?"

"Something like that. And I didn't know about the knife, then. You still have it, don't you?" I nodded. "Now we can see what happens when we get up close to him. I'll bet you anything it reacts."

It was a tempting idea. If the knife remained neutral, it would settle things once and for all. If it reacted, well, I'd deal with that when and if it happened.

"Where are you meeting him?" I asked.

"I don't know. I'm supposed to call him back, just before midnight. He'll give me instructions."

Byron was being cautious. That would leave no time to set up a welcoming committee beforehand.

"And if I don't go with you?"

"I don't know. I guess . . . I don't know." What could I say?

"Okay," I said. "Call me as soon as he gets hold of you and I'll pick you up."

JO CALLED THAT NIGHT, AND FIFTEEN MINUTES later I was in front of her apartment building. She was waiting outside when I pulled up. She jumped in the passenger seat, all flushed and excited, holding a piece of paper.

"Where to?" I asked. She held up the paper and read from it.

"Go up to Fourth Street and get on the freeway. One-oh-one South."

I swung the van around and followed directions. When we hit the freeway she folded up the paper, keeping it tight in her hand.

"Get off at the Monster Park exit," she said.

She hunched down in her seat and stopped talking. I kept stealing glances at her, but she never moved. It looked like she was doing some heavy thinking.

"Monster Park is the next exit," I said, warning her as we passed the Cow Palace. I pulled off the freeway at Monster Park and followed directions. Straight, right, left, and right again, through deserted streets.

"Wait a minute," I said, suddenly realizing where we were. "We're on our way to the city dump."

Not a bad choice, actually. Away from inhabited areas, deserted at night, lots of places to hide and scope out arrivals.

"Can we get in?" she asked.

"I'm not sure. It's locked up at night, and there's bound to be a watchman."

"Ahh. Locked gates and security guards. No practitioner could possibly overcome such odds."

But when I pulled up to the gate across the access road, it was wide open. There was no sign of security people.

"We'll park here," I said. "We don't want to be announcing our arrival."

The dump complex consisted of dirt roads and low gray buildings of corrugated metal, like a surrealistic army base. The wind kicked up as we walked down the main roadway, blowing trash past our feet. Aluminum cans and dented metal containers clanged up against the sides of the buildings. The moonlight was just bright enough to see by, but not bright enough to be positive what you were seeing.

Off to the left, around a huge pile of oil drums and bins filled with dead vacuum cleaners, was an open hillside. Scattered throughout, a ground cover of prickly pear cacti and a collection of bizarre objects, presumably rescued from the dump, dotted the hillside.

They were grouped in some sort of aesthetic order. On the near hillside were the animals: a giant kangaroo lying on its back, several chipped llamas, and an assortment of other things too difficult to identify in the pale light. A huge tiger, twice life size with paint worn off its head crouched on the lower slope nearest to where we walked. The smell of garbage, rotting greenery, and toxic chemicals combined to produce a musty odor uncomfortably similar to a big-cat house at the zoo.

I viewed the tiger with some suspicion. Ever since a certain incident last year, I've never felt completely at ease around inanimate figures. Toss in a remote location, a fugitive black practitioner, and shifting moonlight, and the chances of one or more of these animals deciding to take a midnight stroll were excellent.

Next to the animals were the plaster saints. Figures large and small formed a semicircle on the hill, silently weighing sins. In the middle of the semicircle stood a lone carousel horse, being judged for God knows what crime. The occasional statues of Jesus scattered through the assembly did nothing to ease their accusing stares.

Another hill rose up past a thick grove of trees. Toy trucks of every conceivable size spread out in a yellow line across that hillside, and lower down on the slope a blue plaster replica of Michelangelo's David stood in lone splendor. Farther on, two Santa Clauses and three rusted stop signs. Elvis himself, but no guitar. And half-hidden in a stand of trees, a giant plastic pumpkin. In the light of a sunny day it would all have been quixotic and charming, but under the pale moonlight it felt downright ominous.

I pulled Jo down behind a large bin filled with old tires.

"What now?" she asked.

"Now, we wait."

She was perfectly willing, but Lou had other ideas. He slipped away and disappeared into the dim light. He can make himself hard to see at the best of times, and his black and tan coat flowed perfectly into the dappled shadows. Even if someone were to catch sight of him, they'd likely think he was a particularly large rat.

For more than an hour we crouched behind the Dumpster. Byron was late. Maybe something had happened to him. Maybe he'd had second thoughts. I was starting to get cold and stiff, but I wasn't going to stand exposed and vulnerable while waiting for him to show. When Jo grabbed my arm and pointed, it was a relief. Halfway up the hill, drifting between the motionless statues, a figure was making its way across the slope.

"There he is," she said, mouth right next to my ear. She turned away and I put my mouth next to her ear in the same fashion.

"How can you tell?" We did the back-and-forth thing.

"His clothes. That dark three-quarter coat is a dead giveaway."

"What's he doing?"

"Hard to say. Looking for a place he thinks is safe, I guess."

I settled back to watch. Byron picked a place about halfway up the hill where he had a good view of the surrounding area and settled himself down. It looked like he was waiting for Jo, but wasn't convinced she would be coming alone. I certainly wouldn't have been.

I hadn't thought out any kind of plan. I eased into a prone position on the ground, disregarding the refuse leavings that covered the pavement. That high up he might be able to see us over the top of the Dumpster, and I wanted some time to think.

You might suppose we would have the advantage since it was two against one. But we needed to catch him, not kill him. I wasn't about to arbitrarily kill an unsuspecting practitioner, even if I'd been convinced of his guilt, which I wasn't. But if he really was our bad guy, he'd have no compunction in killing us.

I almost gave our position away when a wet nose poked itself into my ear. Lou was back, and he'd done it on purpose knowing I couldn't yell at him or even move. Jo wriggled herself over and put her mouth up to my other ear again.

"Can you get Lou to distract him?" she asked. It was a good idea.

"I can try. Then, if we can get close enough, try a binding spell. It just needs to last long enough for me to reach him."

I rolled over and spoke almost inaudibly to Lou. With his hearing he had no problem picking up my words.

"Up on the hill," I said. "Get behind him, up above. Distract. Make him look. Got it?"

His standard reaction is a short bark of comprehension when he understands what I'm asking of him, but luckily he was in his stalking mode. He simply gave two quick wags of his tail and slithered out into the darkness again. I lost sight of him immediately, and with the wind picking up, the blowing trash made enough noise to cover any small sounds he might make going up the hill.

I thought I saw his shadow as he ghosted into the line of thick trees that clustered in the center of the two hills, and then he was gone. A few minutes later, the figure on the hillside straightened up and swung his head around toward the top of the hill. He stayed that way for a minute, then relaxed and slumped back to his original position. A minute later his head whipped around again, and this time he got to his feet. He took a couple of tentative steps upward before stopping again to listen intently. When he started moving again, one step at a time, he was headed for the grove of trees.

"Let's go," I said.

Byron was focused on whatever was up above him. Lou was doing a great job of distraction, never showing himself but making sure his presence was apparent. He was having a great time, I was sure.

We made it halfway to Byron's spot on the hill before he sensed something wrong and turned to face us. Immediately he started chanting an incantation, combining it with grand, sweeping arm gestures. I knew what was coming. Sure enough, the giant tiger to our right stirred, yawned, and rose creakily to its feet. The paint had worn off its face and the plaster had chipped, distorting it. Where the plaster showed through, it glimmered a ghostly white.

Luckily, there was more than enough material around to draw on for several different types of defensive spells. I started quickly gathering energy, but it wasn't necessary. The tiger turned around twice like a dog settling down in a favorite spot, curled up, and immediately went to sleep. Either Byron was not the practitioner he thought he was, or the statue was a lot older than he'd counted on.

Jo didn't pay the tiger the slightest attention. Maybe she was confident I would take care of it, or maybe she instantly realized it was no threat. She scrambled up toward Byron while he was occupied with his spell working, and before he knew it, she was right up on him.

From thirty feet away, I could feel the power Jo was pouring into him. She had gotten close enough to kiss him, using raw power to keep him immobile. It was taking a lot out of her and she wouldn't be able to keep it up much longer. I sprinted up the slope toward them.

"I can't hold him this way for long," she said, gasping for breath.

She was so zoned in that she also didn't hear the quick volley of high-pitched barks coming from up the hill, but I did. They were Lou's warning barks. I looked up just in time to see a rock the size of a cantaloupe come hurtling down the slope directly toward us.

There was no time to yell a warning, only time enough to wrap my arms around Jo and fling us both to the ground, our momentum carrying us down the slope, slipping and rolling. The rock had just brushed the side of her head as we fell, but it struck Byron full on.

As we scrambled to our feet I looked up the slope, fearing another rock. At the very top of the ridge stood another figure. In the moonlight I couldn't make out his face, but his stance was familiar. I had no doubt as to who it was.

"Rolando," I said, pointing up the hill. Jo stood there, speechless.

It was pretty clever of him, an inventive use of talent. No fancy spells, no power blasts. Just a small boulder speeding down the hill, talent directing it precisely on target. It was something he'd always refused to do in his soccer-playing days, but he had no qualms about using his talent now to kill Byron. He was just lucky it hadn't killed Jo as well.

No more stones hurtled down. Rolando slipped off the ridge top and disappeared into the darkness. We made our way back up to where Byron had fallen. The faint hope that he might have survived evaporated the moment I bent down to look at him.

His face was unmarked. He must have turned his head away at the last second. But the back of his skull was caved in and bits of bone fragments were peeking through his hair. Ironic, indeed. He wasn't breathing. There would be no healing for him, any more than there had been for Montague.

Jo sat down next to him and cradled his head in her lap. I walked a short distance away; it was such a personal moment that I felt like a voyeur just looking at them. In the moonlight her face was pale and drawn, like one of the walking dead. She held him without moving, not stroking his hair or touching his face. She just sat there.

"He wasn't altogether a bad guy," she said, but that was all.

I took the Buck knife from my pocket and unlocked the blade. It seemed ghoulish, but I had to know. I crouched next to them and lay the flat of the blade across Byron's face. In the dark of the hillside it glowed its spectral accusation.

"You see?" Jo said sadly.

I saw, but I didn't see. What did it mean? A false positive? Could Byron and Rolando have been working together for some unfathomable reason? How could blood from both of them have ended up on Willy's teeth? Had Rolando killed him out of obsession, or conviction? Or just to silence him? Again, too many unanswered questions.

Going through Byron's pockets was an unpleasant necessity. It's not that I'm squeamish; I'm not. At least not physically—blood and gore are unpleasant but never have particularly grossed me out. Emotionally I'm a wimp, though. Going through the pockets of a dead man reinforces the reality of death and makes mortality painfully apparent.

Still, I'd hate to pass up the opportunity to find a convenient confession, signed in blood and notarized, detailing every motive and wrapping up every loose end. I got Jo away from the body and rolled it over. The right front pocket was empty, but the left was not. No confession, but something damning in its own way. Three smooth green stones, just like the one that had been in Sarah's hand. These stones were not inert and dead, though. They pulsed with their own sort of life.

I held them out, showing Jo. She looked at them blankly, without interest.

"Are these like the stones you saw in his safe?" I asked.

"Pretty much," she said. "I only got a glimpse of them."

Lou had worked his way down the hill from his vantage

on the ridge top, totally unfazed by the night's events. Sometimes I think he believes everything I do is a game, as long as it doesn't affect him, or me.

"We should go," I said.

On the way back Jo sat hunched in the passenger seat with arms clasped around drawn-up knees. I didn't think it was safe for her to go back to her apartment with an unstable Rolando still wandering around, so I suggested she stay with me. She would have none of it, which sadly was a bit of a relief.

"Don't worry," she said. "I can take care of myself. I always have."

"What if Rolando comes back?"

She shrugged. "What if he does?"

When we got back to her apartment I walked her right up to her door, just to be sure no unpleasant surprises were waiting. She told me again she could take care of herself and got annoyed when I insisted, but I didn't care.

By the time I got home, I was yawning uncontrollably despite the still-surging adrenaline. It hadn't been a good night. Any night that ends with death is not a good night, no matter who it is that dies. And it wasn't over yet. I still had to call Victor and Eli with the news about Byron. Not only that, we still had to find Rolando. I didn't understand why he had run off.

I spent almost an hour on the phone with Victor, and almost as long with Eli before I could finally crash. They didn't have any better ideas about it than I did. But at least the main thing was finally settled. It really had been Byron all along, stripping practitioners of their minds. So why didn't it feel settled?

EIGHTEEN

THE NEXT DAY'S PAPER HAD A SMALL ARTICLE ON the discovery of the body of an unknown male at the city dump. Police were following several leads, it said. I hoped that was just the usual PR stuff. All I needed was to have the cops come knocking at my door.

For the next week nothing more happened. Except that Campbell returned. She had taken the news of Montague's death hard. There isn't any other way to take something like that. She couldn't bear to stay at the cabin alone, so we ended up taking a road trip to the Baja desert. We camped out, and the weather was mild in the day but cold and crisp at night. Each evening when the sun went down we built a fire and sat by it, sometimes talking, sometimes just staring into the flames.

During the daytime we mostly hiked, examining the plant life and the occasional small, scurrying lizards that crossed our path. The healing power of nature is a cliché, but it doesn't mean it's not real.

Lou scampered around, having so much fun it was infectious. He has his goofy side, and it was on full display.

He's a very clever creature, though I've never thought of him as wise. But he knew what he was doing; his antics eased Campbell's pain more effectively than anything I could do. At night, he curled up between us, wedging himself into the curve of her body and reaching out a paw to me, trying to make us into his own small pack.

"Sometimes bad things can tear people apart," she'd told me. But sometimes bad things can bond them together as well. We became close, a lot closer in fact than when we'd actually been together. More than friends, more than just exes, we leaned on each other without trying. It had nothing to do with sex; sex would have been unthinkable under the circumstances. But it was something. By the time we returned, Campbell had started to make peace with what had happened. She wasn't all right, not by a long shot, but she would be.

When I got back it was still quiet. No mindless practitioners wandering aimlessly. No mythical archetypes walking the streets. No death, no destruction. Most of all, no sign of Rolando.

Jo had been spending all her time tracking down leads, but nothing. He might as well have vanished from the earth. I had a vague suspicion that she might secretly know where he was, but when I pressed her she got angry and we didn't talk for a couple of days.

She seemed depressed and talked about going back to Portland as soon as she found him. At the same time she actually looked better, healthier and stronger than anytime since that first moment I'd seen her outside of Victor's house. I tried to talk with her about my feeling that something was off-kilter, but she didn't want to listen. Understandably, she was focused only on finding her brother.

I knew I should turn over the stones to Eli, but I didn't. They held a fascination and I was loath to give them up, or even mention that I had them. Not yet, anyway. Lou didn't like me handling them, so I put them away in the bottom of a trunk. I had a feeling I might need them someday.

I mentioned to Eli that I still had some questions, but he was less than encouraging. He wanted things to be over, so for him they were. He admitted a lot of things still didn't quite add up, but it didn't affect him.

"Life isn't a mystery novel," he said. "Things don't always get tied up in a neat package."

"And that doesn't bother you?"

"Of course it does, but what's important is that it's over now. No more practitioners have been attacked. No one else has died."

"And where's Rolando? Why did the blade glow for him? And why has he vanished?"

"I warned you about false positives," he said. "Other than that, I don't know. Sooner or later he'll show up and we'll find out, but until then, there's nothing much we can do."

Victor was less inclined to let it slide. He has his obsessive side, more than I do, but he also admitted there wasn't anywhere to go.

I felt ambivalent. On the one hand, I was more than happy to have things back to normal. On the other, I couldn't shake the feeling I was missing something important.

I was also rapidly heading into a blue funk. Then, to make things worse, Bernie Makoff, the trumpet player from Philly, called and told me he was canceling his trip out west, so the gig was off. That was a drag, since I'd been counting on the money. Name players command some real cash, and it would have paid my rent for a month.

So when Willis Thompson called with a fill-in gig, I jumped at the offer. Not that it was a real gig, and the pay was pitiful. It was at a small club in the Mission, Julio's, where the band splits the door take. That's normal, but it was a very small club with a very small cover charge. If we packed the place, we might take home fifty dollars each.

But that wasn't the point. Julio's is my favorite place to play, and Willis is one of my favorite guys to play with. We'd done a lot of these gigs over the years, and they were so much fun I'd have played for a couple of tacos. It was always casual, and not always straight-ahead jazz. We played anything and everything.

Willis is a guitar player, which made the lineup unusual—two guitars, bass, and drums. Standard for a rock band, but you don't often see it in jazz. But we played a lot of funk originals by Willis, some high-energy blues, a couple of jazz/reggae numbers, and whatever else popped into our heads.

"Who else have you got lined up?" I asked.

"Dave Green, of course." Dave was the bass player Willis used most of the time. "And a new guy on drums, Roger Chu. Dude, wait till you hear him. He's sick."

"Can't wait," I said.

This was going to be fun. Of the two of us, I'm the more technically skilled player, but music isn't just about technique. Willis always burns up the room. Whatever he plays, the man simply grooves like mad. When he plays rhythm, anything you play on top of it sounds great, even if it isn't.

As an extra bonus, the owner of Julio's was an old friend, Maria. Lou was always welcome there, even if the health department said he wasn't. Quiet days or not, I wanted to keep him close by.

I called Eli to see if he wanted to take a break for the evening and hear some music.

"Absolutely," he said. "I have a date, sort of, and I was looking for something to do."

He announced this in a matter-of-fact fashion, but it was big news. Eli hadn't been on a date in a year, as far as I knew.

"Anyone I know?" I asked casually.

"No, I don't think so. Just an old friend. More a friend of Margaret's really."

More big news. Margaret was his late wife, and he seldom, if ever, mentioned her name. She had died years before I'd ever met him, and I never did find out the story. Eli's not one to share confidences, even if you've known him twenty years.

"Well, great," I said. "I'll see you at Julio's. We start about nine."

I picked up the phone to call Jo. Then I put it back down. I didn't want to see her, at least not tonight. Tonight was about old friends, and music, and the part of my life that didn't include monsters and psychos and trouble every day.

I was at Julio's by eight, enough time to catch up with the regulars I hadn't seen for a while and to indulge in a beer. Of course I have that no-drinking-at-gigs rule, but I seem to have abandoned that lately. And an added perk of a casual at Julio's is that nobody cares if you make mistakes. It's more like a party than a gig. Lou slipped in with me, staying close so that no one would step on a paw, then ducked behind the bar where it was safer.

The girl tending bar knew him well. She was no more than twenty-two, with short black hair, tats, and everything else necessary to make a good living on tips alone. Everyone knows her as Jenny P, although her real name is something else entirely. Practitioners aren't the only ones who use pseudonyms, but she actually had reason. Women who work in bars have to be careful, and those who aren't learn in very short order to be so. Jenny P thought Lou was just too cute to live. She'd probably put a pound on him before the end of the night with Slim Jims alone.

Willis showed up twenty minutes later. Willis shaves his head, wears tacky, fake-gold bling, works out daily, is a black belt in Tae Kwon Do, and speaks almost exclusively in a faux hipster slang of his own invention. As you might expect, he's a dorky white guy trying to look black, but he can certainly play.

"Mason! Dude," he greeted me.

"Dude," I said. What other response is there?

"You ready to burn tonight? You ready to *smoke*?"

"Always."

Willis spotted Jenny P, who was wearing a particularly tight top this evening. As usual, he temporarily forgot I existed.

Eli strolled in a few minutes later with his date, or whatever she was, in tow. The bar was getting busy, and with his bulk it's not easy for him to edge his way through a crowd. He usually just pushes his way gently through like an irresistible force, but I think he was trying to be more gentlemanly with a woman at his side. I took pity on him, slid through the crush of bodies, and led him and his friend upstairs.

One of the neat things about Julio's is the small loft room that overlooks the stage. Julio's has a long bar and a separate room on the side for the stage, but it also has the loft. It's like a giant balcony where patrons can look down at the musicians below from behind a curved brass rail. Old movie posters are plastered on most of the walls and behind the stage. Bogie and Bacall stare out at you in their timeless fashion while Godzilla creates mayhem behind you and the Three Stooges create an entirely different type of mayhem on the far wall.

A front table was still open next to the rail. Eli looked dubiously at the tiny chairs before lowering himself gingerly onto one. It squeaked in protest, but held. As long as he didn't shift his weight too often, it should be fine.

"Mason, this is Eleanor," he said as he settled himself in the chair. She smiled up at me.

"I've heard quite a bit about you," she said. That put me at a disadvantage, since I'd never heard so much as a word about her. I used a standard small-talk line in response.

"Nothing good, I hope."

"Nothing but good, sweetie."

Eleanor was in her forties, I'd guess, a couple shades darker than Eli and heavyset, but in that powerful sexy way that only black women seem to be able to pull off. I suppose that's sort of a racist thing to say, but it's true. An open, friendly smile lit up her face, but I could sense a "Don't mess with me" right behind her eyes. A slight head cock, a "Say what?" and all opposition would crumble.

Her hair just brushed the tops of her shoulders, and sparkly rings adorned several fingers, but that's not what drew the eye. Artificial nails, bloodred, grabbed the attention. And they were long. I don't mean just long; I mean *long*, like six inches and curved into complex curlicues. She caught me staring at them and her smile broadened.

"You're not a guitar player, I'm guessing," I said. I could hardly pretend I hadn't been staring.

"No, but you'd be surprised what I can do with these," she said, waggling them suggestively.

Eli shifted nervously in his seat, making the chair groan. It was the perfect opening to give him grief, but I knew if I did, I'd never meet another of his lady friends as long as I lived.

I avoided answering by gesturing down at the stage, where Willis and Dave were setting up for the sound check. The drummer hadn't put in an appearance yet, but a young Asian kid about fourteen was opening cases and setting up the drum kit. Maybe the drummer's son, helping out.

"Sound-check time," I said.

I hauled my amp to the stage and set up in the corner, catching up with Dave about what gigs he'd been playing. Dave looks a lot like Willis, except Dave really is hip and really is black.

"So where's the drummer?" I asked him.

Dave flashed me a grin and pointed over at the Asian kid. "You're looking at him."

"You're putting me on. He's what, fourteen?"

"Seventeen. You're not going to believe him."

"Whatever you say."

I walked over and introduced myself. He mumbled something incomprehensible and stared down at the floor. Not great stage presence, but as long as he could keep time, I didn't care. He wandered back to his kit, sat down on his stool, and wrapped a red bandanna around his head. Now he looked like a teenage video gamer trying to pretend he was a ninja.

Willis started out with one of his funk numbers, a two-chord riff with a hook in between, and a bridge of descending altered chords to give it some legitimacy with actual jazz buffs.

I laid out until Dave came in, along with the drums. The little drummer boy was playing a steady, if unimaginative beat. If he was supposed to be some wunderkind, I didn't see it. We got an easy groove going and I looked over at Dave and raised my eyebrows. He looked back and shrugged.

I started running a solo, and the drummer threw out some interesting polyrhythms without losing the basic groove. Maybe he was better than I'd thought. As I stretched out he followed me effortlessly, picking up the energy without changing the tempo. Pretty soon the drumsticks were exploding off the heads with a mix of rhythms and sounds endlessly changing, never losing the groove for an instant. This was the second time I'd been caught by surprise by a drummer. But where Megan from the Dagger Dykes was good, far better than average for a rock band, this kid was in another world. For one of the few times in my life, I found myself intimidated by another player. I got a grip on myself and concentrated on keeping up. Willis and I traded riffs, then came the drum solo.

Most drum solos are an exercise in self-indulgence. The crowd may whoop and holler, but for the most part drum solos suck. An old musician joke: How is a drum solo like a sneeze? You know it's coming, but there's nothing you can do about it.

Only this was something else entirely. He started out by hitting one stick on the rim of the snare drum, just a simple beat. Then the other, with a tricky rhythm. Then, what sounded like a third stick, though that was obviously not possible. Bass drum, tom, high hat, cymbals, all came in smooth as butter and strong as heavy metal. I wondered for a second if he might not be some kind of mutant practitioner who didn't even know he had talent of a different kind. By the end of the solo, I was leaning against the side of my amp, just listening like any other audience member. I had to jump in quickly to not miss the beat.

We played a few more tunes, one after another, with no pause. Willis would start us off with a new tune before the sound of the last one had faded out. I relaxed, and stopped thinking about the drummer, or anything else for that matter. I just played.

After an hour that seemed like ten minutes, Willis signaled a break. I wiped down my guitar and turned to the drummer.

"Great stuff," I said. "Where have you been playing?"

He gave me a shy smile, muttered something incomprehensible once again, and stared down at the floor. As I headed back to the bar for another beer, I passed by Dave, who was now openly smirking.

"I don't think he speaks much English," Dave said.

"Oh. Where's he from?"

"Taiwan, Willis says."

"Taiwan? With a name like Roger?"

"Hmm. I never thought of that. Maybe he's really from Fresno, and he's putting us all on."

"After hearing him play, nothing would surprise me," I said. "So what's your theory? I vote for a deal with the dark lord, Satan."

"Nah. Reincarnation."

"Of who? How long has Tony Williams been gone?"

"Not long enough to qualify. 1997, I think. I'll let you know when I come up with the answer."

A clear spot had opened at the end of the bar, mostly since a crush of customers had gathered at the other end. Lou, of course. He'd found his way to the back bar and wedged himself between fifths of Johnny Walker Red and Jack Daniels. From there, he surveyed the bar scene with regal elegance. Occasionally he'd stand up on his hind legs and bark until someone threw him a piece of beef jerky. All the women had migrated over toward his position and the men had naturally followed.

I finally managed to snag an Anchor Steam and joined Eli at his upstairs table. Eleanor greeted me with enthusiasm.

"I loved your playing," she said. "Eli said you were good, but I had no idea. But, honey, I got to ask. Who *is* that drummer?"

"Spawn of the devil," I muttered. Eli sputtered as some beer went down the wrong way.

"Mason is always wholly supportive of his fellow musicians," he said.

I took a long swig from my Anchor Steam. "They just keep getting better and better," I complained. "And younger and younger. Thank God I'm not trying to break in these days."

We chatted awhile about music, and young people, and the state of the world, but not about practitioners. After a lull in the conversation, Eleanor put her hand on my shoulder. Her curved nails rested there like a giant brooch.

"Eli says you all have been going through some rough times," she said.

I looked at Eli for guidance. Eleanor was certainly no practitioner, and Eli doesn't make a habit of discussing supernatural happenings with ordinary people.

"I told Eleanor what's been going on," he said. "I've known her for a long time, longer than I've known you, actually. She's a smart lady." She beamed at him, and I swear he'd have blushed if he were physically capable of it. "Sometimes it helps to get a different perspective," he continued. "Occasionally one can be so close to things that it's difficult to see what's obvious to an outsider."

He was probably right, but I didn't feel like unburdening myself to a virtual stranger, no matter how well Eli knew her. I didn't want to be rude, though, so I spoke in generalities.

"Well," I said, "it's true. I have been a bit frazzled lately. I keep thinking I'm missing something. If I could find the missing piece of the puzzle, it would all make sense, I'm sure."

"Maybe there is no missing piece," she said.

"What do you mean?"

"Do you ever do crossword puzzles?"

"Not very often. I'm not smart enough."

"Yes, I'm sure. Well, I do them all the time. And sometimes I get down to just one corner, just a few letters missing, but I just can't solve it."

"That certainly sounds familiar," I said.

"I go over it and over it, but nothing quite fits. And finally, I realize what's wrong."

"You've never heard of the words?"

"No, that's not it. What's happened is that one of the words I thought was right turns out to be wrong. It's 'taffy,' not 'catty'."

I considered it. "What kind of clue could be either 'taffy' or 'catty'?" I asked.

"All right then, 'ponds,' not 'pools.' That's not the point. The point is that my original assumption is wrong. As soon as I realize that, everything else falls into place."

"Yeah, but I haven't made any assumptions."

"Sugar, we all make assumptions. We just have to discover what they are."

It was time for the second set, so I went back onstage and made sure my strings were still in tune. What Eleanor had said was true, but I didn't see how it helped me any. If I knew which assumptions were wrong, they wouldn't be assumptions, would they?

Willis handed me a new chart, something he'd just come up with. Like most of his charts, it was handwritten and mostly illegible, but the chords seemed simple enough. Until we got to the bridge. It was another up-tempo tune, more straight-ahead jazz this time, and I'd read B-flat where he had written E-flat and then confused another flat for a thirteenth. Then logically, a G for a C. Before I knew it, I was lost. What I was playing was nifty indeed, but it bore little relation to what the other players were doing.

I abandoned the chart and tried to get a handle on the tune by ear. Dave had been through this before since Willis is notorious for springing his illegible charts on players, so he helped me out by playing a simplified line, hitting the one on each chord change until I got back on board.

I nodded my thanks to him and got back into the groove. I saw a couple of puzzled faces in the audience, but most people hadn't even noticed, or if they had, thought I was just playing some far-out experimental stuff. There are no wrong notes in jazz, I reminded myself. Just interesting ones. That's what all jazz players say when they screw up.

We played a long set, ending up with an extended jam that had people dancing in the narrow spaces between the tables. But I wasn't enjoying myself as much as I should have been. That first tune, the one I'd screwed up, kept bothering me. Not that I'd screwed up; I do that all the time. But it reinforced what Eleanor had said about wrong assumptions. I'd read a chord wrong, and everything that followed after that one mistake made no sense, at least not from a musical standpoint. It wasn't until I dropped the chart on the floor and started to listen that I got back in sync.

After a while, though, I forgot all about it. The drummer kid kept pumping out energy, and Dave was rock solid on bass, as always. Willis was prancing around the little stage like a madman, and it was impossible not to get caught up in his infectious joy. For the first time in months I was just playing; not thinking, not happy, not sad, just playing with the energy of the music sweeping through me, riding the crest. Meditation has nothing on a good set of music for living in the moment.

And that's when it came to me, unbidden. I realized which clue in the crossword I'd got wrong. One simple readjustment in assumptions and everything suddenly made perfect sense. I didn't have time to consider the implications since I was in the middle of a solo, though. The music took over and I stopped thinking until the end of the set.

After we finished the set, Willis was wound up and hopping around like a frog on meth. Dave was happy but tired, just anxious to get back to Oakland and his family. Our drummer started breaking down his kit, expressionless, but every once in a while he'd make a sort of machine-gun ack-ack noise in the back of his throat, so I guessed he was stoked, too.

I got my third beer of the evening and rejoined the upstairs table. It was less crowded now, easier to talk. The two of them had pushed their chairs closer together, and I don't think it was because of the noise.

"I've been thinking about what Eleanor had to say," I said. Eli, a bit tipsy, nodded gravely. He'd loosened up considerably from his usual professorial image and even had both elbows on the table.

"A very wise decision," he said, enunciating too clearly. "I can attest to that."

"I've been a little slow of late."

"It happens."

Eleanor unexpectedly weighed in. "Congratulations, hon. You look like you've finally solved your crossword."

"Maybe," I said. "I'm not sure."

But I was sure, or at least my gut told me I had the answer. That gut feeling is almost always right, but there was that word again. Almost. And almost wasn't good enough, not for something like this.

The conversation lagged after that, so we all left soon after. Lou waddled out from behind the bar, looking satisfied for once. I hoped he wouldn't throw up in the middle of the night. It wouldn't be the first time.

NINETEEN

I DIDN'T GET A CHANCE TO COME UP WITH A PLAN to test my idea. At eight, the inevitable ringing of the telephone woke me after no more than five hours' sleep. Lou gave a huge sigh of exasperation and burrowed more deeply into the covers. He is even more jealous of his sleep time than I am.

I staggered out of bed, hoping for the first time in my life that it was a telemarketer, but no such luck. Jo.

"Mason, it's Jo. Did I wake you?" I bit back a sarcastic reply.

"That's okay," I said. "I'm awake now." I stifled a yawn. "What's up?"

"I still can't find Rolando anywhere." This was not news that warranted an early-morning call.

"Okay," I said.

"But I have an idea. I thought maybe you could help."

"Me? I would, but I'm not very good at finding people. Mostly I rely on Lou for that."

"I understand. And I know he can't find someone who's

shielding, but what about finding an object? Or can he only find people, not things?"

I looked over to where Lou was gently snoring under the covers. It was sometimes hard to believe he could find anything but breakfast.

"I'm not sure," I said. "I guess he might be able to find an object. I expect it would depend on what the object was and what kind of connection he had with it."

"It's a bracelet, a chain, actually. It's an heirloom of sorts, handed down to me and Ro when we were kids. We used to fight over it all the time until one day we managed to break it in half. Ever since, we've both carried our own half of it as kind of a bond between us."

I remembered the matching bracelets I'd first noticed them wearing at Goldie's.

"Now that's a different matter," I said. "Two pieces of an object that were once whole, connected to both of you? I'd think you could find the other half yourself without any help—that's a pretty basic use of talent."

"You'd think, but the piece I have is too much connected to me. Whatever I try, it just leads back to me."

"What about Victor, then? He's good at that kind of thing."

"I'm sure he is, but I don't want to get him involved. You know Victor—once we found Rolando, he'd be questioning and debriefing him for weeks. It's messy enough already. I just want to find Rolando, forget about all this, and get both of us the hell out of here."

I wouldn't mind finding Rolando myself. "Okay," I said. "Bring it over and we'll see what Lou can do."

I knew if I lay back down for even a minute, I'd fall back asleep, so I staggered over to the coffeemaker and started it up. The smell of brewing coffee is a signal that breakfast is in the offing, but Lou never stirred. He has his priorities and right now getting a little extra sleep was number one.

A quick bathroom visit and coffee was ready. I wasn't hungry, but made some toast so I'd at least have something

in my stomach. I reached abstractedly for a morning cigarette before I remembered I hadn't smoked for years.

Eventually Lou pushed his way out from under the covers. He yawned several times and came over to see what
was on the breakfast menu. He turned up his nose at prof-
fered kibble and ducked out back through the dog door.

"Don't go far," I yelled after him. "We've got things to
do today."

By the time Jo arrived, he was back, licking his lips. I assumed he'd cadged a better breakfast from some softhearted
neighbor convinced that Lou was being maltreated at home. I
hoped that was the case. He might also have found some
week-old pizza in a Dumpster.

Jo sat down and accepted a morning cup of coffee. Her
eyes were fresh and alert, her face youthful again. She was
wearing the same clothes as the very first time I'd seen her:
jeans, dark top, and a light jacket.

She reached into her jacket pocket, pulled out a silver
chain, and dropped it onto the table. It was old and heavy
and slightly tarnished. One side was flat, the other raised
with a delicate filigree pattern, an organic motif that mim-
icked leaves or grass. I called Lou over, who looked at it
without much interest.

"Pay attention," I said. "This is important. We need to
find—"

I broke off because he was no longer listening, and two
seconds later he was no longer in the room. He'd spotted
the neighbor cat using the backyard as a shortcut, something which was simply not allowed. It saw him coming as
he barreled through the dog door, and it took off streaking
across the yard and over the fence.

"Goddamn it!" I yelled. "Get back here!"

He ignored me until he was sure the cat was gone, then
came trotting back as if nothing had happened. I was
embarrassed. Here he was, an Ifrit of supposed extraordinary ability, acting like an everyday dog, and not a well-
trained one, either.

"Sorry," I said to Jo. "He sometimes forgets he's not a dog." She gave me a bright smile.

Lou sat down next to me and looked up at the chain, now with apparent great interest. He knew he had the upper hand because I needed him for something. I decided to follow his lead and pretend the interruption had never occurred. I held out the chain and started over.

"This is only part of the chain," I said. "We need to find the other half. Can you do it? Can you find?"

He sniffed delicately at the chain, then circled the room deliberately, stopping for a moment as he faced each direction. Finally, he came back to his original spot and sat down again.

"No go," I said. "Either he can't do it, or the other half of the chain is too far from here to get a reading on."

"What if he were closer? Would that work?"

"It might. That's the way he operates when he's tracking people."

"Can we try it?"

"It might take a while," I said, "but we could. We could circle the city, and then crisscross it if we didn't come up with anything."

She stood up from the table and looked expectantly at me.

"What, now?" I said. When she didn't say anything, I sighed and signaled to Lou. At least this time it was light out. I was sick and tired of all those late-night sorties.

I drove out 280 and John Daly until we reached the Great Highway, the road that runs along the edge of the ocean, right at the city limits to the west. We headed north, driving slowly, paralleling Ocean Beach. Lou stuck his head out of the open passenger window, questing, and chill air rushed into the van, making me wish I'd brought a heavier coat.

Jo was clearly wishing the same thing, shivering slightly. We passed within a stone's throw of Victor's house, and I had a momentary urge to just pull in and dump the whole mess on him. He was the the one who'd brought them here in the first place.

Lou, meanwhile, hadn't given a sign of anything. When we reached the place where the road turns east, up by the Cliff House, he tensed for a second, then relaxed. Then, a hundred yards farther on, right by the lot where we had parked on the night of our Cliff House date, he abruptly barked twice and pulled his head back into the van.

I pulled into the lot and opened the door. Lou jumped out and ran to the edge of the lot where it looks out over the Pacific. Jo and I walked over to the edge. Gray clouds, almost low enough to be fog, hovered over the gray water. The cold sea wind ruffled our hair and chilled us both. Jo slipped an arm around my waist and leaned into me for warmth and comfort. I felt uncomfortable with it, but tried not to let it show.

Two women, laughing, arms linked, passed us on the way to the Land's End Trail. They looked over at us and smiled. To them, we were just another couple, standing at a romantic spot by the ocean with our faithful little dog. If only life were that simple.

"What is all that?" asked Jo, peering down at the concrete ruins below us.

"The Sutro Baths. What's left of them. They were built around the turn of the century—not this last one, the nineteen hundreds one. Saltwater pools to bathe in, a giant enclosed space with rides and attractions, all kinds of stuff. It was a big draw in its time." I waved my hand toward the ruined pools, filled with filthy water and surrounded by low, broken concrete walls. "This is all that's left of it."

"You think Rolando's down there somewhere?"

"Well, Lou seems to think so. Or at least, the chain is."

She scanned the scene of rocks and crumbling foundations below us. The slope leading down to the baths is gentle and usually there are at least a few tourists wandering around with cameras and camcorders. Today, the dank cold seemed to have discouraged them. Only one figure was visible, a black man sitting by the largest pool, playing a saxophone. He was running scales, one after another, channeling Sonny

Rollins playing on the bridge. Or maybe he'd been driven out of his apartment by angry neighbors.

"I don't see anyone," Jo said.

"There are tunnels in the rock, down by the water," I told her. "He could be anywhere, out of sight. If he's here."

She pulled her arm from around my waist and took a step back.

"Maybe you'd better stay up here. Rolando wouldn't do anything to me, but he might freak out if he sees you."

That's what she said, but she didn't mean it. She knew I wouldn't let her go down there alone.

"Not a chance," I said. "Let's go." I started off down the slope, leaving her to follow.

Lou passed by the pools of stagnant water without so much as a glance. It looked like he was headed for the large tunnel that was cut into the rock at the base of the ruins. It seemed appropriate. That tunnel is the subject of all kinds of ghostly urban legends.

Before he got as far as the beach, he stopped. In front of him was a tunnel opening, all right, but it wasn't the one I knew about. I've spent a lot of time in the area and I would have sworn no such opening existed. Lou sat down in front of it, showing no inclination to enter.

"Is this it?" said Jo, coming up to stand beside me.

"Looks like."

"I don't like the looks of it."

I didn't, either, but for different reasons. I pointed down at Lou.

"He doesn't, either."

"What should we do?"

"It's up to you," I said. "We either go in or go home."

The opening led back into the cliff, widening out into more of a cave than a tunnel. I could see only about thirty feet in before a bend in the passageway hid the rest. I thought I heard a faint scratching noise from somewhere inside, and Lou's ears pricked, confirming it.

Jo nodded, face grim, and abruptly walked into the tunnel

before I could say another word. I followed, liking this development even less. Lou pushed his way ahead of us both, though I noticed his tail was down.

The floor of the tunnel was damp and sandy. The cave probably filled with seawater every high tide. If there even was a cave present then. I wasn't sure this feature of the landscape was a permanent one.

The passage narrowed again when we hit the bend, and almost immediately it divided. Lou took the left fork without hesitation. Fifty feet later, another fork. An underground maze, just what I'd been hoping for. Lou hesitated a fraction, then took the left fork again. The sand grew thicker and scrunched under our feet. Small openings in the roof let in the daylight, but as we continued, the path angled down and the roof grew higher.

So far it was deserted. I was on edge, and when Lou suddenly pounced on something by the tunnel wall, I jumped three feet myself. I thought he'd caught a rat or some other small creature, but what he brought back was something very different. It was a long segment of a familiar silver chain. He dropped it at my feet and stood there, tail wagging, rather proud of himself.

He had a right to be; it was quite a feat. But it didn't help us any. If Rolando was nearby, he was keeping a mighty low profile. Jo bent down and picked it up. She pulled out the other half from a pocket and compared the two, as if there might be some mistake.

"Let's get out of here," I said. "Before we find more than we can handle."

"But the chain," she said. "Ro would never throw it away. I think he might be in trouble."

I wasn't so sure it was Rolando who was in trouble. More likely it was me.

"Just come on," I said.

We trudged back, Lou leading the way. I couldn't wait to get out of there, but Jo kept lagging behind, peering down each offshoot of the tunnel as if she expected to find

Rolando lounging on a lawn chair, smoking a cigarette. I called to her once, asking her to hurry up, but I didn't like the way my voice echoed in the damp air.

I finally stopped, waiting for her to catch up. She was staring intently down one of the side branches and put up a hand to alert me to something. She took a couple of steps into the passage off the main tunnel, and then, with a sudden jerk, disappeared from sight. I ran toward the opening, but by the time I got there she was gone.

I hesitated for just a fraction, fearing a ploy, then plunged down the passageway. I couldn't take the chance I was wrong. The passage twisted and turned, smelling faintly of fish and seaweed, but finally reached a point where it ran straight for a hundred feet or so, and I stopped to get my bearings. Lou, unaccountably, seemed confused as well. He took a couple of steps forward, then backed up rapidly, uttering a low growl.

I could see nothing in front of us but the rock walls of the tunnel stretching ahead, but that didn't mean nothing was there. It only meant Lou's senses were sharper than mine. I started backtracking slowly, keeping my focus ahead, glancing behind me only often enough to keep from tripping over my own feet.

How do I get myself into such situations? Lost underground, in a tunnel system that might or might not be entirely real, unknown dangers ahead of me, Josephine somewhere up ahead, and absolutely no idea what was going on. It was like the old joke: just lucky, I guess.

We eventually ended up in a large chamber with a larger-than-usual opening near the top of the roof. I felt uneasy, not just because of the situation, but more in a physical sense, the way one does right before a thunderstorm breaks. Uncontrolled energy coursed all around, in the walls, in the floor, in the very air, a wild pulse of unfocused talent.

I'd never felt anything like that before, and it wasn't a good feeling. My skin felt like it was on fire. It was like sitting on a fifty-thousand-volt high-tension wire suspended in the air. It's not dangerous as long as you're not grounded, but you can feel the energy surge running through you, and if you should happen to brush up against something, well, that's that.

It wasn't good from a practical standpoint, either. I couldn't send out a probe to check for magical dangers. The background energy would simply overwhelm it. It would be like listening for approaching footsteps while standing next to a waterfall.

Worse, I was effectively defenseless. Any use of talent would be impossible. You can't properly focus your energy when there's a hundred times as much surging uncontrollably through the air. I wanted to take a time-out, go back to Eli, and have him explain to me what was going on.

I must have been slightly dazed, because I wandered aimlessly for what seemed like forever. Lou was shaking. He wasn't afraid, or cold; the energy was affecting him even more than it was me. He seemed confused, and when a dim shape appeared at the far end of a chamber we entered, he didn't even notice.

Whatever was up ahead reeked of magical energy. It saw us standing there and froze, poised halfway between attack and flight. It was motionless, but it wasn't. I saw that same flickering strobe effect that I'd noticed with the bridge guy, except there was nothing remotely human about this thing. It was covered with sleek brown fur, like an otter or a seal, but its head had a vaguely equine cast. A second later, the hair was long and shaggy, and large canines protruded from its mouth. It briefly dropped to all fours, lifted its head, and made a shrill keening sound.

Almost immediately two other figures appeared. The first was short and squat, with powerful-looking arms and a grayish leathery hide. The second was tall and lithe, black furred and with the suggestion of a tail. His head was long, with a pointed snout and lots of sharp teeth.

I began to understand what I was dealing with. The bridge guy, the part troll, had told me about others who were further along the path than he was. There are lots of them, he'd said. The wild ones. These were the ones I'd run into in the fog at Stern Grove, or ones very like them. Those whose talent had eventually taken over completely, those who had become more animal than human. Those who no longer did magic; they *were* magic, so imbued with talent that it leaked out into their surroundings. The archetypes, the sources of human myth and legend. But what were they doing here? Ahh, the wild magic running through the rock. That was what had attracted them.

The squat guy seemed to be a gnome of some sort. The first one? Nothing I was familiar with, but I did remember something about selkies and kelpies and other Celtic folk-lore. And the tall guy with the sharp muzzle? Unless I was very much mistaken, I was looking at my first full-fledged werewolf.

Not an actual werewolf, of course. It had once been a human with talent, a practitioner. There is no such thing as a werewolf. But it was a damn good imitation, and it could rip my throat out just as easily as could the mythical beast.

The minute Lou saw it, the hair on the back of his neck stood up. He growled softly, only this time the growl sounded suspiciously like a whimper. Seeing the werewolf made me remember my wolf talisman. I hadn't even thought to use it up to now. I didn't know if there were any rules about its use, but I had a strong feeling that it was not to be employed except in the direst emergency. Otherwise, I might come to be known as the boy who cried wolf, liter-ally, and when the time came that I really needed it, there would be no answer.

I pulled it out, but as soon as I touched it I knew it wasn't going to work. When I'd used it before, it had been alive, humming and charged with energy. In fact, the very first time I'd used it, my hand got blistered from the sudden heat. Now it was inert, cold and dead, no more a magical object than is an old bottle cap.

While I'd been doing this, two of the figures had slipped

behind us, blocking any possible retreat. The werewolf blocked the tunnel in front of us. He paced back and forth, then suddenly came to a decision and bounded toward us as fast as any true wolf.

Lou showed a great deal of bravado, snarling and warning him to keep his distance, but he didn't try to close with it. The thing reached toward him, and as Lou skittered out of the way, the creature suddenly changed direction and leapt at me, catching me off guard. He grabbed my left arm, and his grip was strong enough to let me know I was in real trouble, not that I wasn't already aware of that. I had a sudden idea, a wild hope. I held up the wolf talisman in my other hand, showing it to him. Maybe it would spark some kind of reaction; maybe he would recognize me as part of the wolf clan.

Except, he wasn't a wolf, no matter what he looked like. He ignored it and took hold of my wrist. Now he had both my arms. I tried to slam my head into his face, but he was too quick for me and jerked his head out of the way.

Lou finally dove in, catching him right below his knee. He let go of my left hand, reached down, grabbed Lou by the scruff of the neck, and tossed him halfway across the cave. I jabbed at his eyes but missed low, cutting my fingers on sharp teeth. He seized my wrist again, bending my arm back. I tried for a knee to the groin, the old standard, but if he'd forgotten about being human, he hadn't forgotten his defensive moves. He turned his hips sideways, deflecting the blow. I was out of options.

His lips curled back, exposing sharp, pointed teeth, strong and white. I couldn't break his grip, but I did manage to pull my right arm down, partially protecting my throat. His mouth opened wider, and then, just before he lunged, he stopped. I felt a burning sensation on my arm. It was my tattoo, energized by the free-ranging talent in the room, glowing like a luminous watch dial. It throbbed and pulsed, distracting me even as I was fighting for my life.

But I wasn't the only one distracted. His gaze focused

on it and a dim comprehension filtered into his eyes. He let go of my arms and stepped back in confusion, unable to take his eyes off it, as if it called to him in some way.

He tried to speak, but only guttural sounds came out of his throat. A stricken expression passed over his face, as if he could hear himself and realized for just a moment what he'd become. I took advantage of his momentary distraction by balling my hand into a knife-hand fist, the only karate skill I know, and driving it viciously into his throat. He gagged, staggered back, and went down on one knee. I was past him in a flash, running full tilt down the tunnel ahead. Lou staggered after me, still dazed, but easily able to keep up.

I took random directions every time I came to a fork in the passageway, hoping to throw off the expected pursuit. Finally, when I couldn't run anymore, I stopped. Breathing hard, I listened for sounds of pursuit. I couldn't hear a thing except my rasping breath. So far, so good. Lou threw himself flat on the rock floor, still a little shaky.

"Good job," I told him. "You're a tiger."

I pushed on, wandering aimlessly again through the tunnels, unwilling to stay put. We still had to find Jo and get the hell out of these caves, but that wasn't going to be easy. The free-flowing magic made Lou's tracking skills as useless as my magic, and he was still too glassy-eyed to find anything even if the magic were to ease.

Then I noticed I was feeling better. My skin was no longer quite so sensitive, and Lou had perked up considerably. The feeling of electrical current was gone. The area of wild magic clearly didn't extend through the entire tunnel complex.

"Lou," I said, getting his attention. "Can you find Jo?"

He swung around and started back the way we'd come. Every time we reached a branch of the tunnel, he took one fork or another without hesitation. I recognized some of the rock formations we had passed on the way in. Lou wasn't taking me to Jo at all; he was leading me out of the tunnels.

"Hey!" I said. "Jo. We need to find Jo first."

He ignored me, and when I reached down to grab him, he scooted out of the way. A couple more quick turns and I saw the entrance, gray sky looming up behind it. Lou headed for it without hesitation. I was getting seriously pissed. I'd never seen him flat-out refuse me before.

He whipped around me, now standing between me and the tunnel complex, and started barking in anger and frustration. Perhaps I was still muzzy from the wild magic, because I'm usually not that slow. My dawning comprehension must have shown on my face, because Lou stopped his protest and started walking out again.

Of course Jo wasn't in the tunnels anymore. She had already left. When I got to the entrance I stopped and called her name, but I already knew there would be no answer.

I squatted down and absently wiped the blood off my hand from where it had been creased by the werewolf's teeth. I stared out at the waves slowly rolling up the empty beach. Now at least I was sure.

TWENTY

THINGS HAD FINALLY COME TOGETHER. IT HAD taken me long enough, but there was no longer any urgency. As far as Jo knew, I was dead, gone forever. Things were neatly wrapped up here for her, and she'd lay low until she finally left to resume her experiments in some other city. But there were still a lot of things I didn't understand, and I was going to find out if it killed me. Which, of course, was always a possibility.

I hadn't been home for more than fifteen minutes when the phone rang. I let the machine answer it, but as soon as I recognized the voice, I picked up.

"Mason! Why haven't you been by to visit? You have to see!" It was Sandra. I had no idea what she was talking about. She didn't give me the chance to reply, just barged ahead. "It worked. It actually worked, and you haven't even been by to see."

"See what?" I asked.

"Oh, come on. You know. It was your idea, after all."

"My idea about what?"

"Ifrits. What else? It worked and now I've got one again."

I got a sick feeling, a quick flash of things crawling out of the grave that were never meant to see the light of day.

"Moxie?"

"No, no. Of course not. Moxie's gone. This is a new Ifrit, just like you said it would be. Why haven't you been by to see?"

"I've been busy," I said, for want of anything better. "But I'm free now. I'll be over in half an hour."

I'd been feeling guilty about not checking in with Sandra anyway. I hadn't seen her for quite a while, hadn't bothered to make sure she was all right. I'd rationalized it by telling myself if she saw Lou after losing Moxie, it would only make her feel worse, but I knew that wasn't true. She loved Lou, and it would have been a comfort to her.

"Mason!" her familiar voice squealed as the door opened. Sandra came flying through the doorway onto the porch like a dust storm, long hair flying and beads trailing behind. She ran over to Lou and started thumping him like he was a stuffed toy dog. He took it good-naturedly; he'd always liked Sandra.

She had put on some weight, which was a good thing. The last time I'd seen her she could have been an after picture for an antimeth ad. She was bubbling over, happier than I'd seen her since Moxie disappeared.

"Hold on," I said, giving her a hug and lifting her off her feet. "What are you so excited about?"

"The Ifrit I made. It's not like Moxie—it's not even a dog." She began to giggle. "Mason, it's a *squirrel*. Of all things. I guess it fits, though."

I guessed it did. We went inside, where she kept bounding around much like a squirrel herself, chattering away and never pausing for an instant. I finally had to grab her and sit her down in a chair at the kitchen table.

"Okay, take it easy," I said. "First of all, what do you mean you made an Ifrit? And how would I have known about it?"

"Because you sent that woman over. Josephine? She said you had some theory and I was the perfect person to try it out." She picked up on my puzzled look quickly. It's not always a good thing when someone knows you well. "You did send her, didn't you? She asked me not to mention it to you, that she was going to surprise you."

She'd succeeded there. But I didn't think this was going to be the good kind of surprise. I didn't want Sandra to think anything was wrong, so I kept quiet. She was just too ecstatic for me to put a damper on things.

"Oh, yeah, Josephine," I said, easily. "That's right. I did tell her about you, come to think of it. I just didn't expect she was going to get hold of you quite so soon."

"Well, I'm glad she did. It worked! I have an Ifrit again! Let me find Roscoe. Oh, and look, look. My latest painting. Tell me what you think."

She was out the back door and down the steps into her garden before I had a chance to answer, leaving me alone with a painting propped against the far wall of the kitchen. It was huge, easily six feet high and wider than it was tall. An outdoor scene, woods, with a late-autumn sky glowing behind a brook that was just breaking through a cover of melting snow.

In the foreground stood a young woman, naked except for a pair of tennis shoes, obviously a younger version of Sandra. Her head was turned slightly to one side, with a pensive look. I couldn't tell if it was meant to be innocent or erotic. Maybe both.

At first it seemed like a giant photograph, hyperrealistic, but closer up I could see the swirl of brushstrokes and blurred color bleeding into the canvas. Sandra had always been a talented artist, but this was a quantum leap beyond anything she had ever done. I wondered if it had anything to do with the Ifrit she had apparently called up.

When she returned, bounding up the back stairs, a large red squirrel was riding on her left shoulder. Lou glanced up and did a double take. He does that a lot; since he usually acts before he thinks, he's always stopping to reconsider halfway through.

This was more like a triple take, though. His first instinct on seeing a squirrel is to blindly charge toward it. But he only got as far as leaning forward when he realized it wasn't a squirrel. His second instinct, the double take, was to walk over to greet a fellow Ifrit. But again, he only got as far as lifting one foreleg before he stopped. He took a second look and sat back down, puzzled. The hair on the back of his neck rose slightly, almost unnoticeably, but I saw it. This was not looking good.

"This is Roscoe," Sandra said. "Roscoe, Mason. And Lou."

I looked at the squirrel. It looked back at me, and I didn't like what I saw. Lou has a whole variety of expressions, way more than an ordinary dog, and dogs can be very expressive. But your basic squirrel has only two. Alert and asleep. Of course, this wasn't exactly a squirrel, but I still wasn't expecting much. And certainly not as much as I was seeing.

It looked . . . sly. Not just clever, but untrustworthy. And at the same time, gleeful, in an unwholesome way. It drew back its lips, exposing sharp incisors. It clearly wasn't any more impressed with me than I was with it. I might have thought I was just imagining it if the hair on Lou's nape hadn't raised yet another fraction.

Sandra noticed the bad vibes in the room and went quiet, looking first at me and then at Lou. Before she could say anything, the squirrel leapt off her shoulder, ricocheted off a cabinet, and headed directly at Lou. Before Lou could so much as blink, it veered off and skittered through the kitchen window with a dismissive flick of its tail.

I grabbed hold of Lou just before he took off after it. Mostly Ifrits get on well together except for the occasional spat, but I could see murder in his eyes, Ifrit or no. Sandra laughed nervously.

"Roscoe's not quite adjusted yet," she said. "I guess I shouldn't expect him to be perfect, not yet. But it'll be fine, don't you think?"

I thought not, but there was no point in saying so.

"I'm sure he will," I said. "Things sometimes just take some time."

I wanted to know how she'd created this . . . thing. I wasn't ready to call it an Ifrit yet.

"It's like asking me how I create a painting," she said. "I could tell you all about paints and canvas, but if you want to know about the creative process, well, that's a bit harder. But you know all that."

I did. Music and art aren't that different, just different expressions of the same thing. But it couldn't have been that simple.

"So that's all?" I asked. "You just pulled, uh, Roscoe out of thin air?"

"Oh, no, of course not. Josephine had an entire ritual set up. I just supplied my creative energy, my spirit. It wasn't easy, though, let me tell you."

Sandra kept glancing out the window every few seconds, trying to catch a glimpse of her Roscoe. It should have been heartwarming, but it wasn't. It was disturbing and slightly macabre.

"It hardly seems possible," I said. Sandra focused back on me.

"I know. I couldn't believe it myself." She glanced out the window again. "Of course, she had that stone, which helped."

Of course. The stone.

"A green stone," I said.

"Then you do know about it? I don't think I was supposed to see it. She was trying to keep it hidden, but I saw it. I don't think she noticed."

I didn't think Jo had noticed, either. If she had, Sandra might well have joined Moxie before her time.

Sandra got up and walked to the back door. "Sorry," she said. "I'm still a bit worried about Roscoe."

"I understand," I said. "I've got to be going anyway. But congratulations."

She gave me a bright smile and rushed out into the back garden in search of her beloved Roscoe.

That night, I got the green stones I'd taken from Byron's pocket out of the trunk and laid them out on the kitchen table. I picked them up and fondled them, feeling the ancient energy coursing through them. Lou didn't like it; he wanted them out of sight and went so far as to actually growl at me until I put them aside.

But I couldn't let it go. Why had Jo helped Sandra create an Ifrit? Jo wouldn't have helped her for no reason. And sure, the Ifrit Sandra had created was distorted. It wasn't like any Ifrit I had ever seen. And yet, she had created *something*. It had to be important, and the stones had to be part of it. I thought I knew where I could find an answer.

I put on my battered leather jacket, slipped the stones in my pocket, and drove downtown. I headed toward the construction site, the one where I'd first seen our friendly neighborhood bridge troll.

I went through the whole routine of scaling the fence, this time being more careful and getting over unscathed. I had gotten only a few steps in when Lou pressed himself against my leg, his way of alerting me when a warning wasn't strictly necessary. Farther in, barely visible in the dark, under the access ramp high above, three shadows lounged.

"It's about time," said the bridge guy. Overhead, cars streamed by, almost drowning out his words.

"I didn't realize I was expected," I said.

"Sure, you did. It just took you a while to figure it out."

His two pals, the same two I'd met before, stayed well back. They seemed even less human than before, almost approaching the level of the transformed practitioners in the tunnels who had almost done me in. Wolf Guy was really starting to look like a wolf. Richard Cory was looking less than human as well, but exactly why I couldn't say. I watched them both warily. Bridge Guy walked over next to me and held out his hand.

"Did you bring them?" he asked.

I didn't ask him what he meant. I pulled the stones out of my jacket pocket and handed them over. He wrapped huge hands around them and smiled. I wasn't at all sure I was doing the right thing. Maybe this was a very bad idea. But I had to know. I had to see.

He walked farther back under the bridge and conferred briefly with his two allies. They broke off the conversation and started gathering objects once again, not stones and pieces of wood this time, but sections of electrical conduit, rolls of duct tape, and broken bits of rebar. Richard Cory glided through the night, while Wolf Guy stumbled occasionally, growling a soft complaint each time. Bridge Guy came and stood beside me.

"She came back later on, didn't she?" I asked.

"Who?" he said, but he knew who I meant.

"What did she want?"

"She wanted to know about Ifrits."

"And did you tell her?"

He nodded, slowly. "What I could. She had something to trade."

"The stones."

He nodded again. "She never brought them, though. I guess she didn't feel the need."

"And you just let it slide?" That didn't gibe with my earlier notion about the dangers of welshing on a bargain.

"Let it slide? No, not really. I'm just in no rush. Sometimes things take care of themselves in the fullness of time."

Fullness of time, my ass. That's like saying in the long run we're all dead. True, but unhelpful.

"Why the hell didn't you tell me about her?" He looked at me calmly.

"You never asked," he said. How perfect.

When the other two were done gathering objects, each

came up to Lou and stared into his eyes, focusing intently. They seemed barely human now, but Lou was less bothered by that than I was. Finally, Bridge Guy handed them each a stone, drew a circle in the dirt around the collected objects, and they gathered round once again outside the circle.

This time their chanting had more focus, or maybe I was just more familiar with it. The red and gold swirl that I was beginning to associate with Ifrits made its appearance, and this time, instead of fading, it grew stronger. It glowed so brightly that it hurt my eyes. Slowly, a form started to coalesce out of the swirling color. Lou started growling softly, not strictly a warning, but more a protest about something he didn't care for.

At first I could see only flashes of what seemed to be a creature of some sort. Then, gradually, the colors resolved into a fuzzy image and vanished as the image became clearer. Finally there was nothing left but a small animal standing in the center of the circle. An Ifrit.

Except it wasn't, not quite. It was huge, twice as large as any Ifrit I'd ever seen, three times as large as Lou. And it didn't resemble any animal I was familiar with. Many Ifrits are cats, a few are small dogs, and there is the occasional large bird. I've even known a rat or two. But none of them are made-up creatures. They all are something, something recognizable.

This creature was the size of a small Border collie, only stocky and powerful. Its fur was thick, dark, and mottled, but its tail was completely bare. A broad and flat face added to the impression of strength. It seemed to be having trouble closing its mouth, though, due to an overabundance of sharp teeth. Bearlike paws with long claws attached rounded out the package.

But it wasn't just some beast. It turned confidently in the circle, surveying each figure surrounding it, coolly and with sharp intelligence. Sandra's squirrel had looked sly. This creature looked treacherous as well. The wolf guy made a sort of chuffing noise and took two steps back. Richard

Cory didn't seem as concerned, but he did something to himself that made it hard to see him, even though I knew exactly where he was standing.

They had clearly evoked something unexpected, something unwholesome and dangerous. This thing was no more an Ifrit than a golem is a tap dancer.

Bridge Guy obviously knew something had gone very wrong. He held up his stone and quickly started chanting again, this time with a different rhythm, hoping to reverse the process and send whatever it was back to wherever it had come from. The creature's outline stared to grow fuzzy, and red and gold flashes of color began to swirl around it again.

The thing in the middle of the circle wasn't about to sit still and be consigned back to oblivion, though. With a sound halfway between a snarl and a hiss, it sprang out of the circle, directly at Bridge Guy. He recoiled, but not quickly enough to avoid a slash to his arm. He immediately dropped down, his entire body reverting to the leathery gray troll persona, and reached for the creature. Too late. It was past him in seconds, headed directly toward Lou.

Lou gave a strangled yelp and took off toward the fence. The fake Ifrit was faster than he was, but Lou was quicker. Just as the creature caught up with him, he doubled back, then reversed direction again, escaping its lethal claws by only a few inches.

They were moving so fast I could barely follow them, much less come up with any help. Lou dashed toward the opposite fence, and it seemed as if he was cornered, but at the last moment be wormed his way among the cracks of a pile of broken concrete and rebar, a safe urban cave. The creature was not discouraged. It started digging, using its powerful claws to pull chunks of concrete up like a bear tearing open a rotten log. Whatever this creature was, it apparently possessed a single-minded hatred of Ifrits.

At least it had finally stopped in one place. I ran toward it, gathering energy as I moved. I got within ten feet of it before it whirled and threw itself at me, all fur and teeth and snarls. I probably would have lost a good chunk of flesh before I could have stopped it, but a figure flashed between us, snarling as angrily as the creature itself. It was my pal the wolf guy, although by now he was hardly a guy at all. He reminded me of the wolf-thing in the tunnels, only this time I wasn't the target.

He pounced, and a maelstrom of teeth and claws swirled around me, sort of like Lou and Maggie, but on a larger and more deadly scale. Then the fake Ifrit broke off, bounced against a nearby oil drum, and bounded away into the darkness. It made it over the fence at the far end and I could hear dirt falling as it sped down the hill.

The wolf guy turned toward me, and for a moment it seemed like I was going to be his next target. Bridge Guy slid in between us and held up his hand. After a long moment, Wolf Guy began to look more human again and moved away back into the shadows. Lou poked his head out of his safe haven, saw that the coast was clear, and strolled nonchalantly over to me.

Bridge Guy brushed back a tangle of hair, dropped the now-dead rune he held on the ground, and smiled ruefully.

"That didn't go quite as well as I had hoped," he said.

"What a surprise. What in God's name was that?"

"Well, it wasn't an Ifrit—that's for sure."

I stared off into the darkness. "No, it wasn't. Maybe we should go look for it. I hate to think of that thing wandering the streets."

He briefly considered. "No, I don't think that's necessary. I don't think it can last long on its own—after all, it was just a construct, not a true being." He shook his head sadly. "I should have known. But I expect it will just fade away over time."

I wasn't so sure of that. The thought of it holing up somewhere in the city was not comforting. But the thought of hunting it down by myself was even less comforting. And right now I had other, more pressing concerns, so I uttered those familiar words, those words I've so often mocked, those words that always turn out to be so dreadfully wrong.

"Oh, well," I said. "I guess it won't be that much of a problem, then."

TWENTY-ONE

IT WAS WAY LATE BY THE TIME I GOT HOME, BUT I called Victor anyway. I knew I should lay it all out for him, but I didn't want to. It was personal. I'd been played for a fool, and I was going to handle it myself. I was going to get proof, proof that even Eli would accept, and then we would deal with it. And in the back of my mind, still that niggling doubt. What if I was wrong? What if, beyond all reason, there was some other explanation? I'd never live it down.

Victor sounded wide-awake when he answered, as always. I don't know if he stays up late or if he just puts on a good front. For all I know he never sleeps.

"Have you got an extra key to Jo's apartment?" I asked, with no preliminaries. It didn't faze him.

"No. I had two and I gave one to her and one to Rolando. Why?"

"Can you get Jo out of the city for a few hours tomorrow, then? Send her on an assignment? Tell her it's something to do with Rolando, maybe?"

"What's going on, Mason?"

"I need to search her apartment, and I don't want to be

interrupted." He was silent for a moment before he answered.

"If I remember correctly, the last time you visited a practitioner's residence uninvited it didn't go so well. And at the risk of sounding repetitive, what's going on? Do you know something?"

"Yes. No. Maybe. It's something I need to do. Can't we just leave it at that?" More silence. "Victor, I'm asking," I said. I could almost hear him shrug over the phone.

"All right," he finally said. "I'll call you tomorrow when I get it set up. And Mason, I hope I don't regret this."

"You and me both," I said. "And if she asks, don't tell her you've talked with me. As far as you know, no one's seen me since yesterday."

WHEN VICTOR CALLED THE NEXT DAY, I WAS READY.

"You should have at least three hours," he said. "By the way, am I going to have to drop by later and pick up your withered corpse?"

"Sooner or later, I'm sure. But not today."

"How reassuring," he said.

When I reached Beale Street I parked about a block away from Jo's building and put Lou on a short lead. I walked up to the front entrance, timing my arrival so that I reached the lobby door at the same moment as a legitimate tenant. She held the door open for me and I nodded my thanks.

"Do you know of a good pet store nearby?" I asked as we passed through the lobby.

She did, several, and proceeded to inform me about the virtues and flaws of each one. The security guard, a guy I hadn't seen before, saw us chatting and naturally we were together. Plus I had Lou. If there's anything more reassuring about harmless intentions than a small dog on a leash, I don't know what it is.

If that hadn't worked, there was always the fallback of a

masking spell, but I didn't want to leave any more traces of talent than necessary. I didn't want to leave any traces of myself at all.

The black shoulder bag slung carelessly over my left shoulder was roomy enough to conceal a pair of large channel locks. Using talent to bypass the warding was all well and good, but there would still be the problem of a locked door. My talent is strongest in dealing with organic things; weakest in dealing with objects of iron and steel. If Jo had latched the deadbolt, it would present a problem, but she wasn't the type to think much about physical locks. Or so I was hoping.

Again I took the elevator to the twelfth floor and walked down two. I was worried about the wards as well. If Jo had bothered to set up new wards, the backdoor I'd created in the old ones would have been wiped away, and I wasn't confident I had enough skill to get past a new setup. But I didn't think she had. I needn't have worried. My backdoor stealth ward was securely in place. Jo hadn't even touched it.

I plugged in and rerouted the energy flow from around the door into my own ward, the one I'd placed there. It was like bypassing a simple alarm system with a loop of wire and two alligator clips, and just that easy.

A firm grasp on the doorknob with the channel locks, a hard, quick twist, and the lock snapped easily. Cautiously, I tried the door, and it swung slowly open. No deadbolt after all. Two seconds later I was inside with the door closed securely behind me.

I stood by the door, listening, ready to get the hell out if things went sour. My previous encounter with Byron's little pet had made me wary of blithely waltzing in to a practitioner's residence uninvited.

It was a full ten minutes before I was satisfied. Lou got impatient long before that, but he could tell from my grim demeanor I wasn't in the mood for argument. Finally I started moving through the apartment.

Jo's room was straight back, and off to the right was another bedroom with the door closed. Rolando's, I assumed. I pushed the door to that bedroom open partway and waited outside the room for another two minutes. I wasn't comfortable about this adventure in the first place, and the longer I was in the apartment, the less comfortable I was going to feel. Eventually I eased in through the doorway and looked around.

The room was neat, almost military in feel. A narrow single bed was pushed against the wall next to one of those high-rise windows that doesn't open. Across from the bed, a computer sat on top of a small desk, papers stacked tidily to one side.

Across from the desk, a closet with wooden accordion doors took up most of the wall. I crossed over and opened the doors, half expecting some demon or monster to fling itself out of the closet depths. Nothing like that was inside, but I did find something almost as disturbing.

A canvas bag. In itself, nothing to cause alarm. But I recognized it. It seemed like years ago since I'd sat down on Victor's floor holding a dead rune stone in my hand with the music of Mussorgsky in my ears. In that musically inspired vision of a dead world, a solitary figure had crossed the landscape collecting random bones. I couldn't make out who it was at the time, but I did remember the distinctive black-and-white pattern of the bag and the sight of bones being tossed into it with casual abandon. Maybe Jo hadn't stolen them from Byron. Maybe she'd collected them herself. I'd never know.

I pulled the bag out of the closet and hefted it. It was heavy. And the muted sound of objects clinking together told me what was in there. I dumped the contents out on the floor. A collection of familiar green rune stones spilled out, identical to the one found clutched in Sarah's unwilling hand and the ones cleverly planted in Byron's pocket. There must have been a hundred of them. The impact of this mass of stones was overwhelming, dwarfing anything

I'd felt from them before. These were live runes, inorganic and organic at the same time. They were bones as much as stones, or at least the remains of mortal creatures. An aura of ancient death hung over them, strong and unmistakable.

As I stared down at the collection of bones, one of the things that had troubled me was now explained. How, I'd wondered, could simple bones contain such power to transform and evoke? Wouldn't it take a practitioner of extraordinary power to actualize them?

But looking at the mass of bones, it became clear. All one had to do was find these remains. A power was embedded in the bones themselves, an ancient and alien life force, coiled and waiting to be released. With just a fraction of my own talent and power, I could have easily unleashed it myself, raised the bones up, bound them with muscle and sinew and blood, and sent them marching off on any mission I desired.

It was necromancy after a fashion, a specialty that even black practitioners tend to avoid. But with things from so far in the distant past, and not even our past at that, it didn't seem as reprehensible. Why use them for simple tasks, when so much more could be done with them? Why not bring them to life? Why not have your own personal minions, servants, and bodyguards, compelled to do your bidding? There was a subtle pull to those archaic bones, filling me with the desire to bring them back to life.

Could I really do it? Think of the knowledge I could obtain, the secrets I could learn. What wonders could I accomplish and how like a god would I be, bringing back to life long-dead creatures from another time and place?

Lou sat nearby, ignoring the bones, looking up at me as if he knew exactly what I was thinking and didn't like my thoughts. I shuddered and walked out of the room, leaving the bones where they lay. Dead objects they might be, but they were heavy with an unholy power. Victor had once said he was surprised I hadn't turned out to be a black practitioner. At the time I'd written it off as just another of his snotty comments, but maybe he understood something about me, something that could have gone either way. For the five millionth time I thanked the stars for providing Eli as a guide for my younger self.

A quick once-over through the rest of the apartment turned up nothing. I pulled out drawers, poked into corners, looked under rugs. Nothing. The only place left to look was in Jo's room, and I was hesitant about doing that. Partly it was simple nervousness. Bad enough to be creeping around the apartment, but if she came back early and caught me going through stuff in her bedroom, nothing would keep me from unfortunate consequences.

I knew I had no choice; after all, that was why I was here in the first place. Still, I stood irresolute until Lou made up my mind for me. He'd been following me around, curious in a detached sort of way but not totally engaged. None of this made much difference to him. Suddenly his ears shot up and his head snapped around toward the door to Jo's bedroom. Now there wasn't even the illusion of choice. In for a penny, in for a pound.

I went through the same routine as before, intending to nudge the door open a crack and wait, but Lou pushed right by me and slipped through the narrow opening. I muttered a bad word, pushed open the door all the way, and walked into the bedroom.

The unmade bed brought back memories, not altogether pleasant ones. The closet on the far wall was identical to the one in Rolando's room except the doors were slightly open. Lou's attention was fixed on the opening, though he didn't seem to have any inclination to go in there. A faint scuffling, scratching noise was coming from the back of the closet. I didn't really want to know what was making it. Still, I could hardly leave now.

Moving as quietly as I could, I reached out for the small wooden knob that would open the doors all the way. With one quick pull I opened the door and the noise stopped. Clothes on hangers crowded wall to wall, making it hard to see inside. A few cardboard boxes cluttered the floor, and wedged in between them, incongruously, was a black garment bag. I reached down, pulled it from between the boxes, and dragged it out into the room. It was heavy, disturbingly so.

I knew what I would find even before I unzipped it. I had known what I would find before I'd ever entered the apartment, for that matter. I just hadn't wanted to admit it to myself. The zipper snagged momentarily and I worked it carefully, showing insane patience. When it finally came free, it opened up with a swift rush, revealing the contents inside. Sure enough. Staring up at me, wide-eyed and blank, lay a perfectly preserved and very dead Rolando.

TWENTY-TWO

ALL MY SUSPICIONS AND ALL MY WORST FEARS were confirmed in that instant, but instead of triumph I felt only an overwhelming sadness.

"Sorry, Ro," I said to the empty shell that had once been my friend.

You idiot. You fucking idiot. You don't know who you're dealing with, do you? he'd said. No, I really hadn't.

As I stood over his body, something small and quick crawled out from inside the closet and skittered past me before I could react. It moved fast, but in an odd, unnatural fashion, like a crippled rat. Not fast enough, though. Lou pounced as it bolted for the door, pinning it down, teeth fastened on the back of its neck. It squealed in pain and Lou immediately let go, stepping back a pace but ready to pounce again. It retreated to the farthest corner of the room and curled itself into ball.

I moved over to get a good look at it and immediately wished I hadn't. It was the size and shape of a small cat, but not a cute and furry one. Its wrinkled skin was a blotchy gray, hairless and covered with open sores. Tiny red eyes, like those of an albino, stared up at me in fear and defiance. Half-formed, ill-defined ears dripped from its skull. Its feet were so deformed it had trouble standing properly.

Worst of all were the tumors that bulged over every inch of its body. Its neck was swollen in several places, and down along its back grotesque lumps and growths sprouted like malignant fungi. They seemed to writhe with a life of their own every time it shifted position.

Lou's warning bark came far too late to be of any use.

"I see you've met Isobel," said a voice behind me.

I'd been so focused on the thing before me I'd forgotten I had broken into a practitioner's home. I automatically looked up at the mirror on the wall. It was no surprise to see the reflection of Jo standing in the bedroom doorway.

"What is it?" I said, turning around slowly to face her.

"Why, it's an Ifrit, of course. My Ifrit."

"Sandra," I said. "You used her as a test case, helped her to create an Ifrit, and then tried one for yourself. But you don't have her creativity, do you? So this was the sad result."

"Oh, no, not at all. At first, Isobel was fine. Creativity? You have no idea just how creative I can be."

"But why?" I asked, and as I said that, everything fell into place. I looked down at the pitiful creature riddled with tumors and covered in sores. Then back at Jo, radiating health and vitality.

Most people use logical chains of evidence to reach a conclusion. Homicide detectives, for example. But the really good ones rely more on intuition. Oh, they assemble the chains carefully, but it's all done after the fact. The real solution comes like a bolt of lightning—*My God, he did it*. Great scientific discoveries sometimes happen the same way, by instant epiphany. All of the mathematical proofs come later, as a necessary afterthought.

I operate the same way. My musical compositions are a gift from the muse, and although I can later analyze why they work, that's not the starting point. This realization came more slowly, but just as surely. It was like a deck of cards falling one after another, faster and faster until the entire deck was complete.

The practitioner in the doorway by Goldie's Bar? Jo, of course. And I'd always assumed the visitor to Montague had been a man, but that visitor had been shielded and glossed over with illusion. Later, when Jo returned in her natural guise, he might well have made the fatal mistake of turning his back on her. An attractive young woman always seems less of a threat, even though that's ridiculous if you stop to think about it.

All the signs of physical sickness were there, but I'd missed them. After the phony attack by the Cliff House, the one that she so astoundingly escaped, she'd been left with one pupil larger than the other. I'd assumed it was from a concussion, but there are other causes for such things. Like a brain tumor. The sex, with her total loss of control, and then the uncontrollable vomiting after exertion. Not psychological after all.

And the knife blade, the ultimate proof? Oh, it had lit up all right when it was next to Rolando. Only, Jo had been just as close. No wonder he wanted me out of there. It wasn't himself he was worried about. It was me.

Rolando wasn't jealous of me at all. He was scared and didn't know what to do. Even before the knife blade glowed, he must have had his suspicions. But he couldn't have been sure. She was his kid sister after all.

The next time the knife had glowed was when it was placed on Byron's skin. But of course, at the time his head had been in Jo's lap. What a coincidence. And that rock hadn't been meant for Byron at all. By that time Rolando had understood the monster she'd become.

She must have killed him that very night, after I'd left her. And of course, the final straw, one last attempt to get rid of me, leaving me alone in those deadly tunnels of rock.

And her Ifrit? That was the key. She had created it all right, but not as any companion. It served, quite simply, as a receptacle. All the sickness, all the pain from the cancerous lesions that were invading her body and brain had been poured into it, leaving her whole and healthy once again.

Jo crossed the room and sat down on the bed, moving the tangled sheets out of the way.

"If I'd known you were going to drop by, I'd have straightened up a bit," she said. "I knew something was up when Victor tried to send me on a wild-goose chase, but I didn't expect you. I should have known you'd escape from the tunnels."

"Sorry to disappoint," I said.

"It's a shame," she said. "None of this had to happen. If I'd had Isobel from the beginning, no one would ever have been hurt. But I didn't—I only just figured out how to do this, you know. Until then, I'd been getting sicker by the day. It was beginning to take all my energy just to hide my condition from people." She stretched luxuriously. "You have no idea how good it feels to be healthy again."

"I'm very happy for you," I said.

"Thanks," she said, smiling. Among other things wrong with her brain, she'd apparently lost the capacity to recognize sarcasm. "Anyway, if I hadn't come up with this idea, I'd be dead by now. And you should take some credit, you know. You and Sandra. It was your theory about Ifrits that gave me the idea in the first place. If I could just break off the part of me that was sick, I thought, just funnel it away, then everything would be fine again.

"It didn't work out quite the way I'd hoped, but it's good enough. I supplied the power and the evocation spell and the rune; Sandra provided the technique. I just wish I could have discovered it earlier on. If I had, there wouldn't have been all that unpleasantness."

"Unpleasantness?" I said. "What unpleasantness? What's a few dead and mindless practitioners compared to your problems?"

"Come on, Mason," she said. "You know I'm not like that. I thought I had a way to switch bodies—my sick one for a strong and healthy one. I didn't want to die. Who does? And the tumor—" She shuddered dramatically. "You have no idea what it's like living with a thing like that in your head. You can't really blame me for trying to find a wholesome body for my own. But I couldn't pull it off, even with the rune stones. People are stronger than I thought."

"And if you had? Then what?"

She smiled ruefully. "Well, I couldn't just let someone run around in my old body telling what I had done, now could I? Besides, it's not like they were friends of mine or anything."

"Lovely," I said. "And me?"

"You? Ah, well. You were different. At first I tried to catch you unharmed. I thought you'd be a particularly good subject for the switch, what with your health and talent. So I sent the dhougra, but she failed. Lou here wouldn't let her win you over." She glanced at him, almost fondly. "And with Lou hanging around all the time and you on your guard, it was going to be difficult to trap you again."

"He does have his points," I said. "So then what? You finally decided to just save yourself some trouble and just get me out of the way?"

"Well, yes, but that was before I knew you that well. I was afraid you'd figure it out. Ro said you always do, eventually. Remember? So you had to go. I thought when you went off that cliff it would be the end of it. I still don't understand why my little pet saved you. I would have punished her, but I couldn't find her."

"How did you control her?" I asked.

"The stones. Even Byron didn't understand their full potential, even though he was the one who found them. They're control enhancers, among other things. The dhougra couldn't be controlled without them.

"But after that, I changed my mind about killing you. I was never that happy with the idea anyway. I thought I could finesse the situation, right up until yesterday even. You see, I became rather fond of you. I really did, you know."

"And the creatures in the tunnel? How did you know they were there?"

"They weren't. I lured them there. Our friend up by the bridge told me all about them. Of course, he had no idea what I was going to do. They can't be controlled, you see—they've gone all the way over. Unless you have the rune stones. I used the stones to boost the magical energy in the tunnels, and it attracted them like moths to a flame. I can't believe you got out of there."

"And Rolando?" I asked. "He tumbled to it eventually, didn't he? So, good-bye, Rolando." I looked at the bag still lying on the bedroom floor. "You just left him in the closet, I notice."

She giggled. "He's been in the closet all his life," she said. "Didn't you wonder why he never had a steady girl-friend?"

I hadn't realized just how crazy she had become until I heard that giggle. It gave me chills. But crazy could be a good thing. There was no way I could come out on top if it came down to a test of talent. For one, she had home-court advantage, and that's a bigger edge for practitioners than it is for a basketball team. And with the stones, she was stronger than I was anyway. A lot stronger. But if I could throw her off balance . . .

"I did wonder," I said. "But I thought it was just because he was more interested in *you*."

I'd hoped to make her angry, to distract her, but it didn't work.

"He was, wasn't he," she said, thoughtfully. "Poor Ro. Maybe I shouldn't have let him . . ."

She trailed off, with a faraway look on her face. That was the moment of opportunity, but I wasn't quick enough to take it. She focused again.

"He tried to stop me. You saw—he actually tried to kill me, up at the city dump." She shook her head in amazement. "After that, well . . ." She smiled again. "I couldn't let that pass, even if he was my brother. I mean, how could he?"

All the while we'd been talking I kept glancing around, looking for energy sources, preparing to launch any attack I could. Jo might well be fond of me in some twisted way, but she wasn't about to let me live. Not after everything she'd gone through to get where she was.

"He was just ungrateful, I guess," I said, trying to keep her talking. I had an idea. "Now what?"

"Now I go away. Maybe back to Portland. The troubles have stopped, and after a while, everybody will forget about them. Now that I've got Isobel, I don't need anything else."

"You're cured?" I reached out for the vast and empty sky right outside the high-rise window, arching quietly into the void. I reached out to Rolando, sleeping the dreamless sleep of death.

"No, not cured. It keeps coming back. In fact, it seems to be getting worse ever since I started this. But every time it does, I just siphon off the sickness into little Isobel here. Poor baby. Honestly, I don't know how much more she can take."

"And what happens to you if she dies?" I kept my voice even and nonjudgmental, just having a casual conversation with an old friend. I sent out a trickle of energy, calm and soothing, not enough for her to notice. She yawned.

"I'm not sure. But I made her; I can make another. And another after that if I have to."

"It must be hard for you," I said.

I increased the energy flow. Calm. Peace. Sleep. Her eyes started to droop, and she yawned again in spite of herself.

"It's not so bad," she said, voice thick and sleepy.

"No," I said. "But it must make you tired sometimes, so weary."

"Umm," she agreed.

I upped the energy flow. She'd be asleep in moments, and as I kept pouring in power, she'd sink into a coma as deep as death.

I was having some trouble maintaining, though. Fear

and sickness emanated from the pitiable creature huddled in the corner, threatening to break my concentration. So much sickness emanated from its corner that I had to damp it down before it overwhelmed me and unbalanced my own spell. Jo must have been pouring illness into it nonstop for days.

Suddenly, the wave of sickness ceased. In its place was a feeling of peaceful calm. I glanced over; I couldn't help myself. The Ifrit was curled up, sound asleep. Jo's eyes snapped open and she was suddenly as wakeful as an owl at midnight.

"You son of a bitch," she said.

She reached into a pocket and pulled out another green rune, not dull and inert, but glowing with power. She poured energy into it. The stone amplified the energy and concentrated it into a tight packet of death. With one quick motion she flung it out toward me.

It was too strong to block, but I did manage to deflect it, like a soccer goalie tipping aside a hard shot with his fingertips. I guided it right into the mirror over the bed, concentrated on her reflection, and sent it back where it had come from.

It should have killed her, but I had forgotten about the Ifrit. Isobel woke up instantly, screaming in pain. Jo staggered, but stayed on her feet. For a second I had a window, a brief moment where if I had put enough rage and conviction into some spell, it might have overwhelmed her even with Isobel to help. But I didn't have the requisite hatred in me. The tumor that had eaten away at her brain had damaged it beyond repair, long before she discovered this bizarre way to leach out the sickness. She might be healthy now, but she was far from well and always would be. She was dangerous, she was devoid of emotion, and she had done some very bad things. But she wasn't evil; she was sick. Or maybe the difference was simply one of semantics.

In any case, I hesitated just a moment too long. She recovered quickly. She took the energy I'd thrown back at her, spun it through the stone again, and sent a condensed pulse right back at me. This time I didn't react quickly enough.

My head felt like a stun grenade had gone off inside. I dropped to my knees, so weak I could hardly think, much less stand. Worst of all, I felt sick, sick unto death. Imagine the worst flu you've ever had, one so bad you almost think you might die, and double that. And then double that again. And that would have been an improvement over the way I felt.

"You horrible little man," she said dispassionately. "And to think, I actually thought I liked you once."

She pumped in more energy, and the sickness intensified. I slowly toppled over until I was lying on the floor, on my side. I couldn't even muster enough energy to turn my head to look at her. My field of vision started to narrow and darken. A profound lassitude spread throughout my body. Lou's face came into view, his expression concerned.

I wonder where he'll go? I thought. When a practitioner dies, no one ever sees his Ifrit again. Would he fade away once I was gone? Or would he slip away and live out his remaining days in some other dimension, a sort of Ifrit heaven?

I might have been ready to go gentle into that good night, but Lou had other plans. He uttered an angry bark, or at least I think it was angry. It sounded distant and hollow and very far away.

He whirled, and I thought he was going to fling himself at Josephine, which of course would have been suicide. But instead, he darted into the corner where Isobel was cowering. Isobel squealed, a piercing shriek of fear that cut through my dulled senses. In my dazed and altered state I could have sworn I heard her scream the words, "No, please." I'm sure it was my distorted senses that caused me to hear that. I hoped to God that was all it was.

Whatever it was, it didn't deter Lou for a second. She tried to put up a defense, but it was a feeble effort. He went right through her guard, ignoring her weak teeth and grabbing her by the neck. As soon as he got a grip, he shook her from side to side like a terrier with a rag doll. Then he let her fall and instantly lunged back at her now-defenseless throat, this time slashing and tearing. Blood welled up on her hairless neck and drained down the front of her body, pooling on the floor. She staggered once, then collapsed and lay motionless except for the spasmodic twitching of a rear leg.

From what seemed like a great distance I heard a scream of rage. Jo was finally showing some emotion. The bone-drenching weariness ebbed away, and I found myself able to sit up, just as Jo, magic and spells forgotten, came charging across the room in a desperate attempt to save her Ifrit. Lou ducked under the bed before she got close enough to get her hands on him, and she collapsed next to Isobel, cradling the lifeless body in her hands.

I was still in that hazy dreamlike state that comes just before you lose consciousness, so I can't swear that what I saw was real. But that state is very much like the one you're in when viewing on the psychic plane, and God knows that's real enough.

A slight phosphorescent glow appeared, a halo effect around Isobel's head. It spread until her entire body was enveloped, and then, as if something slowly questing, colored tendrils started to reach up toward Jo. She was oblivious to it, still focused on grieving, or as close to that as she was now capable.

Even after everything that had happened, my first instinct still was to shout a warning, but I never had to make that choice. The best I'd be able to manage right now would be a hoarse and feeble squawk, and I wasn't keen on drawing attention to myself anyway. So I watched, fascinated and horrified, as the tendrils crept higher and higher. Eventually they reached the level of her head and slipped into the base of her skull like some vampire plant. A flow of color pulsed madly through the connection, but unlike a vampire, something was flowing out, not in.

At first it had no visible effect. But gradually I noticed a change. Jo looked suddenly tired, something around the eyes as if she hadn't slept for a couple of days. Purple splotches appeared on her neck and face. Her long hair turned dry and lost all sheen, and when she abstractedly put up a hand to scratch at it, large clumps dislodged and drifted to the floor.

By this time she became aware that something was terribly wrong. She tried to stand up but managed to get only halfway to her feet before her legs buckled and she had to sit back down. Her body started shaking and a horrible whimpering sound came from somewhere deep inside.

Slowly, tumors began to emerge on her face, swelling it and distorting her features. Then on her hands and the backs of her arms, all the while growing faster and larger. More hair fell out, and sores appeared on the skin of the now-naked skull. All the sickness she had poured into her created Ifrit was coming back on her, redoubled in spades. It was like watching a sped-up version of *The Picture of Dorian Gray*.

She tried to speak, but her ravaged vocal chords could no longer function. She could only emit little mewling sounds, horribly reminiscent of Isobel. Worse, as her skin withered and puckered and the last of her hair vanished, she began to resemble a giant version of the Ifrit she had created to save herself.

Her breathing became labored. She would take several deep breaths, then stop completely. No one should have to die alone, but I couldn't make myself go near her. But it didn't matter. She was no longer aware I was there, and when she reached out for help, it was to something or someone only she could see.

I finally had regained enough strength to climb shakily to my feet. Lou crawled out from his sanctuary under the bed and stood by my side. He kept spitting and coughing as if he'd eaten something particularly nasty. We watched in silence until, after a long spell of rapid breathing, Jo finally ceased breathing altogether. She was still sitting cross-legged in an obscene parody of a meditation stance, but she was gone. Her body was shrunken, insubstantial, a far cry from the vibrant and powerful woman of only a half hour ago.

There were probably things I should have done there to tie up loose ends. I knew Victor would have gone about it with his usual efficiency, but I couldn't bear to stay in the apartment a second longer. I did stop and pick up those green stones from Rolando's room. They weren't the kind of thing you wanted to leave lying around.

I rode the elevator down to the lobby. No point any longer in cautiously taking the stairs. Through the glass lobby doors, I could see the blue sky and people passing by, talking and laughing, living their lives. As we walked out through the front door, I held it open for an elderly couple coming in. The woman bent down to give Lou a pat on the head.

"Oh," she said. "What a cute little doggy."

ABOUT THE AUTHOR

John Levitt grew up in New York City. After a stint at the University of Chicago, he traveled around the country and ended up running light shows for bands in San Francisco. Eventually, he moved to the Wasatch Mountains and worked at a ski lodge in Alta, Utah. After a number of years as a ski bum, he joined the Salt Lake City Police Department, where for eight years he worked as a patrol officer and later as an investigator. His experiences on the job formed the background for two mystery novels, *Carnivores* and *Ten of Swords*. For the last few years, he has split his time between Alta, where he manages the Alta Lodge, and San Francisco. He owns no dogs, although his girlfriend now has four.

When he's not working or writing, he plays guitar with the SF rock band The Procrastinistas and also plays the occasional jazz gig. If you wish to hear the entire song the mythical Dagger Dykes play in *New Tricks*, go to www.jlevitt.com and click on "My Songs" and then on *In the Night*. Fellow band member Steve McNamara is the hot guitarist, though.

John is currently at work on the third book in the Dog Days series.

THE ULTIMATE IN FANTASY!

From magical tales of distant worlds to stories of those with abilities beyond the ordinary, Ace and Roc have everything you need to stretch your imagination to its limits.

Marion Zimmer Bradley/Diana L. Paxson

Guy Gavriel Kay

Dennis L. McKiernan

Patricia A. McKillip

Robin McKinley

Sharon Shinn

Katherine Kurtz

Barb and J. C. Hendee

Elizabeth Bear

T. A. Barron

Brian Jacques

Robert Asprin

penguin.com